The Miss Education of Dr. Exeter

BOOKS BY JILLIAN STONE

The Seduction of Phaeton Black

The Moonstone and Miss Jones

The Miss Education of Dr. Exeter

The Miss Education of Dr. Exeter

JILLIAN STONE

KENSINGTON PUBLISHING CORP.
www.kensingtonbooks.com

BRAVA BOOKS are published by

Kensington Publishing Corp.
119 West 40th Street
New York, NY 10018

All Kensington titles, imprints, and distributed lines are available at special quantity discounts for bulk purchases for sales promotions, premiums, fund-raising, educational, or institutional use. Special book excerpts or customized printings can also be created to fit specific needs. For details, write or phone the office of the Kensington special sales manager: Kensington Publishing Corp., 119 West 40th Street, New York, NY 10018, attn: Special Sales Department; phone 1-800-221-2647.

ISBN-13: 978-0-7582-6900-3
ISBN-10: 0-7582-6900-5

First Trade Paperback Printing: July 2013

10 9 8 7 6 5 4 3 2 1

Printed in the United States of America

First Electronic edition: July 2013

ISBN-13: 978-0-7582-8912-4
ISBN-10: 0-7582-8912-X

Prologue

Excerpted from the journal of Tim Noggy:

28 November 1889. Phaeton Black is officially missing. He has been gone for 60 days.

2 December 1889. In the aftermath of the invasion (of Prospero's army) of Reapers, I have managed to repair a section of the Portal Fabricator, the part Lovecraft refers to as the Inter-Dimensional Injection Portal (iDIP).

5 December 1889. Mr. Ping paid a visit today and brought with him a horde of diminutive test subjects. He calls them "flies on the wall." I have begun limited testing of the iDIP and shall see to the dispersal of Ping's flies. Ping would not divulge where he acquired the clever, spying insects, but they are impressive, and I am hopeful they will hasten our search to find the missing Moonstone and its keeper.

7 December 1889. It took several days, but we injected squadrons of flies into the greater Outremer. Since there are no reliable maps of the other side, we assume our local convergence of time and space is a far greater territory than London proper. I'm hoping the flies will disperse widely from here. Each spy fly is fitted with a camera and listening device.

8 December 1889. Jersey Blood and Valentine Smyth volunteered for the first mission into the Outremer since the portal connections were shut down. We anxiously await their report on the state of Prospero's aether plant as well as his drone factory, which are located in the section of the grid marked *island.*

(Again, I have no idea how accurate this map of Lovecraft's is but it seems we will soon find out.) Per Gaspar's instructions, first priority is the whereabouts of Phaeton Black. Find him, and the Moonstone cannot be far afield. Jersey and Valentine will have twenty-four hours before the machine will extract them.

9 December 1889. (2:47 a.m.) Cheers! Jersey and Valentine have returned unharmed. Since the attack, I have taken up residence behind Lovecraft's laboratory. I had fallen asleep and awoke when the portal engine whirred to life—the auto function on the machine had begun the extraction. I was relieved to see Jersey and Valentine tumble through the portal—bedraggled and in need of rest. They left in a hurry for Half Moon Street, but promised to return in the afternoon to debrief.

I overheard a smattering of talk between the two—something about transmogrifying. The expression they used was *mogging*. Some people use the term *shape-shifting*. Call it whatever you want. I've been told Jersey Blood is a half-breed, part demon part human, but I've never seen any evidence of it. You'd think I might have caught a glimpse. A horn might have popped out of his forehead. Something. But I've seen nothing, not even a flash of red in the pupils of his eyes.

9 December 1889. (4:15 a.m.) A spy fly in the Outremer quadrant marked "island" picked up a conversation, one side of which appears to be Phaeton. And—I've got map coordinates! It seems the island on the map that we thought was London isn't London . . .

Chapter One

22 Half Moon Street, Mayfair
London, 1889

MIA CLAWED AT HER BALL GOWN as she climbed the stairs. There it was again, that tingling feeling—more of an itch than an urge, as if her skin was stretched too tight over the wrong body. At the first signs of a metamorphosis, they had made their excuses, left the ball at Stafford House, and returned home. "Coming to bed, darling?" Her question was a flippant snarl, not a sultry invitation, for she knew he would not condescend to answer. She reached the landing and turned, surprised to see him just a few steps behind her.

As her guardian drew close, her nostrils flared. The scent of Royal Lime No. 5 layered with hints of his shaving soap assaulted her senses. She was drawn, however, to a more intoxicating musk—the very masculine essence that was Doctor Asa Exeter, enigmatic half-blooded Persian prince and English baron. "Will you let me help you, Mia?" He stood one step below her, bringing them eye to eye.

"You know that is impossible." A momentary flash of fantasy intruded—her bare breasts exposed to his anguished gaze, nipples peaked in anticipation of the brush of his thumb. Mia shivered. The sudden surge of arousal could have caused an instantaneous shift. She shook her head gently so her tears would

not spill. "The change comes faster now. You could be injured."
She lifted her chin. "Let me be, Om Asa."

She turned to leave, and he caught her hand. "At least let me mix a powder for the headache."

Exeter had spent a week in the library of secrets studying her condition. He well understood that her migraine warned of an impending, involuntary shift. The pain had quickly become intolerable, and he had escorted her out of the ballroom. In the carriage, she had tried to make light of it. "It seems this is my coming-out season—in more ways than one."

Now, here on the stairs, she met his gaze, that of a protector, of caring and affection. The same look of concern she had known since childhood. The one that now caused her heart to break. "The discomfort will pass, shortly."

Exeter rattled off a litany of symptoms. "Neuralgia, generalized body aches, a sinus drip—not sniffles from a cold, but the kind one gets from exposure, when one is out in the snow for too long." He examined her carefully. "Typically these signs begin within a few hours of the transformation. Are they all present?"

She rolled her eyes upward. "Yes, Doctor Exeter." The wild thing inside her stirred. The beast humped its back and stretched, languidly.

The headache had eased somewhat, which was all the more terrifying. This meant the reshaping of her body was imminent. Mia's gaze lingered on the seraphim painted on the ceiling. God's burning angels. "We were fortunate tonight," she murmured. Sometimes, there were no warning signs—the shift just happened. "Jersey says as I gain experience I will be able to better anticipate the onset of change."

As intimate as it was to be alone with Exeter, things had felt a bit desolate this evening, without the Nightshades. She had grown used to having bodyguards most everywhere they traveled. Jersey Blood and his consort, Valentine, had been assigned to her and Exeter. Jersey was a seraph shifter who rarely allowed himself to transform. He had become something of a mentor in these early months of her transformation.

"Gradually you will learn to manipulate these shifts; then you may change at will, if you so choose," Jersey had assured her. His promise of control cheered her some, even as she fought back the urge to rip off her dress and expose herself—to rub against Exeter and purr.

"I must go." She ran the rest of the way up the stairs and down a length of carpeted corridor. This longing to mate with her guardian was not new, exactly. But there were times now, when her desire was almost too strong to bear. Upsetting to say the least, and beyond perplexing for the good doctor. The untamed feline urge was so strong that, on one occasion, she had used coarse language and disrobed in a provocative way. Shocking behavior on her part. Now her belly trembled at the memory of Exeter's palm cupping her breast, the moment when his thumb had stroked and she had exhaled a low, throaty rumble.

He had stepped away in horror.

Mia shook off the painful memory and burst into her bedchamber. She made it as far as her dressing table before she realized her mistake and turned back. Exeter stood in the open doorway holding an oil lamp, his gaze penetrating, measured. "I believe you need me to undress you."

She bit her lip and nodded. Several weeks ago there had been a close call with Lucy, her maid. One evening, as she helped Mia ready for bed, a sudden, unexpected shift had happened. No warning signs. She had hissed so ferociously, the terrified girl had fled the house in the middle of the night.

Exeter entered the room and set the lamp on her dresser. "Come, Mia." She hadn't noticed how dark it was—mostly because her night vision was extraordinary now. She could read the ancient codex at her bedside without illumination, if she cared to be illuminated.

Placing her hands on her hips, she turned her back to Exeter.

"Please assure me you will not frighten the Metropolitan police on patrol in Green Park . . . again." Exeter's fingers moved down the row of hooks and eyes that fastened her gown.

"I often have no control over her . . . she's—" Mia shifted away and he pulled her back. Persistent, gentle fingers loosed the strings of her corset. Even as her cheeks flushed with heat, cool air wafted over skin moist with perspiration. His knuckles brushed against the flesh of her back, causing a shiver she failed to conceal.

A hand slipped around her waist and he turned her toward him. "As the codex advises—assert yourself but do not force her to your will."

"She always wants . . ." Mia avoided his gaze, until she couldn't any longer. "You know what she wants." Exeter's exotic green eyes, the color of imperial jade, stayed with her. The stubble on his chin and jaw made him look swarthy, and exceedingly masculine, and yet he was also her protector.

"Gentle persuasion, Mia. The more you struggle with her—"

Inexplicably, before she could gain control over her hand, she reached out and stroked the dark, tempting ruff of his whiskers. She traced a faint, cream-colored scar that ran along the edge of a powerful jawline. Her touch stopped his conversation mid-sentence.

What inexplicable behavior! But this is how she had become with him. Heat flushed her cheeks and she withdrew her hand from his face. Shaking her head, even managing an uneasy laugh, she apologized. "I don't know what came over me, please excuse . . ."

"No, please, continue." Covering her hand in his, he guided her fingers over the stubble below his cheekbone to his handsome, well-formed mouth. Her gaze lingered on his generous bottom lip and the upper, with its strong Cupid's bow. Another scorching flush of heat crept up her neck. Gently, he turned her hand palm up and brushed his lips over the faint pulse on the inside of her wrist. "Forgive me, Mia."

A tingle shivered through her body, curling her toes. She had never seen him smile, not like the one she now experienced, and she was positive he felt her tremble. Sweeping a stray wisp of hair off her cheek, he took a long moment to examine every feature on her face.

"You are changing, Mia, from a precocious, adorable girl into a most sultry beauty. From here on out, I will have to keep a close watch on myself." Exeter backed away and shut the door quietly.

Mia blinked. She wasn't quite sure what to make of his speech—apology, confession, or warning? All she knew was the ends of her mouth tilted upward.

She disrobed and left nothing on, having learned the hard way. Any clothes on her body would end up in tatters. The evening chill was soothing, even sensuous. She moved to the tall paned windows and opened French doors. A waft of air hardened her nipples and prickled her skin. Touching herself, she imagined his fingers . . . there.

The shift was instantaneous. Painless.

Lean sinew rippled under a coat of sleek, black fur. Exeter stood on the rooftop and admired the panther's agility and stealth as she dropped down between buildings and into the alley north of Curzon Street. A gray ghost of fog crept over stone pavers. "So, the huntress is on the prowl."

Any time now, she would return to human form. These involuntary shifts never lasted long. Exeter hooked a finger into his waistcoat pocket and tipped out his watch. Nearing the stroke of three.

Less than an hour ago, a large blue-black cat sprang from Mia's bedchamber window to the roof of the town house. She had put up a merry chase, and he had followed after, hurdling gables, vaulting chimneys, using potent energy for the impossible jumps. Still, it amounted to vigorous calisthenics, keeping up with the agile feline.

Exeter leaned against the steep pitch of an attic roof and

squinted. The dark cat crept down the mews lane, but he could not make out what she stalked. Farther away, a dustbin toppled to the ground with a crash.

Mia froze, fixing on something down the narrow row. Shoulders hunched, she crouched low and waited.

He suspected rats or alley cats, until he heard the scoffs and shouts that followed. Exeter stepped out from behind the chimney for a better view. Three young street rowdies sauntered down the row, up to no good. One of them emptied the last of a whiskey bottle and gave it a toss. The glass shattered against a wall.

Mia backed into a corner and hissed.

"Well now, what 'ave we here?" A brawny young man stepped closer and she took a swipe at him. "Watch yourselves—this pretty puss has claws." The drunken sot swayed backward, then pitched forward. One of his mates had the good sense to yank him away and prop him between cohorts, who hung back. "Look at her—big, ain't she?" Another boy gasped. "Some big green eyes on her . . ."

She curled her lip with a snarl.

"Fangs, as well." The bolder, drunker lad stuck a thumb under his cap and scratched. "What do you suppose?"

All three ruffians stared as one spoke up. "I say this pussycat likely escaped from some rich lord's private zoo, don't you know." The rowdy beside him nodded. "Mattie works fancy balls at a duke's house in Belgravia. She says he's got a leopard—one of those big cats with spots. Rides 'im in an open carriage through Hyde Park."

Exeter stood at the edge of the roofline and observed the cornered panther that was Mia. She paced back and forth, eyeing the young men. Jersey Blood had warned him about tracking Mia in her shift-state. "Unless she's in dire straits—leave her be. She needs to learn her own strengths, how to defend herself."

Mia lunged at the doddering bullies and hissed. She was testing them.

"You suppose this one's escaped?" one of the boys asked.

"There's a bloke named Jamrach, has a shop over on Radcliff Highway in Shadwell—Jamrach's Menagerie. He deals in wildlife, birds mostly, but large cats as well. I wager she'll fetch a thumping-good sum." The boisterous de facto leader kicked over an empty dustbin and picked up the lid. "Hand me a stick and grab one for yourselves, lads."

Using the lid as a shield, he tried poking and prodding at her. "Let's see if we can get this pretty puss into the bin. Go around to the side there—don't let her give us the slip."

A gnash of bared teeth ended in a snarling growl that quickly grew into the loudest call of the wild ever heard in the borough of Westminster. She leapt directly at the large bloke, teeth bared. At the last second, as the bully boy staggered to one side, the sleek cat veered off and took a jaw-dropping spring into the air. She jumped from window ledge to roof and landed not far from Exeter.

If he wasn't mistaken, Mia had incorporated a bit of what Ping referred to as relic dust and champagne, or potent energy, to assist in those breathtaking leaps. Until now, he hadn't seen such skillful maneuvering from Mia. And she had manipulated the physical universe in cat form.

The wild creature stared down at the astonished hooligans below who dropped their sticks and lids and hurried out of the alley.

"Impressive, Mia."

The cat turned, flashing green eyes of . . . was that recognition? His heart thumped hard inside his chest. He stood his ground and held his breath as she crept closer. At the last moment, she turned her head and rubbed against his leg, arching her back. Glancing over his shoulder, he watched her curl back around for another pass. He descended to his haunches and she allowed him to rub her neck and scratch behind her ears—with one hand, then both. Her robust rumble modulated into a low purr as she closed her eyes and collapsed into his body.

A flesh-and-blood young woman lay in his arms. Exeter removed his coat and covered her. She opened her eyes momentarily and shivered. Lifting her up, he bent the physical world just enough to make it home in several leaps—from rooftop to rooftop, until he dropped down onto the balcony of her room. He pushed open the window and was greeted by Mr. Tandi, who waited beside a small copper bath. His manservant poured a steaming kettle of water into the tepid bath, as he angled Mia through the French door. "That will be all, Mr. Tandi."

Exeter lowered Mia into the warm bath and stayed until she was revived enough to begin to bathe herself. "Are you well enough, Mia?"

She looked up and nodded. Still he waited until she smiled softly. "Leave me—you look tired, Om Asa. Get some rest."

His servant stood in the corridor holding a brandy on a silver salver. These strange middle-of-the-night rituals had become routine of late. Exeter slumped onto one of upholstered chairs in the hallway. For months now, the Nightshades had kept vigil from these chairs—only tonight it would be Mr. Tandi.

He took a sip of the warm amber liquid. "How long has it been since you and Mia announced yourselves at my door, Mr. Tandi?"

His manservant's eyes lit up at the memory. "My word—seems very long ago—ten years, I believe, sir." Exeter recalled the tall, soft-spoken African man standing in the foyer, holding the hand of a doe-eyed waif of a child, the young Anatolia Chadwick. Mia, as she was called even by her parents, was at best a distant relation. But, it seemed, he and his father were all the child had left in the world.

Mr. Tandi had recounted a hair-raising tale of a bloodthirsty raid on a small town built around a mining operation. Wearing the clothes on their backs and carrying a hidden pouch filled with diamonds, they had made their way to Cape Town, sold a few gems, and booked passage on the first ship bound for London.

A last swallow of brandy slipped down his throat. Exeter

closed his eyes and remembered the scrawny little girl and the African man—as dark as midnight—standing at the door. He set down his glass and rose from the comfortable upholstered chair. At Mia's bedchamber, he tapped lightly on the door before slipping inside to check on her.

Silently, Exeter stood near the edge of the canopy bed. He swept back a veil of diaphanous curtain and watched her breathe, tempted to get out his stethoscope and listen to her heart. She had always looked like an angel in her sleep; since when had she become the devil's own temptress?

For several months now, there had been provocative moments between them, including a few ardent displays of affection. Some of Mia's advances had been quite shocking and affected him deeply. So much so, he wasn't so sure he could still say that the attraction was entirely one sided. This evening, as was his custom, he had waited on a neighboring rooftop for her. From this vantage point, he had spied Mia seconds before her shift. Her nude figure bathed in soft moonlight . . . so breathtakingly beautiful, he had thought her as stunning as a painting he had once seen by Jules Lefebvre in the National Gallery of Victoria.

Just hours ago, she had stood on tiptoe and stroked the stubble along his jaw. He had captured her hand, and his lips had found the sensitive flesh on the inside of her wrist. His tongue traced a light blue vein, and her pulse had quickened. "*Carus Deus,* you are torture."

How long was he going to be able to resist her?

Chapter Two

EXETER PUT DOWN THE MORNING PAPER. "I didn't expect you up this early." He studied his charge over the rim of a tipped cup. She appeared entirely too chipper as she poured the Earl Grey and stirred in a dollop of milk and a lump of sugar.

"I must apologize for our hasty retreat from the ball last night." She paused to sip, silently. "You and Phoebe Armistead were having such a lovely time dancing together."

It seemed *chipper* had quickly merged with *testy*. Mia was nearly always out of sorts after a shift. Exeter set down his tea. "I danced twice with Phoebe. Once because I asked, the second time because—"

"Once was enough, I should think." Mia scraped a pat of butter across her toast with excessive vigor. "Phoebe is three months my junior, and yet you appear transfixed by her."

"More like three years your senior—and I was not, in the least, captivated." Exeter paused as he forked up a bite of smoked fish. "Phoebe's mother pushed me on to her. What was I to do, exactly, dance with you all evening? Even if we were . . ." Exeter stuffed the kipper in his mouth rather than finish his thought out loud. No sense encouraging Mia's lovesickness. For several months now, she had made him the focus of a girlish, adolescent admiration. He had hoped, once she became more settled with her new dual identity, this infatuation would diminish and her foolish behavior would ease. At the moment, it seemed Mia struggled less with the powerful changes to her body and more with her adjustment to her social life.

He chewed slowly and swallowed. "It would be rather selfish of me not to allow the attending bachelors a chance with the loveliest young woman at the ball, would it not?"

"Very kind of you, but which young man do you imagine might enjoy a lifelong companionship with a wife in daylight and a feline in the dark?" She bit into her toast and chewed. "Gilbert Sackville, Henry Madigan—perhaps Charles Mercer Fitzmaurice, Marquess of Shelburne?" Mia dabbed her mouth and returned the cloth to her lap before meeting his gaze.

"Mia, you must try to take this adjustment one waltz at a time—so to speak." Exeter lowered his fork and exhaled. "I suppose there is a part of me that hopes for some semblance of . . ."

"Of what, Om Asa?"

He shrugged. "Normalcy, I suppose."

She fixed a stiff, close-lipped smile. "Is there such a thing for a creature like me?"

When she spoke like that—softly, with that wistful look in her eyes—his heart ached inside his chest. Even now, when she was trying her best to needle and provoke, he admired her spirit, knowing it was this inner strength—this resilience of hers—that would see Mia through this most difficult time of her life. And he would do anything for his ward—short of what she wanted, which was unthinkable. No matter what his friends advised, she was his charge, and he would not take advantage of her—no matter how often or provocatively she threw herself at him.

"Never apologize, Mia. Your kind are brought in to this world for a reason." Exeter fashioned a reassuring smile. "You have a destiny to fulfill, my dear."

Mia chewed her toast and swallowed. "Is my new—difficulty—the reason Phoebe is old enough and I am not?"

He forked a bit of soft yolk onto a flake of fish. "Why do you keep bringing up Phoebe?"

Mia slanted sparkling dark eyes, full of devilish mischief. "Because she fancies you. She called you wickedly dashing, and once said she'd like to come upon you in a dark corner of the gallery behind the ballroom."

Exeter nearly choked on his bite of kipper and egg. "Since when does this kind of unseemly chitchat go on between young ladies of quality?" Mia's chortle of laughter destroyed his attempt to appear stern and disapproving. "And what about that poor young man—Cecil? You were rather rude to him, Mia."

His slightly forlorn ward sighed. "It was unkind. But he's always lurking about. I can't have a glance across the ballroom without him staring at me."

"That's because he's smitten." Exeter softened his scrutiny, but continued to stare at his lovely ward. "And your prowl about last night, after the ball? Are things . . . getting any easier?"

Her expression darkened before she looked away. "You should know—you followed me from rooftop to rooftop."

The door opened and Mr. Tandi entered the dining room. "A message, sir." Exeter picked up the envelope from the silver tray.

> Early this A.M., iDIP's tracker picked up the following transmission from the Outremer:
>
> Voice identified as that of Phaeton Black: "What is this insatiable lust for the Moonstone all about? According to Ping, even if I wanted to help you, the force inside this stone has a moral compass . . . (static) . . . no new army of snake heads. I'm afraid . . . (static) . . . sorry to disappoint."
>
> More static before an unidentified voice speaks: "Whose morals—yours or mine?"
>
> Voice identified as Phaeton: "And no snidely trickery."
>
> Transmission cuts off.

A hurried postscript was added across the bottom of the message in Tim Noggy's hand.

Doc—you won't believe where the message came from: 48°53'59"N, 2°17'59"E

Mia swallowed. "What is it, Om Asa?"

He read the message again, this time out loud. Her eyes widened at the mention of Phaeton Black. "Do you think it's really him?"

He shook his head. "If it is, it's a miracle. The odds of finding him this quickly . . . Let's not get our hopes up too high, as yet." Exeter stood. "Come, let's find this location."

Mia was out the door, through the hall, and down the corridor. If only she could see herself as he did in this moment. Mia thought of herself as a woman, and, in the technical sense, she was. As he watched her fly down the corridor he was tempted to call out, "No running in the house," as he had so often done during the past ten years.

He stood in the doorway of the study and rounded off the map coordinates. "Forty-eight degrees north by 2 degrees east. If I'm not mistaken that should place us on the Continent." He moved in beside her at the globe.

Placing her finger on the line of latitude, Mia turned the globe until he found longitude. Their fingers met over—"Paris, France." Mia jerked upright. "Our Paris, or an alternate Paris?"

"Mr. Noggy has advanced the idea that there may be touch points—places where one parallel universe connects with another. Just as we have discovered an alternate London, there may indeed be another Paris." He moved his finger westward, over the globe—across the channel, over the fertile plains of Kent, stopping at London. "A few months ago, before we lost Phaeton, he suggested a new wardrobe for you, Mia. Something less ingénue. Gowns that are more—sophisticated."

"I love that man with all my heart." Mia sighed. "Not as much as I love you, of course. But there are certain things Phaeton knows . . . mysterious things . . . and so understanding of the female temperament—our dreams and longings . . ." She tilted her chin, exposing a graceful length of neck as she turned to him. ". . . our desires."

And then there were moments with Mia, like this one. Sensuous moments when she was so utterly desirable his body ached for her. Caught off guard, his gaze lingered too long on her lips, which parted ever so slightly. Her large, liquid brown eyes returned his gaze honestly, openly.

He cleared his throat softly. "I thought we might . . . make a trip to Paris—have a look about for Phaeton, and order a new wardrobe for a beautiful young lady."

Even as she struggled to remain composed, her eyes lit up.

Exeter grinned. "One who doesn't scamper down hallways and say rude, upsetting things to well-meaning young men who just wish to waltz with her."

Mia exhaled a deep breath, but didn't roll her eyes, even though he knew she wanted to. "When might we leave for France?"

"I shall arrange travel this morning. We could leave by tomorrow morning if my agent can book passage." Exeter checked his pocket watch. "We'll give the Nightshades some time to sleep in. Jersey and Valentine got in very late last night."

Mia nodded. "I saw Valentine briefly—sneaking out of Jersey's room."

Exeter twisted a look of irony into a faint smile. "In a few more hours, we can all ride over to Lovecraft's factory together. America should be up and about by now—go check on her, would you?" Mia turned to leave and he caught her hand, placing the message about Phaeton in her palm. "Be sure to caution America about the news."

Mia smiled. "After all these months, she'll likely weep for joy."

"And Mia."

She turned back. "Yes, Om Asa?"

"Perhaps you should drop the Om in Om Asa. As charming as it was for you to adopt Mr. Tandi's honorific"—Exeter felt his jaw twitch from nerves, though he wasn't sure why—"I believe it's time to let it go."

She lingered near the door of his study. "May I call you Asa privately and Jason or Exeter among company or in public?"

He returned her smile. "I'd like that very much."

She whirled around, tossing a second thought over her shoulder. "And I shall call you 'the good doctor' when I'm cross. Or when I'm being minxy."

The moment Mia was down the hallway and out of earshot she paused for a muffled squeal of happiness and a bit of fancy footwork. A new wardrobe, designed by couturiers in Paris! The smile she had started with Exeter crept though her entire body.

Exeter. Jason. And perhaps Asa, when they were intimate together.

Of course she hadn't phrased it quite that way, in front of the doctor, but a lady could enjoy a momentary flight of fancy, couldn't she? She lifted her skirts enough to ascend the stairs. Reaching the third floor, she checked to make sure no one was looking and raced down the corridor to America's room.

At times like this she felt completely normal and estranged from the part of her new life that frightened her, terribly, at times. But when those dark urges came—always in the evening, and always so . . . irresistible. At the fifth door on the left, she rapped quietly and poked her head in the doorway. "America?"

Phaeton Black's exquisitely beautiful paramour waved her into the bedchamber. "Come in, Mia." America Jones stood near the tall windows in her room. Her profile was haloed briefly by morning light. She was large and round with child—an earthy fertility goddess—and she had never looked lovelier.

Exeter had made the remark the other afternoon at tea. And Mia wholeheartedly agreed. America had put on a bit of weight, and her cheeks glowed a rosy peach color, The effect over fawn skin tones was stunning. Everything about her spoke of the new life growing inside her. Phaeton's child.

Mia thought about the hopeful news she carried in her hand and smiled. She opened and shut the door quietly. "Exeter received a message from Tim Noggy." She paused, making sure to measure her words. "It seems Mr. Ping's flies on the wall have captured a conversation . . ."

America searched her face. "What are you saying, Mia?" Her voice was hesitant, as if she already knew but wouldn't dare let herself hope.

"One of the voices has been identified as Phaeton's." Mia held out the folded paper. She felt the tremble in America's hand as she passed her the note. "Perhaps you should sit down." Mia guided her over to the settee.

America held onto her hand as she read and Mia bit back the urge to speak until she could stand it no longer. "Well? I do think there is room to be hopeful, even though Exeter advises caution."

America held up a finger. "Shh! Let me read his speech again." Her gaze slid back and forth across the notepaper and stopped. "Snidely trickery." Her eyes sparked with light. "That certainly sounds like Phaeton vernacular—don't you think, Edvar?"

Large yellow eyes blinked as the gargoyle gradually made his appearance. A snort or snuffle from the leathery gray beast ended in a whiny, high-pitched yuk-yuk. America grinned. "There is always a little bit of no in every yes from Edvar, " she explained. "Phaeton claims Edvar is contrary by nature, but I have come to believe he's just a grumbler."

"Contrary and curmudgeon do go hand in glove." Mia agreed. She had only recently become aware of Edvar's presence, though Exeter had always been able to see the little fiend. Not much larger than a medium-sized terrier, the gargoyle had been Phaeton's companion since he was a child. Mia thought it quite charming and wonderfully protective of the creature to remain at America's side all these months. Mia squeezed her hand. "Tim was able to get map coordinates."

Near breathless, America looked up and whispered, "Where?"

"Paris!" Mia could contain her excitement no longer. "We're going after him."

America's gaze searched her face. "How—when?"

"Very soon. Tomorrow, if possible. I've sent messages to Tim Noggy, as well as my travel agent at Thomas Cook & Sons." Exeter stood in the doorway. "May I come in?"

"Please." America waved him in.

"Jersey and Valentine are downstairs breakfasting." Exeter cocked his head and examined her breakfast tray. "I see your appetite remains hearty." Gently, he took hold of America's wrist and removed his pocket watch. "Strong pulse—perhaps a bit fast, but after the news"—he smiled at her—"understandable."

America wiped away a tear and smiled. "Phaeton is alive."

Chapter Three

LAST ONE IN THE CARRIAGE, Exeter took a seat between Mia and America. Across the aisle, their bodyguards sat rather cozily together. He studied the two Nightshades, both darkly beautiful and private beings, who had revealed little about themselves until recently. Valentine Smyth and Jersey Blood had been wonderfully helpful in the first days and months of Mia's shocking transformation.

Jersey was a strapping male half-breed, tied by birth legacy to an aristocratic line of Normans, who in ancient times had consorted with fallen angels. The result was a race of demon shifters. To his credit, the captain of the Nightshades appeared to be very much in control of his inner Beelzebub, who had never been seen by any of the other members of the clandestine order of sentries with the exception of Valentine, the stunning female Nightshade, who was also Jersey's consort.

"His kind are known as watchers." Valentine had once explained, after Jersey had left the room. "Rebellious angels in ancient times—they roam the earth in search of duties to perform. No matter what you may hear about them, they are warriors and heroes among men."

Sensing Exeter's notice, Jersey lifted his gaze and tried to probe his thoughts. When this Nightshade gazed at you, it was as if he met your soul, not your eyes, and if he was not mistaken, the very private man under the cloak was a surprisingly compassionate creature.

Exeter dipped his head to see out the carriage window. They were passing Green Park. He settled into the plush squabs of the spacious town coach and smiled at the bodyguards across the aisle. "Was it a good trip into the Outremer?" His gaze moved from one to the other. "Safe journey, I take it?"

"We had an informative meeting with an Eden Phillpotts—double l, double t—proprietor of the Antiquarian Bookshop, 77 Charing Cross Road." Jersey's gaze shifted to Mia, who raised an inquiring brow. Before she could question him any further, Exeter addressed her directly. "On a private matter."

This was nothing he wanted Mia to know about—at least not until he heard what they both had to say in detail. Valentine had briefly mentioned something of their findings at breakfast. She and Jersey had apparently met with a shopkeeper who claimed to be able to help shifters acclimate to their new dual personas. Exeter had found her brief cap sum both alarming and, frankly, salacious. "Hard to take anyone seriously with a name like Phillpotts." Exeter coughed a bit and changed the subject. "I don't believe you have ever told us how you and Valentine met."

A smile cracked the ends of Jersey's mouth. "She tried to kill me."

Valentine grinned. "Back in my novice demon-slayer days."

"Novice as in novitiate," Jersey added, "Sister Valentina."

"It's true. I was a Sister of Mercy for a month or two. I spotted Jersey one evening in the garden. He was wearing black robes. Mistook him for a possessed priest I was tracking and endeavored to—"

"As I said—you tried to kill me." Jersey's gaze moved over Valentine Smyth with such intimacy, Exeter was forced to look away. He had seen that same expression on Jersey's face before the two had left for the Outremer.

Several evenings past, he had met with Jersey and Valentine in his study to discuss a method Mia could learn to use to control the time and place of her transformations. Jersey had talked about a little-known technique practiced by ancient shape-shifters, and a rare and collectible bookshop on Charing Cross Road. There had also been talk of a strange proprietor, not of this world.

"Who told you about this creature?" Exeter had asked.

"Tim Noggy." Valentine offered, quite seriously.

He had shaken his head. Since Lovecraft's death, the rotund Mr. Noggy, inventor and pseudo scientist, had overseen the repair of the professor's underground factory and labs. And he had done an admirable job of it—case in point: the message that had arrived at breakfast this morning. But what did Noggy know of such things as shape-shifting?

Frankly, Exeter found it exasperating. Still, what could it hurt to inquire? So it was agreed that, while in the Outremer, Jersey and Valentine would pay a visit to the proprietor of the bookstore recommended by Noggy.

Before leaving his study, Valentine had intimated the involuntary shifts were caused by pent-up desire, and stressed Mia's need for release. The number and frequency of her transformations suggested that she was—for lack of a more delicate description—sexually frustrated.

Exeter must have appeared unconvinced, as Valentine went on to explain: "Have you ever seen a cat that has been kept indoors, away from prowling toms in the alley? Pussy lifts her rump and cocks her tail to one side. If you stroke or scratch her scruff she'll go into raptures. Doctor, you admit seeing the panther assume the lordosis position—she was soliciting you to mount her."

Exeter had stared at Valentine. "What can be done about it, short of marrying her off?" He had wanted to add "and to whom" but the thought disturbed.

The carriage turned onto Lower Thames Street and hit a pothole, rousing Exeter from his troubled thoughts. Mia brushed against his shoulder. She wore a dark blue high-crowned hat, set at a jaunty angle. She looked up and met his gaze through the netting over her eyes. Once again he experienced a momentary falling sensation.

What was he to do with this brave and lovely young woman? The question continued to remain unresolved. He hoped that by the end of this day, he'd have some answers.

Exeter read the sign above the door. "*Deus Ex Machina,* God in the machine." Metal letterforms circled the large initial *L*—for Lovecraft. The insignia appeared to be scorched, and the *x* in *Ex Machina* hung askew, but the factory entrance was otherwise tidy and presentable. All the debris from the invasion had been cleared away. In fact, there was barely a trace of the mayhem and destruction that had taken place here just months ago.

He gestured his small coterie inside and followed them down into the bowels of Lovecraft's late, great enterprise. The elephantine Inter-Dimensional Injection Portal or iDIP sat on the old underground train tracks looking, oddly, as magnificent as ever. As they passed by the iron portal enclosure, Exeter suspected they were all thinking the same thing. The last time any of them had seen Phaeton Black alive, he had been sucked into the gigantic engine and blasted off to . . . France.

Exeter bit back an unexpected grin. Only Phaeton could get lost in Paris. He approached the round, unkempt, and affable young scientist who waited for them on the platform outside the laboratory. "Mr. Noggy."

"G'day, Doc." Tim Noggy nodded to Jersey and the ladies. "Nightshade and Shade-ettes." The heavyset young inventor smoothed back a wild bunch of curly hair, only to have it spring back in his face. He gestured the group inside the lab. "As some of you already know, we moved Gaspar to an underground surgery at Black Box—my brother's facility." Tim rolled his eyes a bit, an expression he used with some regularity. "That would be the technology genius brother, not the short rebellious one."

"May we speak with Gaspar, briefly?" Exeter inquired. "There must be some sort of Outremer device we can use to communicate."

The largish inventor shook his head. "He's being kept alive—in stasis—until we find Phaeton and reunite him with the Moonstone." Tim exhaled a heavy sigh. "Ruby and Cutter keep a close watch."

Exeter nodded. Gaspar Sinclair was the organizer and de facto leader of the Gentlemen Shades. The man was also unraveling. In order to preserve his brain, the decision had been made to move him to a facility in the Outremer where the disintegration would be greatly slowed, if not halted entirely.

And the security was impeccable at Oakley's underground facility. Even in his decrepit condition, the man was still the leader of the Nightshades and, as such, was vulnerable to abduction by Prospero's forces.

"I understand . . . Jersey mentioned that he's cognizant for a few minutes a day." Exeter's inquiry was more of a statement.

"Only for a few moments. They raise him to near consciousness—keeps the brain synapses firing. I realize this sounds more like sorcery than science in this world." Tim added with a shrug. "Ruby tells me he seems reassured that she and Cutter remain by his side."

Ruby and Cutter, as well as Jersey and Valentine, were the foursome who made up the Nightshades guard. Normally detailed to Gaspar's security, they had been reassigned to watch over those closest to Phaeton, which included Mia and himself, and—the gruesome truth was—anyone who might be abduction and torture worthy. The stakes were high between desperate, competing forces whose world continued to disintegrate. They would find a way to motivate Phaeton, for it was he alone who controlled access to the powers of the Moonstone—in the service of which, according to Mr. Ping, were unlimited.

There was a kind of genius on the part of the Egyptian goddess who bestowed keeper of the Moonstone on Phaeton. He was the least likely character of any of them to control such power, and yet Qadesh could not have made a wiser choice. Disdainful and delightfully dissipated by nature, Phaeton was also utterly incorruptible.

"And Professor Lovecraft's disabled son?"

"Lindsay Lovecraft? He's working with Oakley and Cutter."

Tim raised and lowered his shoulders. "It seems they've uncovered a large cache of aether buried under Prospero's headquarters. Enough to keep the Outremer powered a while longer. They're currently working on a way to redistribute the fuel." Tim moved over to a tall worktable that had been cleared off.

Jersey looked about the room. "Blimey—the lab is brighter than ever."

"The bulbs run off a turbine, electrical power converted from a steam engine in the rear of the iDIP," Tim explained. He rolled out a huge sheet of paper. "This is the most current map I could find. According to Lovecraft's manual, the iDIP isn't capable of giving map coordinates outside of our own planet, which means that the location has to be—*our* Paris." Tim hauled his hulking frame around the end of the lab table and spread out the street map.

"Forty eight degrees . . . fifty-three feet . . ." Tim mumbled the coordinates as he swept his hand through the streets of Paris, over Pont Saint-Michel, slowing near the University of Paris. "Puts us . . . here, Sorbonne Square." A sausage finger, tipped with a ragged nail, stopped in a small blind court.

Exeter joined the others around the large table. He pointed up the Seine, to the larger of the two islands in the middle of the river. "Île de la Cité. A short distance away." He traced a path across the Pont Neuf to the west end of the island. "Our base of operations." Exeter thumped the map. "Trust the Parisians to nickname Place Dauphine *'le sexe de Paris'* because of its suggestive V shape."

Everyone leaned over the map to observe a perfect triangle, surrounded by uniform homes and apartment buildings. America looked up from the map and grinned. "Phaeton would approve."

Exeter straightened. "I've arranged to take over the largest apartment available in the L'Hôtel Claude, Place Dauphine." He looked around the room. "I'm hoping there will be seven of us. Jersey Blood, Valentine Smith—Mia and myself—Mr. Noggy and Mr. Ping . . . if we can locate him."

Tim looked up in surprise. "I'm going to Paris?"

"Pack a bag, Mr. Noggy." Exeter swiveled toward the ladies. "And America."

America squeaked a cry of happiness, even as he narrowed his gaze. "You're invited along for one reason and one reason only—I don't trust you to stay put in London. If labor should start and you're on the road somewhere alone . . ." Exeter shook his head. "As it is, we'll have to sneak you into France—just keep that traveling coat on."

He caught an exchange of winks among the women. "And let's try to keep this trip discreet—we take as few people as possible into our confidence." Exeter exhaled and looked to Tim. "Have there been any more transmissions?"

"Static. Garbled words, mostly." A sly grin twitched at Tim's mouth. "Then this, just before you arrived." Tim held up a paper and cleared his throat. "There's bit of transmission static, then a voice: 'that's because sexual perversion—kink—as you call it,' . . . more static . . . 'is only kinky the first time, and just because I'm interested in pornography, doesn't mean I'm easy.' "

America grinned. "Phaeton has always been rather fond of titillating language and subject matter. He often borrows picture books from Mrs. Parker's collection of erotica."

Mia's eyes widened slightly, and she moistened her lips. Exeter quickly read his ward's response to America's remarks and changed the subject. "What about map coordinates? Anything new? A number that might indicate a third dimension—height or depth? It would greatly narrow our search, would it not, if we knew to look on top of a building or below ground?"

Jersey sparked to his queries. "It's obvious Phaeton is being held by unsavory elements of the Outremer. And if his captors are unraveling, they would likely hole up underground."

Exeter nodded. "Tim's reports indicate that deep, below-ground shelter affords residents of the Outremer some form of protection."

Tim leaned over the map and *tsk*ed. "Those nasty, destructive cosmic rays."

"Catacombs!" Mia perked up. "At university, we spent nearly a week on the catacombs under the city—more than 180 miles of quarry tunnels snake through the foundations of Paris. I believe nearly all of them are off-limits, though I understand the ossuaries are open for public viewing. Rather fascinating, though eerie—piles of human skulls and bones arranged into columns and walls."

Exeter's gaze moved around the table. "A trip to the Drunken Lizard may be in order. Pop in on a cartographer by the name of Potter. If I recall, the man spent several years digging around below ground in Paris, as a surveyor for the proposed Métro—an underground rail system. For the price of a pint or two . . ." Exeter quirked up both brows. "Shall we, ladies and gentlemen?"

Mia held on to her hat as the group emerged from the abandoned train station. A strong wind whipped off the Thames and through the looming construction girders that currently made up the Tower Bridge. Would the impressive overpass ever be completed?

America trotted up beside Exeter. "Would you mind dropping me off at Mrs. Parker's? I'd like to make arrangements to close the office. Better now, before we leave, I should think. I'm nearing my last month and it's to be expected that I would take a bit of time off."

America smiled sheepishly. "Once we find Phaeton and our pea in the pod arrives, we can reopen Moonstone Investigations. Try to get back to normal—if such a thing is possible for us."

A lopsided grin tipped the ends of Exeter's mouth, telegraphing his skeptical amusement. "The pairing of a daughter of a Cajun witch raised by a sea captain and a gifted investigator of psychical disturbances." He shook his head. "Such a couple could hardly enjoy a mundane life." He helped America into the carriage and then turned to Mia. As luck would have it, he failed to notice the flush on her cheeks—thank God. Because she wasn't about to answer his prying questions.

At the very mention of Mrs. Parker, Mia's pulse had elevated. Over the years and especially these last few months, she had either overheard or been privy to conversations that paired Doctor Jason Exeter with Mrs. Esmeralda Parker, madame to a bawdy house of notorious reputation, and home to Phaeton Black's below-street flat.

Something raw and envious roiled around in her gut, and by the time they turned onto Shaftesbury, she was nearly afire with curiosity about Madame Parker. Lost in a preoccupation of lurid thoughts, she listened absently to snippets of conversation, until she caught Exeter's stern look. "You are and will continue to be the most sought after of any of us, America. Phaeton is obviously being held by someone—whether it is Prospero or some other unknown force . . ." Exeter frowned to emphasize a point. "You must listen and obey my orders at all times or I cannot protect you."

Mia tilted forward in time to catch an upward flutter of eyelids from America. She well knew the feeling. Exeter could be insufferably protective at times.

In front of 21 Shaftesbury Court, America was soon out the carriage door, and Valentine followed after. At the last moment, Mia stepped out of the carriage. Exeter grabbed hold of her elbow as she descended.

"This is rather irregular, Mia; where might you be going?"

"I believe I'll tag along here while you and Jersey have a pint or two at the Drunken Lizard." Mia followed after America and Valentine. "Be sure to ask Mr. Potter if he might have a copy of the original quarry map—as I recall, there are several unauthorized entrances." She tried a smile, something to warm the scowl on Exeter's face.

"Mia, I'd rather you didn't . . ."

A low iron fence encircled the below-stairs office. "Didn't what?" She hesitated at the gate. Turning to Exeter, she arched a brow. "Why would you object to a visit with Mrs. Parker? She's a friend of yours, is she not?"

Chapter Four

MIA FELT THE COOL DISAPPROVAL of Exeter's gaze all the way down the stairs to the below-street shop America and Phaeton rented from Mrs. Parker. She tilted her head back to read the writing on the plaque above the door knocker.

Moonstone Investigations
No uncommon psychical disturbance refused,
no matter how perplexing.

The mental image of her guardian's icy stare melted away as she opened the door and viewed the space that had recently been refurbished. The walls were papered in a subtle paisley of warm caramel tones, and the furniture, though not ornate, was quietly professional. Two upholstered wing chairs were angled toward a desk that had recently been polished to a gleaming luster. "I quite love the smell of beeswax." Mia sniffed. "My word, this is, so"—she searched for the right words—"very professional. I would guess it to be the office of a solicitor, if I hadn't read the sign on the door."

America beamed. "Phaeton insisted we not look like a couple of gypsies out to hoodwink a frightened client who has just seen an apparition."

Mia examined a smaller secretary positioned under a high-set window. A Franklin Typewriter perched upright on a small desk no larger than a vanity, and beside the typewriter, a gleaming wood box. A brass armature cradled a handle with a speaking cone at one end and a listening cone at the other. "And this is the telephone I've heard so much about," she exclaimed. "May I?"

America showed her how to hold the receiver and crank the handle. "One short ring for the exchange." Mia's eyes grew wide as she listened intently. "The gentleman is asking for a name?"

"Tell him you wish to speak with someone at the order desk of Fortnum and Mason," America whispered with a grin.

Mia nodded, speaking somewhat stiltedly. "I should like to speak with the gentleman at the order desk at Fortnum and Mason, if you would, please."

While she waited for the call to go through, they discussed their favorite Fortnum's hampers—something to take on the train with them tomorrow. Mia's eyes suddenly grew wide. "Yes, hello? Is this Fortnum and Mason?" She smiled. "My name is Anatolia Chadwick, calling on behalf of Doctor Jason Exeter, Twenty-two Half Moon Street, Mayfair." Mia nodded her head again.

America grinned. "You must speak!"

Mia returned the grin. "Yes, yes . . . that is correct. I'd like to order the Park Lane hamper—the one with the smoked salmon and the cheese . . . yes, the one with the Scotch eggs . . . lovely." Mia winked at both women standing close by. "And a tin of cinder toffees, please . . . dipped in chocolate." Mia's head bobbed. "That will be all . . . first thing in the morning—twenty-two Half Moon Street." She smiled broadly at the group, which now included a very attractive woman who had entered the office through a rear door. "Yes—thank you, sir."

Mia set the receiver handle down gently. "My word, that was . . . so . . . simple." Wide-eyed, she turned to the ladies surrounding her. "I want one."

America laughed her musical, tinkling laugh. "Even though the installation was costly and the phone rarely rings, I must say it is a marvel. Though I suspect if Phaeton were here, he'd sit in that desk chair and glower."

"Phaeton does so love to glower." The attractive woman spoke, and, tilting her head slightly, she smiled at Mia. She didn't appear to be a prostitute. She wore a high-necked blouse and skirt—afternoon attire, not unlike the blouse Mia herself wore under a fitted jacket.

The woman moved closer. "Could this be . . . ? I am guessing by the company you keep . . . you must be Doctor Exeter's ward."

America also stepped forward. "Silly and rather rude of me. I did not realize you two have never met. May I introduce Anatolia Chadwick? Anatolia, please meet Esmeralda Parker."

She shook Mrs. Parker's hand. "Please call me Mia."

Madame Parker had lovely blue eyes, a good deal of ash blond hair arranged in a topknot on her head . . . and . . . Mia lowered her eyes . . . an ample bosom. How cruel of Exeter to have an affinity for large breasts, something she would never, ever have.

Esmeralda took both of her hands. "What a pleasure to finally meet. Jason has told me so much about you—how proud he is of all your scholastic accomplishments." Mrs. Parker stepped back and studied Mia as though she were a new doxy to offer her whoremonger clientele. "He never once mentioned how beautiful you are."

A wave of shame descended like a heavy, wet woolen blanket over Mia. Mrs. Parker was being kind, even as her own thoughts were resentful and envious. Short of breath, Mia gulped for air as quietly as possible.

The appealing Madame appeared to sense the awkwardness of their situation. Was this uneasy tension between them as difficult for her as it was for Mia? And Mia certainly did not wish to be thought of as a smitten, jealous child, inappropriately taken with her guardian.

"America, why don't you and Valentine put a kettle on in

the flat, while Mia and I get acquainted?" America and Valentine opened a door and disappeared down a hallway that, presumably, led to Phaeton's old flat.

Mia cleared her throat. "Exeter . . . the doctor . . . never . . ." She realized she had nothing to say to Mrs. Parker—she knew nothing about the woman. Exeter had never spoken of her directly, and why would he? According to her friend, Phoebe Armistead, a gentleman never discussed his mistress. Oh, there might be an inference or the occasional whisper at his club, but nothing more.

Her entire body wanted so badly to turn away—run from this intimidating woman of experience. Mia willed herself to stay put and not—repeat not—bite her lip. She lifted her chin. "You are his mistress."

"Jason has a standing weekly appointment." A faint smile tugged at the edges of Mrs. Parker's mouth. "Although, I must say he has not been as regular of late. I was hoping you might have some idea why. The last time I saw Jason, he seemed on edge, as though something weighed heavily on his mind." The woman quirked up a brow. "And now that I see you, Mia, I am harboring a suspicion. Might his preoccupation have something to do with you?"

So . . . as it turned out, the Madame was intrigued. Mia slid an equally curious look back at her. There were, in fact, many things she would like to know about Exeter. Intimate, personal things. The doctor likely had sexual preferences . . . proclivities.

Back when Exeter's father, Baron de Roos, was alive, they had spent a good deal of time at the baronial mansion on the Thames. Mia didn't know much about sex, so she had gone exploring for books on the subject. Since childhood, she had called the huge two-story room in the manse the library of secrets, as it was perhaps the most extensive, private library of arcane knowledge in all of Great Britain.

Mia had found a number of illustrated texts edited by Sir Richard Burton. Sitting on the top step of the spiral staircase, she had pored over the exotic sex manuals for hours—until her bum hurt. She had also grown more and more aroused, to the point that she called for a bath and had a good long soak. Afterward she had touched herself—in exploration—and thought of Exeter. She had awoken the next morning in an irritable temper, harboring the distinct impression that there was much more to know about her bodily desires.

Mia's cheeks flushed with heat, even as she dared to look the worldly Mrs. Parker in the eye. "I expect Doctor Exeter's disquiet may have a great deal to do with me."

"Would it help any to talk about it?"

She began to shake her head no, deny her agony again, like she had so many times before. Perhaps . . . not this time . . . not with the answers to so many of her questions standing right in front of her.

"Even as a child I adored him. Exeter was barely out of university when he took me into his care. I thought him the finest, handsomest man in all the world—with his long dark romantic hair and green eyes. Later, I grew to greatly admire his brilliance. Both his dedication to the arcane sciences, as well as his work in practical medicine—blood grouping and the like." Mia fingered a stack of blank pages beside the typewriter. "I expect most everyone thought I'd grow out of my childish romantic attachment." Mia sighed. "But it is not so easily done, I'm afraid."

"Have you told him?"

"Not in so many words." She resisted a frown. "He is aware of my admiration"—Mia lowered her gaze—"awkward as it is."

Mrs. Parker ventured closer. Something in her eyes spoke of trepidation, but there was also a gentleness in her manner, as if she had expected this moment might come for some time. "Jason loves you dearly, Mia."

"I'm sure you're right—just not in the way I would hope to be loved." Mia swallowed, "I was rather hoping you might help me in this matter. After all, you know all the things he most . . . enjoys."

The moment she said the words, Mia understood the shocking boldness and impertinence of the request. The Madame stared for a moment. Then the moment turned into a very long moment. Frankly, Mia wondered if the woman was going to laugh or slap her hard across the face. She braced for either one and received neither.

"Shall we join America and Valentine for a spot of tea?" Mrs. Parker slipped an arm through hers. "You must realize, Mia, that whatever transpires between Jason and I is a private matter. But I might suggest to you something I have learned about men, over the years."

Mia exhaled a breath, brightening somewhat. "That being?"

"Most of them, the strong virile ones anyway, like to do the chasing—part of the hunt I suppose, it gets them wanting . . . needing more."

Mia nodded. "Yes, of course. I have been too obvious. I must learn how to beguile him."

Mrs. Parker slanted an amused gaze her way. "Jason is a man of fine character—but I suspect you are a great temptation."

Exeter rocked gently with the sway of the carriage and observed the agitated behavior of his ever vigilant, unflappable bodyguard. Tucked into a corner, Jersey Blood stretched out on the opposite bench seat of the coach and glared out the carriage window. The scowl deepened, however, when he fixed his gaze on Exeter.

"You're going to have to face facts, sooner or later. Someone needs to administer some relief to Mia—she needs to learn to control that inner wildcat."

Exeter returned Jersey's glare with one of his own. "We'll discuss the matter this evening with Mia. The proposed measures are quite extraordinary and frankly, somewhat deviant. She not only should be apprised of this unusual therapy but she must have a choice in the matter."

"We are about to embark on a mission that is not without its dangers." Jersey persisted. "This is a way for her to quickly gain control over the shifting."

Exeter narrowed a menacing gaze at the Nightshade. "As I said, we'll take this up after supper." He had hoped for a method less carnal for Mia. But even the ancient codices had alluded to the control and release of sexual pleasure as a way to manage aberrant transformations.

He inhaled a few deep breaths and fingered the rolled-up map on his knees. Using his own method of mind control, he moved his thoughts to something less perturbing. Their trip to the Drunken Lizard had turned out to be timely as well as fortuitous. They had easily found the cartographer, Potter, in the pub. An angular hollow-cheeked man, with pointed ears that protruded between locks of hair, making him seem all the more . . . elvish. After several pints, Exeter convinced the spindly bloke to sell him his map of the proposed Paris underground. Leastwise, that was what the map's legend purported. In actuality, the map also included the labyrinth of interconnected limestone quarry tunnels—better known as the Paris catacombs.

"There are a number of ways down into the catacombs from the colleges and there are likely many more." Potter was on his third or fourth pint and still seemed perfectly alert—not a bleary eye or a slur out of the man. So when he suggested they move to the rear of the pub, they all followed him into a small private dining area and watched the mapmaker consume yet another glass.

"See here . . ." Potter held the translucent parchment map up to an oil lamp that afforded a whole new view of the catacombs. "Secret passageways and pass-throughs only a rare few know of, but be wary"—Potter had flashed a warning look—"not all of these byways are safe to use." The flickering wick behind vellum paper barely illuminated his face. "Some of these larger alcoves are new, relatively speaking, dug within the last fifty years. Nowadays Red-shirt anarchists and the like hold meetings in these spaces . . . store arms and explosives—so take care. By now there could be miles of underground fortifications that are mined and booby-trapped."

Exeter mulled over Potter's warning as the carriage slowed

outside 21 Shaftesbury Court. It seemed myriad worries filled his head this afternoon. The trip, the tunnels—and Mia for another. He had left his ward in excellent hands, yet he could not help but worry. The tic in his jaw muscle signaled his underlying concern. Would Mia and Esmeralda talk? And if they did—what, or more specifically, who would they discuss? Mia was curious right now and looking for answers, as were they all. He tried shoving the troubled thoughts into a dark corner of his mind with no success.

Jersey leaned forward and pressed the door latch. "I'll collect the ladies if you wish." His bodyguard exited first, and Exeter joined him on the sidewalk. "Would you see the ladies home in the carriage? I intend to speak with Mrs. Parker on a private matter—pop in at Thomas Cook, check on our travel arrangements. I'll hire a cab outside Drake's. I shan't be far behind."

Inside the brothel, Exeter checked his pocket watch. Not yet four in the afternoon, well before peak hours, and business appeared to be brisk. Exeter glanced at two attractive females sitting in the parlor. They looked for all the world like well-bred young women—not the doxies they actually were. Part of the appeal, and Esmeralda's secret to success, was appearances. Mrs. Parker's looked to be more of a quality boardinghouse than bawdy house. No doubt it was even more titillating that way.

"Jason, this is a pleasant surprise." He turned toward the familiar voice. The Madame approached, looking lovely, but also a bit flushed, and no doubt curious.

"Esmeralda." He nodded formally, quickly shifting his attention to the young women who stepped up beside her. His gaze landed on America. "I gather you have made arrangements to close up shop temporarily?"

"Yes, I've written up a notice and posted it on the door." A glow radiated from Phaeton's darling paramour. "The paperhangers just finished the nursery."

He'd seen the small room she referred to as a nursery in the flat, and it was no bigger than a pantry closet. Still, her smile was infectious. "Fairies and gnomes?" he asked.

America shook her head. "Butterflies and honeybees . . . in a meadow . . . with rainbows."

"Lovely picture—the babe at play in Elysian Fields." He broadened his smile, before turning to the madame of the house. There had been little or no contact between him and Esmeralda in months. Not since his battle of wills with Mia had begun—how could he have possibly taken an evening off with Mia's episodic, involuntary shifts on the rise?

Exeter made eye contact briefly with Mia. "Jersey will see you home." He nodded to their imposing bodyguard, who gently steered the young women toward the exit. Mia paused at the door, suspicion written all over her face. "You aren't coming with us?"

He shook his head. "I shall follow along after I finish here." He quickly signaled Jersey with his eyes, who took Mia by the arm and escorted her out the door.

"Your ward is lovely, Jason."

He turned back to study her expression, which had not changed, much. The hint of color that had blushed her cheeks earlier had faded, leaving her a bit pale, though the curious expression remained—eyes full of questions, not knowing where to begin.

"Might we go somewhere private, where we can talk?"

"My apartment?"

He shouldn't have hesitated with his answer. During his brief moment of indecision, storm clouds gathered behind those lovely ice-blue eyes of hers. "Yes, why not?" He shrugged in surrender and gestured up the stairs.

Inside her rooms, she turned up the gaslight and moved to a breakfront. "Whiskey or cognac?"

Esmeralda's boudoir was inviting, familiar—filled with books and art. Looking around at the furnishings, he could not think of a sofa or chair they had not . . . taken pleasure on.

Exeter set his hat down on the side table. "Nothing for me."

She turned away from him, and poured the whiskey. "One for me." She poured another. "And one for me."

Exeter moved closer, so close he nudged the back of her bustle.

"Your charge is lovely, Jason." Sweeping her skirt to one side, she turned to face him.

Slowly, without taking his gaze away, he reached around her. "I believe I'm thirsty after all."

"I shall try a third time. Your ward is love—"

"Mia needs me."

She inhaled a breath and spoke on the exhale—barely a whisper. "I need you."

He tossed the smoky spirit down his throat, savoring the liquid amber burn. "We do not need each other, Esmeralda—we enjoy each other." The whiskey loosed a slow smile.

Though her lips remained pressed together, she responded in kind. "A good deal of enjoying . . . as I recall."

"I assume you and Mia spoke." He gentled his voice. "This is going to sound terribly intrusive, but I must know what you discussed."

"Besides you, or including you?"

Studying her, Exeter exhaled. "Naturally, Mia is curious . . . about us."

Esmeralda pushed away from the breakfront, bringing her lips to within inches of his, but she didn't move to caress him. At the last second she moved away. "Among other things, she asked me for the address of Etienne Artois, a well-known male prostitute—a young *amoureux des femmes* in Paris."

Exeter pivoted toward her slowly. "And your reply?"

Chapter Five

THE SLICE OF CHERRY TART DID NOTHING to soothe the tempest in Mia's roiling stomach. She gathered her napkin and set it beside the slice of barely touched dessert. If she was not mistaken, Exeter appeared to be rushing dinner along.

For a time, conversation had been lively at the table, what with talk of tomorrow's travel itinerary—trains, the channel crossing, and a hotel suite in Calais. Even Exeter's packing instructions caused a stir of excitement. He had advised Mr. Tandi to have several empty trunks shipped separately for the new clothing items they would return with. "At this point it is hard to estimate the length of our stay—though I suspect we will be there long enough for you to have at least one fitting, Mia."

Somewhere between the turtle soup and rib roast, she had caught him staring at her across the dining table . . . with angry eyes. In her youth, she knew what that coal-black stare meant. A strongly worded lecture or worse—a paddling. Oddly enough, a vivid recollection of one of his paddlings caused a flush of heat to rise from her chest to her cheeks. Good Lord, the thought was—titillating.

As shocking and disturbing as the changes taking place inside her were, something else had shifted these past few months. Her feelings for Doctor Exeter had transmogrified, as well. She no longer thought of him as her guardian—far, far from it.

Exeter was the first to stand. "Brandy in my study." He nodded briefly to the ladies at table, yet his gaze lingered on her. "You may join us, as well, Mia."

The pounding of her heart doubled the pace of her footsteps as she was escorted down the polished parquet floors leading to the doctor's study.

What was this all about? Exeter had stayed behind to talk to, or have relations with, his mistress. She had a sneaking suspicion it was the former. One, because that was the way Exeter was, controlling to a fault. It was his forte, as well as his favorite pastime, to nose about in her business. If it was possible to huff or harrumph quietly in one's thoughts, Mia harrumphed. Secondly, she imagined a man who had just had a boff with his mistress would convey a relaxed frame of mind, and Exeter was decidedly unsettled this evening.

Inside the dark, womb-like comfort of his study, she took a seat and watched him pour brandy into three snifters. "Would you like me to warm yours, Mia?"

Puzzled, she raised both brows. "I'm not sure—yes, I suppose so."

Holding the snifter above a candle flame, he turned the glass. As he warmed the brandy, he related a story that was shocking, yet not entirely without hope. Glancing up from the glass, he studied her. "Sorry to put it so clinically, but there you have it."

Mia quietly repeated what she thought she had heard. "You're saying I could gain control over the shifts by using my own arousal, paroxysm, and release. And as I learn to control these physical urges . . . I will also be able to shift at will." She swallowed.

Exeter handed her a warm brandy. "Drink me."

Mia looked up into eyes that had warmed slightly. He quoted *Alice's Adventures in Wonderland*. Brandy fumes tickled her nose as she sipped. The warm Armagnac slipped down her throat. "Mmm . . ."

She was tempted to answer in Alice-speak, something memorized from childhood. But was he baiting her? Exeter often accused her of being immature, but in actuality, it was *he* who was uncomfortable with the notion of her maturity. She slid a sultry smile his way. "As long as it's not poison, wot?"

Emboldened by several sips of brandy, Mia turned to Jersey. "And what more can you tell us of this—bookshop proprietor, Mr. Eden Phillpott?"

Jersey puffed slowly on his cigar. "Valentine and I were escorted into a small room in the back of the shop. He sat in a large chair with his legs crossed—part human with the head of a lion."

Mia stared. "Like the Egyptian goddess, Hathor, or . . . male equivalent?"

Jersey cracked a lopsided grin. "He wore a tweed shooting jacket with elbow patches and smoked French cigarettes, lighting one from the butt of the other."

Mia leaned forward. "You mentioned his teachings—knowledge that must be imparted to my body. How might this be accomplished?" She looked from one man to the other. "I take it that someone—must instruct me, personally?"

Exeter set his brandy down. "How are you feeling this evening?" Gently, he took hold of her arm, placing his thumb on her wrist. Hooking a finger into his waistcoat pocket, he slipped out his watch. Mia waited for him to finish taking her pulse. He asked the same set of questions every evening.

"Somewhat agitated, I suppose." She exhaled, a bit loudly. "There is this—I don't know how describe it. It feels like tension. And sensations of hot and cold—as if something is building inside me."

"Your pulse is up, slightly, from last night." Exeter released her wrist. "No headache?"

She shook her head no, then yes. "There is a dull pressure in the back of the skull. Nothing painful, as yet."

Exeter settled into the wing chair opposite. "Mia, there is a doctor on Harley Street. In fact there are several physicians who treat women's hysteria with a massage therapy. I thought we might consider—"

Mia cut in. "But, what if something went badly wrong—a shift in the middle of treatment?"

He sighed. "That is one of the complications."

Mia's cheeks flamed with heat. "This is all so humiliating." She slid her gaze from Jersey to Exeter. "Why couldn't you do this therapy?"

When Exeter hesitated, Jersey snuffed out his cigar. "Someone has to relieve her, Jason. If you won't do it, I will."

Exeter's frown darkened into something truly menacing. "You will do no such thing." The two men stared each other down.

Finally, Jersey broke the deadlock. "Mr. Phillpott kindly provided us with instructions—a version of this very technique has changed things dramatically for me. I believe it will work for you, as well, Mia."

"And yet, we actually know very little about this therapy," Exeter's argument was more of a warning.

Jersey stood and stretched. "I'm off to play a cutthroat game of backgammon with Valentine." On his way out of the study, he tossed a conspiratorial wink at her just to irritate Exeter. "Ask him for Valentine's notes."

Mia smiled. Everything about this brave and stoic Nightshade had always seemed a bit dark and tormented. But lately he was less morose—as if a great burden had been lifted. "Good night, Jersey."

"It's good to feel human again." Jersey shut the door softly.

Exeter poured them each another brandy and settled into a wing chair. He studied her with steely eyes. Not his usual evaluation, this was more like the way he studied a chess piece when his king was threatened, and there were few moves left on the board.

Mia finally released a sigh. "You've been staring at me all night with those angry eyes, like I was in for a good paddling."

No answer from him, not a peep, just the ticking of the wall clock.

He sipped his brandy and continued to stare over the rim of his glass. Finally, he lowered the snifter. "Oh, I'm not going to paddle you, Mia. I'm going to make you climax."

She gulped hard and his eyes dropped to her throat. He

raked a strand of hair behind his ears, and something wild and thrilling stirred in her belly. All she had thought about these last few months was this man—so calm and reserved—so completely and perfectly handsome. He was her protector. Her teacher. Her knight in somewhat tarnished armor.

He was . . . her Exeter. And he was everything she had ever wanted in a man.

She had dreamed about doing things with him—wicked fantasies that were about to come true . . . only in the oddest way possible. She would experience intimacy with him, even though he did not love her passionately.

That he cared for her deeply was a certainty—just not in the way a man loved a woman. These physical intimacies were being foisted upon him. Mia sighed. If she took into account his most recent behavior, there were signs he might be reevaluating their relationship—like last night. Exeter had kissed the inside of her wrist, and then quickly apologized. "From here on out, I will have to keep a close watch on myself." And there had been a flicker of desire in his eyes—she was sure of it.

"I take it you are talking about a kind of release." She raised a determined chin and met his gaze. "I will reach some kind of apex of pleasure, after which the involuntary urge to shift will diminish."

With a flick of his eyes Exeter read the mantel clock. He reached inside his dinner jacket and handed over a piece of folded notepaper. "Here, take this."

"Valentine's notes?

He nodded. "Read them in your room."

Mia rose from her chair. "When shall I expect you?"

"I am going to finish this brandy. Make an appearance in the parlor, and retire early." He looked up at her. "Will that give you enough time?"

"Good Lord, Exeter." Mia rolled her eyes. "Could we please get this small matter over with? Don't leave me pacing."

He swirled a slosh of amber around his glass. "This is not a small matter, and you will see me—when I get there."

She shut the study door louder than necessary. Not a slam, but something good and testy.

Exeter closed his eyes and lay his head back against the tufted upholstery of his wing chair. He pictured Mia reading Valentine's notes and immediately fell to massaging his temples. At least the notes would prepare her, but it made his task no less precarious.

He was already teetering on the edge of lasciviousness with his lovely ward and yet he had held back. He was twelve years her senior—nothing new in that, of course. And this certainly wouldn't be the first time a gentleman formed an attachment to a younger cousin. In fact, marriages of this kind were almost commonplace.

So what held him back? Mia had grown into one of the loveliest creatures he had ever set eyes upon. There were times when all he wished to do was look upon her. Once or twice she had caught him admiring her and he had not shifted his eyes, but had allowed his gaze to linger, even caress her.

His gaze moved to the chess table in front of the hearth. Several nights past, she had opened with the queen's gambit and immediately sacrificed a pawn—only to get her pawn back seven moves later! He was quite sure it would not be long before she would beat him at his favorite game.

That same evening, Mia had called him stubborn to a fault and he had called her recalcitrant. Exeter exhaled a silent sigh. All he had ever wished for Mia was a happy, normal life. Grow up, meet a solid young man, and marry. Establish a home of her own and children. Everything that was no longer possible for her.

He drained his glass and tried not to think too hard about what he was about to do. Leaving his study, he noted the jump in his pulse, well beyond its usual sixty-eight beats per minute. He checked in with his guests in the parlor. Just Valentine and Jersey hunched quietly over a backgammon board. America had retired early. He walked the perimeter of the room in silence, not unaware of the fact that he was poor company this evening.

Exeter pivoted on his heel and said good night.

He climbed the curve of the grand staircase slowly, not in dread, but with considerable caution. It was very likely this night would change his relationship with Mia forever. They would have to find a new path together, a new way of seeing each other, relating to one another.

There was a possibility, if he handled this experience right, it could open up a whole new life for her. But if things went badly—if she shifted unexpectedly—the experiment could end in heartbreak.

Exeter didn't bother to turn up the gaslight in his bedchamber. He found his dressing room by feel and removed a freshly pressed cravat from the highboy. Raising his chin, he loosened the tie he wore and slipped it through his collar. With both neck cloths looped in one hand, he collected his medical kit and made his way to Mia's room.

He rapped quietly before he slipped inside. It was to be expected Mia would be nervous—but he could palpably feel his own anxiety heighten, as he pressed the door shut. He turned around and found her standing near her four-poster bed, wearing nothing but a pale damask counterpane. As she turned, the gossamer quilt fell off one shoulder and the loosely wrapped coverlet parted. Exeter inhaled sharply. A deep angle of exposed flesh invited his gaze. Rounded breasts, and lower—past her navel—a darker hint of curls. She had removed all but the pillows and sheets from her bed, and had lit several lamps and a number of candles. The effect against the pale peach skin tones of her body was mesmerizing.

Twice this evening he had seen her swallow hard. Now it was his turn. "This won't require a complete disrobing—unless . . ."

"And if a shift happens?" she asked.

"In a heightened state of arousal? I should think I'm either dead or badly maimed." Exeter winced a bit. "Sorry. You must forgive my poor attempt at gallows humor."

Mia managed a soft, skittish laugh. "And here I was trying for lovely and seductive."

"And you are all of that." He closed some of the distance between them. "But this is not a seduction, Mia—this first time is to be a lesson in how to use your sexual release to control the inner beast."

She glanced up at him shyly. "I read the notes, Exeter. There is some kind of connection, a state of being that happens during the shifts which correlates to the act of pleasure."

"If it wasn't for the fact that you could injure yourself—or me—I would have given you the notes and let you experiment in private. But we need to be careful here. You read the example of the young man who died?"

Mia nodded. "It happened during a partial shift. He stopped breathing and never recovered. The lion-headed creature, Mr. Eden Phillpott, advises there be a mentor or guide present, like yourself."

"Someone with experience." Exeter bit out, making sure she understood their relationship—that of instructor and student. He leaned over the sheets and stacked a number of pillows near the middle of the headboard. "I believe it would be most comfortable for you if you would lie back—in the middle of your bed."

As he straightened, he became aware of Mia's gaze locked on the ties in his hands. Her eyes quickly darted back up to his face. She nodded weakly as the color drained from her cheeks.

Hoping to appear less stern, Exeter raised both brows. "I am obliged to ask, what would pleasure you most? I am willing to do whatever it is you need of me tonight."

She turned her back and stepped out of the coverlet, letting it fall to the floor. "I thought this wasn't to be a seduction."

He took in every inch of her lovely lithe body—the curve of

her spine, and soft shoulder blades—not too angular. He reached out to caress her round, smooth buttocks, and stopped himself. "Perhaps you might order me to do things to you . . . if the thought excites you."

Her skin glowed in the candlelight—not the typical rosy porcelain of the winsome English lass, but something warmer, sleeker, in pale tawny-colored tones.

"Something like . . . look at me, Exeter." Unpinning her hair, she pivoted, slowly, arching her back as she turned toward him. He felt as though his eyes devoured her breasts, which were small and perfect with brown nipples set high on the slope of the curve. Stunning. Arousing.

Last night, he had glimpsed her standing in the open window, so achingly beautiful bathed in nothing but the pale moonlight. Then later, so vulnerable—in a shivering, insensible state—her rigid body as cold as ice. He had cared for her many times in the aftermath of her return shift to human form—carried her home and placed her in a warm bath. During those times, he was her protector or her doctor—not the man who was about to become her . . . Exeter exhaled a silent groan.

Waves of chestnut hair fell down her back. Yes, he had seen her before, but this was exquisite, and sensuous. He cleared his throat and yet his voice remained husky. "Or . . . you could ask me to be more forward—more aggressive."

Her eyes gleamed with the heat of a young woman whose sexual interest was building. "Then do to me with your hands, what your eyes are doing to me now."

Exeter brushed a thumb over her bottom lip. "Open your mouth."

He pushed deeper and her tongue swirled around the tip as he slipped in his thumb. She wrapped her lips around the thick digit and sucked. Exeter closed his eyes, momentarily, to temper his pleasure. He knew this would be difficult beyond measure, but he was wrong.

This, in fact, was the trial of his life.

He dropped his hands down to her breast and rolled a nipple between slick fingertips. She swayed forward, moaning in pleasure.

He cautioned himself. She must not become overwhelmed, consumed by sensation. He could not let passion overtake either of them. The doctor in him asked, "How are you feeling?"

Mia's lovely dark eyes shimmered with light.

"So, the cat prowls." Exeter withdrew and studied her for other signs of a shift. "What I am about to do is primarily for my safety, though it may also help to discourage a transformation." He helped her into bed and she reclined at a comfortable angle against the pillows.

Exeter could not help but stare. "You look like a nude by Edgar Degas—one of those ballet girls he so loves to paint." Exeter loosed one of the ties looped through his fingers. He reached out for her hand, winding the cloth around her wrist several times before he made a knot. "Too tight?"

Gleaming eyes looked at him—eyes that were aroused. She exhaled a sigh and her belly shuddered. "I'm fine."

Exeter pulled the neck cloth taut and wrapped it around the bedpost. "Are you cold?"

She shook her head. "When the cat is near, the elements don't seem to bother me." Exeter removed his jacket as he walked around to the far side of the bed. "Do you want the candles?"

Her smile was shy, and so beguiling. "I want to see you—and everything you do." Exeter looked up from his wrapping and tying. "Would you like me to disrobe? That might make you more comfortable—or no?"

Mia moistened her lips, scraping the bottom lightly with her teeth. "Odd, I suppose, but there is something wonderfully wicked about being undressed, on display as it were, for my fully clothed instructor."

Exeter smiled at her candor and her irony. "That is because everything about this intimate little tableau is erotic." He finished tying her other arm to the bedpost. "Your initiation into physical intimacy is happening too quickly for any young lady.

But I also must be honest. As experienced as I am, this is arousing for me, as well."

A slow smile curled up the ends of her mouth. "That makes me glad."

He sat down on the edge of the bed, and rolled up his sleeves.

"There's warm water in the washbasin, and soap—are you planning on doing surgery?" She was teasing him—making light of the situation. Perhaps he should follow her lead.

Exeter reclined onto an elbow. "No, but we could play doctor."

He enjoyed her round-eyed look so much he allowed himself a grin. And something else—this wasn't nearly as awkward as he had thought it might be. "I could place my stethoscope to your heart. Or I could take your temperature . . . rectally." When her mouth dropped open, he chuckled out loud. Good God, this might even turn out to be pleasurable.

She looked wonderfully naughty—her cheeks flushed with desire as her mouth opened to him. How he wanted to ravish those lips. Exeter knew he was riding a fine line, and he was dangerously close to taking her—giving in to every carnal thought he'd ever had about Mia. And there had been so many of late.

She interrupted his lustful thoughts with one of her own. "You were being serious—about the . . . the thermometer?"

"Entirely serious. Much of arousal is in the mind as well as the heart." He traced the curve of her breast and tweaked a nipple. Her entire body jumped, then shuddered from his touch. "As you can see, some of it is pure anatomy. The human body has a number of arousal receptors, including the anus." He moved to the other breast and circled the areola so lightly he barely touched her, yet the nipple quickly puckered into a hard point. "What do you feel when I do this?"

Mia's only answer was a sweet gasp for breath.

"Of course technique plays a role, as well." Exeter trailed a fingertip down her torso, over ribs barely felt, and lingered for a teasing swirl around her navel. "Where does your body tell me to go, Mia?"

She raised her heavy-lidded gaze from his hand to his eyes. "Lower."

Exeter hesitated just long enough to elicit the cutest growl. "Was that the panther or Mia?" A testament to the veracity of Phillpott's notes. As her arousal grew, she would likely exhibit signs of an emerging shift.

Her pupils were round and black, and she smiled slyly.

So far, he thought they were managing well. The trick was to keep the arousal slow and steady. When Mia drew close to her climax, he would help her focus—keep her sharp and present, even as she surrendered to pleasure. If she didn't transform—if she kept the cat at bay—that meant this system of shift management was going to work. With practice, she could use these same techniques to shift back and forth at will.

He plunged though a tangle of moist curls, palming her Venus mound and parting her labia majora. His fingertip found the pearl-sized spot that would soon become the focus of her entire being. "This is your clitoris." He stroked slowly. "Pay close attention to what I do here, Mia—as this is something you can do on your own."

Mia's brows crashed together. "Why would I wish to do this on my own if I have you?"

He wasn't going to argue with her, not in this moment. "As you well know, you must learn to self-modulate this experience—ultimately." Slowly, he ran his fingertip down between her labia minora and was greeted by flood of wetness. He would not break her hymen—not tonight. The doctor in Exeter steered lascivious thoughts to something more clinical, like a vaginal exam. "Lift your knees, Mia."

Chapter Six

MIA PULLED HER KNEES UP. "Wider, love," Exeter nudged them apart, dominating her gently, as was his way. "Let me see how beautiful you are." His voice gravelly and low—nearly a whisper. He ran his fingers down the inside of her thighs. "Try to relax."

He was doing things, saying things she had dreamed about for months. She could only hope that the words and deeds came from his heart. Her eyelashes fluttered as she closed her eyes. "Take a deep breath and exhale." He entered her most private place, and stroked. His fingers were slippery from the moisture her body had made for him—wetness he was using to arouse her. "You will feel the pleasure build quickly, now." She was aware of a delicate scent in the air—musky and primal. For an instant, she was a wild creature in the woods, thrusting up to greet her lover.

He stroked, adding pressure as he circled a place that made her cry, "Yes." And, "More." Her belly trembled and she thrust upward as he probed into her secret female places. Her hips grinding to the rhythm of his strokes. There was something clinical, yet tremendously exciting about Exeter's detachment. A deliciously naughty connection moving back and forth between them. His stoicism had always intrigued her, for it was so perfectly Exeter. She could not help but wonder what this man might do, if and when he ever lost all control.

He taught her something of the anatomy of pleasure with his

touch. Using his thumb, he stroked lightly and very fast, which made her moan.

He moved his finger lower and entered her woman's passage, probing gently. "This ring of delicate membrane is your hymen. Lovely and pink. Virginal."

She strained at the ties, which had grown taut and somewhat painful. Exeter stopped and slipped his hands under her bottom. He lifted her up and nudged her closer to the headboard. "More comfortable?"

"Much—thank you."

He paused to look at her, brows slightly furrowed, signature frown. "I would never wish for this to be any young lady's initiation to sexual relations."

"Then make it better for me." Mia looked at him. "I need you closer, Exeter."

He returned a nonplussed, dumbfounded blink and promptly ignored her request. He applied himself to her swollen place—the magical spot that made her gasp and moan and cry out for more. Momentarily, all her thoughts returned to pleasure. Her cheeks burned from humiliation. She was asking for something he did not wish to give—himself. There was intimacy in closeness—lovers' arms and limbs entwined, lips touching, tongues swirling. No doubt Exeter worried that he would lose control, and that such abandon could spell disaster. Or worse, he might begin to feel something.

As if he sensed her heartache, he lowered himself over her torso and locked into her gaze. Dark, gleaming hair, nearly shoulder length, fell forward. His eyes dropped to her mouth as he leaned closer. "You want me to kiss you." His breath warmed her lips.

She nodded. "Very much."

He brushed soft, pliant, kisses over her mouth and pressed her lips open. "Give me something deeper, love." He used his tongue to swirl and mate with hers. A tight, urgent heat spread from her lips through her body to that place—the small spot that created so much desire. A pleasurable tension was rising inside—taking her to a place of exquisite, nearly unbearable sensation. His fingers plucked at her clitoris, and she moaned as if she were a taut string on a cello. "Exeter . . ." She murmured.

"Your eyes are dilated, Mia—flashes of green warn me to stay vigilant." Words spoken between harsh, shallow breaths. Could Exeter be aroused? She wanted him to be.

"The notes say we must tempt the tiger—get her close." She exhaled her answer against his cheek. "Kiss me again, Exeter. Wrap your arms around me, please—"

This time he took complete possession of her mouth. His tongue reached deep and filled her up, his sensuous lips roamed over hers. "Good God, Mia—you have bewitched me."

"Harder. Bite me." He caught her bottom lip with his teeth and drew blood. She bit him in return, and she felt the cat inside stir. They were tempting her, plenty.

"Let go for me, darling." Then he added forcefully, "But don't leave me—ever." His fingers returned to her clitoris and stroked faster as ecstasy swelled inside her. Pleasure that demanded to arrive.

She lifted her head and roared. "Don't stop!"

He positioned himself directly overhead, as tears came to her eyes. "You are going to climax soon. Look at me, Mia." With his free hand he tilted her chin. "Stay with me, love." Even as his fingers danced and circled, pleasure broke inside her—pleasure she might die of—another wave of pleasure—and then suddenly, without warning the cat inside was loose.

Or at least partially so—for the panther was also constrained. Mia tugged at her bindings even as her snout elongated and her fangs materialized. For some inexplicable reason she lashed out at Exeter. Liquid crimson dripped down his neck.

She heard him call to her, faintly. "Come back to me." Slowly, the wild thing inside relented and Mia was back—body and soul. Every cell in her body vibrated with pleasure—wave after wave of euphoria, until she fell into a state of insensibility. "That's it—very good, Mia, stay with me." His reassuring voice was near, coaxing her return to him.

Mia blinked and she was in her bedroom again, and there was Exeter, poised over her. Her heavy eyelids closed and she drifted off to sleep. She was not sure how long she remained in a partial stupor, drained, euphoric, incapacitated from her climax, but at some point—whether it was seconds or minutes—she reopened her eyes.

Exeter sat back on his haunches, with his hand to his throat. Blood ran down the side of his neck. Alarmed, Mia sat up, only to be yanked back. Bother! Her hands remained bound to the bedposts. "Did I hurt you, Exeter?"

"I'm fine—it's just a scratch." She was quite sure he forced a grin to reassure her. "Some sharp fangs you've got there, young lady."

"Sorry." She made eye contact with the man who had just . . . "So much happening at once, I could hardly . . ." Mia shook her head in wonder. "Exeter, it was so . . . there aren't words to describe it." She lay back and smiled rather provocatively. It must have been alluring, because Exeter returned her flirtatious gaze—not with his usual overprotective mentoring look, but with eyes that smoldered—something that caused a shiver of delight to run through her. And he appeared charmed—could that small smile signify . . . a touch of surrender?

Another shiver ran through her—this time from the chill in the air. She was beginning to feel herself again. "Before we discuss the wonders and side benefits of this new therapy, might you untie me, sir?"

Exeter reached for a bedpost, and then hesitated. "On second thought, I like you tethered—where I can keep an eye on you." He climbed out of bed and poked up the fire, adding more coals.

Was Exeter teasing? Perhaps even flirting with her? Mia narrowed her eyes. "And to think I was about to compliment your mentoring. Now you've saved me the trouble."

He circled the bed and unwrapped her bindings, taking time with each arm to massage her wrists and circulate blood back into her fingers. His hands were large, with elegant tapered fingers. Those lovely digits had sent her to paradise this evening. She looked up into laughing eyes—as though he could read her mind. "You were about to tell me what a pleasurable experience you had under my tutelage . . ."

She turned her hand within his and pulled him near. He sat down beside her so she could trace the dark red scratch along his neck. "Rather vicious of me—or her—to lure you in so close."

The ends of Exeter's mouth twitched upward again. "And my reward for braving the black panther for a kiss?"

Her finger moved from his neck to his upper lip, to the cut she had made from her bite. Mia gently kissed his lower lip. "Pay us no mind next time."

Exeter, in turn, passed his thumb over her swollen bottom lip—the one that displayed his mark. "You need a tincture for this scratch and some ice from the cold closet." He reached for his medical bag.

Mia sprang out of bed and opened her wardrobe. "Since we both need tending—shall we visit the kitchen together? If there's an ember left in the stove, I'd like to heat some milk—for hot chocolate." She was not unaware of Exeter's gaze as she pulled on her dressing gown with a chinois motif. "Come." She tugged on his medical bag. "And you shall have a dash of crème de menthe in yours."

In the kitchen, Exeter lifted her up by the waist and sat her down on top of the long kitchen worktable. He unwrapped a clean piece of gauze and dropped a number of ice chips into the cloth. "Place this on your lip—put a bit of pressure on it."

Mia held the cold, soothing compress and watched Exeter pour milk into a saucepan and leave it to heat on the stove. "I think I have some iodine . . ." he mumbled, rummaging about in his kit. "Ah—here we are." He dipped a stick with a cotton tuft on one end into the small, amber-colored bottle.

Mia lowered the compress. "Looks better already." He swabbed her bottom lip. "Ahh!" She cried.

"Don't lick your lips—let it dry."

Mia nodded and took up the swab and bottle. Exeter leaned close to let her dab a bit of tincture on his mouth and along his jawline. "Are you in much pain?"

"Pain? Not really." Exeter's mouth twitched. "Frustration, yes—pain, no."

Mia lowered the swab. "I'm well aware of the sorts of things you did in my room—those . . . pleasures are intended to be mutual." She raised her gaze to meet his.

"My satisfaction, or lack thereof, is of little concern right now. What is of utmost importance is that you learn the basics as quickly as possible."

Mia nodded. "Valentine's notes were quite clear. The trick is to let go and at the same time remain in control."

Exeter skirted the table and moved the pan to a warming plate. Mia joined him at the stove. "I'll stir." Exeter grated shaved chocolate into the steaming milk, turning the cream a rich shade of dark brown. Mia poured the hot chocolate in two cups. "I've seen Mr. Tandi do this hundreds of times—you receive half the sugar, and a jigger of Menthe-Pastille." Mia stirred in the doctor's mint-flavored liquor. "There, something sweet to distract us from the sting of the tincture." She set both cups of hot chocolate on the worktable.

Mia quietly drank the warm, bittersweet confection, and contemplated the man sitting on the stool beside her. There were moments, like now, when she couldn't imagine her life without him.

Exeter sipped his chocolate and gazed at her over a tipped cup. His piercing green eyes were warmer than usual. "Did you know peppermint is sometimes regarded as the world's oldest medicine?" When he looked at her as a woman, as he was doing now, something fluttered in her secret intimate place—the place they could share together, someday.

"Earlier, in my bedchamber, you said I could order you to do things—ask you to pleasure me in certain ways."

"Whatever arouses you—I am happy to do your bidding."

"Next time, I would like to pleasure you, as well."

Without taking his eyes off her, he set his cup down and reached for her, pulling her close. "Mia, think carefully. You do realize what this means?"

Mia nodded. "Things have changed for us."

Chapter Seven

EXETER PACED THE LENGTH OF THE TRAIN PLATFORM waiting for the most unpunctual of all the Nightshades, Tim Noggy. Even at this ungodly early hour, St. Pancras station was bustling. Exeter scanned the gallery for any sign of the rotund young man. Pale shafts of light passed through a canopy of steel beams and skylights, spotting the platform with light. He tucked several morning newspapers under his arm. All of them predicted rain.

Absently, he went over the day's itinerary in his head. They would travel in close proximity to one another, but not together. He had seen his fellow travelers into two first-class compartments. The idea was to get to Paris quickly, drawing the least amount of attention to themselves as possible. Also, if one group ran into trouble, the other could either lend assistance or have a chance to escape.

Mia waved to him from inside their compartment. Exeter paused close by the window of the passenger carriage and dug for his pocket watch. Last night had been somewhat disquieting, highly erotic, and perhaps . . . the most enchanting night of his life.

A faint prickle of arousal ran through his manly parts just remembering. Mia had been wonderfully responsive sexually and had climaxed, something he was not altogether sure she would do. This had been her first intimate experience with a man, and a decidedly odd one at that, considering he had bound her hands and kept the first session as clinical as he possibly could.

In the harsh light of morning he had awoke to a humbling thought. His insistence on being so clinical had more to do with protecting himself than it had been about Mia.

He flipped open his watch. Seven fifty-five. "We leave on the stroke of eight, Mr. Noggy," Exeter muttered to himself. He turned toward their compartment. Mia and America were sampling a tin of biscuits from the Fortnum's hamper, delivered to the house just as they set off that morning. Mia had seen the delivery van and stopped the carriage. Bloody bold of her, and yet thoughtful to have a large basket made up for the journey.

His mouth twitched and he felt a twinge of pain from the mending cut on his lip. In the kitchen last night he had tugged her into his arms and she had kissed him, running a pink tongue along the underside of his upper lip. "Mmm, you taste just like a yuletide truffle, Doctor Exeter."

"G'day, Mate!" The call traveled down the platform, jarring Exeter from his reverie. The large-framed Noggy huffed up beside him. Disheveled, as usual, behind schedule, always, and carrying no luggage.

"Oddly enough, there is a kind of predictability to your lateness, Mr. Noggy." Exeter greeted him with a frown. Tim's cheeks were flushed pink from exertion along with a few beads of ever-present perspiration. "Have you ever considered dropping a few stone? Your circulatory system would thank you for it."

The look he received from Noggy could be described only as nonplussed. "You don't approve of my triple-x, big and tall size, Doc?"

"Outremer gibberish, Mr. Noggy. I am concerned for your health." Exeter asked about the obvious lack of luggage. "Don't tell me you've forgotten your valise."

Tim swept back a tangle of wild hair and answered in his odd parlance of Outremer English. "I'm not coming with you—but, give me a day and a few more tweaks to the iDIP, and I'll meet you there."

He stared at the young inventor. "You've got the portal maker working . . ."

Tim's grin was as wide as a crescent moon and as sly as a Cheshire cat. "Both ins and outs. Accurate to within inches of our map coordinates. Oakley helped install a new computer—the brains of the engine." Tim was obviously enthused and nearly tripping over his words. "Just give me a day or two and we may be able to extract Phaeton from wherever he is. Just—*whoosh*! And he's home again."

Exeter clapped his mouth shut and stared. "How likely might this be?"

Tim's eyes rolled upward as he considered his answer.

"Last call, all aboard for Dover Priory." The conductor's shout accompanied a low whistle and blast of steam as the train began to leave the station. Exeter checked up and down the deserted platform. "Quickly, Tim."

The large young man fished in his pocket and produced a tubular device encrusted with toggle switches. "Here—take this." He pushed the contraption into Exeter's hand, as he jumped onto the first step of the passenger car. "It's a new and improved portable transporter, programmed to send you all back home." Tim trotting alongside the moving car. "Not Outremer London—1889 London."

Mia lowered a window. "Are you both mad? We're about to leave without you."

Exeter opened the compartment door and climbed in. "Mr. Noggy will be joining us in a day or two."

"Chocolate-covered cinder toffee?" Mia leaned out the window and dropped a few chunks of honeycombed toffee into the man's palm. As Exeter settled down beside her, she waved. "*Au revoir,* Tim."

Mia opened the tin. "Cinder toffee?" To please her, he bit into a piece as he unfolded his newspapers. "Why isn't Tim joining us?" she asked.

Exeter snapped open his news sheet. "Because . . . it appears he may be joining us in Paris via the portal maker." Exeter lowered his paper to speak to both young ladies. "Mr. Noggy believes we may be able to locate and extract Phaeton using the iDIP."

America perked up. "Much safer in some ways. But do you believe he can do it?"

Exeter smiled. "That is why we continue on to Paris, undeterred." America was skeptical. Frankly, he couldn't blame her. Her distrust was natural, and rather shrewd. She and Phaeton had survived a myriad of trials recently—put to the test, so to speak, by a powerful entity known only as Prospero. Was this creature man or beast? Magician or scientist?

The trip to Dover started out pleasant enough. Somewhere past Chatham Station, the skies opened up, but the rainstorm proved mild and the young ladies excellent company. As they traversed the lush greenery of Kent, Exeter tried to relax. He was edgy, more so than usual, and he was quite sure his discomfiture was caused by the lovely young miss beside him. With each lurch or sway of the car, her shoulder brushed against him. And with each rub, the faint scent of carnation soap wafted in the air. Mia had simply become a torture to him. In fact, if he continued to have such lascivious thoughts about her he was going to be irritable the entire trip, and that would not do.

He felt a nudge as the minxy, adorable young lady pressed close. "Have you given any consideration to our sleeping arrangements this evening?" Mia whispered.

Somewhat taken aback at her choice of topics, he checked the young woman across the aisle. America had made a pillow of her travel duster and had drifted off for a nap. He leaned close to his ward and changed the subject. "America is no doubt expecting her usual inclusion in this operation, but I must protect her from herself. Phaeton would never forgive me if she or the child were injured—what am I saying? I couldn't forgive myself. If I deny her participation, she's likely to balk or, worse, strike out on her own."

Mia arched a brow. "So . . . you want me to stay close, shadow her without making her feel as though she's being mollycoddled."

Exeter nodded. "There will be times I will ask you both to stay behind. Other times, I will want you and her to take up the rear guard. If America sees you cooperating she is more likely . . ." He shrugged, and let his words drift off.

"I see." Mia flashed a wary smile. "If I docilely go along with your plans, she might be less inclined to make trouble."

"I wouldn't put it that way." Exeter frowned. "Exactly."

Mia pressed her Cupid's bow to her bottom lip to suppress a smile. Unfathomably, he seemed to amuse her again. "I suppose I could be hornswoggled into this scheme, Exeter."

"Hornswoggled?" Now, he was amused. "By any chance, is that in the Oxford English Dictionary?"

"To cheat or trick; bamboozle," she answered his jibe. "I see through your cleverness, Exeter. You wish to keep us both out of harm's way and you mean to do so by enlisting me as a co-conspirator."

Her pout caused a further grin. "You've found me out, Mia. Now, if you will please just agree to my stratagem—?"

"Oh, very well," Mia sighed. "But you now owe me a singular and prodigious favor."

"Done."

She raised her chin. "You never answered my question about sleeping arrangements."

"We have a three-hour respite in Calais. I have reserved a suite at Le Meurice where we can all refresh ourselves during the layover."

Mia stared at him. "And what about the night train to Paris?"

He quietly exhaled a deep breath. "Two sleeping compartments. You and I have one to ourselves. America can ride with Valentine and Jersey."

She moistened her bottom lip, and he noted the red scrape. The one he made when he had momentarily lost control. "So—you intend on giving me another—what would you call it, a lesson, I suppose?"

In the light of day, this had all suddenly become awkward again. Exeter rocked his head. "We could call them training sessions."

"There is no mention in Valentine's notes with regards to the duration of these"—she cleared her throat—"lessons."

Exeter peered over at her. "You're a quick study, Mia. I suspect it won't take long for you to learn to control your body to manipulate the shifts."

Mia lowered her voice. "Odd, don't you think, that the two are tied so closely together?"

Exeter inhaled a breath, squinting absently into the unknown for answers. "Sexual gratification and transformation? Odd, perhaps, but understandable, and certainly no less shocking then say . . . a proper young English woman asking after the address of a male prostitute." He raised a brow. "Who gave you the name Etienne Artois?"

He nearly chuckled when her jaw dropped open—only he didn't. The very thought of Mia asking after a male prostitute stirred up a hornet's nest of anger in his chest.

She clapped her mouth shut. "Mrs. Parker told you."

"And well she did, though I have no particular worry over it, since you shall never be without escort in Paris." He flicked his gaze upward before narrowing it on her. "Why, Mia?"

Her eyes darted a bit, avoiding his scrutiny. "Silly of me I suppose, especially now that you have become my . . . instructor."

"That was the reason? To become experienced?" Exeter was flummoxed. "A young lady's innocence is to be preserved at all costs."

"Why?" She flicked her eyes upward. "I can't think of a single reason to preserve such an antiquated idea of purity."

Exeter marshaled his reasoning. "What about the question of pregnancy—legitimacy?"

"Blather and poppycock. Affairs go on between married ladies and gentlemen of the ton with such frequency—frankly I haven't a clue how they manage to sort through who sired what to whom."

Sharp as a whip and capable of pointing out the maelstrom

of social hypocrisy that was the peerage of Britain. Mia might have joined the Oxford Union debating society, if women were accepted as members. He veered off subject, slightly. "Who on earth gave you his name?"

Mia turned to him. "How long have you and Mrs. Parker been lovers?"

Exeter stared at her. "This may come as a shock, but there are aspects of my life that are none of your business."

Mia tugged off both gloves and opened the hamper beside her. She lifted out a tray of dried fruit and sampled. "Apricot?" she offered.

"No, thank you." Exeter watched as she selected a candied fruit. "Was it Phoebe Armistead?" Almost from the start, he had discouraged the friendship. Both Phoebe and her married sister, Lisbeth, Countess of Bath, had reputations. This past summer the wicked little countess had lured him out onto the veranda and made advances. He hadn't mentioned it to Mia—but he had quietly steered her away from the Armistead sisters.

"How is it you seem to have no compunctions nosing about in my personal business, while I must refrain from inquiring about yours?" She sniffed. "It isn't fair."

For the last two days, ever since Jersey and Valentine had returned from the Outremer with Phillpott's disturbing instructions for shift control, he had felt as though he was on the losing end of a sticky wicket—or was he schussing down a slippery slope? Whichever, it really didn't matter.

His sigh was long and loud. "Even though nothing in life is ever fair . . . and it's none of your business, I shall deign to answer you. Esmeralda and I have been acquainted for something over a year, now."

Mia nibbled on a dried cherry. "How did you come to meet each other? You aren't the type of gentleman who frequents brothels."

Exeter relaxed some. If he could assuage her curiosity by answering a question or two . . . what could it hurt? "We both attended a private lecture by Sir Richard Francis Burton."

"On the Kama Sutra or The Perfumed Garden?" Mia blurted out the words and then halted, abruptly. Before he could raise a brow, a swath of pink blushed her cheeks, followed by a grin. "It took me all morning to find them in the library of secrets."

He may have been wrong about "what can it hurt?" Exeter proceeded with caution. "Burton addressed the Kama Sutra. Contrary to popular perception, the Kama Sutra is not just a sex manual, it is a guide to virtuous and graceful living that discusses the nature of love and family, as well as the pleasure-oriented aspects of our lives."

Mia put the sweetmeats away and closed the hamper. She appeared to carefully consider his words. "And . . . have you two explored all the *pleasure-oriented aspects* of the manual?"

Unbelievably, he found himself grinning at her—and in a lusty flirtatious way. What else could a grin mean after such a question? Rather alarming, but he couldn't help it. Mia had always known how to elicit a smile, particularly when he was on the verge of becoming exasperated or cross.

And she looked enchanting today, dressed in dark blue and cream stripes—a formfitting navy blazer and a small high-crowned hat set at a jaunty angle, she was the very picture of a vivacious young woman. Phaeton had been right. She needed a new wardrobe—sleeker, rich in color. Without exception, at every soiree they attended, Mia drew heated stares from the young bachelors. A half dozen new evening gowns in gemstone colors with plunging necklines. Good God, he'd have to fight them off her.

He caught a glimpse of silver-gray ocean out the compartment window. "We're nearly to Dover Priory." His words were punctuated by a hiss of brakes as the train slowed. "We can take this up again once we're—"

Mia's face had drained of color. He followed her line of sight back out the window. Something—strands of dusky black whisked away as he stood up to see more. Craning his neck, he caught a glimpse of a whirling tangle of filaments—thousands of tendrils in motion that promptly disappeared.

Exeter opened the compartment door. "Stay with America." Using a bit of potent lift, he landed on top of the passenger car roof, and widened his stance. The apparition perched on the edge of the railcar, like some strange bird with ragged wings, an amorphous mass of dark metallic fibers merged together, then whipped apart. He took a step forward and the strange entity dispersed into the buffeting winds with a hiss and an eerie, high-pitched wail. A banshee's moan.

A few scattered raindrops fell on his cheeks; the storm had passed. Not far ahead, rays of sunshine slanted through a break in cloud cover. Exeter lowered himself down the side of the railcar and slipped back inside their compartment.

"What did you see?" Mia sat beside America, who was wide awake and curious, having slept through the initial disturbance.

He shrugged. "Not much, I'm afraid—a glimpse at something odd wearing a ragged cloak of tangled fibers. The tattered threads made hissing noises. Whatever it was—it's gone." He shut the compartment door and turned back to the young women.

"Reapers make hissing noises." America's voice was low, almost a whisper. "Prospero knows we're coming."

Chapter Eight

"A STRONG STEEP OF ENGLISH TEA, and I shall be restored." Mia curled up in a comfortable corner of the settee and stirred a lump of sugar into her Earl Grey.

Their brief voyage across the channel had gone smoothly and uneventfully. Exeter had spent most of the hour's journey speaking in low tones with Jersey and Valentine, while she and America enjoyed a brisk walk around the deck.

The moment they stepped foot in Calais, they were greeted by a cloudburst and had made a mad dash to L'Hôtel Meurice. Their suite turned out to be wonderfully inviting and would be a comfortable place to rest and regroup while they waited for the train to Paris.

Mia sipped her tea and sighed. "Out with it—You three have been conspiring ever since the *Princess Beatrice* left Dover Harbor."

"Prospero toys with us. It's the only explanation for why he might send such an apparition." Jersey popped a delicate tea sandwich in his mouth and chewed with such purpose, it caused her to grin.

"Yes, well, thank goodness we don't terrify easily." Mia's smile dimmed somewhat at her next thought. "I suppose this means those snippets of Phaeton were a deliberate transmission?"

"A lure from the start. He wants us in Paris." Exeter's jaw was flexing.

America leaned forward, clearly alarmed. "We're not calling off the mission. No matter what, I'm going ahead—"

"We are proceeding as planned, but doubling the guard on you, America. As soon as Noggy has the portal ready, we'll bring over Cutter and Ruby."

Mia bit her lower lip. "Cutter and Ruby are needed to care for Gaspar—as well as Lovecraft's son."

"What about Mr. Ping?" America offered. "He knows many of the secrets of the Moonstone and is a powerful jinni."

"I have sent urgent cables to the four corners. Hopefully, he will meet us in Paris." Exeter groused. "I had hoped we might get a few days to ourselves—scout the catacombs, start formulating some ideas about where Prospero's lair might be—whether it's in our time or some future realm."

Mia loved watching the wheels turn in Exeter's brain. She sampled a smoked trout deviled egg and wrinkled her nose. "I imagine there is an alternate Paris, just as there is an alternate London."

"There is also the matter of an exhaustive and expensive shopping excursion." Mia looked up from the platter of delicacies and found him staring at her—and not in the way she was used to her guardian viewing his charge. His gaze sent a tingle running from her breasts to her womb. Something in his eyes spoke of secret kisses and velvet touches, and suddenly she knew. He was remembering last night.

The woman inside Mia met his gaze and held it. "I very much look forward to spending a vulgar amount of your worth at the House of Worth."

Exeter's mouth slowly curved upward. "I'm quite sure the results will be—well worth the price."

"Shall one of us send a wire?" America asked, setting down her cup. "Try contacting Ping, again?"

Exeter rose from his chair. "All this talk of my dwindling income reminds me to contact my solicitor—I want to make sure he's wired an ungodly amount of British Sterling to Lloyds in Paris." Then he did something he rarely, if ever, did. He winked at her. "I will also wire Mr. Noggy about the matter of Mr. Ping."

The moment Jersey and Exeter were gone, America and Valentine called Mia into the bedroom. "Out with it, Miss Chadwick," America teased. "Something is different between you and the dashing doctor."

Mia could hardly contain herself. "Is it obvious? Oh, I do hope so."

Valentine shot her a sly mile. "Exeter has never looked or acted more romantic. You both exude, well, to be frank—there is an evident underlying sexual tension, Mia."

"Just seeing you both . . ." America sighed. "I miss Phaeton, so very much." Mia hugged America tight, or as close as she could. Mia rubbed her roundness. "Exeter refers to this as your 'goddess belly.' "

America's eyes brightened, then narrowed. "And this very pregnant goddess would like an arousing and delicious tale now. You must tell all, Mia."

"From the start—he was so worried about losing control—and I was so worried he wouldn't." She supposed the look on her face gave it all away—because a squeal went up into the air. All three of them piled on top of the giant four-poster bed. Mia shared as much as she thought seemly—with perhaps a few tantalizing bits just for fun.

The fruit was sweet, the pastry as light as a cloud, and the roast duck, succulent. In other words, they were in France, and the diner fare was perfect. Unfortunately, Mia picked through the lot of it. There was an agitation that gripped her belly—the cat stirred inside and another thing . . . she and Exeter shared a private compartment together.

Lifting a fork, she could not help but admire the large gemstone that sparkled from her ring finger. An oval-cut emerald surrounded by diamonds, and a de Roos family heirloom. Not long after they boarded the train for Paris, they had freshened up for dinner. He had fastened her dress, complaining softly about the number of small covered buttons. Fumbling a bit, she had helped with his cuff links. Reaching into his portmanteau, he produced a velvet box and slipped the dazzling emerald on her finger. "As a precaution, you are Mrs. Exeter for the duration of the trip."

She had lifted her hand to admire the ring—as well as the fit. "The emerald was part of my mother's dowry." He had spoken softly, with a good deal of emotion evident in his voice. "The baron had the ring made for their first wedding anniversary."

She had met his gaze. "It's . . . perfectly . . . stunning."

He had nodded, smiling gently. "Family legacy has it the gemstone comes from an ancient mine in Upper Egypt, and was worn by Cleopatra." He had taken her hand and placed it in the crook of his arm. "In keeping with its history—the emerald adorns yet another beauty." They met their cadre of friends in the club car and made their way to a crowded dining car. She and Exeter were seated at a table for two, while Jersey, Valentine, and America dined together several tables away.

She nibbled on a tender piece of duck breast. There was something daring and naughty about this ruse. Mrs. Jason Alexander Exeter, Baroness de Roos. Another glance at the ring forced a hard swallow past the lump in her throat. She angled her bustle to one side of her chair and lengthened her back. She felt like stretching—or prowling.

"How are we feeling this evening?" The doctor in Exeter didn't miss much, and she was beginning to exhibit signs of a shift. A distinctive flush to her chest, neck, and cheeks along with restlessness.

"The cat stirs—and my head hurts." She lowered her eyes. "Would you mind, terribly, if I retire early?"

Exeter reached for her hand across the table. "Stay with me—just a few more minutes." He signaled the waiter. "Cognac." He looked to her. "Darling?"

Stunned, slightly, at his endearment, she ordered a Cointreau. *"Avec eau gazeuse, s'il vous plaît."* Exeter brushed his index finger along the inside of her wrist. "Can you describe what it was you saw, or thought you saw, through the train window as we approached Dover this morning?"

Mia pieced together a careful description before answering. "A hooded face, not unlike the Nightshades when they wear their warrior gear and cloaks—and the cape swirled about, trailing strands of glittering particles. There was a flash of iridescent green in the creature's eyes as they passed over me."

"Any recognizable facial features?"

"It was a specter that came and went so quickly, I could almost believe the apparition didn't happen at all, but for the eyes . . ." An icy shiver ran through her. "Strange beams of light passed through the glass, but I felt as if there was no life behind them—like the moving images Tim receives from the Outremer. The ones that act and talk like a human being, but are in fact, particles of light." Tim Noggy often communicated using this form of science, or magic. Frankly, it all seemed rather Jules Verne to Mia. She looked up at Exeter. "What do you make of it?"

"An automaton from the Outremer." Exeter added, "It is possible there is a flesh-and-blood maker who manipulated the—let's call it a wraith—from a remote location like Paris." He ordered another cognac.

Mia pressed her lips together and remained neutral. She was quite certain he was avoiding being alone with her. And yet, some part of her knew . . . it was all he could think about. The thought not only gave her comfort—but strength. Mia rose from her chair. "Might I have the key?" He shot up from his seat and handed over her request. "Take your time, perhaps you might enjoy a cigar in the lounge car . . ." Clasping the key, she smiled a patronizing, wifely sort of smile. ". . . darling."

She made her way down a narrow aisle to the door that matched the number on the key fob. Weeks ago, America had cautioned her. "Men love the hunt—the chase, whatever you wish to call it. If you truly love him, don't deprive Exeter of the joy of capturing you." Esmeralda Parker had offered similar advice.

A silver half-moon illuminated the compartment interior as well as the passing countryside. Mia moved to the window. It would not be long now, they traveled on *Le Train Bleu,* a luxury French night express train that traveled from Calais to Paris and on to the French Riviera. If there were no delays, they would arrive in Paris before dawn.

As the train crossed over a river, the image of the moon traveled with them, reflected in the calm waters below. "The Seine is quite broad here." Even though Exeter spoke softly, she started at his words.

Mia glanced back. "Rather stealthy of you." She returned to the river. "I'm a bit jumpy tonight, I'm afraid."

"Mia, I never expected last night to feel so . . ."

"Awkward?" she offered, cynically.

"Right." He was close—so close the word warmed the tip of her ear. He wrapped an arm around her. "All morning I've had to fight off a reverie of licentious urges—thoughts that might consume me if I let them."

She leaned back against his chest. "Undo me, Exeter."

Long, tapered fingers patiently unbuttoned and removed her dress. She unbuckled her bustle and stepped out of silk petticoats. Silently, in the moonlight, they performed the kinds of duties a husband and wife traveling without servants shared—a delicious intimacy suffused the air. "And how are you both?" He asked softly.

She pivoted within his arms. "She is aroused." A blush flamed up her neck. "As am I." Exeter lifted her hand to his chin, and rubbed playfully. "Untie my cravat."

Gas lamps from a passing rail station briefly lit the side of his face. His heavy-lidded, primitive gaze spoke of a wildness inside him that matched hers—something she hoped to let loose.

She slipped the tie from around his collar.

"Hand it to me."

Her gaze lowered to his mouth. "Kiss me, first." Even in the dark she knew he smiled as he tugged the neck cloth from her grip.

"I believe you do need to be kissed." He pressed against her camisole and corset, and her nipples peaked. "Hands together—in front." He wound the cloth around her wrists and then lifted her arms overhead. He tied the ends of the cravat to the brass rail of a luggage rack.

Loosing her pantalettes, he pushed them down an inch at a time, until they fell below her knees. He wrapped an arm around her waist and she lifted one leg, then the other, stepping out of silk drawers. His hands skimmed her naked hips and buttock cheeks. Cupping her bottom, he brought her pelvis against him and rubbed in a lazy way—back and forth, as he nuzzled her neck. "Open your legs." He whispered his demand and inserted his leg between hers. "Wider, darling."

As he massaged her bottom, a finger slipped down between her buttock cheeks. "I want to know exactly how hot you are right now." Exeter reluctantly backed away. "I think it's time I take your temperature."

Mia blew a few stray hairs out of her face and glared. "Take my word for it—hot." Exeter struck a match, lifting the chimney on a wall sconce. The compartment glowed with warm flickering light. He blew out the match. "Not that kind of hot—I want a reading on your internal body temperature." Exeter opened his bag and removed several instruments. He poured rubbing alcohol over his fingers and dried his hands with a sterile cloth. He shook a long thin instrument several times and held it up to the light.

Her lower anatomy was completely exposed; all she wore was the briefest camisole, corset, and striped stockings. And another thing—she was quite sure she was wet—dripping wet.

He dipped the glass temperature gauge into a jar, then wiped it clean. Exeter turned and ran his gaze up silk stockings, stopping at the apex of her legs—the dark triangle of her sex. "If it makes you feel any better, Mia, you have aroused me to the point of agony."

Good God—this was so disturbing and yet . . . she was also aroused.

He approached her slowly. "I intend to make this as pleasurable for you as possible." He tilted her head and kissed her lips—teasing out her tongue, with soft pillowed kisses. His arms went around her and a slick finger moved down between her buttock cheeks, where he gently circled the small tight opening. Her knees trembled as his finger penetrated her anus. A wave of pleasure shuddered through her body.

Exeter angled back. "Now, open wide and lift your tongue." He inserted the thermometer into her mouth and flipped open his pocket watch. "Five minutes—keep your mouth closed." Glancing up, he smiled. "You were expecting something else?" Mia thought better of a glare, flicking her eyes upward and away from him.

"I realize this is difficult, but do keep in mind—you are not alone." He moved up beside her, nearly straddling her hip. "As the pleasure climbs and you find yourself at the edge, try to use the last waves of pleasure as a release—from her. Use the power of your climax to settle her down."

His hand traveled lower, past her navel and through her curls. Expert fingers parted her labia, while his other hand stroked her bottom. "Four minutes." His words buffeted against her ear and she swayed against him—gyrating her hips—she couldn't help it. He answered her with a deep groan, as two fingers circled her clitoris. His mouth grazed her neck even as his teeth ravaged her earlobe. "I am going to explore every intimate part of you." His gruff promise sent a shudder of arousal through her. "And you are going to give me access."

He tilted her backside toward him. "Open." His hand moved between her legs from the rear, collecting the slick essence of her arousal. As he pressed against her hip, his fingers invaded, from both sides. Stroking from the front, he circled the throbbing center of her pleasure, while gently tracing the seam between buttock cheeks, a single digit played with the small sphincter muscle, creating such a pleasurable sensation Mia wanted to release a great hiss, or growl. Instead, she whimpered softly, barely able to hold the thermometer between her lips. *My God, my God—Mon Dieu, mon Dieu!*

Three minutes. Mon panthère. Exeter answered.

She understood his words, yet she was quite sure he hadn't spoken. Mia's heart raced at the thought. She was aware of his thoughts. She was also aware of those skillful fingers coaxing out more pleasure, making her belly tremble and her hips thrust. Exeter looked as though he might eat her alive, just as soon as he got his temperature reading.

"Two minutes." A slick finger probed deeper. He stood beside her and seduced with every touch. "Come for me, Mia." His hands stroked and then teased, deepening the intensity of her arousal. Exquisite pleasure danced along the edge of her climax. His finger delved deeper and then pulled out—playing with the ring of muscle at her opening—all the while his thumb circled her clitoris. *N'arrêtez pas!* Her thoughts warned him not to stop, as he brought her arousal to yet another level of intensity.

Less than a minute. Engulfed in pleasure and barely aware of the world, she thought she saw the expression on his face move from joyful to aroused lover as he witnessed her surrender. He massaged lightly through the bucking and shuddering of her climax.

As her thoughts gradually returned to the world, she opened her eyes. "She obeyed, Exeter." Reverently, he leaned over and kissed a latent belly quiver.

Righting himself, he tugged on the thermometer. "Let go, Mia." She had not realized how tightly she clenched the glass tube in her mouth. She relaxed her lips and he removed the instrument, squinting at the glass tube. "One hundred point four. Nearly two full points."

She wondered if she should tell him about the telepathy. Was it mutual? He had seemed to comply earlier with her rather emphatic order not to stop. But, if this ability was mutual, he wasn't saying anything either.

"Was that really about my temperature?" Her voice was husky, dry.

Exeter stared at her. She returned his stare—in fact, she squinted. She was hoping to hear his thoughts—find out if there were hidden motives. Nothing.

"Even as your lips quivered and your belly trembled, you remained in control and held her back."

She thought he looked slightly amused. "I'm going to get you back for this, Exeter."

His eyes lowered to her corset. "I very much hope so."

She glanced down and noted rosy tips peeking over the lacy edge of her camisole. She swallowed. It was suddenly so obvious; he wasn't done yet. He dipped his head and ran his tongue over the mound of one breast—then the other.

The small hairs on her neck and arms stood on end—the whistle of the wind outside the compartment windows grew louder—until the wind whooshed and snapped against the side of the railcar. Two intense green lights beamed through the glass and moved through the small room. Whatever it was searched the compartment methodically.

Exeter.

Without a word, he reached up and untied her bindings. *Find Jersey and Valentine. Stay with them—do not come after me.*

The beams of light moved over scattered garments, stopping momentarily on the open medical bag. Exeter slipped over to the window and turned the latch. A blast of chill night air rushed into the compartment as he lowered the window—papers and clothing fluttered about the small space. He pulled himself through an open section of window.

Mia crouched between the berths and followed the dual shafts of light as they searched in vain. Exeter was gone.

Chapter Nine

EXETER DROPPED DOWN ONTO HIS HAUNCHES and let the bracing cold air revive his sensory faculties. Wispy tendrils under the apparition's shredded cloak appeared first, then dual beams of green light. He traced the rays under the hood to orbs hidden under the shrouded head. His powers sensed cameras capable of transmitting images, not unlike the holograms Tim Noggy received from his brother.

The swath of light found him soon enough. It seemed to Exeter the staring contest went on interminably. He rose to his full height, only to be struck down by a wave of potent energy—a force that traveled within the energy field of the light rays.

The pair of beams swung back and forth, searching for others. Exeter studied the ephemeral creature. An automaton, of sorts. And very large. Exeter was nearly two inches over six feet, and this creature towered over him. He reached deep and drew in enough potent energy to stop a charging rhinoceros.

The blast sent the ominous visitor sliding back down the roof of the railcar. He walked through shredded tendrils of garment—the substance of which was not made of cloth but particles of matter in constant motion.

The strange golem whirred and clicked as it reassembled itself. This being was no messenger; it was some kind of scout. No doubt this creature had been sent by Prospero to test their strength. Exeter's pulse quickened. He had a good idea who the technology wizard was interested in, and he wasn't going to get her.

"I am Exeter." He peered directly into the beams of light. "And who are you?"

He silently gathered energy into his celiac ganglia and waited. For a moment, the luminous eyes drew him in. He made out a nose, mouth, and chin—even a hint of ear as the creature turned to face him. "Miss Jones." On several occasions, Exeter had heard the demonstrations of the phonograph—the voices tinged with metal and a crackling hiss—like now.

"I'm afraid Miss Jones was unable to travel. Her pregnancy is nearly full term. I wouldn't allow—"

The blast hit his solar plexus region and knocked the breath from his diaphragm. Exeter crawled to his knees, gasping for air. Before he could stand, he took a second hit—a blow to his side, which rolled him far down the roof of the passenger car. Finally, air rushed back into his lungs and he rapidly gained enough strength to stagger to his feet. He turned around to face . . . three of the creatures, all identical in shape and size.

"Reinforcements? Rather flattering, wouldn't you say?" When in doubt, use bravado. A valuable lesson he'd learned from Phaeton. Exeter shot a bolt of powerful energy at the trio and leapt into the air, over the trio of wraiths. He landed several feet behind them.

His attackers turned in unison. He was also aware of yet another presence—something moved behind him. It would appear he was surrounded. Exeter hurled a ball of potent energy at the hooded trio and readied to make another jump. A black shadow emerged from between railcars and leapt past his shoulder.

It was the panther. It was Mia.

Stunned, he watched the cat knock the creature over and rip off the cloak. Claws and fangs slashed into the downed wraith. Exeter let loose a blast of potent force, sending the others sliding across the narrow roofline. He leaned over the cat as she tore off the wraith's hood, exposing a metal skull and skeletal body. *I'll bring them down—you take them out.*

In answer, the cat raised her head and hissed.

An orb of violet-colored particles swirled larger and larger in his hand. Exeter opened his palm and fired the ball at one of the wraiths trying to crawl away. Mia sprang from one kill to the next, using her teeth and claws to rip off bony limbs, scattering them across the roof.

"Save one for us." Jersey and Valentine landed on the roof with a thud. Daggers drawn, the mechanized knives unfolded into long swords, crackling with powerful aether.

Exeter nodded toward a wraith staggering upright at the end of the carriage. "You can have him." While the Nightshades sliced and diced, he and Mia finished off the other.

The fray was over as quickly and unexpectedly as it had begun. Nothing but the wind and chug of the train through the darkness—and the clink of disintegrating body parts. Even after the wraiths had been chopped to bits, they continued to shiver and slither about the roof. He picked up a disembodied arm and tossed it over the side. Easing back onto his haunches, he watched Mia chew on a glowing green eye until the light faded. Tentatively, he reached out for the lens mechanism and her lip curled. Risking his fingers, he opened his palm. Long, ivory fangs glistened in the dark. She dropped the dead orb into his hand. Exeter smiled. "Come, pussy."

The sleek panther rose, lifted a paw, then hesitated. Jersey and Valentine edged closer, swords drawn. He signaled the Nightshades to stand down. She crouched, before the pounce. Gleaming black fur gave way to pale flesh as the shift happened in midair. A black cat leapt and a beautiful young woman landed in his arms.

He cradled the trembling girl in his lap. She was in a cold sweat, and her teeth chattered. She opened glazed eyes that held his. "We got them, di-didn't we?"

Against his orders she had come after him. He should be furious with her. Exeter took in the ethereal beauty of her pale face—so innocent, so fearless. "That we did, Mia."

Had she shifted at will? Or had the cat escaped? He had experienced every mewling whimper of her climax—he was sure the cat had been tempered. Exeter lifted her in his arms. Was this unprovable therapy working or not? He was inclined to hope so—for Mia's sake.

"Over here." Jersey stood at a juncture between railcars. Exeter hugged her tight, and followed the Nightshades' lead, descending to the coupler bridge. The bodyguards cleared the aisle in the sleeping car, stopping at their compartment door. "Bollocks, the key is inside," Exeter grumbled.

"As our rotund Australian friend would say—no worries." Jersey fired up the tip of his blade and ran it down the seam in the door.

"And as Mr. Ping would say—'Open, O'sesame.' " Exeter gave it a kick and stepped into their compartment.

He turned back briefly. "Where's America?"

"We've got her locked away somewhere safe, and she's not happy about it." Jersey grinned.

"Seal us in." Exeter shut the door and closed the window. Working methodically and quickly, he lay Mia on the narrow sleeper bed and covered her in blankets, adding an extra coverlet from the berth above. A bit of color returned to her cheeks, but she continued to shiver uncontrollably. What she needed was a warm bath.

His fingers flew through the buttons of his waistcoat. He removed his waistcoat and pulled his shirt off over his head. She needed heat, something that would penetrate the surface level and warm the deeper muscles and tissues. He shrugged out of his suspenders and removed his trousers and drawers. Lifting the sheets, he climbed into the berth and took her in his arms. "Wrap yourself around me—tightly." He melded his body to hers and waited. Gradually, the shaking muscles quieted, and her supple body clung to him. He ran his fingers through a tangle of soft brown hair—sweeping the waves off her face. "There, Mia."

Her eyes barely opened, but she smiled softly. "I'm so tired."

"You often go right to sleep when you come back."

"Mmm." A sweet breath wafted over his shoulder. Her hand lay against his upper body and her fingers softly brushed his chest hair.

One extremity at a time, Exeter rubbed down every part of her body, while she drifted in and out of sleep. Though he had no watch, he pressed his lips against her jugular vein. Her pulse had gone from scarcely perceptible to strong and steady.

Gently, he rolled her onto her other side, so he might spoon against her. She awoke long enough to whisper. "Don't leave me." She reached back for his hand, which he took in his and pulled her close.

"I'm here." He nuzzled the nape of her neck. There wasn't a place on her body that didn't arouse him. Her skin was as soft—as he was hard. She was so strokable. And he was so in need of stroking. Exeter was sure he'd never get to sleep, not with that velvety bum rubbing up against a blistering erection. And then again . . . he closed his eyes and slept.

A warm, gentle breeze brushed her cheek. Exeter's breath. His arm was around her and she could feel the rise and fall of his chest against her breasts. Mia lowered her eyes. Exeter was lying beside her fast asleep, and he was—she took a sneaky look further down—wearing nothing but his God suit.

She explored slowly, taking in the smallest detail—from the mole on his shoulder to the light covering of fuzz on his upper torso. She ran her fingertips through his chest hair and lower, across the pale golden skin of his abdomen. Exeter had always been handsome of countenance and stature, but his body was also lovely. Wickedly so.

Her gaze traveled over an exposed hip and a fascinating curve of muscle that disappeared under the bed sheet. Mia had studied Greek sculpture and architecture extensively, including the Doric, Ionic, and Corinthian columns . . .

Her gaze returned to his sleek, muscled groin and she wondered, dare she?

She stole a furtive glance at his face. Exeter appeared years younger in his sleep, unencumbered by all the worries and responsibilities he took so seriously. She lifted the covers slowly, enough to view . . . an impressive phallus at rest.

"It is called nocturnal penile tumescence. The spontaneous occurrence of an erection of the penis during sleep."

He was awake.

Caught in the act of peeking, Mia dropped the sheet. Her cheeks flamed with heat, still she was filled with curiosity and more than a little trepidation. Her need to know, however, trumped any fear. "This is normal for men—this size and stiffness?"

She dared to meet his gaze and wasn't exactly sure how to read his expression. Something between sleepy arousal and amusement. "Fully erect, a man's penis varies in size. Some are larger than others—all of them get the job done."

She folded back the sheet. "I see." Her gaze traveled up his torso. "You are handsomely made, Doctor Exeter."

"As are you, Miss Chadwick." He cupped her buttocks and brought her pelvis against him. How easily this man thrilled her. Even now her body tingled from the feel of his hard penis pressing against her belly.

He had mentioned his discomfort last night, which had set her wondering about his pleasure. About exactly what happened when a man climaxed. She understood the mechanics of procreation—but this was different. No one had ever mentioned the part about pleasure—except Exeter.

She placed her hands on his chest. "May I touch you here?"

Exeter nodded.

Her fingertips moved down his torso. "Here?"

Exeter's eyes narrowed. "Mia."

She nuzzled the dark stubble of beard on his chin. "May I please touch you . . . ?" She moved lower and he caught her hand in his and brought it to his lips.

He brushed a kiss over her knuckles. "I'm not sure that should happen right now."

A sharp rap preceded the sound of Jersey's sword reopening the door latch. Exeter leapt out of bed and grabbed his trousers from the floor. Propped on her elbows, Mia nearly gasped. He shoved a long limb into a pant leg and covered a nicely muscled buttock cheek. Even as he hopped into his trousers he aroused her.

A pale pink glow suffused the room. "It's dawn," she mused aloud. Exeter dipped to peer out the window as he buttoned his pants. "We should be in Paris."

Jersey stuck his head in the door before he entered the room. "A drawbridge went out last night—the train was held up for nearly two hours."

Exeter opened his valise and pulled out a fresh shirt. "When do we arrive?"

"We're on the outskirts of the city—no more than twenty minutes." Ever the vigilant bodyguard, Jersey stole a quick glance around the room. "They're serving pastries and coffee in the dining car—join us."

Chapter Ten

"OH, MY"—Mia poked her head out of the carriage—"this is lovely." L'Hôtel Claude exuded an Old World charm with its gated yard and striking dark blue awning over the door. Topiary trees planted in carved stone containers made charming sentries to each side of the hotel's entrance.

Everything about their temporary residence was elegant and understated—very much like the man who handed her down from the carriage. She took note of the quiet courtyard's neatly trimmed, ivy-covered stone walls and tall iron gates. It was also a fortress.

Exeter checked in and distributed room keys. "We've got two connecting suites on the sixth floor with four sleeping chambers. If we require more rooms, the hotel assures me they will make every effort to accommodate us."

During the trudge upstairs, Jersey calmly laid down a few security rules. "I'd like to request that no one leave the hotel alone and never without either Valentine or myself as an escort. Report any strange occurrence, no matter how insignificant. And I must ask everyone to leave their rooms unlocked, in case Valentine or I have to get to you quickly."

On the sixth floor, before Exeter could turn his key, the door to room 19 opened. *"Bon jour, mon amis."* Mr. Ping bowed politely and ushered them inside the suite. "The rooms are perfectly situated, Doctor Exeter." Ping swept back the pale under curtain behind a swag of sumptuous drapery and opened French doors. "Come, have a look."

The view from the hotel room was spectacular. Her gaze traveled across the Quai des Orfevres and the Seine to the Latin Quarter on the left bank. A telescope mounted on a tripod had been set up on the narrow balcony, which hardly had room for the window box planted with red cyclamen. Exeter leaned over to take a look, adjusting the eyepiece. "What am I looking at, Ping?"

The attractive and somewhat whimsical character folded his hands over his chest. "Latin Quarter. The east wall of the Sorbonne. There is an underground entrance to a student dinning hall—mostly used by delivery people to the kitchen." Exeter motioned Jersey in for a look.

"Directly below the kitchen," Ping continued, "is one of your long-lost entrances to the catacombs." The gifted genie was in shirtsleeves and waistcoat; he apparently had been there for some time, preparing the room for their mission. Of all the Nightshades, Mia found Ping the most fascinating. He was also a powerful, magical force who was said to transmogrify between male and female at will. She had never seen him in his female form . . . Jinn. There was something intriguing about this beautiful, androgynous character, whom she found to be deadly handsome in a most exotic way—with his liquid silver eyes and long black hair. She had once had a discussion about him with America and Valentine, more of a girlish giggle, but she was surprised to learn they all felt the same attraction to Ping.

"What about the other locations?" Jersey looked up from the eyepiece to the river.

Ping sighed. "The view is blocked from here, better from the rooftop—we can set up there if need be."

Mia hadn't taken her eyes off the iron spire across the river. "By Mr. Eiffel's Tower?" she queried. "It is rather . . . intrusive." They all turned to study the daunting edifice.

"I'm not sure I like it—yet." Jersey muttered. Exeter added a grunt of agreement.

"Why the surveillance?" Mia asked.

Exeter turned to her but spoke to all. "It is my understanding that Tim will be bringing several new gadgets with him—radio communication devices modified for our world. These will allow us to speak to one another, no matter where we are in the city. The telescope is a precaution—an aboveground lookout, to keep us apprised of either the French police or Prospero's patrols."

Ping nodded. "The other device will track us underground, and keep us from going in circles." The young man crossed the comfortable sitting room and pushed apart pocket doors to a dining area. "I thought this would make for a kind of war room. We can tack up the maps and store all of Tim's equipment in here"—Ping gestured to the table—"and enjoy a meal."

A number of covered dishes were placed on a table set for six. Mia and America both lifted domed lids. "Thoughtful of you." Mia thanked the jinni.

He turned to America. "Phaeton has been a great friend to me as well as a brave protector of us all. I sense his time with Prospero has been difficult"—when America looked up in alarm, Ping smiled a mysterious Ping smile—". . . for Prospero."

While Exeter and Jersey pinned up the map purchased in London, Mia fixed a plate for Exeter. She piled on his favorite foods, including lamb braised in a luscious ratatouille. Exeter sat down at the table beside her. "This looks perfect, Mia."

"Of course it is." She grinned, digging into her salade niçoise. "Is there a bellpull about? I know I'd love a good soak and a nap, after luncheon." There were nods from both America and Valentine.

"Enjoy your meal, ladies, and allow me to order your baths." Ping exited the room, returning some minutes later holding a plainly marked tin, and a tubular device, of the kind Tim Noggy carried about.

"Tim asked me to bring these on ahead." Ping pushed a toggle switch on the side of the cylinder and a vibrant green line shot out from the end of the tube and into the air. The narrow light beam snaked up and down, sometimes curling back on itself, sometimes dividing into two lines to make a rectangular box, then merging into a single line once more. The beams traveled up and down, side to side, forming a labyrinth of glowing green lines in the air.

"A map of some kind?" A wide-eyed Mia looked from Exeter to Ping.

Ping positioned the projection over the map on the wall. Almost at once they all realized what was happening. The new semitransparent grid was aligning with the much older map, at least in most places.

Exeter set his fork down. "Another version of the catacombs?"

Ping nodded. "From the other side."

"The catacombs of the Outremer," Mia whispered.

"Using both maps, and the locator bugs, we should be able to triangulate the most likely spots Prospero has hidden Phaeton."

America's gaze fell on the plain metal box. "Locator bugs?"

Ping nodded. "Open it."

America used two fingers and gingerly lifted the lid. Simultaneously they all peered inside. A great number of black beetles—mechanical creatures the size of a tuppence—swarmed about inside the tin. "I've been working with the tech wizard, Oakley."

"Tech wizard?" Jersey asked, holding up a wine bottle. "Anyone wish to finish the last of this fine vintage?" Seeing no takers, he poured the remaining claret into his glass.

Ever the professor, Exeter elucidated. "From the Greek word, *technologia*. Meaning a systematic treatment of an art—

from *tekhne?* art, skill plus *logia*. Used to describe applied sciences, like engineering."

"Tim often calls Oakley a tech wizard, who in turn refers to Tim as the Big Brain." Ping appeared both amused and impressed by the eccentric brothers, and it was difficult to awe a creature like Ping, whose very existence was the antithesis of technology and science. He was a supernatural force.

"Oakley designed the flies on the wall, as well as these creatures," Ping explained. "Rather unique little bugs—they're heat seekers. They'll scurry straight for anything with a temperature of thirty-five degrees centigrade or greater." He closed the lid on the tin.

"And when might we expect Mr. Noggy?" Exeter inquired.

"He's here, in Paris." She did not believe she had ever seen Ping smile—actually it was more of a grin—and it was lovely. His silver eyes crinkled. "Actually, he's below Paris—in the Outremer. He's taking in the sightseer version of the catacombs. He intends on making a break from the tour and have a sneak about."

"He's here, but he's in another dimension—an alternate Paris, and he expects to reconnoiter—when?" Exeter rubbed his temples, not a particularly good sign.

Ping arched a brow and coupled it with a half smile. Mia thought he looked devilishly like Phaeton Black. "Tonight."

"Let's hope he doesn't get lost down there." Exeter leaned back in his chair and looked around the table. Mia supposed they all looked a bit ragged.

"No one got much sleep last night. Now that Ping is here to keep watch, I recommend we all get some rest." Exeter the doctor advised. "We begin the search for Phaeton tonight—two groups of three—that way each of us will have a Nightshade with us. We'll enter the catacombs from two different map positions and turn the bugs loose."

Exeter entered the room and shut the door quietly. He was immediately struck by the sights and smells of their bedchamber. Their bedchamber. His heart pounded out of control at the thought of Mia's next lesson. Truth be told, he was both excited and disturbed by his role as Mia's sexual initiator.

Recently, Mia had matured considerably in his eyes—exactly the kind of perception adjustment Phaeton had mentioned months ago. Even better news, she was learning to use her newly sexualized body to control the wild creature inside. This most unusual therapy from an eccentric bookshop owner actually appeared to be working.

Mia had drawn the drapes to keep in the warmth. The room glowed softly, from a candelabra placed beside a copper tub. She lay back in her steaming bath, a washcloth covering her eyes. Pale flickering light cast a warm glow over her glistening skin. She was partially submerged in a froth of bubbles and aromatic bath salts. One knee angled out of the milky water. His gaze followed the line of a long shapely leg to the end of the bath. Her toes curled over the rounded edge of the tub.

"Water's lovely, Exeter—care to join?"

He pushed off the door and headed straight for the center of the room. Circling the heavy poster bed, he let down the side curtains. If they were to leave the door unlocked, the least he could do was assure them some privacy. He removed his coat and lay it across a side chair. "You're certain there's room for the three of us?" He untied his cravat, as he approached the bath.

The beauty in repose lifted the washcloth and looked him up and down. "Pussy wants her back scrubbed."

He stood at the end of the tub and undressed. Cravat and collar, shirt, trousers, hose, and low-topped boots—finally he stood in front of her with nothing but a dancing erection. Her eyes lowered to his penis. "You are stimulated?"

"What does it look like?" Exeter reached behind his head. Most often, he wore his hair tied in a queue that emphasized his noble forehead and elegant cheekbones. He pulled off the ribbon and his hair fell in loose waves to his shoulders. "And how is the minxy she-devil this afternoon?"

"She stirs about—but, I feel as though . . ." Mia appeared to be searching for the right words. "The urge to shift is a bit like a sneeze—you can wiggle your nose and interrupt the itch, but sometimes it can't be stopped."

"Scoot forward." He climbed in behind her, wrapping his legs around her. He quickly washed his chest and shoulders, then soaped a washcloth and scrubbed her back. "Mmm," she murmured.

"Lay back, Mia." She leaned against his body and he nuzzled the topknot of luxurious hair piled on her head. "I must admit, there is something wonderful about being naked with a beautiful young woman in a tub filled with soap bubbles." As he luxuriated in the bath, she scrubbed his legs, one at a time, down to the soles of his feet.

Exeter groaned. "I never thanked you and pussy for your assistance last night—you are quite powerful in feline form. There is potent force in the cat."

"I have flashes of memory—leaping onto the roof of the passenger car—a bit of a scuffle—gnawing on wraith bones." She handed him a mildly scented soap and cloth.

"Nothing on how you got there?" He worked carefully over her anatomy, starting with firm, plump breasts and working his way down every inch of her body.

Mia moaned softly. "I remember feeling rather ferocious and protective"—she reached back and rubbed the stubble on his jawline—"of you."

He pulled her knees up and extended her leg into the air. "A test to see just how flexible you are. Good God, love, you're a ballet girl."

He imagined the arch of her brow. "You know ballet girls intimately, Doctor Exeter?"

Exeter turned on his side against the wall of the tub, and at the same time, angled her body toward his. She easily tucked herself to one side. "Throw a leg over my hip—that's it." They lay in the warm bath, breathing in the layer of hot steam that floated just above the glistening surface of the water.

Mia reached up and ran a wet finger over his upper, then lower lip. "Tell me about the ballet girl."

He studied her for a moment. "I was on break from university, trying to decide if I would push on for a medical degree. I met a few chums at the theatre—each one of us ended up with a young lady that night."

"Did you . . . love her?"

Exeter's mouth twitched, ever so slightly. "I'm afraid with young men, the urge to mate is not often governed by the heart—alas, not even the head. It is a much more primal urge."

"Oh yes, I know about urges." Mia furrowed her brows. "Does that make me a wanton?"

Was it the protruding lower lip or the genuine look of worry on her face that so beguiled him? "It makes you—Mia." He leaned forward and kissed her lightly. A simple brush of his lips to hers, and all he could think about was more.

She toyed with the washcloth. "I want to touch you tonight."

He angled away. "But you are touching me. Look, we lie together in this bath—every part of us is touching."

Even though he smiled gently, her expression darkened. "What do you do with your desire, Exeter? Where does it go? I do not wish you to think of me as a torture." He was near speechless as she explained. "America says Phaeton becomes unbearably irritable when he is . . . pent-up."

He did his best to suppress a grin, which proved impossible, because her dimples were out. "I could suck your lingam like a mango fruit . . . if you wish."

He stared for a very long time, before he rose from the bath and yanked her upright. He tried not to linger too long on the rivulets of sudsy water trailing over her sleek curves.

She continued to quote the Kama Sutra. "Let me put the whole lingam into my mouth and—"

"Stop that," he ordered, and promptly swept her up in his arms. Parting the bed drapery, he lay her out on top of the counterpane. She used her heels to dig in and inch away from him. "Stop what, Exeter?"

As predatory as a great cat himself, he leaned over her. "Stop tempting me so." His voice was gruff, and he imagined he looked as though he might eat her alive. Perhaps, he would.

"Turn over—on your stomach." Mia raised a brow, but obeyed. He held her wrists together against her back. "You need to be taught a lesson," he whispered, and slapped her bottom. With his free hand, he gently stroked her clitoris. He alternated his stinging slaps with his pleasuring touch. The objective was to have her begin to be excited by both. And he didn't stop, not until her breath came in short, harsh gasps. The spanking, the scent of her arousal, her lovely mewling whimpers urging him on—all signaled her escalating pleasure.

Exeter broke away, gasping for air himself. Dear God, how he wanted her. "Do not make this harder for me, Mia." What on earth was he saying? He was making it just as hard on himself. Aching balls hard.

He let go and flipped her over. Facing her, he brought her face closer, inch by inch. Then he did something inexplicable. He kissed her. Christ, how could he resist her? He covered her mouth with his and sucked her tongue into his mouth. He meant for his kisses to be punishing—ravaging. He wanted to see her lips swollen and slightly open—imagine how she might take him in her mouth.

He was on the brink of losing complete control. "Open your legs."

Mia drew her legs up defensively and then teased him with just enough resistance, until she allowed him to push them open. "I'm going to taste you, Mia."

He brought both knees up high, and trailed soft kisses along the insides of her thighs. He understood what she wanted, what she desperately needed. He would replace the measured sting of the spanking with his tongue.

Gliding his mouth over the most sensitive parts of her, he laved and flicked with a rhythm that invited her hips to rock with him. His face was wet with her essence when her legs and belly began to tremble. Sweet, mewling sobs of pleasure begged him not to stop. "Oh yes, Asa," she gasped. All it took was one last lick and she was over the edge of her climax, crying out in unrestrained ecstasy.

Exeter picked her up and moved her under the coverlet. Nestled in the warmth of the feather bed, he wrapped her in his arms and squeezed her tight. "What is it about you, Mia?"

"Me or my bottom?" She wore a curious, slightly vexed look on her face. "Feeling a bit itchy and sensitive back there."

He kissed her neck. "Good."

Chapter Eleven

MIA NARROWED HER EYES. This man had taken her over his knee, in the most erotic sense. He had positioned her facedown—buttocks up—held her hands in his vise-like grip and spanked her. Not as hard as a paddling, she supposed, but she was quite sure he'd left his mark.

He'd also aroused the wildest, wickedest thoughts. More. And harder. She moistened her lips and pondered her first question: *Me or my bottom?* Exeter watched her closely. She suspected he was interested in her reaction to his shocking behavior. "Was that supposed to be arousing—or punishing?"

Exeter bit back either a grin or frown. "Perhaps a bit of both."

Mia hooked a leg over his body and placed a hand on the hard, rippled surface of his torso. "You must let me pleasure you." She wanted to gaze on his handsome face—see his eyes darken and glaze over from her touch—how empowering it would be to give him pleasure.

"No."

"Why not?" Mia growled, and tossed off the coverlet. "Then touch yourself—but you must let me watch."

Exeter appeared to consider her idea, and a thrill rippled through her. He punched up a few pillows and settled back against them. "And how is pussy feeling?"

"Well pleasured, Doctor Exeter." Mia grinned. She watched in fascination as he took his cock in his hand. He stroked slowly, from the base to the tip, occasionally running a finger along the cleft of the helmeted tip. A lightning bolt of pale blue veins zigged and zagged down the length of the powerful shaft. She could only imagine what he might feel like deep inside. The very thought caused her womb to clench. "May I . . . lend a hand?"

He gazed at her from under heavy eyelids. "There is a jar of paraffin jelly in my kit."

Mia slipped from the bed and returned with the ointment. Opening the jar, she gobbed a bit of the slippery substance on the end of her fingers.

Sensing her intentions, he eyeballed her. "I have not had a woman in months—you dare to touch me, and I promise you I will explode." His speech was a hoarse whisper. She had come to know the timbre of his bedding voice, and his gravel-laced speech sounded like a man who was greatly aroused.

Climbing over his legs, she straddled his thighs. "Where, first?"

"Spread it on the tip." She circled the head of his penis with her finger. "Like this?" Exeter groaned his answer and it thrilled—such a primal, speechless utterance. Golden green eyes, glazed over from desire. "Lower." He held the shaft still, while she spread the slick clear jelly over his member. Covering her hand with his, he showed her how to stroke. Up and down, once, twice . . . She moved slowly at first. "Now, faster." She pumped faster. "Harder." She pumped harder. His hips thrust up to meet her and his head angled back into the pillows. "Good God—I'm going to come." His face was so beautiful—chasing after his pleasure—no other thoughts, no worries—just her next stroke. "Do not stop now, Mia—whatever you do."

"I will not." Her hands, slippery with emollient, were running up and down his straining shaft. She followed his instructions—slightly harder and a bit faster—until he growled loudly. In that moment, his pulsing hot seed spurted high into the air. Even as waves of pleasure consumed him, he managed to watch her with half-open eyes.

Mia sat back on her haunches, stunned.

Still in the throes of a convulsive finish, his shoulders heaved as he finished his release with a long exhale. Gradually, his breath returned to normal, and he made eye contact. One side of his lips twitched upward before he stuck his head under a bolster. She was quite sure she heard muffled laughter.

She pushed out a lower lip. "Not comical or amusing, Exeter."

He lifted the pillow. "You didn't see the look on your face."

She imagined her large round eyes and her mouth hanging open; no doubt she had looked like a babe in the woods as the big bad wolf slathered sperm over his chest and stomach. She slid off the bed and fished a washcloth out of the bathwater. "I had no idea." She used the cloth to wash his chest and the banded muscles of his stomach—she could not help but think him handsomely made—lean and hard.

"You had no idea . . . of what, love? The force of the eruption? The amount of seed—?"

"All of it." Her voice almost a whisper.

He tugged the cloth away, and dabbed her cheek. "You missed a spot."

"Is it always like that?"

Exeter grinned. "Perhaps not quite as effusive—as I said, it's been a while." He lobbed the washcloth into the tub with a splash.

"But . . . when you remained at Mrs. Parker's. I thought—"

Exeter frowned. "You thought wrongly. Mrs. Parker and I are not lovers." He eased his expression. "Leastwise—we haven't been for some time now."

Her chest swelled a little and her eyes watered. But before her heart could soar with happiness, he added. "I am still curious, though, as to why you asked her for the address of a male prostitute in Paris."

Mia shifted her eyes away from his darkened gaze. "I did not think she'd be such a tattler—"

"What a brazen little chit you are. Asking after Etienne Artois." He pulled her up beside him and tucked the coverlet around her.

Mia rested her head on his shoulder. "Phoebe got his name from her sister. We were curious."

"I might have known the little minx put you up to it." He sighed, adding a gruff, Exeter sort of *tsk*. "Lisbeth has amounted to nothing but trouble for Henry."

He referenced the Earl of Bath. And she'd heard the rumors, as well. Most of the gossip had come from Phoebe herself. In fact, she had taken delight in telling Mia that her sister, Lizbeth, Countess of Bath, had approached Exeter suggesting a weekend tryst at one of the country manors. Mia nuzzled his shoulder, which muffled a growl. "I do not like it when you refer to me as a chit."

He reached under the covers and hooked her leg over his thigh. His slumberous, half-lidded gaze traced the curve of her hip. "Then don't act like a chit."

Exeter motioned Jersey ahead. "The lock is ancient and rusted—quick work for your dagger." He reckoned they were at least fifty feet below the square, yet they had not yet reached the catacombs. Barely an hour ago, they had slipped through the locked gates of Place de Sorbonne and ventured down a narrow stone stairwell. He glanced over at Mia—who watched the captain of the Nightshades fire up his dagger and go to work on the padlock. She met his gaze over Jersey's shoulder. "Will we avoid the ossuary, or do we head straight for it?"

"Having second thoughts?" Exeter kept his grin wry. "Correct me if I'm wrong, but didn't you refer to this escapade as a great adventure?"

"An adventure in men's trousers, no less." Mia returned his grin with a wink. Good God, what was he to do with her? He had raised a termagant—wild, dangerously brave, and completely arousing in trousers and jacket with her hair tucked under a paperboy's cap. A few hours ago he had taught her how to stroke his cock—something she had proved wonderfully adept at, for a novice.

Exeter exhaled the resigned sigh of a man on the verge of complete surrender. The unthinkable was happening. From the very start, he had adored Mia. But he was in danger of falling in love all over again. Good God. Exeter pushed the thought back—far back—and concentrated on the task at hand.

The plan was to place the locator bugs in and around the north end of the catacombs, while Ping, Valentine, and America sprinkled their heat seekers in an old lime quarry below the Luxembourg Gardens. They were to reconnoiter at a third secret entrance—a brewery hundreds of years old. Tim Noggy would also try to make the rendezvous, from the Outremer.

The beam from Jersey's dagger easily sliced through the lock, and they made their way down a twisted hallway of mortared stone. Taking up the rear guard, Exeter motioned Jersey and Mia ahead. They had agreed to travel light, which meant no lanterns. Jersey's dagger would provide plenty of illumination and Exeter carried a battery torch with him. It was a miraculous gadget Phaeton had procured for him months ago from Scotland Yard's Secret Branch. Exeter hoped the experimental dry cell batteries were still good. The torch was their only backup.

A half dozen candle feet of light spread out from Jersey's weapon. "Dagger, sword, torch—quite a utility you've got there, Captain Blood," Mia teased their stoic bodyguard.

The Nightshade set a blistering pace through the darkness stopping once to help Mia negotiate a length of passage undergoing repair work. "What's that noise?" Mia asked.

Both he and Jersey slowed to listen. "There is a complex network of springs under Paris." Exeter listened a moment longer. "Aqueducts travel alongside some of these tunnels. If we hear an underground train, that would likely mean we have crossed into the Outremer."

Mia shook her head. "No—it wasn't a gurgling sound, nor a

train. More like a zephyr—a singing wind." Wide, liquid eyes moved from him to Jersey and back again. "You don't hear it?"

"Does the cat hear this strange wind or does Mia?" Exeter probed, gently.

Mia chewed her lip. "I'm not sure." He thought he knew the answer but signaled Jersey to push on.

"We're almost there." Jersey swung the luminous sword forward, and they followed after him. The narrow passage gradually widened into a large chamber. They found themselves standing before a stone portal at the entrance to the ossuary. Above the doorway there was an inscription: *Arrête! C'est ici l'empire de la Mort*. Jersey read the words aloud.

Mia translated, "Halt! This is the Empire of Death."

They entered a cavern lined with carefully arranged human bones. Bones heaped high behind retaining walls made up of femurs and tibias, skulls and mandibles. Some of the arrangements were artistic in nature: a heart-shaped outline in one wall, a cross of skulls on the opposite side of the room. A number of intricate designs were fashioned using skulls surrounded by a pattern of stacked femurs and tibias.

They stepped gingerly at first, and then more rapidly, as Jersey ushered them through one connecting cavern after another. Mia turned to back to him. "Dear God, Exeter—so many lost souls."

"Millions, I'm afraid." As if his answer wasn't grim enough, Jersey pointed to a placard mounted on a wall that estimated the number of dead. Near six million. They entered a round room circling a huge central pillar carefully crafted out of an arrangement of bones.

Jersey pointed the end of his blade at one rusty gate, then another. Both blocked passages led to other parts of the catacombs. Signs posted on the iron bars warned of possible cave-ins—that the passages beyond were either under renovation or unsafe to navigate. The Nightshade looked to Exeter. "The next tunnel is crucial if we are to meet up with the others."

Exeter opened a satchel strung over his shoulder and removed a tin with half the heat-seeking bugs. Mia helped Exeter spread the inert bugs around the cavern. "What did you do with my cinder toffees?" Mia asked suspiciously.

He searched in another pocket and unwrapped a pocket square. Two large pieces of the honeycombed toffee lay in his palm. Before she could reach for a piece he pocketed the handkerchief. "If we get lost down here this could be our only sustenance until we're discovered by either Tim Noggy or Prospero."

"I'm not about to get lost down here." Mia's hand plunged into his pocket and retrieved the candy. She selected the smallest piece and offered up the other.

Nodding toward one of the gates, Jersey popped the honeycomb in his mouth. "Somewhere south of this room, we need to make a right turn."

Exeter folded up his map. "No matter what, we maintain a southwest heading. If a passage takes us off course, we double back." Leveling his compass, Exeter confirmed the direction Jersey was pointing.

Mia sighed. "Worst case, Ping will find us."

Jersey fired up his dagger and made short work of the gate lock, ushering them into the next passage. Up until this point the tunnels had been tall enough for even Jersey and Exeter to traverse upright—now there were long stretches of low ceilings. Jersey frequently called out, "Watch your head."

As the passage lowered and narrowed, Mia began to appear agitated. Twice she stopped and whispered, "Shush!"

Jersey slowed. "We've got a dead end ahead."

"Shush!" Mia's harsh whisper was more adamant this time—enough to warrant a long silence. A moaning sigh—something decidedly unnatural—whimpered through the cracks and crevices of the limestone walls.

Mia's eyes were large and round. "Did you hear that?"

Exeter looked up at Jersey who nodded. "I say we track back to the gate and look for another tunnel south."

The singsong voice whispered again. Exeter whirled around, looking for a being or face. He'd even settle for a smile—but found none.

A second wave of hushed quavers filled the air. "Circles-s-s-s, circles-s-s-s—you move in circles." The musical, airy voice hissed. He checked his compass again. "The needle is spinning." Jersey and Mia both leaned in for a closer look.

Exeter drew on his gut instinct, something he had learned to trust when confronted by the supernatural. "Talk to the wind, Mia." He smiled softly and nodded to encourage her.

She scanned the rock walls on both sides of the passage. "Who speaks?"

"Who-o-o asks-s-s-s?" the voice sputtered and hissed.

"You talk as though you were out of breath, but you are made of air—you are the wind."

"Alas-alas-alas-s-s-s, not wind . . . per s-s-s-se. I am the last breath of the souls who are buried here."

"Oh dear," Mia exhaled a sigh of solidarity. "Would you tell us, please, which way to go from here?"

"That would depend on wh-wh-where," wafted the whisper, "you were going."

"We make our way southwest to join our friends," said Mia.

"Then, you must s-s-s-top moving in circles-s-s-s. If you continue to circle, no matter which way you journey, you will only return to me."

Exeter frowned; this strange wind whispered in riddles.

"No, that won't do—we need to get *somewhere,*" Mia insisted adamantly.

"Oh, you're s-s-s-sure to do that," mocked the wind. "That is—if you are contrary enough."

Mia checked with Exeter. "Contrary?" she mouthed silently. He shrugged. Mia must have felt as though she was getting nowhere, because she tried another tack. "What sort of beings live here about?"

"In *that* direction," a breezy zephyr blew by their noses, "lives an old rock troll and in *the other*"—the whisper abruptly reversed course and rushed down the passage they'd just come from—"there is a magician. I don't advise you visit either one—they're both mad."

A whimpering moan whirled into a cyclone of wind, tossing up a screen of dust particles. Mia squinted—they all did—as sand and dirt swirled around them. In warning, Jersey pointed his sword at the twister. Using all the seeing power he could muster, Exeter made out the shredded robe of an ethereal being. The creature turned tail and vanished down the narrow corridor.

Exeter suspected a deception—something whimsical and unthreatening—to distract them. He broke the silence. "What kind of down-the-rabbit-hole trickery was that?"

Jersey slashed his sword as he started down the corridor. "One of Prospero's hirelings. We'd better move on—in a hurry."

He checked his compass. "Magnetic north has returned."

"Humor me for a moment, gentlemen." Mia blew a few strands of hair off her face. "What if she . . . the entity . . . was trying to be helpful?"

"She?" He and Jersey asked in unison.

"Whatever it was, it felt like a she, though I suppose it might have been a he." Mia shot them a bug-eyed "pay attention" look. "When I said—'but we need to get somewhere,' the wind answered—"

"If you're contrary enough." Exeter repeated the zephyr's words.

"Exactly!" Mia's eyes brightened. "What if your compass is not reading true north? What if, in effect, we have been traveling northeast, instead of southwest?"

Exeter's gaze rose from the instrument in his palm. "You're suggesting we follow a course contrary to the compass."

Mia pivoted in place, peering into the blackness of the crudely carved passage. "It's possible we missed a much smaller tunnel—one that heads in a northeast direction."

"Why don't you two have a look about," Jersey grunted.

"I'll double back to the round room—get to work on the next gate."

Exeter reached in his coat pocket and produced the experimental torch. He toggled the switch. Nothing. "Hold on, Jersey." He slapped the metal cylinder against his palm and a circular beam of light spread across the tunnel. "Open every gate you find, and keep a sharp eye," he called after him, "we could be walking straight into a trap."

"May I?" Mia tugged on the torch.

Exeter didn't let go—not at first. He just wanted to take a moment and admire her. *That was rather brilliantly intuitive, Mia.*

No compliments—not yet. She smiled up at him. "If we rendezvous with Tim Noggy you can buy me breakfast at the *crêperie* on Boulevard Saint-Michel."

"It would be my pleasure." She had read his thoughts, again. There was an intimacy in knowing another's thoughts—as well as a disturbing invasion of privacy. Exeter released the torch, and followed close behind Mia as she swept the beam across the corridor, from one wall to another.

Taking their time, they explored a few smaller tunnels that either grew too small for passage or turned back on themselves. Up ahead, the spit and hiss of Jersey's sword reverberated through the passageway. Mia stopped to examine a makeshift scaffolding constructed over a chasm. Joining her, he peered into the depths of the pit. Some sort of cave-in had collapsed the floor. When combined, both maps had shown quarry tunnels dug at different depths—he sensed another passage directly below.

Mia glanced back at him. "I'd like to have a look under these boards."

They found an open spot that led down into the cavern—not steps exactly, more like a few toeholds. Using potent energy, Exeter jumped first and waved her down. Following right behind him, she lost her footing and began to slide.

Exeter brought her down the rest of the way, wrapping his

arms around her possessively. "You might have used a bit of relic dust and champagne," he murmured. She nuzzled his neck and purred—yes, he was quite sure of it. "And how is pussy this evening?"

"She wants Exeter." A hint of cat whispered in her throat.

He pressed his mouth against her temple. "Good God, Mia, not here."

Mia pushed away. "Then help me undress, for she is coming."

Exeter quickly weighed his options. Bring her to climax or chance letting the panther loose to roam the catacombs. Both were inopportune choices, but one was also unthinkable. There were hundreds of miles of tunnel—layer upon layer of ancient limestone mine. If the cat emerged and darted off she could easily get lost. He might never find her again.

He backed her into a wall of crumbling rock, and held up his index finger. The tip sparkled with warm light. "A bit of potent energy—set on pulse."

Chapter Twelve

"WHAT DO YOU PLAN TO DO WITH THAT FINGER?" Mia snarled as he pulled off her trousers and yanked down her pantalettes, She was so close . . . so close. She might shift any second. But she didn't—instead, she let him tear at the lace edge of her camisole.

He plunged into her labia and she jumped from the sensation. His finger was warm, almost hot, and the tip vibrated against the place he called clitoris. She arched away from the wall as her eyes rolled back in her head. The sensation was so intense, she thought she might climax on the spot.

"Open to me—wider." The panther's tamer used his finger like a whip and chair. He roughly parted folds, exposing more of her to pleasure. Whimpers deepened into moans as her stomach fluttered with arousal. "Exeter," she gasped, pushing against the finger that hummed and flicked, coaxing her raw need to the very edge. He reached under her camisole, rolling a nipple between his thumb and index finger.

Dropping to his knees, he hooked her leg over his shoulder. "Bloody gorgeous clitoris," he groaned, and buried his face in her. She was completely exposed from the waist down—deliciously naked and vulnerable—and completely open to him. "Exactly the way I want you, Mia." She rocked with each stroke of his tongue, urging him on as he licked his way around her swollen spot using that wickedly skillful, tormenting finger of his.

This was only their fourth intimacy—was she counting? Yes,

she was. It was if he already knew the secrets of her pleasure. How to make her whimper and beg for more—grind into him like a wanton shameless hussy. He reached behind and cupped her buttocks, pressing her into his mouth as he flicked his tongue and sucked her throbbing clitoris.

On the verge of climax, he rolled back on his haunches. He was teasing her—leaving her pleading for one more stroke—the one that would send her over the edge. "Please, Exeter," she begged. He shook his head, breathing hard. His beautiful eyes, slightly glazed—his mouth and chin wet from her arousal. She had done that to him.

"Lift your camisole above your breasts." She did as she was told, as he angled the torchlight against a large rock—his lips moved from her glistening thighs and lingered on the hollow, trembling curve of her belly. He moved his hands higher, over her ribs to the peaks of each mound—he rubbed softly at first, and then harder—tweaking both nipples into hard points.

He rose to her chest and swirled a nipple into his mouth—he nipped and she cried out. The fingers of one hand raked through her hair—pressing her head back so he could kiss . . . the tip of her nose. "You are near paroxysm, Mia, and I will watch your pleasure." Two fingers massaged a nipple, while his other hand—the one with the devilish, vibrating index finger—delved between her legs. He kept the magic finger on her clitoris, while two fingers stroked the length of her—toying at her entrance. Her virginity was still very much intact. He had not entered her yet, but she wanted him to.

"Look at me." His whispered.

Her eyes locked with his golden green gaze. Eyes that had turned into burning embers. Her arousal was climbing in force, pounding through her, pooling in her womb. God, how she loved him for this—not just because he gave her such astounding pleasure, but because he risked relieving her here—in the middle of the catacombs.

"Exeter—Mia, are you down there?" Jersey's voice filtered down from above.

His finger did not stop, but continued to pulse. "There's another tunnel, lower down," Exeter called up. Then he leaned close to her ear. "Come for me, Mia."

Aroused to the point of climax, she drew in gulps of air as quietly as possible. "We've found a tunnel—be right there."

There was a silence. "Is everything all right?"

"Answer him." Exeter insisted, as his finger insisted she climax. With each stroke, the cat readied to make her leap—unless she held the great cat back. She dug her fingernails into his shoulders, and tossed her head back. "We're fine—I just want to get a bit closer."

She glimpsed a hint of a grin on Exeter. "You couldn't get any closer."

"You wretched man—you're enjoying this." She thought about his penis as she crashed over the edge of her pleasure—the great length and width of him—the arousing fantasy of him inside her. As sheer bliss consumed her, she bit into the fabric of his coat to muffle a cry.

"You think you're the only one this is hard on?" His words rushed past her ear, causing a second shudder. She reached down and found a rock-hard shaft straining at his trousers—proof of his discomfort. "Obviously not." She stroked him lightly as he pressed his forehead to hers.

"You're sure you don't need me down there?" Jersey called again.

Exeter shoved her hand away and pushed back. He was a most inscrutable character, often hard to read, but tonight his breath was harsh, and he wore a look on his face that spoke of agony and ecstasy. If she could put words to his expression it would be "what did I ever do to deserve such torment?"

He helped her back into pantalettes and trousers. "Button yourself." Exeter removed a pocket square from his coat and wiped his face. Stepping away, he brushed against the torchlight and it fell off the rock, illuminating something they'd missed—a good-sized hole in the wall of the pit. Mia could make out less and less in the dark as her panther vision faded—still, she sensed something at the far end of the passage. Their own shadows, perhaps?

"Exeter," she whispered, nodding to the newly exposed hole in the ground. "There's something moving beyond the end of this shaft."

Jersey landed between them, with a thud. She was quite sure he paid particular attention to her. "Before I venture into that hole in the ground, please assure me the cat is sated."

"For the time being," she murmured, grateful for the cover of darkness, as a flush of color swept over her cheeks.

Exeter frowned. "How long were you up there?"

Jersey almost never smiled, and rarely laughed. But he released a dry, throaty scoff. "Since bloody gorgeous clit—"

"Never mind." Exeter swept the flashlight off the ground. "Why don't you fire up that sword and forge the way?"

They entered the hole in the ground single file, on hands and knees. At one point, the ceiling lowered, forcing them to crawl on their bellies. Mia balked, as a sudden sensation of panic nearly overwhelmed her. She tried to reverse gears and run—only she backed straight into Exeter, who sensed her alarm. "Your hysteria is temporary—you're experiencing a bit of claustrophobia. Take slow breaths—rapid shallow breathing causes your heart to race. Slow down and push on, Mia."

Mia managed to squeeze a look back at Exeter. He rubbed her leg. You're doing fine."

She exhaled and faced forward. Jersey had already cleared the passage. Up ahead she heard talking, she was sure of it—and something that sounded like a bit of backslapping. Overcome with curiosity, she ignored her anxiety and moved forward. Thankfully, the ceiling of the tunnel was also growing taller again.

"Hey—cheers in there." A familiar voice greeted them.

"Is that you, Tim?" Up on all fours, she shuffled toward the voice at the end of the shaft.

Jersey reached in and pulled her out. It was Tim Noggy, all

right—in all of his largeness. A wonderful sight, indeed. Mia dusted herself off as Exeter crawled out of the tunnel.

"Gadzooks, it's good to find you all. My compass is broken." Noggy pointed to a small device that flashed illuminated numbers and letters.

Exeter passed his compass over. "When the needle isn't spinning it appears to point in the opposite direction." Tim studied the dial as he pivoted in a circle. "Which would make sense if we were in the Outremer."

"Is it possible we *are* in the Outremer?" Mia asked.

Tim shrugged a shoulder up and down. "I'm pretty sure I just came from there." Their large inventor friend checked his portal device. "December eleven, eighteen eighty-nine."

Exeter glanced at the date. "Have you any idea where Ping and the young ladies are?"

Tim shook his head. "I just got here, mate."

"What about Prospero? Any sign of him?"

Tim's gaze crinkled and his grin widened. "I've got some news on him, all right, but first let's find the others." From one of the many pockets in his greatcoat, the young inventor pulled out yet another contraption. "This will set off the bugs—they'll find our missing party in no time."

"No need to waste battery power." They all whirled around to find Ping standing in the middle of the cavern. Valentine and America peeked around the corner of a passage that led south, that is, if south truly was . . . north. Good God, they really were down a rabbit hole.

"I do hope your tour of the catacombs was as interesting as ours." America smiled, as she and Valentine joined them.

Exeter sucked in a breath, exhaling quietly. They had managed to find each other more by accident than by design. Still, he was greatly relieved. "I promised Mia I'd buy her breakfast—shall we debrief?"

Tim brightened. "I almost forgot, we're in Paris—*Croque*

Monsieurs!" He gazed at the raised brows surrounding him. "It's kind of like a grilled ham and cheese—only better."

Mia lead the way out, with Exeter right behind her. They found the ancient brewery without much trouble, and the third secret passage. Tim ushered them ahead while he set off the miniature locators. As it turned out, they had surfaced in the basement of an apartment building just south of the Luxembourg Gardens. Finally, Tim poked his head aboveground and declared: "The bugs have been animated."

It was well past dawn before they tucked themselves into a corner of Le Procope, 13 rue de l'Ancienne Comédie. *"Bonjour, mademoiselles et messieurs.* Café or tea?" Their waiter was wonderfully patient with Tim as he struggled to describe a *Croque Monsieur,* a café staple that hadn't been invented yet. "A jovial French waiter at this hour of the morning." Exeter winked, and ordered savory crepes. Once everyone had ordered and settled in with tea or coffee, he encouraged Mia to relate her encounter with the chatty creature he called the breath of lost souls.

"We conversed in Lewis Carroll speak," Mia poured milk into her tea. "Oddly diverting—and I'm almost certain I saw a cloaked figure recede into a maelstrom of dust."

"An entity unknown to me nearly abducted America." Ping shared. "I was distracted momentarily by a strange gust of wind and debris—not unlike the one you describe, though we had no conversation. Whatever it was, came and went quickly."

America's almond shaped eyes grew round for a moment. "Prospero?"

"Very likely." Exeter exhaled an impatient sigh. "It seems to me we know very little about Prospero—just the most cursory of facts, actually. For instance, we know that he is a titan of industry in the Outremer—part scientist, part wizard. You have often described him as a tyrant and a hoarder of aether. I assume that operation is gone now that Victor's rebellion blew up Prospero's refinery plants." Exeter scrutinized the young inventor.

"What do you know of Prospero, the man, Mr. Noggy? For instance, is he well known for his exploits with the ladies?"

"There are reports he's bisexual—not like Ping—not sure what to call it in 1889," Tim shoveled a spoonful of sugar into a second cup of coffee.

"He enjoys the company of men as well as women," Exeter clarified.

Tim nodded. "Victor obsessed on it for a while. He thought he might be able to get to Prospero using prostitutes."

Exeter suspected Tim Noggy knew more than he was telling. Originally, Tim had identified himself as an Australian, but as it turned out, he was brother to two very powerful men in the Outremer. Tim's twin, Oakley, ran a highly successful technology company called Black Box, and the dwarf, Victor, self-proclaimed conscience of the three siblings, was a wily political tactician and rebellion leader. Exeter remained convinced the brothers had not revealed half of what they knew about Prospero, nor the history of the troubled, unraveling world they hailed from. He had shared his concerns about the brothers with Mia on several occasions. "Is Victor still in self-exile?" Exeter queried.

Tim slurped his coffee. "He checks in from time to time—he's planning an outright assault on what's left of the wizard's resources. Victor believes we've got him on the run. Prospero is down to rationing his aether, and since it fuels everything in our world, including his own powers, he's been forced underground."

"Into the Paris catacombs." America mused aloud.

A round face bobbed up and down. "Looks like it." Tim's eyes shifted back and forth, with a sparkle of mischief. "I've got something to show you when we get back to the hotel—something Victor recorded."

Mia had ordered eggs scrambled in butter and chives. The corner of her mouth glistened—tempting him to taste. Instead, Exeter reached up and dabbed a napkin at the edge of her lip.

"A bit of butter—" he winked, as his gaze swept across the table to Noggy. "So you do manage to communicate with Victor."

"You asked about Prospero's proclivities. They're sort of . . ." Tim rocked his head back and forth. "Pornographic ."

Exeter stared at Tim. "Sort of?"

Tim eyed the young ladies at the table. "Okay, not sort of."

America swallowed. "Have you . . . received any word of Phaeton?"

Tim nodded. "He's holding his own—for the time being."

"How long will it take the bugs to home in?" Exeter forked up a bit of ham and crepe in Hollandaise sauce.

"I expect to see some bug clusters by late afternoon—hard to say for sure. There's a hundred and eighteen miles of quarry tunnel. And those are just the ones on the map."

"You believe there's more, off the map?" Exeter asked.

"I know it, mate. The bugs are going to find more than one or two warm bodies, especially the bugs I laid down in Outremer Paris. There's an underground nightclub, art galleries—all kinds of illegal stuff going on in the catacombs. Prospero will have a hideout in both worlds—likely close together."

Ping shot a piercing look over the rims of his dark glasses. "And how is Outremer Paris?"

The question stopped Tim's fork midway to his mouth. "The Eiffel Tower is looking more like the leaning tower of Pisa—it has a few weeks at best." He shoveled food and shrugged. "Just a guess."

Exeter settled back and returned the genie's uneasy gaze. If Prospero enjoyed relations with both sexes, he would be unduly intrigued with Ping and Jinn. "We're going to need all your talents for this one, Mr. Ping."

Ping smiled as he sipped his Darjeeling tea. Mysterious silver eyes met Exeter's over the edge of his cup. "Truly."

Mia finished her breakfast in relative silence—as they all did. Afterward, she and Exeter trailed behind the others as they crossed the Seine on the Pont Neuf. "We have an appointment for a showing at the House of Worth this morning. Would you like me to cancel?"

Mia paused to admire dark and light swirls of water rush under the bridge. "Call it a premonition, but I keep picturing a hasty retreat out of Paris. It might be best to get the shopping over with."

"I hate to rush you, but . . ." Exeter pulled her close, rocking her gently in his arms. "Let's get your new wardrobe selected and purchased, Baroness de Roos."

His reference to her title caused a flare of heat to sweep over her cheeks. Mia glanced at the emerald on her ring finger. "I'm quite a tireless shopper, Baron de Roos. We shall get the job done in one day." Exeter grabbed hold of her hand and maneuvered through a tangle of carriage traffic to the tree-lined quay that ran along the Seine.

"I believe it might be time to discuss the next phase of your training, my dear."

He hadn't let go of her hand; in fact, he wove those long tapered fingers through hers. Mia's heart did a bit of dancing about in her chest. "And that would be?"

"It is time for you to get comfortable in your cat suit." His eyes crinkled, slightly. "Valentine's notes were quite adamant about the fact that these metamorphoses are hard on the system, at least initially. To give your body a chance to recover from each shift, you must try to remain a cat for a few hours at a time."

Exeter stopped beside a low wall overlooking the river. "We have yet to acknowledge this to one another, but we have begun to communicate telepathically." He curled a finger under her chin and tilted her face upward. "When you are the panther, I am quite sure you recognize me—and you understand what I say. On the roof of the train, you knew Jersey and Valentine as well, did you not?" He moved closer, searching her face. The harsh morning light played across his dark beard stubble. He appeared tired, though ever her handsome, stoic protector. The man she loved with all her heart.

"Of course she knows you, Exeter." She smiled to reassure him. "She understands instinctively who is friend or foe." In fact, the cat was a rather excellent judge of character; she found Exeter to be the most intriguing male in all the world. "While I am the cat, I am completely present—aware of all the elements, some of them beyond my ken. Her sensory abilities are raw and unfiltered and she is both wary as well as enthralled by . . . everything."

For a moment, she could feel her feline essence; a dazzling bit of sunlight off the Seine caused her pupils to narrow into slits. "I am seeing the world again, through new eyes."

"We might encourage you to shift for several hours tonight." Exeter smiled somewhat wistfully. "But, I must ask one thing of you, Mia."

She searched his face. He appeared hesitant, as though he was embarrassed to ask. "What is it, Exeter?"

"May I collar you?"

A flush of heat moved across Mia's cheeks. "You would put me on a leash?" The wild feline inside stirred.

"Only because . . . I don't want to lose you. The cat often runs off, you could get lost in the catacombs." Exeter swept a stray wisp of hair away from her face, and tucked it under her cap. "My word, you are provocative in newsboy attire."

Mia chewed on a bottom lip. "I'm not sure she will take to it—but I suppose we must try." Myriad thoughts, many of them wild and wicked, accompanied this strange idea he proposed. The flutter in her stomach reminded her of their first night together—when he had fastened her wrists to the poster bed. Mia leaned against Exeter and rubbed her cheek against his.

"We will continue your lessons this afternoon. This time, at the edge of climax, you will let her shift." He used his husky bedding voice—the one that encouraged moisture between her legs, even when he hadn't touched her.

"Might that be dangerous? Her fangs left you marked."

"A mere scratch." He kissed her lightly. "My darling, Mia, you have taken possession of me body and soul."

Her pulse thrummed a strange, erratic rhythm as his soft kisses and sensuous bites angled back and forth across her lips. And she had neither solicited nor cajoled him into such affection. She badly wanted to ask, even as she repressed the thought.

But what of your heart, Exeter?

Chapter Thirteen

IN THE WAR ROOM, *née* "dining room," of their hotel suite, Exeter studied the image maker intently. "What is a hologram, exactly?" he queried, as Tim set up yet another odd contraption.

"In this case, it is a moving photograph of an interference pattern that, when suitably illuminated, produces a three-dimensional image." Tim's shoulders bounced up and down. "This little portable player doesn't really do the transmission justice, but you'll get the picture."

At first, there was nothing but a voice in the dark. "If there is a way to crack open Pandora's egg, I will find it." The voice was soft, gravelly—measured.

Phaeton Black sat behind bars and yanked absently on his bindings. "You are persistent, I'll grant you that, but you cling to myths, Prospero." The cell appeared to be shallow, enclosed by an old iron gate. Exeter squinted at a rather daunting lock mechanism. Absent a keyhole, but adorned with colorful lights, the device blinked in the dark. "Ping was quite clear," Phaeton continued, "the Moonstone knows your intentions. You cannot trick the stone with your wily wizardly ways."

A figure moved through shadows like a wraith in the dark. And a face, in profile, appeared inches away—nose to nose with Phaeton. "If that is the case, why hide it from me?"

A grin that was pure Phaeton Black lifted Exeter's spirits. "Might I suggest more sex torture? Might loosen my lips a bit—and mind I get a bit of anal play this time—before you bugger me. Or perhaps you might suck my cock?" Phaeton boldly stared the wizard down. It was as if they were two sides of the same coin—the cruel emperor on one, the court jester on the other.

"Continue to prevaricate, Phaeton, and I shall be obliged to use additional force. If I cannot have the stone, you will be kept . . . subdued." Exeter concentrated on the man called by many names—scientist, sorcerer, the tinker, the master—the lathe and plaster in Skeezick speak. The Nightshades had settled on the name Prospero for this enigmatic foe, and the isolated character from *The Tempest* appeared to suit. The enemy even answered to his name.

These captured images, along with snippets of conversation, had been sent to Black Box in London. According to Tim, his brother Oakley had personally extracted the transmission. Exeter could not shake the thought that Prospero continued to spin his web and he was drawing them in. Surprisingly cat and mouse, for such a high-stakes game.

Phaeton appeared irritated, and somewhat bored, but otherwise hearty enough. From what he could surmise, they were watching part of an interrogation. "Phaeton must have attempted an escape and been recaptured," Exeter mused aloud.

Valentine nodded. "He's got fresh marks on him—some bruising and a cut over his eye." He and Mia sat at the table, along with the other Nightshades, analyzing the strange, disturbing imagery. Phaeton was strung up—nearly naked as far as he could tell.

"There—another look at Prospero." Taken aback, Exeter caught his breath. Younger than he imagined.

Even Mia gasped. "Rather attractive. Strong, symmetrical features—except for the eyes, which are most unusual, wouldn't you say?"

Mia's admiration of another man's looks sparked a touch of—well, it rankled—yet Exeter had to agree. The eyes appeared to be both light and dark at once. Not unlike Ping's eyes—only a good deal more menacing. "Can we see that again?"

Tim nodded and pushed several switches.

The hair on the tech wizard's head was shorn extremely short; no more than a stubble of growth formed a widow's peak in the middle of an otherwise intelligent brow. Exeter did not believe Prospero could be much older than himself.

Black eyes flashed with silver. "What am I going to do with you, Phaeton, short of killing you?" The image crackled with static and flickered out altogether.

"That's all there is." Tim said.

Exeter scanned the uncomfortably quiet room, stopping on Noggy. "Once more from the beginning?"

America stood up to leave. Exeter caught her hand. "I'm sorry, I should have—"

"Do whatever you need to do to bring him back, Exeter." Tears welled in her eyes, and spilled over. She appeared to wobble a bit on unsteady legs. Exeter shot up from his chair and caught her as she collapsed in his arms. She cried the first tears he had seen from her since the day Phaeton was lost to them.

As her pregnancy advanced these past few months, she had been wonderfully courageous. They had given her work to do, and she had proven herself an excellent nurse to Gaspar, whose unraveling body had kept them all busy trying to find ways to arrest and repair the damage.

They had left Cutter and Ruby behind with Gaspar, and the urgency of getting to Phaeton could not be more compelling. They must return to London with the Moonstone—they were dangerously close to running out of time to help the Nightshades leader, while courting cataclysmic disaster for the Outremer. And if they failed—it seemed likely that both worlds would cease to exist.

Indeed, they needed Phaeton and the Moonstone to restore both the future and the past. Like it or not, they were inextricably linked—one could not exist without the other.

Exeter rocked America in his arms. How dearly she loved Phaeton and how terribly she must miss him. They had all spent these past months wondering if they would ever find the extraordinary, incorrigible Mr. Black. Given the odds, the prospects were beyond dismal. Ping and Noggy had worked quite tirelessly on locater gadgets and by trick or accident of fate, the flies on the wall had brought them to Paris.

Parts of the transmission had been rather graphic—too graphic for the ladies, yet America had insisted on watching. But he could not, for the life of him, think of a reason to subject America or Mia to a second viewing. He caught the eye of Mia, who put her arm around America. "I ordered baths the moment we arrived. Shall we find a nice hot soak somewhere?" As if in answer to Mia's suggestion, a knock on the door produced a number of attendants carrying copper tubs and buckets of steaming hot water.

Exeter rolled the doors to the dining room closed and signaled for a replay.

Tim hesitated. "That wasn't the end of the recording."

He pulled up a chair. "Some lurid scenario, no doubt."

Tim nodded his head slowly. His eyes darted over to Valentine, who defiantly arched a brow and crossed her arms over her chest.

"This is shocking as well as vividly salacious," Tim warned, as he pressed the play button.

Exeter leaned forward. He sensed something purposely voyeuristic about the way the scene had been captured. Due to the poor image quality, Prospero could be heard, but he was always in shadow.

The unseen wizard paced around the small cell—lingering behind Phaeton, presumably ready to sodomize him. "You can take my cock in your mouth anytime." Phaeton was purposely baiting the man to perform fellatio, while a shapely female figure dressed in black leather entered the cavern.

Exeter grinned. "Phaeton appears to be holding up brilliantly—devoted hedonist that he is."

The image broke apart and resolved into a picture of an ebony-haired woman—attractive in a jarring, severe sort of way. She was scantily clad in leather, with a great number of tattoos scrawled over her body. Leather holes cut in the front of a bustier displayed pointy nipples and bulbous breasts.

Exeter didn't quite know what to make of it. "Good God—are those real?"

"Surgical implants." Tim offered. "They make an incision and stuff plastic bags filled with saline in there."

He continued to stare, though he was not sure why. Horror? Fascination? Lust?

The female stepped into the light snapping a riding crop against tall boots. Up until now, all they had seen were breasts. "Domina Valor." Tim uttered the name in a hushed tone.

"Who is she?" Jersey leaned forward.

Tim paused the image. "She's a porn star in the Outremer. Victor recognized her immediately; he owns a big collection."

Exeter stared. "A collection of pornography?"

Tim nodded. "She once did fifty guys in a hour in *Domina does Dallas*."

Jersey snorted. "Does she flagellate them or fuck them?"

"Both . . . I think." Tim's eyes darted about. "Okay . . . I . . . didn't actually *see* her do it—I just heard about it."

"Well, I know I've seen enough." A wary, slightly amused Valentine rose from her chair. "You boys enjoy yourself. I'm off in hopes of finding another hot bath."

"Ready?" Tim punched the button again.

Phaeton was speaking. ". . . No? Then how about a spanking—or a few love bites, right there on the tip?" Exeter could not help but think Phaeton's openly lurid taunts made him vulnerable to harsher treatment—still, there was often method to his madness. Methods that could only be guessed at, if one reached into the darker corners of one's sexual fantasies.

"But for the restoration the Moonstone can bring—I would not waste my time," Prospero sneered as he circled Phaeton.

"Handsome cock you've got there, Mr. Black—and ramrod hard by the looks of him." Domina dropped to her knees. A long pink tongue unfurled from ruby-red lips.

"If only we had run into each other earlier, Prospero—I

would have gladly handed it over." Phaeton looked down and groaned. "*Domina flagellates Phaeton* . . . be sure to send Victor a copy . . ." He exhaled a groan of pleasure. "That's it—suck the tip, love."

As Domina Valor alternated whip and tongue, Prospero grew more insistent for information. The erotic imagery cut in and out as Phaeton's pleasure turned more and more to pain. There was no way to tell if the scenes were contiguous or not, for they often seemed oddly truncated, causing Exeter to grow even more suspicious. "Prospero certainly has in mind an insidious carrot-and-stick reward scheme. And I believe Phaeton is aware that he's being recorded."

"That's all there is." Tim flicked off the machine and turned toward the wall. Hundreds of tiny green specks dotted layers of catacomb maps. "See here," Tim pointed to a very small cluster of bugs. "This may develop into something significant, or it may not. We're looking for a much larger mass." The rotund young scientist turned to Jersey and Exeter. "I don't think we're going to see anything definitive until late this afternoon."

"Is there a way to hurry them along?" Exeter exhaled an impatient sigh.

"They're stealthy little bugs, mate, what do you expect?"

Exeter left the dining room in an irritable frame of mind. The bugs were moving at a snail's pace, and he was overstimulated in the way a man becomes aroused by viewing French nudes in a stereoscopic. He loosed his cravat. Hopefully Mia would be near to completing her toilet. He enjoyed a momentary fantasy. Mia, naked in her bath. Good God, such a wicked thought. I am the beast, otherwise known as Mia's guardian.

In truth, he had become her lover. And it was a guilty pleasure, one that he had not completely reconciled, as yet. He knocked quietly and opened the door. Two young women were having a bath in a familiar copper tub—what a sight to behold.

With the curtains drawn back, sunlight warmed the room. The young ladies' singsong laughter brought to mind two woodland sprites having a splash in a pond. The lovely sight eased both his mind and spirit. He paused a moment, with his back to the door, just to enjoy them.

Mia noticed him first. "Oh dear, it's Exeter."

America shrieked a laugh and sunk deeper into the water. Amused, Exeter ventured closer. "Actually I find this most timely. I've been meaning to do a late-term exam on you, America."

Exeter shrugged out of his coat and held up a bath sheet. America rose from the bath and he wrapped the towel around her. "Why don't you lie down on the bed?" He helped America out of the tub and turned to Mia.

"I hate to hurry you along—but you might begin to dress, while I have a quick look at mother and child?" He covered Mia in a Turkish towel, redirecting his attention to America. "Having Mia here should make you all the more comfortable with the exam, I would hope." He opened his medical bag and removed a jar of paraffin jelly and a sterile cloth. "Have you felt the baby move today?" Rolling up his sleeves, he scrubbed his hands in a nearby washbasin.

"Oh yes, with some regularity all morning."

"This shouldn't take long—I am curious to see if the child is engaged." He scrubbed vigorously with soap and water.

"Engaged?" America raised up on her elbows.

"When the head drops down into the pelvis, it is called 'engaged.' In first-time mothers it usually happens in the last two to three weeks." Exeter propped several bed pillows under her lower back, tilting her hips up. "And you, my dear, are nearly thirty-seven weeks, if our original estimates are correct." He lifted the towel covering her belly. "I'm going to place one hand on your lower abdomen and two fingers inside you."

"She's quite a bit larger than a pea in the pod." As Exeter palpitated, he smiled down at her. "At this point, you may be feeling more pressure and an occasional, sharp little twinge—that would be the infant turning her head."

America nodded. "Yes, I have felt both the twinge and the pressure."

"All completely normal, nothing to worry over." He slid his fingers up into her vaginal canal. A bit wide-eyed, America inhaled a breath. Exeter gently palpitated. "Your cervix has softened a good deal—I suspect there may be some dilation, as well."

He glanced at Mia, who was leaning over his shoulder, all round eyes and flushed cheeks. Her towel had slipped off a shoulder, exposing a lovely shaped breast and a hint of beige nipple. "And how are you holding up, my dear?" he asked.

"I'm . . . completely and utterly . . . enthralled, Doctor Exeter." Mia moved up beside him. "Might I—watch?"

"Even better, I shall put you to work." Exeter reached for his bag and pulled out a bar covered in paper. "Extracted from the cacao bean. Cocoa butter." He peeled back the wrapper and placed the waxy square on America's distended belly. He gently pressed it to her skin and circled slowly. "Her body heat will cause the bar to melt as you stroke her skin." Exeter showed Mia how to use her fingers and massage. "This conditions the skin and prevents striae—red marks from the skin being stretched." Exeter handed Mia the cocoa butter. "The baby will enjoy the rubdown, as well."

"Mmm, like a cup of hot chocolate." Mia inhaled the scent as she smoothed the bar over America's belly. A sudden bump sent Mia upright. "Oh, my!"

Chapter Fourteen

"I BELIEVE I AM IN A STUPOR OF EUPHORIA." Mia sat comfortably beside Exeter as the carriage turned onto Rue de la Paix. "America's belly ripe with child, tight as drum—when I massaged her with the cocoa butter and the baby kicked, oh, Exeter, I felt so close to the life inside her."

She suspected she looked a bit glassy-eyed, even dreamy, and for some inexplicable reason, she could not let go of her reverie. "Apologies for rabbiting on, but . . ." Mia caught Exeter staring at her over the top of his news sheet. "Did you feel it, too—during the exam?"

"There is great delight in the birthing of babies." Lowering the paper, he used his enigmatic smile—the unbelievably attractive one. "Something stirring about a new life, I suppose." He calmly returned to his reading. How could he possibly be so nonchalant about such an experience? She could only wonder at how miraculous a birth must be.

She blinked at him. "Exeter, you were brilliant with America. Sensitive and thoughtful. I very much suspect those stiff-collared Harley Street physicians aren't half as competent as you are. Why on earth did you decide not to practice? A specialty in women's medicine—relief from hysteria, perhaps?" Mia grinned. "Good Lord, they'd be lined up around the block hoping for a massage by Doctor Exeter."

Exeter snapped his paper, though he cracked enough of a smile to cause a deep crease and a glorious dimple—glorious for its rarity. He lowered his paper. "Did the exam bother you?"

Mia returned his gaze. "At first I was curious—" A thought stopped her speech, and nearly left her breathless. "You've no idea what a marvel you are." There had been a lighthearted reverence in the way he examined America. After locating the baby's head position, he'd taken her hand and pressed it to her belly. "Do you talk to the baby often? My mother sang Persian songs to me in the womb."

Responding to the doctor's query, America had propped herself up on her elbows. "Are you smiling at Doctor Exeter, Luna?"

And when he found the baby's head, he advised, "I suspect it won't be long now. My best guess is a few days . . . or a few weeks." Exeter had smiled at the disappointed look. "Nature nearly always makes doctors look a bit dotty when it comes to predicting the onset of labor, so I leave it sketchy."

After the exam, he'd grinned at America. "So you have decided on the name Luna . . . even if it's a boy?"

America had exhaled a funny, exasperated sigh. "*She* is definitely a girl. Phaeton met our daughter in the Outremer. As he was sucked into Lovecraft's transporter, his last words to me were: 'Her name is Luna . . . let go of me, America.' "

Having never heard this story before, both she and Exeter had exchanged glances. Mia had swallowed a rather large lump in her throat. "You never told us, America."

"I couldn't speak of it until now—without crying."

Exeter had folded America's clothes and helped her into Mia's wrapper. "Take a good long nap—doctor's orders." He had seen her down the hall and returned to their room for a quick bath. They'd dressed in relative silence for her appointment with Charles Fredrick Worth of Maision Worth, the famous couturier of Rue de la Paix.

Mia rocked against him as the carriage braked in front of the salon. "You were born to be a physician, Doctor Exeter—a healer. I've never seen you as joyful in your lab."

He arched a supercilious brow. "That is because my work on blood typing is a serious matter."

"Indeed. So very serious, you rarely leave your laboratory except for fencing twice a week. Or your standing appointment at Shaftesbury Court."

The very mention of his arrangement with Mrs. Parker caused the cat to stir inside her and Exeter to lower his paper. "Do you suppose there will be time this afternoon to purchase pretty matching undergarments for your gowns?" He folded his paper and tossed it onto the seat, opposite. There was a sparkle in his eyes that caused her heart to flutter inside her chest. He helped her down from the carriage.

"A clever way to change the subject, Doctor."

He placed her hand through his arm. "Clever, I think not. I have in mind something more bestial in nature."

Was it just her imagination, or was he flirting with her?

Exeter checked his hat with a footman in House of Worth livery and helped Mia out of her coat. Her essence had changed recently. He no longer considered her his charge. Instead, he thought about her night and day, in the most carnal ways possible.

"Ah! Baron de Roos, you have arrived." They both turned toward the effusive gentleman wearing a velvet beret over thinning gray hair. He flourished a courtly bow and turned toward Mia. "Charles Worth, at your service."

Exeter was faintly amused. "Allow me to introduce my wife, Lady Anatolia Exeter, Baroness de Roos."

"Baroness." Worth kissed the back of her hand. The couturier batted his eyelashes and continued to view Mia with a good deal of regard. "The salon is right this way." The man gestured and led them through a gallery that opened onto an elegant room, styled after a lady's boudoir and papered in an intricate chinois motif. Several settees were arranged around a low dais that ran the length of the room.

A matronly lady of obvious aristocracy sat on an opposite sofa, attended by a handsome gentleman many years her junior. "May I introduce La Contessa di Castiglione, and her escort, Etienne Artois?"

Exeter's bow stiffened as Worth made introductions. The modiste continually returned to admire Mia's lithe frame. *"Quelle beauté!"* he murmured. "May I?" He lifted her chin and turned her cheek. "Observe the length of curve from shoulder up the nape—*très élégant*—a swan."

"She will make a show of your gowns in London, Charles," the Contessa remarked. "And you will make another fortune this season."

Mia nudged Exeter with her elbow. "You're glaring."

"Indeed." He murmured under his breath. "*Escort*—is that what they're calling male prostitutes in Paris these days?"

Mia leaned into him. "If I'm not mistaken, the Contessa is a former mistress of Napoleon the third."

"Quite the pair." He harrumphed.

"Mmm, almost as scandalous as you and I." Mia sipped her tea and sneaked in an eye-roll.

The first model entered the salon from behind a curtained backdrop. "A vision in apricot." Charles Worth spun a mesmerizing tale of exotic fabrics and intricate embroideries as gown after gown was presented for their approval.

As models traveled through the room, they came close enough for Mia to examine the exquisite artistry, impeccable drapery, and tailoring of the House of Worth. She chose several morning frocks, afternoon and tea gowns, as well as a sleek champagne-colored evening gown. It was cut narrow with a draped apron that gathered above the bustle, in the shape of a rose.

Exeter was quite taken with the evening wear and chose a black velvet opera cape, embroidered with graceful sprays of gold and red flowers. *"Tulipes Hollandaises,"* Worth called it. He also fancied a daring gown with plunging neckline, front and back—and a corset so beautifully embroidered it was designed to be seen.

The Italian countess admonished Exeter with a chuckle. "You will have all of London ogling the baroness."

Mia sat up, pressing her hand to his arm. Something blue was headed their way—an understated froth of a gown strolled through the room. Embroidered silver dragonflies shimmered through a thin layer of transparent overdress. And the décolleté? Exeter imagined perky round globes and a hint of cleavage. His sudden surge of arousal, however, was very real. He turned to Mia, who tore her eyes off the dress long enough to meet his gaze. *Yes*.

After a near endless parade of evening wear, the showing was finally over. Mia was shuttled into a fitting room to be measured, as Exeter finalized their purchases. He inhaled a quick gasp—twice as much as he imagined. He nodded to Worth, "I look forward to seeing Anatolia in the loveliest gowns money can buy."

"*Absolument!* Stunning on such a beautiful baroness." Worth took him on a tour of the back rooms, ending in the fitting area, where Mia was being measured by two female seamstresses. She stood with her arms out, in camisole corset and petticoat, and she was listening quite intently. There was to be a fitting in the next few days—and another, in London, by a House of Worth–approved seamstress, who would unpack the wardrobe and make final alterations.

"Ah, here you are!" The Contessa wove a path around stacks of fabric rolls and cutting tables. "You must both come to my soiree—*très intimate*—this evening, eight rue de Talleyrand."

Following close behind the Contessa, Etienne Artois hadn't taken his eyes off Mia. "Baroness, you would not, by any chance, be an acquaintance of the Countess of Bath?" Exeter quickly made his way to Mia.

"Why yes, I know Lisbeth, as well as her sister Phoebe."

"Ah, Phoebe—she is a minx, that one, but also enchanting."

The Contessa's *prostitué* stepped forward, just as Exeter swept Mia off the podium. Gripping her elbow, he led Mia to a smaller stall and pulled the curtain. "Any additional measurements will be taken in the changing room."

Artois reluctantly backed away. "I did not mean to offend Baron de Roos."

The Contessa chuckled, "*Anglais,* always so serious! Please do bring your lovely wife tonight and help us celebrate, *oui?*" The bold woman snapped her fan shut and left the room on the arm of her escort.

Mia opened the curtain enough to poke out her head. "I'm so sorry, Exeter—I didn't think—until it was too late." Her cheeks flushed with pink.

He could kick himself. "This is my fault, I should not have continued the Baroness de Roos . . . ruse."

Mia's brows lifted in amusement, then crashed together. "But what are we to do? Our elopement—"

He winced at the word *elopement.*

"Exeter, you know that is what they'll call it. The gossip will be all over Mayfair."

He could almost hear the tittle-tattle being tapped out in Morse code, traveling by undersea cable, arriving in Mayfair days ahead of them. In no mood to think about the scandal they had just created, he shrugged. He would think about it later.

For the rest of the afternoon, he escorted Mia up and down the Rue de la Paix, dutifully carrying hatboxes and opening shop doors. But whenever they were alone in the carriage, he managed to do a great deal of grumbling.

"Exeter, I have apologized profusely, I don't know what more—"

"This is my problem—I'll figure something out."

"Why can't it be our problem? I can ignore the snide remarks and whispers if you can."

Exeter looked at her for a moment. "Just let me grouse a bit, Mia. I am responsible for your well-being and happiness and—"

"*And,* I'd be a great deal happier without your grousing and grumbling." Mia appeared exasperated—then her lips curled upward, and her eyes crinkled. "Are we bickering, Exeter?"

He could not resist her. Locked in her impish grin, he cracked a half smile. "Where to now?"

Mia checked her list. "Hermine Cadolle. Seventy-one, rue de la Chaussée-d'Antin."

"More hats?" He didn't groan, exactly.

"Lingerie." Mia stuffed the notes in her reticule. "We don't have to—"

"Skip the one shop I've been looking forward to all day?" He tapped on the trapdoor of the carriage. "Seventy-one, rue de la Chaussée-d'Antin."

Madame Cadolle's proved to be well worth the wait. Not only were there exquisite corsets and brief pantalettes made of silk and handmade lace, but the woman had invented something new—a two-piece undergarment called *le bien-être.* The lower part was a corset for the waist and the upper supported the breasts by means of shoulder straps.

After an arousing, near naked fitting for Mia, his smile had returned, though he was perhaps more on edge than ever. He had sat in rapt attention as Mia's breasts were stuffed, plumped, and lifted into corsets, camisoles, and yes, even *le bien-être.*

On the way back to their hotel, he exhaled a breath and checked his timepiece. "After four o'clock."

Mia gazed out the carriage window. "There is almost no place in Paris one can travel and not see the Eiffel Tower." She looked a bit pale in the afternoon light.

"You must be exhausted from all the shopping and fittings." Exeter noted the furrow in her brow, a sign of a headache. "How are the two of you feeling?"

Mia continued her gaze out the window. "Soon, Exeter."

Good God. He was hard from her answer. The hot blood of pure lust burned in his veins. He'd spent the day admiring beautiful gowns and underthings—imagining Mia in all of them. No wonder he was irritable. Yesterday, he had let her handle his cock, bring him some relief, and already he thought of her as his concubine.

Inside the hotel, Exeter arranged for their packages to be brought up. He pocketed a few messages and joined Mia at the stairs. On the sixth floor, Tim Noggy answered the door looking a bit deflated.

"What's wrong?" Exeter asked.

He shook his head. "The bugs are on the move—it's just that they're slow. We're not going to have a bead on Prospero's hideout until morning." Tim led the way to the dining room. Jersey, Valentine, and America already sat at the table. "Sorry we're late." Mia sat down.

"You haven't missed much." Tim rolled the pocket doors closed. "As I said—the bugs are slower than anticipated."

Exeter moved around the table to get a closer look at the activity in the catacombs. The electronic map displayed a flurry of tiny green dots moving at a snail's pace. "How long before they run out of power?"

Tim stuck his lower lip out. "Ten, twelve more hours."

Exeter turned away from the map. "Cutting it close, Noggy."

The big man's eyes flicked toward the ceiling and over to the map. "You're telling me . . . Doc."

"Where's Ping?"

"He's having a walk through the catacombs from the Outremer." Valentine offered.

"I expect Prospero has some sort of forbidding presence in the Outremer." Exeter fished in his pocket and opened a gilt-edged envelope. "A formal invite from the La Contessa di Castiglione . . . who likely worked as a spy for Napoleon the third—no doubt she—"

"Got the hotel name from Charles Worth." Mia pressed her lips together and stifled a laugh.

Exeter moved on to the next message, but not before he shot Mia a look across the table—the spanking look. "This one is—

ah! We are all welcome to visit the exhibits at the exposition grounds, including Mr. Eiffel's Tower, compliments of L'Hôtel Claude."

Exeter crumpled the notepaper and opened the next. He read the words once to himself, and then read them again, out loud. " 'Meet me at L'Enfer tonight.' Signed, Phaeton Black." Exeter surveyed the room and didn't bother to pose a question. It was obvious the note was a tempting trap of some kind.

America's tawny cheeks drained of color. "Phaeton wants us to meet him in Hell?"

Chapter Fifteen

"IT APPEARS HELL HAS A STREET ADDRESS." Exeter handed the missive to America. "Fifty-five Boulevard de Clichy."

Valentine read the note over America's shoulder. "If memory serves, Boulevard de Clichy is in Montmartre."

Exeter searched for the bell pull. "Perhaps one of the staff can enlighten us further."

"A café of ill repute, messieurs." The young maid stated in a whisper. "In Montmartre—the Pigalle—*le secteur de lumière rouge.*"

"The red-light district." America's almond-shaped eyes perused the ceiling. "Phaeton shall feel right at home."

"As well as the devilishly wicked Prospero." Exeter handed the girl a few coins and saw her out of the suite. This last invite was intriguing, but more than that, the message felt . . . diabolical. It deliberately dared them to come after Phaeton. As Exeter paced the dining room, he noted a small black dot, high up on the wall. The dot moved—just a fly. He changed direction, and halted.

Just a fly . . . on the wall.

Pivoting slowly, he lifted his index finger. A flash of potent energy struck the tiny intruder. "I believe this may be one of ours." Exeter picked up the smoking insect and turned to a table of openmouthed Nightshades.

Tim Noggy pulled an enlarging glass out of his coat pocket. "Blimey! He's one of ours all right. You zapped him good—not even a twitch."

"This would indicate we have more than one spy in our midst—Prospero has likely turned the flies against us. God knows how long he has been listening in on our plans, feeding us transmissions that were sure to lure us to Paris." Exeter scanned a room full of sober faces.

Jersey rose from the table. "We'll do a sweep of the apartment. You and Mia need to get some rest."

Exeter grunted. "The nightlife in Paris starts fashionably late and goes well into the early morning hours. Shall we meet here in the parlor, at say—the stroke of nine?"

America brightened, as her gaze moved from Jersey to Exeter. "We're going then—to meet Phaeton."

"I'm afraid this evening's adventure is fraught with danger, but it is our best chance, thus far, to extricate Phaeton." Exeter eyeballed the supra-metallic daggers Jersey and Valentine carried. "I do hope those things are fully charged."

Tim Noggy pulled out a revolver. "Just in case Prospero knocks out our aether."

A sharp rap at the door brought them all into the parlor. Jersey's hand was on his dagger. *"Entrez."*

A bellhop opened the door. "Delivery for Baron de Roos."

Exeter waved in the man, who dipped a bow and presented a red leather case stamped in gold roman letters.

There was a quiet gasp and a full complement of stares from the ladies, who spied the Cartier's jewelry case from across the room. Exeter dug in his pocket for a tip. This was excellent timing indeed. He tucked the box under his arm and turned to his . . . wife. "Shall we try to get some rest, Mia?"

Those same large eyes followed them, as Exeter escorted Mia through the parlor, down a short hallway, and into their room,

Being together, alone in a bedchamber, was beginning to feel . . . normal. Mia sank onto the settee and unbuttoned her shoes, while he moved to the windows. He released a sheer under drape and the effect was—just enough light.

"I don't suppose you care to attend La Contessa's soiree

tonight?" Mia pulled up her skirts and wiggled her toes before tucking long limbs beneath her.

"I have every intention of crying off." Moving across the room, his gaze narrowed. "Do you wish to attend?"

She moistened her lips and tilted her head. "No, but I believe you might be less averse to her invitation were it not for the likely attendance of Etienne Artois."

He came to a glaring stop in front of her. "Why are you so fascinated by him?"

"Why are you?" She met his gaze for an angry moment, and then looked away with a sigh. Exeter placed the jewel case on top of the counterpane and took the seat beside her. Lifting her feet onto his lap, he massaged small toes through silk stockings. "Mmm." She exhaled a soft moan. "I thought there might be a strategy in attending. Quiet the gossip." Mia swept a few loose hairs into her topknot and refastened a hairpin. "Would you say Etienne Artois is dashing to look at?"

Exeter stared. "No doubt the Contessa thinks he's a crusher—for a gigolo." He felt a surge of . . . he was not sure what he would call it, certainly not jealousy. Alarmed by the very notion that he might harbor covetous feelings for Mia, he changed the subject. "That lovely diaphanous blue confection, we purchased today will be stunning on you. All your young suitors will wish to ravage you on the spot." Exeter loosened his tie and removed his collar.

Mia opened her mouth, then quickly pressed her lips together. She appeared to consider his words. "Do you say these things to torture me, or is it more of a punishment—for the feelings I inspire?"

Exeter stared. "You're keyed up from shopping."

"*I am not* . . . keyed up from shopping." Her eyes flashed with anger. "I am displeased with you."

"I've just spent a king's bloody ransom on your wardrobe." He sagged against the damask stripes of the settee. "What do you want from me?"

Mia reached over and grabbed him by his waistcoat. "I want you, inside me," she hissed. Luminous dark eyes flashed green, as pupils narrowed into slits.

His gaze dropped to her lips. "I see." A pink tongue swept the pert curve of her upper lip. It seemed he was speaking with the cat.

"Whether you wish to admit it or not,' she murmured, "these intimacies between us are real, and far beyond the physical." Mia slid a fingernail down his jawline.

"Let's get you out of these clothes." He unbuttoned her dress and helped her step out of the several layers of overskirt and petticoats. Tossing the gown across the sofa, he scooped her up in his arms and made it as far as the dresser.

Good God, he wanted her so badly he was near delirium. Using the nearby wall to steady her back, he cupped her buttock cheeks, and brought her pelvis against his. "Put your legs around me, Mia."

"Do not refuse me, Exeter."

"Mia—we have been over this." He groaned, still denying her—denying himself.

"Stop flogging yourself over your attraction to me—I like it—I *want* you to want me . . . and I will not ask again." The cat nuzzled his neck and licked his ear. "Please, Exeter, it has to be you," she whispered, her trembling body underscored her raw desire.

"Mia—of course I want you. You are quite the loveliest young woman in all the world." He inhaled a harsh breath and exhaled ready to surrender. "But—"

"No buts—or I will go out and find a certain young gentleman who will be happy to service me."

"That popinjay?" Exeter's dark gaze sparked to angry life. "Never, Mia."

"Then . . ." She ripped open his shirt and raked sharp fingernails over his chest. "I believe some ferocious sex and no arguing would be lovely right about now." She tugged off his shirt and brushed her lips against his chest and neck. She licked his nipples, biting and suckling until he groaned his surrender.

Her hands moved lower, unbuttoning his trousers. The stroke of her fingers caressed his phallus like a whisper of wind. "You are ready for mating, sir. So hard and yet this broad sword feels like velvet," she purred.

Exeter swallowed. "Use your nails—lightly." His entire body quaked with mounting pleasure. He tore at her corset, lifting a breast to his mouth—tonguing her areola, he sucked the tip into his mouth and nibbled. She arched and cried out as he moved from one nipple to the other—he needed to see red from his suckling—his mark, his possession of her.

Sliding down his torso, Mia knelt in front of his rigid member. *"Mon Dieu,"* Exeter rasped out the words, for he was breathing hard from the feel of her tongue on his lower anatomy. Gazing down, he watched moist lips move timidly over his tightly drawn, engorged flesh. Sweet, crescent-shaped eyelashes resting on flushed cheeks. Her pretty lashes lifted, revealing such . . . wide-eyed loveliness. He could not help but plunge deeper into her mouth and quickly shot to the edge of climax. "That's enough," he gasped, and drew her up from her knees.

"Do I not please you?"

"You pleasure me too well." He tipped his watch out of his waistcoat pocket. "We have hours, Mia—let's take this slow and easy." Standing in the center of the bedchamber, he removed her corset and camisole. He tugged on the ribbon of her pantalettes. "You're very sure you want this—me?"

Her lingerie slipped off her waist, and rode her hips far below her navel. Silk fabric billowed around her legs. Playfully Mia shook her hips at Exeter. "I never wanted anyone but you, Asa."

A part of him delighted in her erotic flirtation. "You are the picture of an eastern belly dancer, perhaps even more provocative. I am reminded of a poem—'she has a way of walking like a gypsy and she smiles like a sultan.' " Exeter disrobed as she unpinned long ringlets of hair. Humming quietly, her hips swayed to an imaginary rhythm. A mane of loose tendrils concealed and revealed her breasts as she twirled.

Mia arched her back and veiled the lower part of her face with her hands. "I believe Eastern dancers push one hip forward and give it a shake? And then the other?" Her dancing became so erotic, his body ached for her. She held her mouth slightly open and drew close, her dark eyes smoldering with desire. She rubbed her hips, first one then the other, against the tops of his thighs. Her nipples rasped lightly across his torso.

He yanked off her pantalettes and turned her around. "Shake your lovely ass and rub against me." She rubbed the firm, bouncy flesh of her buttocks against his body. Placing his hands on her hips, he guided her back and forth across his groin until he could stand it no longer.

She had tempted him beyond all reason—and now he had to have her. "Let me first make you wet for me." He would use his fingers to rub and then pinch her nipples and massage her clitoris. And he would continue the manipulations until his hand was sopping. Only then would he impale her here, against the wall. He slid his tongue up the side of her neck and took her earlobe in her teeth. "Mia, your first time shouldn't be so rough."

She pivoted in his arms, and took his face in her hands. "Promise me you will be ungentlemanly." She kissed him hard on the mouth—winding her tongue around his as she continued to rub against his aching need.

He had denied his growing hunger for her, pushed her away, suppressed his desire, and now he wanted more than a brief coupling. He wished to pleasure her in new, exciting ways and watch her passion mature—demand more of him. "Once I am inside you, Mia, you will experience new pleasures." As he cupped her breasts with his hands, her nipples ruched at the brush of his fingers. There was a quick intake of air before she could respond to his question. "You bring me such pleasure—how could there possibly be more?"

"Oh, my dear . . ." His gaze met beautiful dark eyes glazed with desire. "There is so much more for us." Using his thumb and forefinger, he coaxed translucent, silken flesh to harden and peak. She guided his hands lower, past ribs barely felt, down a smooth belly, to the soft nest of curls below. Urging him to explore the moist flesh of her sex, she shifted her stance wider to accommodate his probing finger. Her shiver of pleasure and a throaty moan prompted him to add another finger—delve deeper. Gently, he massaged her hymen—stretching the thin membrane. "The loss of one's virginity comes down to a small prick, nothing more."

Her hiss signaled he had penetrated her body.

He responded with gentle, reassuring words and soft kisses. Her supple, nubile body responded by pressing against him. *Yes, Exeter.*

Christ, he was as hard as a stone and ready for mating. "Wrap your legs around me." He lifted her up from the buttocks, using the wall to steady her back.

Bracing one hand against the wall of the bedchamber, he pressed her slowly onto his cock. The slippery, tight fit of her was enough to edge him ever closer to climax. He pushed past the broken hymen, filling her a little bit more with each thrust.

"A kiss, Mia?" She covered his mouth with hers. "More tongue," he whispered and received. Holding her against the wall, he drew himself in and out, using the throbbing tip to slip free and move over slick folds—to rub, tease, and make her moan. Slowly, one plunge at a time, he penetrated deeper, until he had planted himself to the hilt.

"Oh oui! Mon Dieu, oh oui!" She spoke to him in the blasphemous language French lovers understand. Her voice was breathy and edging toward the peak of her excitement. His own gasps and guttural cries increased along with the speed of his thrusts.

He held himself deep inside her and carried her across the room to the bed. Her legs remained tightly wrapped around his waist and she arched up to receive him again and again as he slipped in and out of her with greater urgency. At the peak of his pleasure, he remembered. And groaned.

Exeter slowed his pumping and lifted himself off the beautiful body beneath him. He trailed kisses from the hollow of her diaphragm to her belly, lapping up small beads of sweat with his tongue. He tasted salt and hotel soap—French lavender. Best of all, he tasted Mia.

Breathing hard, he sat back and rather methodically slipped off her garters and stockings. Cupping her leg at the crook of her knee, he kissed the sensitive flesh of her inner thigh. Mia propped herself up on her elbows. "I don't understand—why are you stopping?" Exeter closed his eyes and continued to softly stroke the inside of her trembling thighs.

Having allowed himself a moment to recover, he reached for his medical bag, which he always kept on the nightstand when traveling. He removed a palm-sized tin and opened the lid. She lifted her chin for a better look. "Condoms?"

"Used primarily for the prevention of venereal disease. However, the doctor also recommends their use for contraception." Exeter removed an individually wrapped latex sheath and set the tin aside.

Reaching over her, he picked up the red leather case and placed it on the flat of her abdomen. Mia ran her finger over the embossed gold leaf letters and smiled, shyly. In the dusky light of early evening there was a sultry look about her—disheveled, and so very beddable. He leaned forward and kissed her lightly. "Open your present."

She fiddled with the small latch for a moment or two and then lifted the lid. Exeter never took his eyes off her. He wanted to read every nuance of her expression—good or bad.

"Exeter," she whispered. "So many emeralds."

Chapter Sixteen

MIA LIFTED THE NECKLACE out of the velvet lined case. On closer examination she arched a brow. Three rows of sparkling green stones studded a black leather collar. "Is this for me . . . or her?"

"You are one and the same, Mia—not either or." Exeter scolded lightly. "I must confess, I have been colluding with Cartier for over a week now." He wore a happy conspiratorial look on his face. "Julian Cartier and I were schoolmates at Harrow." He appeared as fascinated by the gem-studded choker as she was.

"Ah, there's a note." He opened the small crisp envelope and removed the card. "This is a first sample—sent over for approval." His gaze met hers. "Does it . . . meet with your approval?"

How was it this man could thrill her one moment and anger her the next? The collar was beautiful, but it was also disturbing. "I'm not sure—what do you intend to do with it?"

"As I explained earlier today, you are learning to control the emerging cat, but we also must work together to train her, when you are not in human form. I'm hoping this collar can restrain as well as persuade." He reached for her and she flinched, involuntarily. "Mia, let me help you."

"I'm afraid of her."

"I know you are." His demeanor shifted from tutor to something gentle and intimate. "Perhaps, and this is just a theory, but what if we can get about together in daylight? The Tuileries, for instance, a gentleman and his exotic pet out for a walk together. Might it not help you settle into your new alternate persona?"

Dear Exeter! He was always trying to create some sense of normalcy for her, as if such a life was possible. She had become a creature who existed in the half-light.

"So I am to be your curious pet. I suppose it is all the rage in London." She had seen the Duke of Grafton and his magnificent Peruvian jaguar riding in an open carriage in Hyde Park. And the Marchioness Woburn, who never went anywhere without her pet ocelot. She shrugged a bit and sighed. "Is this behavior also fashionable in Paris, or might we get arrested?"

One side of his mouth twitched upward. "It might be wise to do a few late-night strolls before we promenade on a Sunday afternoon."

Exeter pressed her further. "You need to be with your cat for longer periods of time. Your body needs a chance to recover—you're dragged out and far from lucid when you return, Mia. You suffer hot and cold chills, a faint, rapid pulse—all signs of shock. It's worrisome." Exeter hesitated, which meant he was holding something back.

Mia swore the cat licked her upper lip. "What . . . ?"

He swept a tangle of waves away from her neck. "This time, when I bring you to orgasm . . . instead of pacifying her, I want you to let her loose."

Mia sucked in a breath. What little control she had gained over her shifting was about to be sorely tested. She felt as though they were headed into dangerous territory. Fearful thoughts deluged her. "Exeter, you've seen how she is. You could be injured—severely this time."

Mia wasn't quite sure how to say this next bit—so she blurted it out. "And . . . as stunning as this collar is, I am put off by the notion of being treated like a pet." She suspected her distaste for the gorgeous collar came more from the feral feline, than herself. A snarl gurgled through her body at just the thought of being led about—even if it was by Exeter.

"You're angry with me." He was taken aback. His brow wrinkled in concern.

"What if she leaps out at you—like the first time? She came dangerously close to your jugular vein with those fangs. I take it you mean to control her with the collar, but she will also have her claws this time." Mia moistened her lips, nervously. "She's very strong. How will you hold onto her?"

"She is part of you, Mia—you have more control than you allow yourself to believe. On the roof of the train to Paris—you shifted and came to my aid. We fought the wraiths together."

She ran a bare foot up and down the quilted counterpane. "You held the spooky creatures down and she tore them apart."

Exeter studied her. "I can only image how miraculous and how terrifying it must be to coexist with a wild creature—and yet, I always feel you inside her."

He pulled a loop of satin ribbon and revealed another layer, beneath the velvet-lined tray. "My hope is that your affection for me will be enough to control her fright at being tamed." Strands of delicate silver mesh twined together, forming a long leash. Exeter tugged, then snapped the leash harder. The flex and bulge of his upper arm muscles reminded Mia of how wonderfully fit and muscular he was. Her body stirred.

"All these small silver rings linked together create a resilient length of chain mail." He attached the lead to the collar. "May I?"

She stared for a long time before nodding.

He slipped the leather around her neck and fastened the buckle. "Too tight?"

She swallowed. "Fine for me. Shall I ask her?"

But for the lust in his gaze, Exeter appeared slightly amused. He turned the collar so that the silver chain fell down between her breasts. The feel of slithery metal sent shivers through her—or was it this man who made her pulse leap? She reclined onto her elbows. "How do I look?"

He crawled on top of her and pulled on the leash—enough to raise her lips to his. "Edible." His gaze moved over each feature of her face, memorizing the smallest detail. He even touched the tiny mole beside her upper lip. "Before I ravage you, my lovely black panther, you will kiss me." His body was hard and warm against hers and so close she could easily detect the subtle musk of his scent. "Now," he demanded.

Her breasts rose and fell against his chest as she caught her breath. "Make me." Slanting her eyes, she turned her face away.

He tightened the silver chain until her lips were nearly upon his. "I am so ready for you it hurts." His kisses began as soft, openmouthed busses, his velvet lips passing gently over hers. A sensuous, probing tongue teased her lips open and invited her tongue to meet his own. And she returned his passion with a surprising amount of intensity. Her lips brushed back over his, both tongues playing a tangled, thrilling chase, heightening their desire—plowing into each other as if to simulate what was to come.

Breaking the kiss, Exeter perused her body as though he really did wish to eat her alive. "You are even more beautiful dressed in nothing but emeralds." His penis appeared to enjoy the view as well, as it pitched about like a ship's mast in a storm. He tore the paper wrapper off the condom and rather expertly tamed his twitching member long enough to roll on the rubber goods.

His gaze was heavy, eyelids half-closed by desire. He reached through moist folds and found her throbbing center of pleasure. Her arousal rose quickly, as his finger circled and flicked over her swollen secret place—the one he so expertly manipulated.

"Make it pulse," she whispered. He placed a warm, vibrating fingertip against her clitoris until her hips ground against his hand. He knew how to make her shudder and yet he also held back enough to keep her from experiencing satisfaction.

"Open wider, love." He wound the silver leash around his hand and hooked her legs over his arms. The collar tugged at her neck, sending a delicious jolt of arousal straight to her womb. He used the tip of his penis to tease and stroke her entrance as he pushed in.

In a shocking move, he grabbed hold of her hair and yanked. *A warning to the cat, love.* His fingers pressed into her buttocks as he plunged deeper, filling her so completely she moaned. With each thrust, he rubbed slick places that quivered and quaked to life. The combination of rapid thrusts and his finger on her clitoris sent deep waves of arousal through her. "Let her go, Mia."

"Ah-h *non,* do not stop, Exeter." She bucked up to meet his throbbing shaft as she crashed over the edge of pleasure.

"I am with you," he gasped, grinding out the last of his climax even as the cat took a swipe at him, claws extended. She scratched his chest, and four red tracks emerged over his right pectoral muscle. Exeter fell back, groaning in ecstasy.

Horrified at her feline behavior Mia retreated to one side of the bed with a snarl. Exeter slowly settled back on his haunches. As the panther retreated, the silver chain tightened. *Steady, Mia.*

She drew her muzzle back with a hiss, revealing long white fangs. She was always somewhat fearful after a shift.

The cat smelled blood. *Exeter, you're bleeding.* Mia thought she might cry—but this wildcat shed tears for no man.

He looked down at his chest—rivulets of crimson ran down his chest. A few drops dotted the tops of his nicely muscled thighs. She placed a tentative paw out and crept closer.

She says the sight of your handsome legs makes her feel like frolicking.

Exeter grinned. "Shall we do some frolicking together?" He pulled gently on her collar and after a bit of hesitation, she came to him. Crooking an index finger, he scratched under her jaw, then the back of her ears—finally she allowed him to pet her all over. A rumble emerged from deep inside her body.

While Exeter washed up, Mia pawed at the discarded condom. Something about the slimy rubbery thing reminded her of a half-dead worm. When the condom appeared to slither away, she pounced on it. This caused a snort of laughter from the doctor as he washed his chest and applied a tincture. *It's twilight—shall we go out on the rooftops? Perhaps drop down into an alley or two and see how we manage the collar and leash together?*

She watched Exeter dress with a great deal of interest. He eschewed a tie, pulling on a woolen waistcoat and jacket. It was winter in Paris and though the days had been sunny and mild, evening brought on a chill.

He sat down beside her and pulled on his boots. The cat leaned in rather affectionately and rubbed against his upper arm. *We shall stay on Île de la Cité, tonight, have a quiet romp around the island.*

She raised a paw, licked, and washed her face. *Catch me if you can, Exeter.*

Exeter cracked open an eye, expecting to see Mia lying beside him. Nothing. Nothing but darkness and the faint glimmer of emeralds. A snuffled breath repeatedly brushed his ear. Or was that panting? Something moved on the mattress.

He lifted his head. A lazy paw stretched across his torso, triggering a return to alertness. He recalled a few of the evening's earlier events. Mia had loosed the cat at the paroxysm of pleasure, and she had taken a good swipe at him. Four dark red parallel marks grazed his right pectoral muscle and upper diaphragm.

He eased back down onto his pillow. So much for a quiet frolic over Parisian rooftops. Their evening constitutional had quickly turned into a lively dash through the city and a trip to the top of the Eiffel Tower. They had raced through the exposition gardens of the Champ de Mars, and made it to the top of the tower in four powerful leaps—assisted, of course, by a bit of potent energy.

Perched above the romantic city on the Seine, he and Mia had become enthralled by the flicker of gaslights and evening stars. Lowering himself to his haunches, he scratched behind her ears.

The purr is both soothing and restorative to the cat's nerves. Mia had shared, mind to mind. Her control over the cat grew noticeably stronger with each shift.

Exeter had rubbed her back. *If we are attacked or captured, I want you to shift, Mia. Promise me you will shift.*

As you wish, Exeter.

The cat curled up beside him stirred. Languidly, she lay her head on her paws. Had she been sleeping beside him all this time? Luminous, pale green eyes blinked in the darkness. Her steady breathing gently permeated the air. Exeter tried a thought to see if she was awake. *Since you have marked me, I believe it is only fair that I be given the privilege of naming you. You must be tiring of cat or puss.*

A pink tongue unfurled, followed by a ferocious yawn and show of fangs. Warily Exeter inched away. Mia was shifting—much slower than he had ever witnessed. Sleek black fur faded to pale tawny flesh, fingers protruded out of paws. A nose as black as a coat button receded along with her snout and whiskers. Dark, coffee-colored eyes reemerged on the face of the beautiful young woman he cared so very much about.

"I like the name Mia—it suits us." She smiled up at him, somewhat shyly. "We are, as you say Exeter, one and the same."

"Mia it is." He propped his head up using a pillow. "I suppose if we need to clarify we could specify two- or four-legged Mia."

She snorted a laugh. "Or you might ask, was Mia wearing a fur coat at the time?"

Exeter examined her carefully. No fever. No cold sweats. Even her skin glowed with color. He retrieved his pocket watch, and lifted her wrist. "Eyes bright and shiny—pulse is . . ." He watched the seconds tick off. "Pulse is normal." Exeter met her gaze. "I could not have hoped for better, Mia."

She returned his smile. "I feel fine—a bit tired, is all."

"We have time to eat and bathe before Café L'Enfer—or we could catch a few more winks and bathe. Which would you prefer?"

"Sleep." Softly, she kissed each scratch on his chest. They rested for another hour in a kind of twilight slumber, She hooked a long leg over his thigh, while he ran his hand along the curve of her hip and across a rounded buttock cheek.

And the bath was . . . stimulating.

They took turns washing each other. Mia, the water sprite, with a slippery bar of soap in her hands, caused a good deal of tumescence under milky water. For his part, he kept his fingers soaped and on her clitoris until she quivered and moaned.

By nine, they were squeaky clean and thoroughly pleasured. They dressed in a rush and met the Nightshades in the dining room just past the designated hour. "Everyone accounted for?" he inquired.

"America and gargoyle are off having a visit with one of Edvar's relations, the chimera, Le Stryge," Valentine advised. "At Notre Dame Cathedral . . ."

He must have blinked.

"I believe he resides above the Northeast Façade—along with a few more of Edvar's kind." The female Nightshade fashioned a pretty eye-roll. "He was quite insistent."

"The *gargouille*—they are waterspouts, are they not?" Mia asked.

"Turned to stone, centuries ago. Edvar was correct about that." The gentle, mannered voice came from behind them.

Exeter pivoted. "Mr. Ping, you have returned to us."

Ping appeared slightly more male than female. Exeter had witnessed the immortal jinni vary his gender on several occasions. It was . . . stunning, to say the least.

"Doctor Exeter. Mia. You're just in time for my report." Ping slanted silver eyes as he pushed a lever on Tim's projection map. "Several tunnels have been lost and others gained." The genie pointed out the best and worst of what they might face, if they decided to enter the catacombs from alternate, Outremer Paris. "I ran across a troll by the name of Gobb Filkins who knows the catacombs and moves quite comfortably back and forth through the warples."

Exeter frowned. "Good God, trolls."

"Says he's glad to help us." Ping shrugged. "Apparently,

Prospero elbowed him out of his favorite niche, and Gobb is . . . perturbed."

"Warples?" Mia queried.

"Short for Trans-temporal warp portals—wherever both worlds touch. Oakley's going to use the warples to prove his Uncertainty Principle. The more precisely one measures the momentum of a particle, the less precise one's measurement becomes." Tim rubbed sweaty palms on his trousers. "It helps explain why the portals tend to drift." The young inventor's anxiety level was palpable. Clearly he was agitated.

"What's wrong, Mr. Noggy?" Exeter had never seen the young inventor in such a state.

"The wizard container is ready." Noggy removed a dingy-looking pocket square and wiped the perspiration off his brow. "Oakley's latest device . . . I thought I mentioned it in London . . . designed to capture and contain Prospero—for a few minutes. Actually, we're not sure how long it might hold him. Kind of hard to run beta tests, if you follow." Tim scanned blank stares. "Guess not. Anyway, once we've got him in the trap, we have to get him to Black Box headquarters, where there's a permanent cell that will hold him indefinitely."

Exeter suddenly understood the level of anxiety in the room. He had never met Tim's twin brother, an inventor in his own right, but he had heard enough . . . Oakley was a genius and a recluse, with a talent for making money. Bazillions, was the word Tim had used.

At one time, Oakley had been a competitor of the powerful Prospero, maker of strange and sundry creatures, who also controlled the aether supply in the Outremer. To Exeter's mind, their much reported rivalry had always begged the question—where exactly did Oakley fit in—and who, exactly, was the enemy? Whatever the answer, Prospero had presumably forced Black Box underground. The details were fuzzy. Exeter continued to scrutinize Noggy. He disliked fuzzy details, and he greatly disliked this dangerous, sideways shift in their mission. "I take it we are going to have to lure him in?"

The corpulent young scientist nodded.

"Well, this is a good deal more than we bargained for." Exeter checked the mood around the room. Sober, indeed. "However, it may also be the only way to free Phaeton and protect the Moonstone."

Tim hesitated. "Uh . . . about the Moonstone."

Chapter Seventeen

MIA SENSED AN UNDERCURRENT OF HYSTERIA in the dining room; conspiratorial forces were at work. Exeter arched a brow and she answered him silently, shifting her gaze to the cherubic young scientist. "What exactly are America and Edvar doing with those old stone waterspouts?" she queried.

Tim mumbled something she could barely make out.

Exeter leaned forward. "Sorry, did you say—setting a trap?"

"I suspect they're not visiting with Edvar's distant relations." Mia scanned the room and didn't receive much eye contact.

Finally Ping spoke. "We tried to bring you in on the plan, but found your bedchamber empty. One of the tall windows was open . . ."

Exeter swept his frock coat back, resting his fist on his hip. "Mia has reached a point where she can control her shifts." His gaze connected with hers. "A real breakthrough, actually. We were out together this evening, as an exercise."

"That is wonderful news." Valentine approached them both. "America believes Phaeton entrusted the Moonstone to Edvar, and that the gargoyle hid the stone in one of the creatures at the cathedral."

"Please tell me Jersey is with her." Exeter raised his voice.

Tim licked the droplets of sweat on his upper lip before speaking. "America got a bit ahead of plans—Jersey went after them the moment we discovered the note."

Valentine handed over the message. "Ping and Victor both

advised Phaeton to entrust the stone to someone of great loyalty. A person or creature who could not be swayed." Mia thought the female Nightshade stood up rather well under the doctor's severe scrutiny.

Exeter crumpled the notepaper. "You realize America is in grave danger, especially now . . ." Nodding to something behind the inventor, he lowered his voice to a whisper. "Step aside, Tim." He pointed a finger at the low-flying spy, zapping the small intruder with a pinpoint beam of energy. Mia quivered involuntarily at the memory of his extraordinary touch. Exeter noticed, and winked.

"We need to find them quickly, before Prospero can act." He motioned them out the door, and down to the lobby.

No matter how angry he was, Mia had to admit that Doctor Exeter was the most reassuring of men, at times. Somehow, no matter how great the difficulty, she knew he would see them through the trials ahead. In the courtyard, he helped the ladies into the coach and waited for Ping and Tim to climb inside. He poked his head in the door. "What's the address again—of the café?"

Valentine leaned forward. "Fifty-five Boulevard de Clichy." Exeter looked a bit sheepish. "I apologize for raising my voice earlier."

En route to the cathedral, Tim quickly laid out the situation. "If Edvar has loosed the Moonstone, the logical place to store it would be in the incarcerator."

"The only way to lure clever game into such an obvious trap. I take it America has the device with her." Exeter's jaw twitched as he studied Tim. "Tell me truthfully, Mr. Noggy, was it in your brother's plans to *incarcerate* the Moonstone as well as Prospero?"

Tim's mouth flattened into a thin, grim line. "More than likely."

Mia was curious. "Rather a neat trick—capture two for the price of one. But how could anyone possibly know it would work—the device, that is?

"Several years ago, during a brawl, Oakley whacked some skin off Prospero's skull." The mental picture of Tim's brother engaged in knives and fisticuffs with the evil wizard caused several mouths to drop open.

"It was brutal. A fight to the death, only . . . it didn't exactly turn out that way." Tim shook his head. "Prospero fled with some of my brother's top-secret designs and Oakley ran his DNA profile." The roundish young scientist read the look on Exeter's face. "Chill, mate—it's a medical identification procedure that doesn't get invented in your world for another hundred years."

"Anyway, if we can get Prospero within a few feet of the incarcerator"—Tim pursed his lips and made a siphoning noise—"he gets reduced to subatomic bits and sucked right in."

Mia clapped her mouth shut and checked Exeter, who continued to stare rather pointedly at Noggy. "And you're quite certain the device will hold both the Moonstone and Prospero."

She caught an upward flicker of exotic silver eyes, as did Exeter. "Thoughts, Ping?"

"Any calculations for the Moonstone would be guesswork. As for Prospero . . ." The jinni did not appear overly concerned. "Remember the Moonstone senses intentions."

Tim craned his neck for a glance out the window. "We're at the western façade of the cathedral—does anyone see them?" The cathedral's doors appeared to be open, though it was hard to make out much detail, as the impressive Gothic structure was dimly lit. A number of visitors lingered near the entrance.

"There—up in the gallery of chimeras." Valentine pointed to the figure of the smallish gargoyle perched on the head of Le Stryge. Edvar bounced up and down on his larger stone cousin in the most insistent way, as if he was attempting to dislodge—one might surmise—the Moonstone. In a burst of color and light, a globe-shaped object emerged from the head of Le Stryge. The glowing object hovered momentarily in midair and then dove for the concourse. The diminutive comet whooshed its way around clusters of tourists, who cried out in alarm at the strange, low-flying object. A cloaked character chased after the fireball—almost certainly Jersey.

As the carriage slowed Exeter leapt onto stone pavers and headed for the dark side of the cathedral. Valentine followed after, but stopped at the front entrance. Using a push of potent energy, she jumped to the balcony. Mia squinted to separate living figures from stone gargoyles on the upper tier. In a triumphant gesture, America held up a shiny metal tube and followed Valentine onto the roof behind the towers.

Ping joined Mia as she made her way around Notre Dame and onto a darkened pathway. Valentine slid down the arch of a flying buttress and waited for Edvar and America to follow. It seemed to Mia that the gargoyle and America were sliding at a worrisome speed—perhaps too fast. Mia picked up her skirts and ran alongside the nave. "Valentine, don't let her fall!"

And suddenly, Exeter was there. He caught Edvar first, then America as they slid off the buttress and into the deep shadows of the great cathedral. "Nice bit of potent leaping, ladies." Mia joined them at the bottom of the buttress. Exeter set America down. "As well as a rather excellent bit of rescuing," she smiled at him.

"America, do not try to keep pace with Valentine," Exeter grumbled.

"Has anyone seen Jersey?" Mia asked.

"The object disappeared over there." Exeter rasped, slightly out of breath. He nodded to a stand of trees.

Mia nodded. "I'm almost certain I saw him run after the Moonstone when it . . . *whooshed* off the balcony."

"Oh, that's not the Moonstone, the Moonstone is in here." America held up a cylindrical device—presumably the portable incarcerator.

"The orb with the dazzling tail was a decoy." They all pivoted toward the familiar craggy voice. Jersey stood in between a row of poplar trees. "In case Prospero's wraiths were lurking about."

Tim caught up to the gathering. "Now that the trap is set, all that remains is to lure Prospero in close."

"And, I have someone special in mind." Exeter turned to Ping, who sauntered up to join them. There was something about Ping in a top hat and evening coat that was both delicious and strange. Or perhaps it was the blue-tinted spectacles that turned his eyes violet—the color of relic dust and champagne—the ethereal jinni's term for potent energy.

Ping smiled pleasantly, and nodded a bow. "How may I be of service?"

"I need you to seduce Prospero." Exeter was deadly serious.

Ping's long lashes fluttered slightly as he cocked his head. "As Ping or Jinn?"

Exeter cracked a grin. "Perhaps, both."

"Entrez et soyez condamné!" The café's doorman, dressed in a Satan suit, welcomed them to le Café de l'Enfer.

"Enter and be damned—warm greeting." Exeter escorted Mia inside the gaping devil's mouth that made up the front door of the café, which had to be the most eccentric, and quite frankly bizarre nightspot in all of Paris.

If any of you tire of sin, you can always dash next door for a bit of Heaven.

Mia distinctly heard Phaeton's voice in her head. She looked at Exeter—nothing—he was occupied with the maître d'. She looked back at America, who appeared a bit fidgety standing beside Ping. "Was that him?"

America shrugged a bit warily. She had heard the voice as well, but looked to Ping. Peering over the rims of his spectacles, his eyes flashed silver. "Watch yourself, we've crossed into the Outremer."

Mia blinked as she took in the crowd at the bar. Yes, the attire was different—so very plain, and informal. She hadn't felt a thing, and now suddenly she found herself in an alternate Paris.

Ping tapped the doctor on the shoulder. "Should anyone

comment—we've just come from a costume ball." After a quick, furtive glance around the room, Exeter nodded.

"This way—*monsieurs et mademoiselles*." The maître d' wore a tuxedo and was normal in appearance, but for the brilliant crimson horns that poked out of salt-and-pepper hair. Mia pressed close to Exeter. "I cannot help but think our costumes will hardly be noticed in such a venue." He gave her hand a reassuring squeeze.

They were led through a standing-room-only crowd at the bar to a larger, dining area in the rear of the café. A soft rhythmic music pervaded the cavern-like atmosphere. In keeping with the motif, lost souls undulated on the dance floor in a macabre burlesque, a queer tribute to the tortured plaster figurines that writhed on the walls and ceiling. Exeter dipped close. "Hellish, indeed," he murmured. Skirting the dance floor, Mia noted musicians of dark skin color, Africans, she thought, but Parisian, as well. A female cabaret singer crooned in sultry tones. Mia listened carefully to the French words . . . a love song.

"Très bon." The maître d' flourished a gesture, as a waiter pushed two smaller tables together. The rather dashing looking devil helped Mia into her chair. *"Soyez un belle coquine, s'il vous plaît."*

Mia turned to Exeter as he slid in beside her. "Did our waiter just call me a naughty girl?"

In a most irregular display of public affection, Exeter placed his arm across the back of her chair. "I believe his advice was—*soyez*—'be a beautiful rascal.' And he was rather polite about it—the young man did say . . . please." His sensuous, heavy-lidded gaze held hers as he leaned close. "I must say I'm looking forward to it." It seemed Hell's Café was already having an effect. As if their lives weren't odd enough.

Several intoxicating drinks helped put a full-tilt spin on the evening. Everything—the sights, the sounds—all seemed enhanced, if a bit fuzzier. And still no sign of Phaeton.

Exeter leaned across the table. "We should break up."

Ping nodded. "I sense wariness. We may appear too formidable." The wariness Ping noticed only made sense if Prospero lacked any kind of battle squadron. Mia found it hard to believe the man could be so lacking in resources.

"Somebody get out there and dance," Tim suggested.

Jersey looked stricken. "I don't dance."

Valentine set down her drink and winked. "I'm working on him."

Strains of piano and the soft rhythm of bass fiddle and drum drew Mia's attention to the dance floor. As the cabaret's entertainers struck up a new tune, Exeter leaned close. "Dance with me."

Mia gaped at him as well as the others around the table. "What kind of dance is this?"

"Give me a minute. I have to think back to cotillion—a painful experience." Chin in hand, Tim's eyes rolled upward. "Fox-trot, I think, but feel free to dance a jig. Just get out there and fake it."

Exeter coaxed her up out of her chair and onto the dance floor. "I believe this dance is close to a waltz, only instead of three-four, we move in four-four time." She had no idea what step came next, but he made it easy to follow his lead. As a small child, he had taught her to dance. "Place your feet on top of mine, Mia." She recalled happy hours spent waltzing around the parlor on a rainy afternoon.

Mia imagined her ballroom slippers on top of his dress boots and concentrated for a turn or two. He was a strong dancer, and she soon relaxed in his arms. "Two slow glides followed by two quick steps."

Exeter smiled. "Exactly." He lengthened his stride, smoothing out the dance. The strains of a smoky, silken voice blended perfectly with the cabaret musicians. Almost effortlessly, he led her around the dance floor, brushing against her in the turns. She felt the power of his legs, the heat of his body as he pulled her closer. "Do you remember how we used to practice for your French exams?"

Mia nodded, adding a shy smile. "You would sing to me in

French, and I would sing the line in English." Exeter turned her about the floor listening to the cabaret singer. "You put your hand in mine . . . and then you smiled hello . . ." He sang softly in a husky voice.

"And I have no words . . . my heart is pounding so." She translated as strong thighs, pulsing with rhythm, whirled her through a labyrinth of other dancers.

"Tweedledum and Tweedledee." Exeter nodded over her shoulder and turned so that she could get a better look. Two identically dressed creatures huddled together in the shadows, vulture-like, bony shoulders hunched over frail bodies. The duo wore coachman's hats over mourning veils to obscure their faces. They turned in unison as Exeter swept her across the dance floor, sending a shiver down her spine.

For some reason, she could hardly sing the French lyrics over the ache in her throat. "Keep going, Mia—"

She swallowed. ". . . I long . . . long to hold you close." Her vision blurred. The song spoke of a burning hunger and unrequited love—entirely too close for comfort.

Exeter shortened his steps. "Mia . . ."

Blinking back tears, she finished the words of the song. "To you I'm just . . . a child . . ." Inexplicably, the tears kept coming.

Exeter appeared stricken. He pulled her into the middle of the floor and turned in slow circles. "Mia, I care so very much . . ."

"No—don't." Choking on her words, she swept an errant teardrop away. She quickly searched the room for a distraction and found one. "Exeter—one of those strange characters is moving toward our table."

His gaze narrowed. It was clear he didn't wish to change the subject. Reluctantly, he stole a glance in the direction of the Nightshades and exhaled. Cursing under his breath, he grabbed her hand and wound a path through the dancing couples. Mia dipped and dodged to try to see what was going on across the dance floor.

America stood up from the table. "Phaeton?"

Both she and Exeter tracked her line of sight. Mia gasped. "Exeter—is it him?" Phaeton stood in the alcove. Before anyone could stop her, America ran toward a fading image.

"Go back, America!" Phaeton's voice echoed from a faraway place.

Chapter Eighteen

EXETER GRABBED HOLD OF AMERICA only to have her break apart in his hands. *Whoosh*. Vanished into the Outremer. The darkness had just reached out and swallowed her up. He whirled around to find Mia and the Nightshades right behind him. "And the Moonstone?"

"Right here, mate." Tim held the incarcerator under his arm.

Exeter exhaled a sigh of frustration or relief—maybe a bit of both. "I'm quite certain those two odd blokes dragged her across. We must follow them, in haste." Exeter retrieved from his pocket the portable iDIP, which Tim had given him the day before in the train station. "How do I work this?"

"I wouldn't, mate." Tim grimaced.

"Why not?"

"Because we can't be sure where she is. We need to get back to the hotel room, see if the bugs have located the hideout—pronto."

Mia grasped Exeter's arm. "Earlier this evening, I heard a voice. Ping heard it, as did America. I believe it was a warning from Phaeton, but there may have been a message, as well."

Exeter turned to Ping. "What did he say?"

"If any of you tire of sin, you can always dash next door for a bit of Heaven." Ping repeated the words verbatim.

Exeter stared. "What do you think it means?" A waiter dressed as Satan took obvious delight in shouting his order to the bartender. "Three seething bumpers of molten sin, with a dash of brimstone intensifier!"

Exeter tapped the waiter's shoulder. "What sort of establishment adjoins l'Enfer?"

The devil snorted a laugh. "How can there be a hell without a heaven, monsieur?

As the Nightshades encircled the man, Exeter pressed the question. "Another café?"

The waiter retreated slightly. "*Oui,* Cabaret du Ciel. Everyone knows this, monsieur—"

Exeter placed Mia's hand through the crook in his arm. "We break up into two groups," he tossed the directive over his shoulder as he headed for the door. "Mia and I will go after America. They can't be far ahead of us, not with a pregnant captive in hand."

Exiting Hell's Café, they were mysteriously plunged back into 1889 Paris. It appeared the veil between worlds was less stable in Montmartre. Mia wobbled a bit—disoriented by the sudden shift in time and space. "A bit of hysteria is all—breathe deeply—you'll soon shake it off." Exeter steadied her.

As they waited for their carriage, he unfolded a square of paper that contained a small amount of white powder. "Derived from an alkaloid obtained from the leaves of the coca plant, valuable as a local anaesthesiant, also used as a stimulant." He took a pinch of the powder and held it under her nose. "Inhale, Mia—as if it were snuff." He passed several packets around. "We are likely to cross over several times tonight—this will help keep our heads clear."

Almost instantly, Mia appeared brighter—more alert. "You will likely experience a kind of visual and mental clarity." She rubbed out a tickle in her nose. "Better?" he asked.

"Rather splendid, actually."

"I'd like Jersey to come with Mia and me." Exeter turned to Tim. "Mr. Noggy, the communication devices?" While Tim dug in his pocket for gadgets, they finalized plans. Tim, Ping, and Valentine would return to the hotel, mark the likeliest spots for Prospero's underground chambers, and promptly relay the locations via the communicators. "Here we are." Tim produced a handful of small devices. "Just like *Star Trek,* only better." One never completely understood what the cherubic young inventor was talking about. Exeter was quite sure he spouted the esoteric vernacular for his own amusement.

Ping removed his spectacles. "You will likely descend into a sketchy bit of old quarry tunnel, which means you'll run into a number of passages that lead nowhere. Some were dug as tests for the Métro. Paris will not have an underground train system for another ten years—so, if you happen to run across tracks or hear trains, you'll know you've passed into the Outremer. Also, anarchists store weapons down there. They often plant explosives to protect their caches. Keep a lookout for trip wires."

Tim handed Exeter a small, curved device. "Two buttons. One is the on/off switch, the other—press to speak, release to listen. Hook it over your ear—that's it."

Exeter pressed the on/off switch and practiced.

"The headset is also a homing device, so leave it turned on. Press when you want to talk and release to listen. These things can communicate across time and space, so they should be fairly reliable underground." Tim swept back a riot of curly, unkempt hair to adjust his own communicator. "Stay in touch—every half hour or so, give us a call."

Exeter helped Valentine into the waiting carriage and gestured for everyone to gather close. "Once we locate the hideout, we'll designate a staging area. Ping will approach Prospero alone, lure him out of his den, so we can move in and collect America and Phaeton." He turned and studied the enigmatic young man. "Hopefully, you have prepared a seduction. Will it be Ping or Jinn?"

The jinni offered quite a mesmerizing smile. "As you advised, I have a bit of both in mind." Regardless of one's sexual proclivities, one would have to be dead or blind not to see the allure of the androgynous creature. "Make your move with

Prospero as soon as possible." Exeter returned Ping's grin. "Beguile him until we are well away from the hideout." He removed a pistol from his pocket and spun the cartridge. A bullet in each chamber. Six emergency shots—just in case there was no aether to draw upon. Exeter crooked an elbow toward Mia. "Shall we look for a few devils in Heaven?"

Inside Cabaret du Ciel, they were greeted by a self-styled Saint Peter, who anointed the inebriated crowd from a basin of not so holy water. "Prepare to meet thy great Creator and don't forget the garçons!"

Gauzy wings fluttered and brass halos bobbed as waiters flitted about the room in white robes. Exeter wove a path through a throng of intoxicated customers. "Heaven appears to be as popular as Hell with the boozy crowd—who would have thought?" Mia murmured.

He spotted a wraith at the end of the bar and nodded to Jersey. "In the alcove behind the bar."

The Nightshade moved ahead. "I see him."

Exeter tucked Mia behind him, protectively. A cloaked specter stood in the shadows in a coat of gossamer rags—tattered and war torn. The elusive apparition reminded him of the hooded Nightshades, who also wore cloaking devices.

"Prospero?" Mia's whisper tickled his ear.

"Possibly." Without taking his eyes off the creature, Exeter reached back for her hand. The wraithlike figure turned, then hesitated. Pinpoints of silver light, where eyes might be, looked back at them. The entity was actually beckoning them to follow. Cheeky phantom.

Skirting the bar, they found no sign of the sorcerer. Exeter examined the alcove for a possible trapdoor, nothing but a shallow niche with a painting of cherubs frolicking in the clouds. "Hold on." Jersey felt around the edge of the gilded frame. "This side is hinged." Exeter pressed the opposite side and the painting separated from the wall, revealing a hidden passageway.

Jersey climbed in first, then Mia. Exeter took up the rear guard. They crawled along in relative darkness, until Jersey fired up a bit of dagger light. "The passage grows larger up ahead." Jersey lengthened the dagger into a sword and increased illumination. "Looks to be part of the old limestone quarry." Jersey crawled out and helped Mia and Exeter down.

Pivoting in a circle, he counted two passages, traveling in opposite directions. Straight ahead, a set of stairs led one way—downward. Strange harmonics echoed softly up the stairs from the lower substrata. Jersey pointed his sword toward the echo and something fluttered in a dark turn of the stair. "Looks like we go below."

They descended into more quarried caverns and narrow passages. Occasionally, they caught sight of a tattered wisp of fabric or heard a faint shuffle of footsteps. Reaching a blind turn, Jersey turned to them. "You two wait for a bit, then follow after me slowly—" Jersey halted his speech as a swirling column of dust came toward them. He motioned them all against the wall as the hissing rush of air passed them by. Jersey held up a finger and they waited in silence.

Exeter broke the stillness. "What was that?"

The Nightshade nodded into the blackness. "It's still out there." He'd learned to trust Jersey's instincts—the half-breed demon had invisible feelers. How else had he known about the wraith attack on the train to Paris?

Jersey lowered his voice to a craggy whisper. "Every time we lose sight of this spook, we get some kind of clue—a sound, a footprint in the dust . . ."

Exeter nodded. They were being led. "If we have to run, I'd rather it not be into a trap."

"As I was saying—I'll scout ahead. Make your way forward, slowly. I'll find you." Jersey slipped around the corner and was quickly enveloped by darkness.

Mia stood with her back to the wall of the passage. Exeter pressed close. "How are the two of you?"

"She is present—no headaches—as yet."

"Any urges?"

She didn't have to answer. The hot, smoldering desire in her eyes said everything. She slanted her gaze away.

"Hold her close, but don't let her shift—make her wait. Do you remember what I told you earlier?" He took a few steps forward, and stopped abruptly. Mia nearly ran into him. Instinctively, she flattened her hand against his back. Her touch so stimulated him, he moved her against the wall, and covered her with his body. "Answer, Mia. What did I tell you, earlier?"

"If we run into trouble, I'm to shift—get away and find help."

"First make sure you are safe—then you may seek help." He pulled her to him—so close he located her lips by a gasp of sweet breath. Bracing her face between the palms of his hands, his mouth sought hers with soft, hungry kisses. And she invited his tongue to delve deep and tangle with hers.

His cock rose with each soft, sultry caress. "I want to kiss your navel and move lower . . . to your lips." Exeter broke off the affection before he lost all control. "Know this, Mia. I am coming apart inside." His breath was harsh, labored. "I desire you much more than I can safely . . . control." He exhaled, chastising himself silently. He had seen it coming—this forced intimacy had changed everything. Never in his life had he been this captivated by a woman. Mia's courage and fortitude, the startling combination of physical beauty, brilliance of mind, and purity of heart. It was enough to drive him near mad with want for her.

Something hissed in the dark. Exeter jerked upright.

"What was that?" she whispered.

He rummaged around in an inside coat pocket for the battery-powered torch. "Let there be light," he whispered and flipped the toggle switch. "And there was light." He winked at her.

He shined the beam down one side of the corridor. No creatures. He turned in the opposite direction and shined the beam directly into the face of a hideous fiend he'd never seen before—one that grinned . . . and drooled.

Mia screamed, and they both backed away.

The strange being was human-like. Beady grey eyes, bulbous head, the limbs were skeleton thin. Was this a Skeezick? He remembered a description America had once shared. Gaping mouth filled with needle-like teeth and a good deal of drool.

"Hold on, Mia." He picked up a large rock and tossed it. The figure broke up into shimmering particles and then reformed farther down the passageway. An image, one of those projections called holograms—likely used to frighten people away.

So . . . they were close.

Exeter pressed his communicator button and kept his voice low. "This is Exeter, I believe we may have stumbled upon Prospero's den." Footsteps echoed from behind—running footsteps. Exeter released the button and squinted down the corridor. A pale blue sword bobbed in the dark—it was Jersey and he was coming up fast. "Run!"

"Pick up your skirts, Mia." They ran, half stumbling, toward a fork in the passage. Exeter caught Jersey's eye. "How did you end up behind us?"

"The passage to the right doubles back—go left." The Nightshade pointed with his sword into the dark. No time to ask who was behind them. He urged Mia forward. Rounding a blind corner they both sprinted down the corridor and nearly fell over.

Trip wire.

A bolt of energy shot up his spine. Using potent lift, he tossed Mia far forward as the bomb went off. The shock wave blew them all farther down the passage buffeted by an eerie squall of dust and a blast of orange-red flame. Skidding along the floor, an avalanche of rock and dirt descended on him, forcing air from his lungs. His hearing cut out as debris of all sizes and types rained down in silence. For a moment, everything sparkled—dazzling stars, then a quick fade to a gray haze populated by ghostly figures. He collapsed under the weight of the rubble.

* * *

Mia stretched her neck and moved forward, cautiously. She uncurled a pink tongue and licked the dust off his face. He groaned, and she sprang back—her survival instincts raw and edgy. A quiver ran down the length of her body, lifting a cloud of dust off her coat. She sneezed.

Exeter—I know you can hear me. He groaned again. His head, shoulders, and one arm were free; otherwise he was covered in stone. So why hadn't he been crushed to death? The cat raised a paw and rubbed her face.

I have wrapped myself in a field of potent energy.

Mia sat up straight, on her haunches. *Wake, Exeter.*

Mia—can you—see Jersey?

She remembered now—there was another. Perhaps he was caught in the rubble farther back, or he was behind the collapse of the tunnel. *I do not see him.*

Any of Prospero's men about?

No one but you and I.

His eyelids fluttered. Exhaling another groan, he turned his head enough to see her. "Mia—" With his free hand, he reached out. She lowered her head, and nuzzled his open palm. "Can you see the communicator anywhere?"

Cats don't fetch, Exeter.

Still, she rose up on all fours and sniffed through the surrounding rubble. Exeter appeared to be making a great effort. Grunting and straining, he managed to pull his other arm free. A silver leash attached to an emerald collar was looped around his hand. *Come to me, Mia.*

She dipped her head and after a few attempts, he managed to buckle the collar. *Try to pull me out—use potent force.*

Mia tugged and pulled over and over, but couldn't muster enough lift to move the ton of rock above Exeter. The cat's breath became harsh and labored. *Save your energy to hold off the rocks, and I will go for help.*

"It's too dangerous, there could be more cave-ins."

You must trust me enough to let me go.

He offered a weak smile. *I thought cats didn't fetch.* His fingers opened and he released the chain.

There was a small tunnel opening—an air vent that traveled high above the passageway. Before Exeter could change his mind or talk her into staying, she sprang to the top of a pile of rubble, dragging the silver leash behind her. Eventually, the small shaft would lead aboveground. Mia hunkered down, jumped, and slipped neatly into the opening. Once she reached the surface, she would find her way back to the hotel, and bring back the others.

A chattering, or more like the sound of angry people yelling, drifted down the air duct. Yes, she was almost certain they were human voices. Curious, the cat moved closer.

Be careful, Mia. The cat sent him a purr. The fact that she and Exeter could communicate so well emboldened her exploration. She crawled into a connecting passage that angled down, not up.

"Tell him anything he wants to know—he won't get what he wants, regardless."

She recognized Phaeton's voice. The cat crouched, inching down the shaft until she came to a slatted louver covering. Mia narrowed her eyes.

America sat on a crude wooden bench, her hands bound by leather cuffs. Chains ran through her bindings, attached to rings mounted to the wall. "You must trust me when I say it won't be long now." On the other side of the small space, Phaeton was slumped in the corner of a cell. Heavy iron bars obscured some of her view, but he appeared to be brooding.

"What is—or was this place?" America tugged at her bindings. Mia wholeheartedly agreed, imagining the Bastille a more hospitable situation.

Mia—be very careful. Is there anyone else in the dungeon?

No use hiding her thoughts, Exeter apparently heard them all. The cat froze. A door creaked open. A man of striking appearance entered the room. His head was shaved, or nearly so—she supposed it was more of a close-cropped stubble. He closed the door quietly behind him.

Tall and broad shouldered like you, Exeter.

He wore a long silk robe that was frayed along the hemline and cuffs. The hair along the cat's spine stiffened. He also held a whip—a flogger with a number of knotted leather strands at one end—a cat-o'-nine-tails. As the wizard approached America, the cat pawed restlessly, ready to spring. No one would lay a hand on America—not if she could help it.

Mia, what is happening?

Prospero.

Phaeton rose from his cot and spoke up. "America is prepared to tell you whatever you'd like to know, aren't you, dear?"

The wizard scanned the room for a prolonged period. "No doubt you are both wondering about the explosion—the boom and rumble." He spoke quietly, as he had in the hologram. Rather unnerving, the voice—soft and husky, like Exeter when he was aroused. The imposing man turned from America to Phaeton. "Sorry to rattle your cage."

Phaeton returned his captor's stare. In fact, she had never seen him glare at anyone like this—as if he would tear Prospero limb from limb, rip his eyes from their sockets, then grind him into small bits for the crows to pick over. Phaeton often played his enemies for fools, but she wondered if seeing America so close to her time—her belly large with their love child . . .

"If you touch her, I'll have to kill you."

Good God, Phaeton has lost his wits.

He's in love. Exeter's whispered answer caused her heart to race. It was obvious Phaeton loved America—truly and dearly. A shiver ran through the cat as she shook off his words. The very sentiment Exeter would never feel for her. She instantly quashed the thought.

"It would seem your friends have arrived." Prospero swung the whip handle around. The leather straps whined, stirring the stale air of the chamber. "No body count . . . as yet." Pivoting toward America, Prospero lifted the whip above his shoulder, and let it fly.

The tails wavered above her shoulders. America cried out and Mia burst through the air vent. She landed on Prospero's back, teeth gnashing, and her claws digging into his shoulders. Prospero roared in pain and flung her off. The wizard clutched at his robe and gasped in agony. Mia retreated to a dark corner and blinked. *He must not see me yet—he continues to pivot—looking.* She had never seen Prospero's powers at work—but she suspected he was not so injured that he couldn't gain mastery over her.

Careful, Mia.

The back of his garment was torn to shreds, blood dripped over a back covered in hash marks, most of them old lesions—layers deep. And they weren't battle scars—they were marks made over a prolonged period.

Prospero suddenly whirled around and came directly for her. His fingertips burned with light, the same kind of energy Exeter used to arouse her. But this light was different, it crackled and sparked with hurtful, blinding light. Was Exeter a wizard? The thought flashed and she soon received her answer.

If I was a wizard, would I be stuck under this pile of rock?

The cat leapt past Prospero and sprang off the opposite wall. She added a bit of potent lift and pushed off—only the lift wasn't there. Someone had grabbed hold of the silver chain as she jumped. Despite the violent yank to her neck, she struggled against the leash. Her throat constricted as she stretched, claws splayed, to reach the safety of the air shaft.

"Don't make me hurt you." Another hard jerk forced her into the arms of Prospero.

Chapter Nineteen

MIA OPENED HER EYES. She had shifted. The wizard cradled her like a babe in arms, though his gaze lingered with an interest that was far from innocent. *I am caught, Exeter.*

A very long time passed before Prospero looked into her eyes. "You must be Mia."

Charm him, until I can get to you.

She did not quite comprehend Exeter's meaning. Or perhaps she didn't wish to. "My name is Anatolia Chadwick—or Mia—if you'd like." She lowered her eyelids slightly—offering the sleepy look Exeter had once called sultry. "And you are Prospero."

"To begin my life . . . at the beginning of my life, I was born Alastair Wentworth the third, on a Friday, at the stroke of midnight, I'm told. The midwife declared that I was destined to be unlucky in life; and secondly, that I would see ghosts and spirits. Phaeton and I have this much in common." A corner of his mouth lifted. "But you may call me Prospero—if you'd like."

"Wooing her with *David Copperfield*? It's no surprise you have to create drooling, beady-eyed monsters to keep you company."

The wizard's grin was wicked, or sly. Maybe both. "Phaeton appreciates my literary references. It might even be the reason he's still alive."

Mia looked the intimidating man directly in the eye. "Nonsense. He's alive because you need him to help you wheedle favors from the Moonstone." Mia quickly took in the medieval cavern and cell. "Hello, Phaeton." Her gaze traveled to America, who appeared to be more than uncomfortable, chained to the wall, with only a bench to rest on. "Are you all right?" Something about America's nod bothered her.

"Put your arms around my neck." The wizard ordered in his quiet, contained way. She had expected him to be wretched and cruel—so much easier to detest—but this Prospero was neither of those things.

As yet.

A tug on the leash reminded her who was master. Mia placed her arms around his neck and clasped her fingers. Once again, the wizard ogled her. "You are Doctor Exeter's ward, or concubine. I'm a bit . . . confused of late." The chamber door creaked open on its own. Mia blinked. Had someone opened the door or had the wizard used his wily ways?

Prospero passed through the opening, into another dark passage, like all the others in the catacombs.

"You're dead if you touch her. Exeter will kill you," Phaeton warned, as the door slammed shut. She glimpsed a stare so dark it sent a chill through her. Prospero eyed the henchman walking beside them. "What is it?"

"Three little piggies headed this way." The hideous creature wore a battered top hat stretched over a wispy-haired, bulbous head. The effect might best be described as ill-fitting. And she was quite sure this minion was one of the strange devils spotted in Café de l'Enfer—part of a duo that had abducted America.

"What of Exeter?" Prospero queried.

"Cobbler's awls, Guven'r—he's as good as buried."

Mia's heart hammered inside her chest. Prospero checked her reaction. Could this man be a sensitive intuitive, capable of feeling a racing pulse? Mia found herself tempering a sigh. Somewhere, deep inside, she had let loose a cry. But it was more than that—something beyond her worry for Exeter and his plight. She was almost certain America was in pain.

Doors had a way of opening on their own in the wizard's enclave. Prospero halted at the entrance to a dimly lit chamber. "Would you 'ave Skeezicks finish the job?" The milky-eyed creature blinked.

Prospero lowered his steely gaze from her body to his minion. "Just take care of it."

The hireling bowed and backed out of the small chamber. "What was that? Homunculus? Goblin?" Mia nodded after the retreating servant.

Prospero cocked his chin a bit. "He and his clone are all that remain of a failed experiment."

Her brows crashed together in confusion. "Whatever do you mean?" she whispered.

He continued to hold her in his arms—oddly, as if he never wished to let go. "That would be a question for Oakley."

The man spoke in riddles, which was predictably evasive of him. Mia raised her chin. "I wish to check on America. I will need something to cover myself."

"I might have you walk around as naked as a wood nymph." He appeared amused, but also wary.

She dared to reach up and touch his face. "Please." She stroked a bit of stubble along his jawline, and felt something warm her insides—not desire—more like someone watching over her.

So, you are a voyeur, Exeter, the feline in her teased. Mia pictured the doctor buried under a mountain of rubble. *Use your strength to stay alive,* she scolded. He must use his powers for the cocoon. Whatever was coming between Prospero and herself—a tremor ran through her body, part fear and part . . . Good God. Mia shut down her thoughts. She must try to make it difficult for Exeter to pry.

Prospero lowered her to the ground. He opened the wardrobe and handed her a clean robe.

Mia noted the large flourish of monogram. "Capital C?"

"From Claridge's—my London, not yours—same hotel. In the twenty-first century, they provide guest bathrobes." He helped her into the wrapper.

Mia pulled on the plush, Turkish towel ties. "You stole it."

Those ominous silver eyes sparkled, warmly. "I'm the bad guy, remember?"

Her gaze swept through a room that could hardly be called extravagant. In fact, the furnishings were almost Spartan. The bed was plain, and not particularly large. An old sea chest sat at its foot—with a secretary and wardrobe to each side of the quarried stone walls.

Mia scanned a number of sketches pinned to a sheet of cork above the desk. She squinted at a panoply of frightening designs, which appeared to be more like engineering plans. Good God, more sorry creatures. Some with huge heads, bulging with eyes and tentacles. Others with the stingers and claws of a scorpion—all of them appeared to be armored like soldiers. "More of your creations."

"There is an epic war coming. There will be a need for kick-ass warriors."

"So this is the army of the future . . . monsters." Mia tore her eyes off the hideous living weapons. "You speak like Tim—in that odd Outremer vernacular."

He paced up and down his chambers, slowly. "By my count, there are six of you. Exeter, Tim Noggy, the two Nightshade ninjas—Jersey Blood and Valentine. Phaeton's paramour, Miss Jones . . . and you . . ."

A deft change of subject. But had the wizard let something slip? And he had not mentioned Ping or Edvar. Perhaps, he was holding back. "I count three here at the wizard's outpost. Tweedledum, Tweedledee, and you . . ." As Mia sat back on the chest, the robe fell away from her legs. Prospero's gaze traveled up her bare limbs to a deep v-shaped opening. She let the robe slip off her shoulder, exposing a curve of breast, a hint of nipple peeking out from under the fleecy cotton. Mentally, she tried to prepare for a seduction, unsure whether it would be her or this . . . extraordinary man.

"You are just as lovely in dishabille." She pulled her knees under her chin and drew the wrapper close.

Prospero loosed the ties of his robe—enough for her to see he was impressively muscled—paler in skin tone than Exeter, but similar in physique. And he was nearly naked, with the exception of something very brief and tight covering a bulge of lower anatomy.

"Your arrival interrupted my shower." Prospero turned to a niche in the wall of his chamber and turned a small wheel. Water sprayed from several spigots creating a curtain of fine droplets. Steam wafted out of the shallow space. Enthralled, Mia slipped off the chest and crossed the room. "So you knew I was near. And the whip you threatened America with . . . ?" She held her hand under the warm water.

"I had to get you to show yourself." The man grinned. Not a boyish, innocent smile by any means, but a devilishly charming smile when combined with his soft-spoken voice. Mia was slightly taken aback by this monster called Prospero. At the same time, she hated the idea that she had walked—no, leapt—right into the wizard's nefarious plans, whatever they were.

Prospero shrugged out of his tattered garment. "Those flies on the wall of Tim's? Quite ingenious, even though I've turned them against you, for the most part." Mia noted several ragged slashes she had made to the backside of his robe. On closer examination the garment appeared to be made of silk. He noticed her interest. "An ancient Chinese pattern."

"Oh," she murmured. "Sorry about the damage."

"No need to apologize. The robe will mend itself." He folded the garment carefully and lay the bundle down on the sea chest. Mia gasped as he stepped out of his skimpy unmentionables.

She jerked her gaze up from an impressive phallus at full tilt. "Those have to be Outremer drawers," she blurted out. "Phaeton brought back the briefest of brief pantalettes for America." Mia shook her head. "I can't imagine wearing those strings and triangles—"

"Oh, I don't know . . ." He wore that enigmatic half smile well. "I'd like to see you in a thong."

His eyes were roving again, all over her body, and in a way that made her more uncomfortable than ever. He reached out to remove her robe and she shied away, enough that he hesitated before moving closer. Lifting a hand, he paused for a moment before he untied and unbuckled. He placed the emerald choker and silver chain on his desktop.

Be brave, Mia.

She bit her lip. She must have let something slip—feelings, urges. And she knew what Exeter was up to. He wanted her to live, unharmed, no matter what. His message was clear—let Prospero have his way if need be. Her knees trembled and all she could think was . . . thank God Exeter was alive.

When Prospero offered, she took his hand, and he led her inside the alcove. Following behind him, she could not help but study the crisscross pattern of scars on his back—some pale and flat, others irregular and fibrous. All of them appeared to be old.

The curious cat urged her to reach out and touch—trace the mysterious pattern of slashes down the length of his spine. *Pattern.* She caught herself and held back. What if this hash of disfiguring marks was not evidence of brutal floggings, but a pattern of scars . . . by design? Stunned by the idea, Mia squinted at an intricate web of lines connecting dots—a labyrinth of torment.

Testing the water with an open hand, Prospero turned back and examined her. "You are wondering about the stars."

She started to nod, then stopped. "Stars?"

His gaze cut through a thick mist of steam. "I meant to say scars." He pulled her into the shower. The fine spray of water stung her flesh. "Most exhilarating." Her words, barely audible under the patter of drizzle.

The tall wizard turned his back to the water, and dipped his head under the spigot. He closed his eyes and let the water rain down on his face. Feeling increasingly awkward, Mia watched as he took down a violet-colored bottle and poured something into her hand. The shiny thick substance smelled of wild berries and fresh lavender. "In my world, they call this body wash." He cupped her breasts and stroked, lightly. Swirling the scented soap over each nipple—slippery, and utterly arousing. "Would you rather I not wash you?"

Her sensitive breast tips peaked and she inhaled sharply. She peered up at him through the fine mist. "You are going to give me a paroxysm."

There it was again—that close-lipped smile. He bent low enough to suckle, and when she tried to back away, he held her to him, sucking harder and tonguing the nipple until her knees nearly buckled.

Why was there suddenly no oxygen in this small niche? The steam certainly made the air as thick as a summer day, or had this man just taken her breath away? He reached lower, between her legs. His fingers explored, probed, and made her shudder. How long could she pretend—how much of this charade could she take before it was no longer a charade?

"Please," she moaned.

His silver eyes and black pupils gleamed through warm rain. He pulled her against his body. "Please yes or . . . please no?"

Mia placed slippery hands on his chest. The only way to force another shift would be to climax again—Prospero could enable that shift. If she loosed the cat, she would likely tear him apart . . . or would she? Once more she gasped, "Please, don't."

Droplets fell from his eyelashes to high cheekbones—rivulets of water ran down his muscled torso. "Mia, what you think you've seen. What you've been told about me—"

"I am almost certain America has begun her labor." Mia blurted out. She shivered at the thought of her dear friend having her baby alone—even the steaming rain of water provided little solace. "You must let me check on her."

He stared at her for a very long time. "You are worried—and that worries me." He turned her about and rinsed off the soap, then he shut off the spigots. The look on his face told her everything she suspected about Prospero. They were wrong about him. And if that were so, then whose side was she on?

He opened the wardrobe and handed her a clean robe. "Dee will show you the way." The door banged open to Prospero's quarters. "Hurry up, maker—the girly girl is wailin' awful," the Skeezick warned. Mia tied on the wrapper and hurried out of the room. As usual, the door closed on its own.

"Certainly your name can't be Dee—it must be short for something?" Mia inquired as she trotted after the smallish, bulbous-headed creature.

"Tweedledee, miss-is," the minion stated matter-of-factly. She detected a faint speech impediment.

"Don't tell me, your twin is Tweedledum." The most unexpected feeling surged through Mia. Her heart was nearly bursting with an odd sort of warmth for the enigmatic wizard. And for America and Phaeton—and dear, dear Exeter. And most certainly for this shy, homely bloke that led the way.

"Tweez we call him, as I was cloned from him." The small man grunted, inserting a skeleton key in the lock. Metal ground against metal and the rusty cell door wheezed open. Mia stared at a wide-eyed Phaeton. "Is she . . . ?" She turned to America. "Are you . . . ?"

America wrapped an arm around her belly, and smiled weakly. "I think so."

Entombed under rock and rubble, Exeter fought to stay connected with Mia. Earlier, he had experienced a sensory impression of rain, and the scent of lavender. A part of him was incensed, protective—frustrated he could not help her. And yet another side of him was curious, most disturbingly, in a prurient way. Mia was being touched, and yet he received only fleeting impressions of her growing arousal before she cut him off.

He continued to manifest enough potent force to keep the cave-in from collapsing his lungs, but he would not last forever. In the interest of conserving energy, he had attempted to quiet his mind, and purposely slowed his breathing. Inhales had grown as shallow as exhales. Frankly, he wondered if he was nearing delirium, or worse *non compos mentis*.

He held out hope that the communicator device, no matter where it was buried, still served as a locator. The others would arrive in time to unearth him. He would survive. He would make sure that Mia, America, and Phaeton were safely away. Then he would find Prospero and kill him.

Reaching for deeper stillness, he was distracted by the slightest disturbance of air. A sense of motion, and something else—a presence in the catacombs—an entity of some kind. He resisted the urge to call out for help, until he could resist no longer. Not when there was a possibility that Tim and the others were close by. "Hello—anyone?"

Something skittered along the edge of the wall. Small dark objects with many legs rounded a pile of stone. Exeter squinted. Christ . . . locator bugs. Nearly a dozen of them swarmed over the rubble and came to rest near his head.

"Ah, there you are." The voice came from overhead. A bushy brow and a very large eye peered over the rock pile directly above him—something heavily whiskered and ornery looking.

Suddenly, he had company. Exeter allowed himself a small moment of elation. By the size of the beast, this had to be the troll—the creature Ping had mentioned. "You wouldn't happen to be able to levitate large stones and a good deal of sand and rubble . . . by any chance?"

The troll's muffled reply came from behind the rock. "I was sipping a cup of Earl Grey below Sorbonne Square when I heard the explosion. What on earth happened?"

"Trip wire." Exeter released a loud exhale. A complete waste of potent force, but then again—why not? This large specimen of troll could easily lift some of the bigger chunks of limestone with ease. "Some friends of mine are in trouble . . . I must go to them."

"And you, sir? Would you not call your predicament . . . trouble?" The troll's chuckle loosed rock and debris from the ceiling.

Exeter squinted to keep the dust out of his eyes. "My

friends," he reemphasized, "have been captured by an off-world wizard by the name of Prospero. Know him, by any chance?"

A huge, hairy head rose from the top of the rubble pile and blinked both eyes. "We haven't been introduced, per se, but I do believe I know to whom you are referring." The troll spoke in a deep, refined voice, with a vocabulary that was educated.

"Yes, well, if you would be so kind to help me out from under these rocks and point me in the right direction? I'll be on my way."

"And might there be a reward"—in no hurry, the troll rested his chin on a mitten-like paw—"for the effort?"

"Compensation is not a problem. Name your price, sir." Exeter coughed up a lungful of limestone dust.

"I have no use for money," the troll harrumphed.

"I see." Exeter wrenched his neck to get a better look at the wooly mammoth. "You did mention a reward—might we strike a trade, then? My release for—"

"Arcane knowledge." A large, hairy face dropped down in front of him—nose to nose, only upside down.

"Right." Exeter inched as far away as his confinement would allow. He racked his brain for an offer. "I am acquainted with a gentleman by the name of Mr. Eden Phillpotts, proprietor of the Antiquarian Bookshop, 77 Charing Cross Road. London."

The troll lifted the rest of his hulking frame over the top of the rock pile and took a seat on a slab of limestone. "And might this proprietor—have a knowledge of spells?"

The furry-faced character removed a pipe and pouch of tobacco from a velvet smoking jacket. Exeter noted the elaborate tangle of embroidery covering the shawl collar and cuffs. Rather tony for a troll. "So . . ." A side of his mouth twitched upward. "You are a prince who was turned into a creature of the catacombs by an evil sorceress."

The troglodyte struck a match and puffed, thoughtfully. "Hardly a gripping hypothesis, yet astonishingly accurate in some respects." The acrid stink of sulfur was quickly replaced by the pleasant scent of pipe tobacco.

For a moment, Exeter thought he might be balmy from lack of oxygen. "Or, if you'd rather—I have an extensive private collection—in the library of secrets—the shelves are chock-a-block with spells, as well as counterspells. You are welcome at Roos House on the Thames anytime you happen to be in London . . . in the late nineteenth century."

The troll took a few more meditative puffs. "Counter . . . spells?"

Exeter nodded. "Indeed. For every conjuration there is often an equal and opposite incantation, or haven't you heard?" For a beast under an enchantment, the troll seemed woefully unacquainted with spells. Unless this strange character was acting the dunce. As exhausting as this circular conversation was, he almost smiled. "Newton's laws of spells, actually."

Exeter. The baby is coming.

Chapter Twenty

MIA BANGED ON THE HEAVY IRON DOOR. "We have a young woman in here who is in labor. Open up this minute." Her fist came away covered in red dust, the rusty residue of a door that had to have medieval origins.

"Mia . . . dear . . . you know nothing of birthing." Phaeton's white-knuckle grip on his cell bars gave him away. He was losing his composure.

"Exeter does." She banged on the door again. It was rather touching to witness the unflappable Phaeton Black lose his equanimity. It might even be amusing, were it not for the fact that America was about to give birth. Perhaps to a very special child.

She turned to pound again when a small panel slid back. The grating noise made her skin crawl. Formal attire—including a white bow tie. Prospero ducked to see through the opening. He appeared to be dressed for an evening at the opera, or perhaps a ball.

"Why do you disturb me so?" He asked the question in a rhetorical manner, with a touch of sarcasm in his voice. It might almost be charming if it were not for the fact that her friend was in labor.

"Release us," Mia pleaded. "I need to get America to the hospital—we are in the Outremer, are we not? Exeter mentioned they deliver babies in hospitals."

"I'm afraid I can't do that." His words and tone were clipped, resolute.

"You can have the damned stone—I'll ask for whatever you want—just get her to a doctor." Phaeton shook the bars of the cell so hard they actually rattled.

"Oh, dear," America moaned. "I'm leaking!" Water formed a puddle underneath the bench America lay on.

Her water has broken. Exeter interjected. *The contractions will begin to come at closer intervals, now.* His thoughts helped her immeasurably. Whatever happened, she would not be alone—a doctor would guide her, but oh Lord, could she do this?

"I have a meeting across town—in your time." The wizard's words jerked her back to the small opening in the door. He was not nearly as frightening dressed in a tuxedo and silk opera hat, but the dark menacing look had returned. A look that spoke of mistrust, anger, any number of unspeakable terrors. "So if you'll excuse me, I have business elsewhere." As cavalier as Prospero appeared, his gaze continued to flick past her to America.

Mia looked him up and down. "Conspiring to make more of those ungodly miserable creatures?" She bit her lip, wishing her cheeky mouth was a bit less sharp. Still, she met his gaze and did not falter. "What if I offer a trade? Me, for blankets and pillows, towels, soap and water . . ." She rattled off a list of supplies as fast as Exeter enumerated the items in her head.

Prospero squinted. "I already have you."

"Granted, you have captured me and could take me by force, but honestly, aren't you bored flailing that cat-o'-nine-tails about? I could offer genuine affection. We could start with something sensuous. I could oil some anal beads . . ." Silently, she thanked Exeter's small but exotic pornography collection. "Would that pleasure you? Or you might allow me to caress the scars on your back." She swallowed. "Whichever . . . would please you most." It was her first and only erotic flirtation, and a bit awkward at that.

Mia held her breath and waited. She caught a glimpse of

Prospero's stunned face as the metal grate slammed shut. She turned to her friends, and exhaled a sigh of defeat. Phaeton winked at her. "Bloody, brilliant, Mia. Give him a moment."

She straightened. "Do you think so?"

"He's a bit of an odd duck, very emotional at times." Phaeton shrugged. "Any sentiment hardens quickly, so beware, he's . . . ruttish."

Mia knelt in front of America's large bump and massaged lightly with her fingertips. She spoke in a harsh whisper to both Phaeton and America. "The Nightshades have a plan, which I suspect is going to play out fairly quickly. Let us hope for the best."

America started to wail a bit and gasp for air, as a contraction clenched her belly. *Oh, Exeter, what shall I do?*

Stay calm and reassure her.

"Everything is going perfectly, America. Your water has broken." Trying for cheerful, she managed a tight-lipped smile. Hard to not be terrified under the circumstances. America in labor and Exeter buried under a several tons of rubble. He claimed he was safe for now, having cocooned himself in potent energy, but how long would he be able to hold back the crushing weight of stone? Mia could only imagine the exhaustion he must be experiencing.

She chewed on a raw bottom lip and stopped herself. She must not unduly worry America and Phaeton. They had a baby on the way under the most stressful circumstances imaginable. She would not tax them further.

Grating and creaking noises caused them all to look up. The pair of odd creatures from the cabaret, Dee and Tweez, respectively, carried in blankets, pillows, and towels, along with a large basin of hot water and a cake of soap. Prospero stood in the doorway looking formidable—dashing as well as ferocious. And he was holding a medical kit.

Mia squinted. "How did you get hold of Exeter's bag?"

He set the satchel down next to her. "I used my wizarding ways." His sly grin and narrowed gaze lingered for a moment.

A shiver traveled through her—his essence—an exotic, subtle kind of magic that felt . . . Mia caught her breath. He studied her reaction with interest. "I collected one of your evening gowns and a few unmentionables." He nodded to the folded pile beside the kit.

She was being drawn to him. No doubt a spell of some kind, just like in the shower. She steeled herself and was aided by the interruption of another contraction.

Phaeton strained to hold America through the bars. "I'm here, darling."

"Don't you dare darling me," America gasped as the contraction grew stronger. "You did this to me."

Undaunted by Prospero's wide stance and dark glare, Mia pleaded with the wizard. "Please let him out. He should be by her side—hold the baby, once she arrives."

"Phaeton stays where he is. You can move her closer to the cell, if you wish." Prospero directed the two bulbous-headed droolers to unlock the cuffs on America's wrists. He then lifted America up in his arms. "What are you waiting for? Move the bench." The smallish creatures pushed the heavy wooden seat against the cell bars and Mia covered it with a blanket and sheet, quickly propping several pillows at one end. Prospero set her down gently and turned for the door. "I won't be long."

Mia placed America's hand in Phaeton's. "Squeeze."

A sudden feeling of abandonment came over her—not that this man was much comfort, but he was a wizard. He could make things happen. "Wait. Who are you meeting with?" She was well aware of the audacity of her question. "In case I need to get ahold of you."

He stopped abruptly. ". . . Eight rue de Talleyrand. I have an engagement with a Mr. Julian Ping." He pivoted back to her slowly. "Know him?"

Mia shot upright and stared. She neither confirmed nor denied any knowledge of Ping, but even so she suspected he saw through her silence. A wry, thin smile tugged at the ends of Prospero's mouth. He glanced at America, who was beginning to puff again. "Miss Jones, I leave you in capable hands." He nodded to his henchmen. "Make every effort to provide Miss Chadwick with whatever she needs." The moment the iron door slammed shut, Mia dressed in a hurry.

Prospero knows he's headed into a trap. Her heart fluttered with fear and, oddly, relief—for everyone concerned. Ping was a powerful jinni. He and Tim Noggy would capture the wizard—put a stop this madness—finally get some answers. And the Moonstone, under Phaeton's direction, would restore Gaspar and repair the unraveling worlds of the Outremer.

Mia settled beside America and listened to the man inside her head, who described a huge hairy bloke, a troll, who had begun to move the larger stones and rubble away. *Patience, Mia, I shall not be long.*

America read her expression. "It is Exeter—you are experiencing thought transference."

Mia nodded. *Tell me what to do.*

All right then. Having a child is the most natural thing in the world. Reassure America that I am here and will assist you both.

Mia sat upright. "Assist us?" *Exeter, I don't think I can do this.*

Actually, you have very little to do. America does the hard work. His thoughts were labored, and still he found the strength to tease her—ease her worry. One wrong breath and he could die. *Mia, you can do this.* His whispered coax served to rally her nerves.

All right then, I'm no sissy-baby. She unbuttoned the sleeves of her gown and rolled them back. "Exeter wants me to tell you that he is here with us."

How far apart are the contractions—in minutes and seconds? Very important, Mia.

"Does anyone have a timepiece?" She glanced up at Phaeton, who shook his head.

One of their guards took out his pocket watch.

"I need to know how long each pain lasts as well as the elapsed time between her contractions—do you understand, Tweez?"

"Weez not dunces, miss-is—and the name's Dee," the creature harrumphed.

Mia's gaze moved from Tweez to Dee. "Oh dear, you must stop moving about or I shall never manage to keep you apart."

Get America settled somewhere comfortable—angled in a reclining position.

Mia nodded. *I padded a bench and there's a clean sheet and pillows—it's the best we can do.*

Wash your hands well with soap and water. Mia poured warm water into a hand basin and scrubbed the way she'd seen the doctor clean his hands a thousand times before. Over the next hour he kept her busy with preparations. It was if he wanted to fill her brain with chores, so that she wouldn't have time to be fearful.

Remove any uncomfortable clothing—along with her pantalettes.

Support America's head and back with pillows, and have her lie on her side.

Periodically, Exeter would ask them to time a contraction. "How long?" Mia asked Dee.

"The pain lasted nearly one an' thirty. With two and few between, miss-is."

Mia relayed the times and waited for his reaction. There was a long pause. *What is it?*

She is already in the active labor. As he thought the words, she sensed curiosity in his tone. *Ask her how long she has been feeling these pains.*

It took Mia a while to drag it out of her, but America finally admitted she had felt twinges early in the afternoon. *Good Christ. Mia, you'll need to have a look at her cervix.*

"I wanted to help find Phaeton. If I had said anything . . ." America's lower lip formed a pout. "There would have been a change in plans."

She was right, of course. And she would have been better off right now—they all would, Phaeton being the exception. Exeter would have remained at the hotel—to attend her. He wouldn't be buried under a pile of rubble, near death.

Don't say it, Mia—Phaeton, either.

Mia shot a warning glance at Phaeton, and shook her head. "Yes, well, we must all make the best of it now." She followed Exeter's every instruction to the letter, and he kept them coming nonstop. Occasionally, she allowed herself a moment to marvel. The way a woman's body was so splendidly made for birthing. And how resilient America was, as well as brave.

At the time of delivery, she should lie on her back with her knees bent and spread apart.

I believe we can manage that. The bench America lay on was crude—but as wide as a cot.

Now, have America take deep, slow breaths, particularly during contractions.

Mia looked up at Phaeton, who was doing rather well for a first-time father. He sat in his cell, with his arms extended through the bars. At the start of a contraction he helped America sit up and crooned sweet words, encouraging her to push. Between pains, he rubbed her shoulders.

America's limbs began to tremble—so much so, Mia had to hold onto her feet.

"Is that normal?" From out of the blue, a bit of panic appeared to grip Phaeton. "Honey, I'm not sure I'm cut out for—"

"There now, America." Mia interrupted Phaeton's moment of weakness. Wiping the brow of the mother, she turned to the expectant father. "Phaeton, the leg trembling is nothing to worry over." Mia leaned closer to the cell bars and whispered. "Exeter insists that you not fret out loud—worries the mother."

More than a bit dazed, Phaeton nodded. "Sorry."

She wiped the perspiration off his brow with a cool cloth. "You're both doing wonderfully well—chin up." Mia winked at him.

"Ready to be a papa, Papa?" America smiled at Phaeton and he brought her hand to his lips. Mia smiled at the sight of Phaeton speechless, in awe of America, worried about their circumstances. He was going to be a wonderful father—protective, caring—who would have guessed?

She estimated the cervix opening for Exeter.

The baby is coming fast for a first child—be sure to keep massaging her perineum—we are going to try for no tearing, which means we will bring the baby out gently. And as if his comment wasn't worrisome enough, Exeter let loose a litany of do not's:

DO NOT allow America to push vigorously until you see her vagina bulging with the baby's head. Pushing too early, before she is completely dilated, might tear the cervix.

DO NOT pull the child from the vagina.

DO NOT tug on the umbilical cord.

DO NOT cut the umbilical cord—wait for me. I promise I will be there shortly.

Exeter even had an order for America, which Mia passed along to the young mother: "DO NOT push between contractions."

She breathed a sigh of relief when the head crowned during a contraction. Mia and Phaeton encouraged America to push. *Have her take a deep breath, hold it, and push for a count of ten.*

Until now she had not wished to unduly pressure Exeter. The man was trying to stay alive, while he guided her through the birth of a child. To say nothing of the distraction of being dug out of a pile of limestone. Mia inhaled a deep breath, and exhaled slowly. She had to ask.

When, Exeter?

Time to bring this baby into the world, love.

For the first time in hours, Exeter was able to move his legs. He rocked his toes and stretched his calf muscles to encourage circulation. There was one large slab of stone left on the pile. As soon as the troll lifted the rock off, he wanted to be able to run, not walk, to Prospero's den.

He caught sight of the troll at work, hoisting the chunk of limestone off the significantly smaller heap of rubble. "What's your name, if you don't mind me asking?"

"Gobb Filkins since the spell."

"And your real name?"

"Archibald Dunbar Stuart, formerly the Earl of Moray." The troll tossed a football-sized rock aside.

"Doctor Jason Exeter." There was no doubt the troll could toss a caber or two. "Peerage of Scotland. You're a long way from home."

"That I am, doctor." Archibald peered over the pile of stone. "And how's the bairn coming?

"She's about to be born."

So far, the birthing had been textbook. *Place your hand against the area below the vaginal opening and apply gentle pressure during each contraction.* The pressure would prevent the baby from coming too fast. He instructed her to place her other hand above the baby's head. *This will help you control how quickly the baby's head comes out of the vaginal opening.*

Archibald clapped the dust off his hands. "There now—shall we get you out from under this hill of rock?"

The large troll wrapped his arms under Exeter's and pulled. After a huge exhale and grunt, the beastly character had moved him only a few inches. "Once more, laddie, and see if you can't spare a bit of your power this time." Odd, but he was sure the troll's speech had changed from refined English gentlemen to a brawny Scot with a brogue.

Exeter summoned whatever potent force he had left. "Ready?"

The baby's head is nearly out, Exeter.

Support the baby's head with your hands. And tell America to stop pushing. With the next contraction, the baby should slip out of America. He was vaguely aware that he heard Mia call out to Phaeton. "Look."

Exeter—her head is covered with a—filmy substance . . .

He smiled. *I'm not surprised.* He pictured a thin transparent membrane over the child's face, remnants of the amniotic sac. A veil, some called it—the child would have powers and was destined for greatness. Fitting for a child of Phaeton Black and America Jones. *You may remove the caul and begin to clean the baby's mouth and nose—preferably with the suction bulb in my kit.*

Just one more contraction, Mia.

The troll ran his arms around his upper torso and tightened his grip. "Give us all you got, laddie." Exeter unleashed the potent energy, loosening rock and stone until he felt a sudden release. Archibald landed on his backside as he pulled him free of the rubble.

She is born. Mia's thought was one of awe. He could feel her tears of happiness.

Newborns are slippery, so hold the baby with a towel. Exeter patted the troll's arm. "Good man, Archie." He sucked in a deep breath of air, and let the oxygen fill his lungs.

Archibald scrambled to his feet and pulled Exeter upright. "Can you stand?" The troll held him upright and headed down the passageway. "No need asking—you'll want me to show you the way to the wizard's den."

Even though he could not see the tears of joy on Mia's face, he ought to feel them. An intuition sent a cold chill through his body. *Talk to me, Mia.*

Oh Exeter, she is not breathing!

Mia—DO NOT CUT THE CORD! I will be there shortly. He looked up at the troll. "As quickly as we can." Archibald kept him upright long enough to gain some coordination over stiff joints and wobbly legs.

Stimulate the baby by rubbing her back.

"Up ahead, sir—the narrow passage to your right. Slip through there and you'll come across a cell block—the remains of an old dungeon."

Exeter turned back. "You're not coming?"

"Someone has to keep watch. If you require my services, a shout will suffice."

"Thank you, Archie." Exeter made his way down the dark corridor, feeling his way in the dark. *I'm almost there, Mia. Lower the baby's head and slap the soles of her feet.*

Exeter found a door—then another—this one opened. He stepped inside an empty bedchamber. *Where are you, Mia? No one is here.* A sparkle of green caught this eye. The emerald collar lay on top of a coil of leash. The very idea of Mia alone with Prospero caused a number of lethal thoughts. He stuffed the jewels into his pocket and pictured the randy wizard being sucked into Tim Noggy's trap—the portable black box. As he made his way back down the hallway, a large iron door opened and one of those odd creatures from the café waved him forward.

Mia straddled a kind of makeshift bed, hunched over the infant, while America and Phaeton anxiously looked on. Exeter fell on his knees beside her and turned the baby over—not horribly blue. "My aspirator." Mia handed him the syringe. Prying open the little mouth, he suctioned out any blood or mucus. Clear—Mia had done her work well. Exeter covered the newborn's face with his mouth—two quick, gentle puffs of air into her nose and mouth. "Come on, Luna, breathe."

In between breaths, Mia rubbed the infant with a towel.

Propped on her elbows, America beamed. "Breathe for your papa—"

A shake of tiny fists answered, as if to say "I have arrived" in infant speak. Next came a huge yawn, and a wailing good cry. Hard to discern how loud the babe was, as a number of cheers and cries went up around the room. Even the wizard's minions appeared cheerful. Exeter placed the infant on America's belly and tied off the umbilical cord. A swab or two of tincture and a snip of his surgical scissors finished the job.

He nodded to one of the guards at the door. "More warm water—if you would." Scanning the small room, Phaeton's expression stopped him momentarily. Never had he seen an expression quite like it. Phaeton was in love—smitten by the scrawny, pink little girl in America's arms.

Smiling, he turned to Mia. Tears glistened in her eyes. "She is beautiful, Exeter." A few errant drops rolled down her cheeks.

His arms went around her. "You are a marvel, my dear." He rubbed her back and she loosed tears of relief mixed with joy. The feel of her in his arms again, the warmth of her—good God, even the scent of her reminded him how much he adored her, and how much trouble they were still in. Nuzzling her neck, he stole a peek at the hideous creature that remained in the room.

America groaned. "Another pain," she puffed.

He turned to the new mother. "You are sloughing off the placenta. This last contraction should not be too painful." Afterward, he assigned duties. Mia would clean baby Luna and wrap her in bunting. Exeter would care for America. The other identically hideous guard arrived carrying a pitcher of steaming hot water. Stepping inside the cell block, the poor wretch turned and closed the door. He noted a mighty clunk, but there was no sound of a latch, nor the tumble of locks. It would seem the door could only be barred from the outside.

Exeter quickly formulated an escape plan.

Chapter Twenty-one

EXETER EYEBALLED THE WIZARD'S MEAGER STAFF. "I understand you are charged with the aid and comfort of these ladies." He poured fresh water into a basin and splashed his face. "I would like to suggest a bit of refreshment—hot tea and something light, perhaps a few biscuits and finger sandwiches."

He washed his hands and arms up to the elbow and toweled off. The two horrid little monsters made gurgling and hissing noises at one another—squabbling, he supposed, over who was to be sent off on the errand.

"He thinks you want fingers—actual fingers—in your sandwiches." An amused Phaeton explained to the guards. "Dainty morsels, Tweez, made with butter and jam—with the crusts cut off."

Exeter folded two clean cloths, and removed a bottle of chloroform from his kit. Across the room, Mia sat beside America, cooing and fussing over baby Luna. Everyone, including Phaeton, had been scrubbed clean and bundled into warm clothing. Exeter made eye contact with the new father, who shifted his gaze from the chloroform to Prospero's minions. He acknowledged Phaeton with a nod. If they were to try for a breakout, it would be best to give it a go sooner rather than later. There was a chance the wizard might outwit Ping and return to the den. It was not an impossible idea. None of them knew exactly how clever or devious the man was. No doubt Phaeton would have some insights—but that would have to wait. For now, Prospero remained an enigma.

Exeter stole a glance at Mia, lounging happily beside America. For an instant, he allowed an uncomfortable thought creep into his mind. He wondered what insights Mia had gleaned from her brief encounter with the man. He had found the emerald collar in the man's private chamber. Absently, she swept up a few wisps of hair and pinned them into her topknot. Sensing his attention, she smiled and nodded.

So they were ready.

And it appeared both minions were leaving—which meant the door would be locked. Exeter called after the guards. "One more thing . . ." He caught the door just as it was about to close. Before either jailer turned, he reached over both their heads and pressed the anesthesia-soaked fabric against their mouths and nostrils. Exeter summoned a bit of potent energy, hoisting the wobbly heads, and flailing appendages into the air. "Easy, lads." He used a hushed voice, and soon enough the kicking and thrashing ceased as the frail bodies sagged and legs began to dangle. He propped both guards against the door and tossed a ring of keys to Phaeton.

"There's a code as well." Phaeton reached through the bars, and pointed to a blinking box attached to the cell door. "Fortunately, I have deduced the cipher."

Exeter examined the mysterious apparatus attached to the cell door. Following Phaeton's instructions he pressed buttons marked with letters: P–H–A–E–D–R–A. "Phaedra—the Greek Goddess who hanged herself." As if he had uttered magic words, the blinking light turned green and the device opened, revealing the original lockbox.

"Libertas." Exeter could not help but smile as Phaeton searched for the right key. The man was shaking from the very idea of his imminent freedom. To be able to fully embrace America. Hold his child in his arms for the first time. Exeter dragged both creatures into the cell while Phaeton kissed and

embraced and kissed and cooed and coddled. "Ready yourselves, Phaeton, ladies—we are about to make a break for it."

Exeter locked up the cell and pocketed the key ring. "Off in the land of Nod." He turned to Mia and reached out. The feel of her hand in his was almost too much to bear. He wanted to pull her close, taste that luscious mouth again. But all of that tempting lovemaking would have to wait.

His gaze moved to America. She cradled the babe, and Phaeton carried both mother and child in his arms. "Don't drop them."

"Bugger off. A herd of Prospero's banshees couldn't loosen my grip." The inimitable Phaeton grin had returned, a very good sign. In fact, it appeared to hearten everyone. There was something about the man's attitude, a tour de force of wit and bravado. Exeter realized he had missed him sorely.

Even so, he narrowed his gaze. "Keep an eye out. Plenty of night dwellers lurking about." Squinting into the darkness, he led the way out of the ancient dungeon. Brick and mortar was soon replaced by chiseled limestone, yet he resisted calling out for help. Better to wait and see if the troll was still on guard. A test of sorts.

And he had his answer soon enough. Squeezing through the narrow opening, Exeter searched high and low for his rescuer. "His name is Archibald Dunbar Stuart—claims he's under some sort of enchantment."

"Trolls all want to believe that." Phaeton turned slowly, rocking mother and baby in his arms. "Rather convenient, wouldn't you say? Giant troll pops up in time to dig you out—leads you straight to us—ugly little minions welcome you with open arms . . ." Phaeton didn't roll his eyes, exactly, but the expression irritated.

Exeter sucked in a deep breath and exhaled. "Let us say, for the sake of argument, that Prospero was behind all this coincidental good fortune; what might be his motive?"

Phaeton's gaze darkened as all eyes moved to the babe in America's arms.

Mia was the first to speak. "What if this was never about the Moonstone? I mean, it might have started out that way, and no doubt they all still want to use the Moonstone's inexhaustible aether."

"I'm fairly certain we could place Gaspar, Oakley, and Victor in that bunch." Exeter offered. "But—"

"But perhaps not Prospero." Mia rolled a bottom lip under her pearly white uppers. "We're all thinking it. Luna is special, but what if she's *really* special?"

Exeter knew what they must do. "We have to split up."

Phaeton shook his head. "There is no safe place from him. America needs to rest—the hotel suite will have to do."

Exeter pondered, for a moment, the whereabouts of the others. He still had no idea if Jersey Blood had survived the blast in the tunnel. Perhaps there had been additional cave-ins. Exeter shook off the grisly thought. All he really knew was that the Nightshades were missing. "There's a communicator and a portal maker in the dining room. See if you can't locate Oakley. Tell him to send Ruby and Cutter over."

Phaeton nodded. "I'd feel better with a few bodyguards."

"Mia and I will continue to act as decoys." Exeter chose the widest, most well-trafficked tunnel and headed toward his best guess at north. Using all of his intuitive feelers, he led them in the general direction of the river. They must have covered a mile of quarry tunnel before they encountered the terrifying sound of—quiet. No more Métro trains traveling at high speed down adjacent tunnels.

"I believe we have passed through a portal." Phaeton mused aloud. "We are returned to eighteen eighty-nine."

"Would that be good news, or bad?" America asked.

"Good." Phaeton mused aloud. "While in captivity, these past long months, I've had a chance to study the wizard. He's not as comfortable in our world. Never stays for long and is knackered upon return." Phaeton lifted America higher and redistributed the weight in his arms.

"Do you need a rest?" Exeter asked.

"I can go a bit longer—I was allowed a bit of gymnasium every day—confined to the cell block. Kept me from going barking mad."

Exeter checked over the child, who had begun to fuss. "I recommend we find a defensible spot and take a rest." A chorus of hisses and growls could be heard behind them. "What is that?"

"Something revived from the dead—ghastly creatures." A disembodied voice answered, politely.

"Above us." Exeter nodded upward. Perched in an alcove overhead, two large eyes blinked in the dark. A hairy face plunged forward, tilting a curious chin. Phaeton turned a shoulder to the creature, shielding mother and child, but the troll ignored the rebuff and intruded for a closer look at the infant.

"Careful." Exeter calmed the defensive father. "He won't hurt her."

As if the baby could sense her father's trepidation, Luna ceased her crying and stared.

For a moment, the hisses quieted as well. "There's a horde of them," the troll explained. "Made from catacomb bones, with a few masterful touches by the wizard himself.

"More wraiths?" Mia looked to Exeter.

Exeter had yet to take his eyes off the troll. "You were supposed to keep watch. What happened?"

"Those things—the drones happened. Or wraiths. Whatever you prefer to call them. Wretched creatures like most of his creations." The troll's brogue was gone, replaced by proper British speak.

Phaeton pivoted in place, peering down several smaller tunnels. "What's the fastest way out of here—the closest exit?"

"There's a passage not far from here that connects to an old drainage pipe. The storm drain leads up to a florist shop."

Exeter nodded. "Archie, I need you to get these good people up top. Find the Hôtel Claude, on Île de la Cité." He searched in his pocket and passed the room key over to the only one with a free hand—the troll.

Phaeton's stare traveled from the key up the lumbering hairy-faced creature and over to Exeter. "Hard to sneak him in, but I like the size of him."

"Lock yourselves in the sixth-floor suite. Order room service and a bottle of stout for America." When Phaeton raised a brow, he explained, "Encourages the secretion of milk by the mammary glands."

Mia followed close behind Exeter, who set a blistering pace through a passage that veered off to the east, along the Seine. They did not speak, but concentrated on putting as much distance between themselves and the troll family as they could safely manage. This section of tunnel was older—and piled high with bones. They were headed back into the catacombs. A cold shiver vibrated through her body.

Mia grabbed hold of Exeter's arm, slowing the pace. "What if Prospero knows about the trap?"

Exeter shortened his stride, pulling her up beside him. "You think he suspects something?"

Her nod quickly turned into a confusing shake. "I'm not sure—it's more of a feeling than anything he said. There was something odd about the way he spoke of his appointment—as though he wanted me to know where he was going. He mentioned Ping and an address. Eight rue de Talleyrand."

Exeter stared. "The address of the Contessa Castiglione?"

"Ping and Tim could be in trouble. I say we pay her a visit. We're invited, are we not?" There was something comforting about his wary gaze. She'd seen it hundreds of times over the years. Ordinarily it meant he was on to her—some bit of mischief she was plotting. But not tonight. Tonight his shaded squint felt reassuring.

Emboldened by his interest, she continued. "If I'm right—we might be able to help Tim and Ping capture him. Prospero can't fight us all off."

"We'll make our way to the Contessa's home . . . however . . ."

A caveat was coming. "Yes, Exeter?"

"We will not be announced. We'll find another way in—have a look about. If I deem the situation too dangerous, you will leave immediately."

"And what about you?" she protested. Exeter laid a finger to his lips. The hissing sounds and low moans were drawing closer. She brightened. "A good sign, is it not?" The wraiths had followed her and Exeter.

"How are you feeling?" She sensed his struggle to read the signs of an impending shift in the dark. The telltale wrinkle in her brow and pain in her eyes. The band of headache radiating from temple to temple. He placed a thumb to her racing pulse, so he could feel the elevation in temperature. No use hiding her symptoms any longer. "She wants out."

Exeter massaged her temples. Gentle hands, the hands of a healer. "Better?"

Mia closed her eyes and nodded. "A bit."

"Hold her back, until we arrive at the soiree. We'll find a spare room—or closet. I'll take care of you." She imagined his mouth on a nipple—his fingers slipping inside her. Arousal shuddered pleasantly through her body.

Mia grabbed the lapels of his coat and pulled him back. She kissed him hard, drawing blood. "Don't make me wait too long."

He licked his bottom lip. "We must go."

The hissing noises had grown steadily louder—by the time they found an exit, the wraiths were nearly upon them. Rounding a corner, a bony hand stretched out and grasped at her shoulder. Exeter turned and leveled a blast of energy at the wraith and pushed her up a ladder. "Wait for me topside."

The wraith hordes had reached the level of a howling storm. "Do not try to fight them off by yourself." She turned back to see a large round ball of energy grow in his palm. A squadron of skeletons dressed in rags hissed at the sight and retreated.

"Topside, young lady. I'll just be a moment." Exeter glanced up at her. "Promise."

Mia climbed the ladder and turned the wheel of the hatch. Nothing—no release, just a few creaks and groans. She put her shoulder to the stubborn barrier and pushed. Finally, the door swung open. Mia stepped out into the cold night air and marveled briefly at the unlikely spot. The hidden entrance was situated just below the foot of the Pont Neuf.

Exeter climbed out of the small opening. "Shall we make our way to eight rue de Talleyrand?"

Mia picked up her skirts and jumped over a puddle. "The sooner the better."

Exeter hailed a hansom on the left bank and they were at the Contessa's palatial maison in minutes. Parting the canvas curtain to have a look ahead, he spoke softly. "There's a line of carriages at the gate waiting to enter the grounds." He tapped on the roof and passed the driver a few coins. "We'll be getting out here."

Inside the gate, they meandered past low shrubs and through flower beds. The garden path led to an open door under a sign that read LIVRAISONS. A swath of gaslight poured out the entrance, illuminating several cases of champagne. Exeter grabbed a bottle and nudged Mia through the delivery door, startling a scullery maid. "We seem to have taken a wrong turn. Might you point us toward the salon?"

Following the girl's directions, he opened the door on the right and found the servants' stairs. On the second floor, he turned the knob. Mia wriggled between Exeter and the crack in the door.

"What do you see?" His words breezed past her ear and tingled through her body. Mia caught her breath. "A gathering of rather smart-looking nobs swilling champagne and—"

"And?"

The scene was not unlike any soiree one might attend in London, with an exception. "Not a soul in costume, but some are wearing demi masks—or donning them." Mia shifted to one side, so Exeter could see. "What do you make of it?"

Exeter squinted through the crack. "It appears there is yet another level to this party—on the third floor." He opened the door as a servant walked by, and scooped two black feathered masks off a tray.

"My word, you are a stealthy one this evening," she teased.

He fit the mask over her eyes, and turned her around. "We shall be ravens in the night." His softly spoken words sent a shiver through her. She held the mask in place while he looped the satin ribbons in a bow behind her topknot.

Mia tied Exeter's mask on, but was not prepared for the lurch in her stomach when he turned around. The mask shaded the top half of his eyes, and a glimmer of gaslight played across his face—dark pupils with a glint of emerald in his gaze. Another tremble quaked inside her. The devilish kind of quiver that caused naughty thoughts and made her ache for intimacy with him. "Do you think we're presentable enough?"

A half smile toyed at the edges of his mouth. "Just a guess, but clothing might be optional here."

Mia blinked. "Whatever do you mean—?"

He grabbed her hand and slipped into the crowd. Exeter lifted a chilled bottle out of an iced chiller and replaced it with the bottle he had stolen. "This bottle, a decidedly better vintage, could use a chill, but while we wait . . ." He moved to another table, and procured two empty glasses. "Guzzle a few of these, darling." As soon as she downed the champagne, he poured another.

Halfway through her third glass, she hiccupped. "Exeter, I'm afraid I'm . . ."

"Yes, I believe you're about ready for the third floor." While they finished their bubbly, they both watched the ups and downs, the comings and goings of the guests. "The Contessa has not shown her face. Not a sign of Ping or Tim Noggy." His gaze returned to her. "You haven't seen anything that might resemble Prospero?"

Mia arched a brow. "Might he be a shape-shifter? I didn't get that impression." He emptied the last of the bottle into her glass. "Are you trying to get me sloshed?"

"I am." Exeter took hold of her hand, and angled his mouth

for a kiss, but instead spoke in a whisper. "Do you know what a sexual fetish is?"

Mia shook her head. "I don't believe so." She leaned closer. "What is it?"

"Exotic sexual preferences, you might call them. Sodomy of all varieties, the *ménage à trois*—three usually, though there can be more."

Mia snorted a soft laugh. *"Ménage à quatre ou cinq?"*

Exeter sighed. "There is a subset of the beau mode who enjoy sex orgies—incorporating a variety of different fetishes. The Earl of Shrewsbury is fond of spanking. During the hunting season he hires a number of courtesans out to his country estate, for entertainment."

Mia placed the back of her hand to her burning cheek. All this talk of fetishes and orgies nearly had her wet with perspiration. "One would think his backside would be sore enough after a hard day in the saddle."

His mouth twitched. With his eyes and nose covered, she found herself staring at his mouth. Slightly wide, with a full lower lip and well-formed upper. A girl might lose control of herself. "You're taking this awfully well." Exeter remarked.

"The cat is curious."

"And Mia?"

"She would like to see for herself—what goes on at these orgies."

He reached for the glass in her hand and set it down on a passing tray of empties. "I had no idea you were a voyeur."

Chapter Twenty-two

AT THE TOP OF THE STAIRS, they were welcomed by a man wearing an opera hat, velvet mask, and little else. Leather straps crisscrossed his naked body, leaving the most important parts to dangle. "Raven master, mistress. Name your pleasure." He dipped a bow.

Exeter kept his hand at the small of her back, just above the bustle. "Might there be private viewing rooms?"

The flamboyant greeter pointed to a wall covered by a large tapestry. Exeter whisked her down an aisle filled with the most startling displays imaginable. Agog at the sight of a gentleman performing oral favors, Mia gasped. "That man has a ring in his penis."

"Fetishes often defy imagination, especially if one has no proclivity for them." Exeter pushed back the heavy drape. "Shall I take you behind the curtain, *mon joli voyeur*?"

"And what will you do, monsieur, once you have me alone?"

Grabbing her hand, he whisked her behind the tapestry and into a passageway that connected several small chambers. "I hear moans," she whispered. They passed through a maze of rooms, each one lit by a single candle.

"The sounds of pleasure." Exeter came to an abrupt halt. Craning her neck to see around her tall, muscular escort, Mia could just make out the end of the passageway, and if she was not mistaken, the gasps of heavy breathing.

Exeter moved the candlestick to a nearby ledge and placed her in front of his body. With one arm tight around her waist, he opened a metal shutter that covered a diminutive window to the next chamber.

"Watch." Exeter rasped a whisper, nibbling the lobe of her ear.

A tingle ran down the length of her neck—she felt entirely decadent, but unable to resist peeking through the small opening. A faint glow filled the adjacent chamber, but there could be no doubt who was perched on the edge of a table. The silver feathered demi mask did little to disguise her identity. Mia recognized the Contessa Castiglione with her skirts hiked up to her hips. And that must be Etienne Artois's hand between her legs.

She gasped and Exeter covered her lips with his finger. "Might have known we'd run into them here." He opened a few buttons and pulled the neckline of her dress over her shoulders, effectively pinning her arms to her sides. She felt immobilized, vulnerable—her breasts were completely exposed. Exeter took a small mound in each hand, and they both watched quietly as Etienne dropped his head over the Contessa's bared bosom.

At the instant Etienne sucked the Contessa's breast, Exeter plucked Mia's nipples. She thought she might explode from the intensity of such pleasurable sensation. "Do that again." She leaned back against his chest, and he plucked her nipples until she became weak-kneed.

Gathering the back of her gown, he methodically folded the ruffles of her skirt. "Remember to watch, Mia." Slowly, purposefully, he untied her bustle and placed the contraption on a side table. His hands wrapped around her waist and untied lacy French drawers. He edged them over her hips, and they slipped to the floor.

"Step out of the pantalettes and spread your legs." A soft-spoken demand, but a demand, nonetheless. Mia's heart pounded blood to her nipples and clitoris. She wanted him to touch her there . . . and there. A cool draft of air wafted up the inside of her thighs as she waited for his caress.

Finally she gasped, "Touch me."

"How impatient my little voyeur is." Soft-spoken words—more of a tease than a reprimand, still he covered both breasts and rolled her nipples until she moaned.

His fingers slid up the inside of both thighs, and she trembled as he reached the apex of her pleasure. "Oh, Exeter—please." Her whole body throbbed for him—and the cat urged her on. Skillful fingers entered moist folds, slick and smooth, he stroked back and forth lightly. He uttered a deep, husky groan and nuzzled the hair behind her ear. "You're so very wet, love."

He moved to her side and placed a finger on her clitoris, while his other hand stroked between her legs from the rear. He used his mouth to caress the length of her neck, and his erection rubbed against her side. She answered him by rocking her hip gently back and forth against his straining penis. They were both in a reverie of sensation. "Just as we are enjoying the Contessa and her *homme de fille,* we are likely being watched by others."

Mia stiffened slightly. "You are beautiful; let me arouse you." As if to prove the statement he turned her enough to suckle a nipple, and her pleasure soared to a new heights.

His finger circled her clitoris, while his other hand went deeper—swirling one, then two fingers inside her. He scissored enough to find the spots that made her gasp and moan.

Mia's eyes grew wider still, as she watched Etienne through the opening. He walked around the table and presented himself to the mouth of the Contessa. Mia eyed the handsome penis that sprung from his trousers. She managed to tear her eyes away and turn to Exeter. "Unbutton me."

Exeter hesitated at first. When she raised a brow, he removed the top of her gown. He took a moment to admire her bare torso. A thrilling kind of excitement quivered through her body. She would bare herself, presumably, for all the world according to the Contessa Castiglione. She moved to unbutton Exeter's trousers and liberate the man's impressive shaft.

Now that she had something to compare it to, she thought his penis handsome—and nicely large in scale. In her brief visit to the Contessa's den of iniquity, she had been exposed to more male appendages than she had ever seen in her life, with the exception of Exeter's medical books and pornography collection.

He teased her by removing his hands from between her legs. "Untie me."

"I believe it is also your turn to watch." Sinking onto her knees, Mia took him, not quite fully, in her mouth.

Fully would have been impossible.

Exeter flattened both palms to each side of the window and rocked in and out of her mouth—gently at first. Groaning his pleasure, Mia knew he aligned her ministrations to the scene in the adjacent room.

There was something altogether exotic and mysterious to these sex games, and she found herself, shockingly, an enthusiastic player. And she delighted in giving Exeter pleasure. She ran her lips and tongue over his throbbing, velvet shaft, lightly cupping his sac, and caused the most wonderful utterances from him. Lovingly, he stroked the crown of her head and begged her softly not to stop.

She felt the jerk—the telltale sign of his oncoming climax. And she took all of his seed into her mouth, laving and sucking, draining him, until he bucked and signaled the end of his pleasure.

Pulling her up off the floor and into his embrace, Exeter buried his head in the slope of her neck. "*Mon Dieu,* love." His whispers only served to elevate her arousal, as he turned her toward the peephole and rucked up her skirts. He slipped his shaft between her legs—lubricating himself between her labia, rubbing out more pleasure for himself.

Exeter bent her over and she groaned loudly as he planted

himself deep. She could see through the window that Etienne's cock was firmly embedded into the Contessa, and the comely woman was near tears of ecstasy.

Exeter thrust in and out—still hard, even after that explosive climax. His fingers slid into her labia from the front as he plunged deep inside her from the rear. His manipulations were slow and firm, with an occasional light circling of her engorged clitoris. "Come for me, Mia." A slick finger traveled between her buttock cheeks and pressed into her anus, wiggling, tickling the tight opening. "Give me a climax—I want it now." His fingers quickened their strokes—as he explored deeper and deeper.

The sight of Etienne thrusting into the Countess matched Exeter's deep strokes and light touch. Mia uttered a gasp, unable to stop herself from crying out as she edged ever closer. His fingers invaded every possible orifice; she felt as though three men attended her every desire. The climax ripped through her—shattering her reality, taking her to a faraway place of pure sensation. Her belly shuddered and her knees wobbled at the depth and strength of the pleasure she was experiencing.

Stroking softly, Exeter held her up, drawing out the last of her ecstasy. For several moments, she rested in his arms. "That was—" She could hardly express herself. "I hardly know what to say."

"I take it the cat is sated." There was a smile in his voice. He rocked her gently in his arms. A low-pitched vibration came from the depths of her body and she purred for him.

He snorted soft laughter against her temple.

Mia knew her peak had not coincided with that of the couple in the dark room beside them—her cries of pleasure had come later. Somewhat mortified, she straightened. Eyes wide, she found herself confronted by Etienne. He was peering at her, as curiously as she was looking at him.

The Contessa winked.

Whipping around and shoving her skirts down, Mia knew Exeter had seen the look on her face and had surmised they had been discovered post coitus. Fast witted, as always, he closed the small door to the window and tied up his drawers.

It took only moments for Etienne to drag the disoriented Contessa from their dark little den to the adjacent room. Exeter slipped Mia's pantalettes into his coat pocket and settled her bosom into her dress. Breathing hard, they stared at each other until they both snorted a soft laugh.

"Mes amis!"

She and Exeter pivoted an about-face and stood primly beside one another. The unfortunate part was they were both laughing—which was neither proper nor worldly wise. And certainly not clever. Even so she tried to maintain a stiff smile.

Luckily, Exeter was coherent, for Mia was still flushed and speechless from her pleasure. The doctor nodded formally to the trysting couple. "Monsieur Artois . . . Countess."

Etienne sauntered over to the small window on the wall, opened the diminutive iron door, and peered through it. Turning back, he wore the look of a man with an advantage.

"Well, now, I hope it was as fine and rare for you both, as it was for us."

"Exceptionnel," Exeter offered, perhaps a bit too quickly.

Rejoining his lover, Etienne and the Contessa returned Exeter's compliment with a pleasant nod. "Glad to be of service, Baron *et* Baronesss de Roos."

Mia could not stop the upward twitch to her mouth, and soon the smiles of both she and the Contessa were as much in evidence as were both men's snorts of laughter. Etienne spoke first. "The next time you two choose to become voyeurs, have a heart and let us in on it."

"*Mais oui,* but won't that spoil the enjoyment . . . knowing?" Mia asked with an innocence she did not pretend to hide. There was no use fooling these two.

"Mes no, chouchou, Etienne and I often delight in a bit of—*exhibitionnisme*." The Contessa winked at Mia a second time.

As they exchanged a few risqué remarks and bawdier jokes, Mia and Exeter were escorted out from behind the tapestry and deftly slipped back into the crowded hall. "Enjoy!" The Contessa called over her shoulder. With a snap of her fan she pointed in the direction of a large table of refreshments.

Etienne turned back. "A warning, perhaps? There are some gentlemen here—*Anglais*, I believe."

Chapter Twenty-three

MIA COULD ONLY WAGER A GUESS, but she suspected Exeter ran a worst-case scenario over in his mind. A cloud of perplexed thoughts whirled behind those sensuous, hooded eyes. The *Anglais* Etienne had mentioned would likely be gentlemen of the ton, peers whom Exeter might run into at a social event—or club members. She searched his face. "You're worried."

"Ordinarily, I would call it circumspect. But since we have tossed caution to the wind this evening . . ." He shrugged a shoulder and fashioned a reassuring simile. "We are masked. And from what I understand, no one makes acquaintances at soirees of this nature. Anonymity is de rigueur."

As they circulated among the fornication and flogging, Mia would stop now and then to stare. She couldn't help herself, it was all so . . . titillating. "I had no idea how shockingly wicked I could be and how easily I am brought to such depravity."

"I blame myself for exposing you to such immoral salaciousness. Are you repentant over it?"

Mia hoped her blush was more dazzling than demure. "On the contrary, I am most humbled by my lack of regret."

This time Exeter stopped to stare.

She started to pivot—to have a look at the sought-after, seductive woman he found so beguiling . . . and then it struck her. He was staring at her.

A slow smile, something decidedly masculine and feral, tugged at the corners of his mouth. "Hungry?"

She glanced about, as her hand swept over the buttons of his trousers. "I believe I have what is called—an appetite." She kept her touch light, and quickly found what she searched for. That she openly dared such risqué foreplay appeared to kindle more than a glimmer in his eyes.

She stood with her back to a buffet table, entranced at the sight of a nude woman bound in leather and suspended by ropes in midair. Exeter coated pieces of dried fruit from a chocolate fountain and fed her bites of plum and berry.

"M-m-m." The woman was being denied orgasm by her partner and it made Mia's lower anatomy begin to thrum and quiver. She leaned back against Exeter and whispered in his ear. "Will he ever let her climax?"

"Depends how prettily she begs for it."

Exeter pulled her to one side of the table, to a darker corner of the room. "I almost forgot." He pulled the emerald collar from his coat pocket.

She swallowed. "Where did you find it?"

"Prospero's bedchamber."

A rush of heat flushed her cheeks. "I . . . we . . ." She lowered her eyes.

Exeter tilted her chin up. "For the moment, what happened between you and Prospero is not important—as long as you weren't hurt." He slipped the collar around her throat and clipped on the silver chain. "I thought we could use a fetish."

A passing group of young men all turned around to openly gape at her. A sudden modesty caused her to turn away.

"Hold on, love." He tugged the chain and positioned her derriere against him. Across the aisle, another female was being ceremoniously laid over a paddling rail. A male partner tossed her skirts and petticoats overhead—exposing a peachy, plump bum. Mia pressed against Exeter and he opened his hand. A glow of violet-blue energy swirled in his palm.

He inched up the back of her dress. "I was just thinking you might enjoy another lesson. Something mysterious, arcane—like the use of potent force for a bit of pleasure."

More than curious, she smiled. "I must admit I've enjoyed my lessons thus far."

He closed his fingers around the swirling, radiant force and pressed the tingling egg between her labia. She jumped when the compacted energy began to vibrate.

Exeter chuckled softly. "I've got you." He massaged until she moaned and rubbed her ass against him. When the pulse of energy faded, she groaned. "More, please."

"Not yet." Exeter could be shockingly erotic at times. He was going to keep her begging for more, just like the woman splayed out in front of them waiting for the next pass of the cat-o'-nine-tails. Exeter's fingers remained between her buttocks, gently circling the small, tight sphincter muscle. With each lash of the whip across the aisle, Mia's cheeks quivered.

She leaned against him. "I do remember that spanking of yours being rather titillating—but I can't imagine under what circumstance a flogging might be enjoyable."

Exeter hunkered down close. "If I were to flog you . . . properly . . . I'd use the whip to increase the blood circulation to your skin. You would gradually become more receptive to the sting." His breath carried husky words across the tip of her ear, which he kissed.

Mia shivered. "And I would beg for more."

"You are a surprisingly sensuous woman." He conjured another ball of potent energy and pushed it into her vagina. "Shall we explore further?"

She thought he meant deeper and nodded, barely able to speak. When he tugged playfully at her collar, she realized he wanted her to walk around the soiree with an egg of energy vibrating inside her—stimulated beyond reason—on the edge of orgasm.

An attractive couple approached them and asked for *préliminaires*. "I believe they mean foreplay." Exeter studied her expression carefully before nudging her forward. He unbuttoned the back of her dress, dropping the front of her gown just enough to bare her breasts.

A thrill shot through her body, to be exposed in public like this. The panther inside stirred. The feral creature who longed to run—unfettered by clothes—through fields and forests and bacchanals. Quite before she could control herself, she arched forward to meet their lips. The man and the woman each tasted a nipple—nibbling lightly at first, and then sucking harder. She lay her head back against Exeter and moaned.

Shamelessly, she watched them tongue and scrape with their teeth until both peaks throbbed from their nipping. With each breath, the egg deep inside her rocked from side to side, causing her to clench her vagina. Exeter had increased the egg's potency. "Come for me, Mia—again. I want another." His demand sent a shudder through her body, and a kind of release.

"I am close—*crescendo qui mène à un paroxysme,*" she gasped. Her entire body was racked by an explosive orgasm. Weak-kneed, he swept an arm around her waist and thanked the couple for their assistance.

He held her tightly against him as the last waves of her climax diminished and left her feeling like a rag doll in his arms. He kissed her mouth, his tongue deep and languid. "Such a willing and spirited raven mistress," he whispered.

Across the aisle, a large, ornately framed mirror reflected the ecstatic flogger and his delightful red-bottomed partner. Beyond them she caught sight of Exeter. She watched as he folded his arms around her and buried his face in the curve of her neck. His chiseled jaw and elegant profile nearly made her wet for him all over again. "Good God, I am a wanton."

His lips barely touched her ear—just his breath. "You are the most sensual woman I have ever encountered. Your body delights in pleasure."

Mia sighed, vaguely aware of being buttoned. His knuckles gently brushed the skin on her back as he closed her dress. She opened her eyes to steal another glance in the mirror. Behind them, not ten feet away, a striking man with silver eyes watched, intently. A chill ran down her spine. "Prospero."

"I see him." Exeter checked the exits. Without Ping and

Tim, and Oakley's trap, there wasn't much reason to stay, not with a powerful wizard on the prowl, one who knew they had escaped. They must fall back, regroup, attend to Phaeton and America. The newborn needed protection—more than the troll could provide. He hoped that at least one of the Nightshades was with them at the hotel—Jersey Blood.

Where was everyone? Tim had given him a device earlier this evening, the communicator. At this moment, he'd give anything to have it hooked around his ear. Exeter glanced over his shoulder; no wizard to be found. He didn't like the way Prospero looked at Mia. As if he had come to this soiree for a reason, and was determined to leave with a party favor.

To exit via the grand stair required them to maneuver through a tangle of fornication. He found a side door, which led to a terrace cordoned off from the risqué revelry. After being in a hot house full of writhing bodies, the cool breeze refreshed. Lacing his fingers through Mia's, he guided her along the length of the balcony hoping to find a staircase.

"She is in no danger from me." Prospero shut the French door and sauntered toward them. His expression was neutral enough, though guarded. A slight upturn at the ends of his mouth signaled goodwill, which was almost entirely directed at Mia.

Exeter studied Prospero study Mia, and something clenched in his gut. From the moment the wizard entered the room, he hadn't taken his eyes off her.

"I enjoyed watching your bliss." He continued to admire her. "Not nearly as much as I would have enjoyed giving you—"

"What do you want?" Exeter cut in.

Reluctantly, his gaze finally met his. "Hello, Doctor Exeter."

When he didn't respond in kind, Prospero exhaled a sigh. "Do you mean—what do I want besides the Moonstone and the child, Luna—and of course, Mia?"

"You can't have them."

"But I already have—all of them—even Mia." There was a cruel twist to his smile and those silver eyes turned as dark as pupils could possibly dilate. "We showered together in my bedchamber." Rather triumphantly, he returned his black gaze to Mia. "I soaped your breasts."

Exeter lifted a clenched fist and struck Prospero with a blow that would cause most men to stagger backward, and all it did was turn Prospero's cheek.

He moved to push Mia behind him and was struck by a force that lifted him through the air and slammed him against a wall. A cloud of crumbling mortar and dust enveloped him as he landed in a crumple on the ground.

"Your potent force is badly depleted, Exeter," Prospero loomed over him. "I have no quarrel with you—nor do I wish to punish you needlessly. Unlike what many say about me, I am not a heartless fiend—you listen to Noggy and his twin Oakley. Just give me what I want." The wizard appeared to tire—he was after all in their time, not his own. "Give up the girl, and we will leave peaceably," Prospero's quiet voice returned.

As he struggled to regain his breath, Exeter scanned the balcony. Mia was nowhere to be found. "Like I said, you can't have her."

Where exactly was Mia? Something sprang from the roof edge—a black shadow flew across the moon and knocked Prospero down. She pinned the spread-eagled wizard to the terrace, her large paws locking his arms in place with the aid of potent force. *Careful, Mia.*

The cat snarled her reply.

"Allow me to do the honors." Ping stood behind the wizard dressed in the most stunning black dressing robe ever seen.

Exeter rose to his feet, and Mia quickly retreated to join him.

Intricate, knotted closures remained open on the velvet wrapper. Mandarin collar and cuffs were embroidered with yellow and red flames. Ping wore a waistcoat of crimson silk without a shirt underneath. The vest was unbuttoned enough to display two delicate mounds—Jinn's breasts. Her long dark hair blew about the finely featured face under a black opera hat.

Perfectly arousing and so very androgynous. Completing the exotic picture, Ping wore a velvet demi mask.

Lips blushed with rose opened to full effect, as the fascinating creature spoke in singsong harmony. "Greetings, Prospero."

The wizard picked himself up off the floor. "We meet at last, Julian Ping—or is it Jinn?"

The jinni dipped a curtsy, parting the velvet robe like the wings of a butterfly. A theatrical display of erotic delight, starring Ping's penis.

Exeter had never seen such an exotic androgyne. In the past, the jinni was either Ping or Jinn, but this creature was something even better—a stunning hermaphrodite. As a doctor, he was enthralled. A quick glance at Prospero revealed a mesmerized wizard. The panther backed away, with a hiss.

Displayed for all to see, Ping's manhood angled upward with a good deal of bobbing and waving about. Nearly twice as large as one might have guessed, given his stature and build. The perfectly helmeted head was pierced with a golden ring and run through with a red satin ribbon, which Ping tossed into the air.

Spontaneously, Prospero reached out to catch the ribbon. There was a sudden yank—and for an instant Exeter glimpsed the surprise in the wizard's eyes. He'd been hooked. A great, mysterious fish on the end of a powerful jinni's line. Ping stepped aside as a violent force dragged a disintegrating Prospero across the balcony floor and into the cylindrical tube, which opened and banged shut with a reverberation that shook the balcony.

It was over so quickly, no one spoke for a moment, not even Ping. The three of them stared at the trap—wordless, motionless. The curious canister turned blacker than black, and appeared to absorb all light, while reflecting none. Not more than a foot long—and yet it held one of the most powerful wizards of the Outremer.

Exeter caught up the silver chain attached to the emerald collar and inched forward for a better look. The tube shimmied across the floor, causing Mia to hiss and Ping to place his foot on the rollicking apparatus. Exeter had been assured the trap was strong enough to hold the formidable wizard—but for how long?

Ping read his mind. "Oakley is fairly sure this will hold him. We even got a thumbs-up from Gaspar, at least—what could be seen of his thumb."

"Fairly sure?"

Ping shrugged, rather good-naturedly. "The trap works on the same principle as an oil lamp or bottle or—jar. All of which are excellent containers for Moonstones or jinn or wizards."

Exeter nodded. There were times when he found Ping and Gaspar's version of the occult beyond mystifying. Still—what they had accomplished was impressive. Exeter shook Ping's hand. "Honestly, I'm not sure how that could have gone smoother."

With a great swish of her tail, Mia sat on her haunches beside Exeter. *We were all mesmerized.*

Nodding to Mia, Ping reached inside his robe. It was no surprise the jinni would be receptive to her thoughts. He removed a familiar Noggy device—the portable portal—from an inside pocket. "Best I return this unit to Oakley's storage facility, posthaste."

Exeter held up a finger. "One more thing—you wouldn't happen to know what happened to Tim and Jersey?"

"They're back at the hotel, with Phaeton and America. And of course, baby Luna." Ping's eyes sparkled just speaking her name. "I have heard her—she has healthy lungs."

The cat looked up at Ping. *She is special, isn't she?*

The jinni tucked the black cylinder under his arm. "Luna is a daughter of the moon and stars—she will become a great healer and peacemaker. It is her destiny." Ping pressed a button and was gone.

Chapter Twenty-four

Green Park, London

"I NEVER THOUGHT I'D LIVE TO SEE Phaeton Black pushing a perambulator about in the park," Exeter goaded. With the panther by his side, he and Mia ambled along with Phaeton and America.

"I cannot believe it myself." Phaeton leaned over the baby carriage and cooed. "Pay your godfather no mind, Luna." The beaming papa looked up at Exeter. "She's got her mother's almond-shaped eyes—did you see them?"

America smiled. "Her father's grin, as well—I saw a hint of it just this morning. And there was mischief in her eyes."

"Let us hope some good comes of it." Exeter teased, giving a nod to the two Nightshades behind them.

Jersey Blood and Valentine Smith strolled arm in arm, some distance away. Until they had Prospero safely locked away, precautions were to be taken with regards to Luna, in particular. No one knew exactly what this child born of the moon and stars meant, as yet, but they weren't taking any chances.

Since they had returned to London, there had been several troublesome episodes at Oakley headquarters in the Outremer. The larger rooms designed to house the wizard had proved less than stable. Oakley had called Exeter over to consult on ways to incarcerate the dangerous, wily Prospero.

"We'll meet in St. George's Churchyard." Phaeton snapped him out of his troubled thoughts. The Blacks and entourage split off at a fork in the pathway heading for Shaftesbury Avenue.

"Bright and early, then!" America called to both of them.

Exeter answered Mia's wave. "At the stroke of ten, Thursday morning." He turned them north, toward Piccadilly, where they came upon a new neighbor, a Mrs. Agnes Lassiter. She was heiress to a merchant fleet, and her personal worth was reported to be in the millions. Exeter greeted the woman as she made her way over to get a closer look at the large black cat walking beside him.

"Is he a *Panthera parda* or *onca?*" Wide eyes stared at the exotic animal. "I'm somewhat of a philofelist—cat-lover."

"*She* is a *parda,* from the southern region of Africa."

The fascinated woman nodded. "Look, in just the right light you can see the spots hidden by the excess black pigment—melanin—the effect is similar to that of printed silk, is it not?" Leaning closer the woman hesitated. "Might I touch her?"

"She is quite tame, but I do not advise petting." Exeter smiled.

The woman straightened with a sigh. "Such a beautiful pussy."

"That she is, Mrs. Lassiter." Exeter tipped his hat.

"The pheasant is delightful—very succulent." Mia chewed quietly. She managed to suppress a growl, but not the glare that shot across the dinner table. It had been exactly twelve days, three hours, and forty-nine minutes since their return to London. She knew this because it had been exactly that long since Exeter had visited her bedchamber or touched her intimately. She had brought up his indifference during the soup course, and he had positioned his lack of affection as a necessary disengagement.

"Paris was lovely, Mia, but—"

"I'd rather not listen to any more buts."

"You deserve to experience the world, meet people, fall in love."

"Have my heart broken." She barely choked down whatever tasteless morsel was on her fork.

"If that is what it takes to make you realize you have your whole life in front of you." Exeter spoke quietly, but forcefully. "I only want for you what every young woman should have. Especially one as bold and beautiful as you are." Exeter paused to pour them each another glass of claret. "Now, we need to see if you can go it alone. See if you can manage your shifts by using all the techniques I have taught you."

She took a sip of claret and then another. "What sort of skills do you mean—exactly?"

Exeter sliced a bit of leg meat off the bone. "We shall continue this discussion after dinner. In my study."

Mia exhaled an exasperated sigh before changing the subject. "Just think, in a few more days, Phaeton and America are finally to marry. And baby Luna will be christened—all in an afternoon." She smiled. "Even though it galls me to say it, well done, Exeter."

Since they were to be godparents, Exeter had gamely contrived to meet with the vicar, an amiable man by the name of Wicklow, to make arrangements. "A small wedding after the christening—what could be simpler? As long as Phaeton and America were in the chapel, I thought it expedient to add a ceremony." Exeter chewed. "Mr. Wicklow agreed."

He made merry eyes across the table. There was no doubt he felt the tension between them, and was trying to cajole her. "How are the reception plans coming along? Sorry for springing all this on you and then dashing off to Cambridge."

"Invitations are printed and mailed. Champagne is ordered. We are to have a light supper around seven—with any luck we'll have the whole motley crew out the door by midnight."

Exeter tilted his head, curious. "You invited Mrs. Parker and the girls?"

"Of course. They are Phaeton and America's friends—yours, as well." She rested her fork and knife on the edge of her plate.

"When I used the expression motley crew, I was referring to those unruly Nightshades, including Gaspar, who should be restored enough to attend." Mia couldn't help a devilish grin. "Though I suspect a few of Esmeralda Parker's girls can be just as unruly."

"I don't believe our guest list has ever been this interesting," Exeter sipped his claret. "I hand-delivered invitations to Oakley and Victor. They said they'd try to make it."

Her brows elevated, then crashed together. "After everything Phaeton has gone through—what he has done for them?" Phaeton's first act of Moonstone business was to restore Gaspar, as well as their world. "I should think they could do better than try." A frown did not quite do justice to how she felt at the moment. "You've made several unplanned trips to the Outremer of late. Something has gone wrong, hasn't it?"

"In a manner of speaking." Exeter hesitated. She knew that look. He was holding back, in a protective way. Finally, he met her gaze. "The Moonstone has turned out to be—temperamental. It's not just about Phaeton asking politely for powers with an open heart. Apparently . . ." He exhaled. "There are extenuating circumstances."

Absently, she twirled her wineglass about by the stem. "More than once, Prospero made references to Oakley and Victor—he claimed they had painted him the villain."

Exeter set his napkin beside his plate. "What else would you expect the man to say?"

"Just—be wary." She met his gaze. "Things may not be what they seem."

"I will keep that in mind, if it eases yours."

She lifted her chin and plastered a smile on her face. "It does."

Exeter studied her false grin, then changed the subject. "I understand you received an overseas cable today. Anything you'd care to discuss?"

She removed the telegraph wire from a pocket in her gown. "You might read it, first."

She inhaled a quick breath as he opened the message. When Exeter had cooled toward her, she had felt confused, abandoned. She had also suffered a bad patch of tears and anger—until this wire arrived.

Exeter looked up from the missive. "You've been accepted to the Boston University School of Medicine."

Mia knew without a doubt that she was beaming. "A women's medical college in Boston. The first school in the world to formally educate female physicians."

Exeter continued to stare, openmouthed. "Are you sure about this?"

"I've never been more sure of anything in my life. I wish to practice medicine. Perhaps forge a specialty in women's health. Seeing you with America, in the hotel—being your eyes and hands for Luna's birth . . ." Since his shocked expression hadn't changed, she continued to state her case. "How perfectly women are made to procreate, to nurture a child in our womb, bear the pain and the joy of childbirth." Mia jumped up and leaned across the table. "It is my calling, Exeter—be happy for me."

"I am over the moon, Mia. The world needs more physicians with such passion and dedication, but . . ."

Her eyes flicked upward. "Yes, of course, you are over the moon, *but* . . ."

She watched him temper a sharp intake of air into a quiet exhale. "Boston is rather far away. I know we could find something closer. I am acquainted with the Dean of the London School of Medicine for Women, an Elizabeth Anderson. I could speak with her."

Mia was stunned at his sudden turn of heart. He had avoided her at every turn, making two trips to the Outremer and one to Cambridge, for a lecture. He had stayed overnight, chumming about with colleagues and friends, and yet now he wished to keep her close.

Mia angled her bustle as she returned to her seat. The tea tray arrived, along with a decanter of Exeter's favorite port. A lemon curd tart appeared in front of her. Without much enthusiasm, she added a dollop of clotted cream while Exeter continued. "There is also a new school of medicine for women in Edinburgh—"

"I am beyond fortunate to have received this offer." Mia cut in. "London has a waiting list, and Edinburgh's program is still very small. I wired the Dean of Boston University School of Medicine on the off chance they might allow a midyear enrollee. They will hold a slot open until the tenth of January. All I need is the tuition." Mia scraped a spoon over her tart, nervously.

Exeter appeared to have no appetite for dessert, preferring to sip on his port. "It's not the money, it's . . . I'm sure you don't want another repeat of Oxford." Exeter was unfairly referencing the start of her women's studies this past fall. She had been found naked in the forest, wandering and incoherent. The incident had marked the beginning of her change.

"I am well past those days." She must have appeared stricken because he softened his argument.

"Indeed, you are. You've made wonderful progress with your feline counterpart." Exeter smiled a simple closed-lipped smile, the kind that brought that long dimple to one side of his mouth. She loved that dimple.

He settled back into his chair. "I arrived home early yesterday afternoon. Mr. Tandi placed a finger to his lips and bade me follow him into the garden. Four-legged Mia was catnapping in a tree branch."

Her favorite shade tree in all the world, the old oak took up nearly the entire garden space, except for a small patch of sunlight that grew roses. The panther loved to snooze on a low-hanging limb, almost every afternoon.

"Did Mr. Tandi happen to mention that while dozing off one day, she slipped off the branch and was quite rudely awakened by hard ground?"

A blush of warmth rose on her cheeks when he barked a

laugh. Exeter hardly ever laughed. "I take it she survived the fall."

"She's a hardy pussycat." Mia returned his grin.

His rather charming, wistful gaze turned a bit edgy. A gulp finished his port and he set the glass down. "Shall we retire to my study?"

Chapter Twenty-five

EXETER OPENED THE DOOR and Mia swept past him in a stunning gown—one of the new evening dresses that had just arrived from Paris. Layers of diaphanous blue silk covered in a swirl of dragonflies. The embroidered silver fairies flitted their way up the bodice of the dress to a décolleté that was stunning. He had watched the curves of her breasts rise and fall throughout most of dinner this evening. Most distracting.

"The dress is lovely on you."

She smiled. "I think it might be my favorite, thus far. A Madame Mateau, here in London, is doing the few nips and tucks." She took her usual chair, while he poured them each a brandy. "The rest of the gowns should arrive by week's end."

He braced himself against the edge of his secretary and swirled two glasses of Armagnac, one in each hand. "Those pretty ball gowns won't get much wear in medical school."

Mia placed her hands in her lap, steepling her fingers. "Medical school in Boston or London?"

She perturbed him more than ever, now that he knew what it was like to lay with her. Her sensuous body, how wonderfully open and responsive she had been with her lovemaking—something he hadn't foreseen. Now that they were home, just being with her had become a torture. He wanted her morning, noon, and night. Just the way she sat in the wing chair, posture perfect, and yet there was an ease about her, the picture of elegance. His gaze flicked down her neckline to the delicate material that barely covered—nay, even hinted at—those rosy tips.

A surge of arousal raged through him as he considered clearing the top of his desk and tossing up her skirts. He resisted the urge to act like a randy schoolboy and caught himself before he slipped deeper into reverie. "It seems you are set on Boston, no matter what I advise."

She thrust her chin out. "Why do you want me to stay . . . so much?"

A very good question. If she was such a torture, why not encourage her to go? If only it were that simple. He returned her stare. "Why do you want to leave . . . so much?"

Mia growled a harrumph. "I believe you asked me here for another reason?" She met his gaze with an arched brow and an air of defiance. Good God. She had no idea how gorgeous she was when angered. Her rich brown eyes smoldered like dark embers, and the way she tilted her chin—as regal as a princess. He marveled at how often she left him close to breathless. The days they had spent together in Paris had been—*ne plus ultra*—the ultimate in romance, danger—and those sensuous, erotic nights. He drew in a breath.

Even before they left Paris for London, he began to pull away. He had acted shamelessly at the Contessa's soiree, baring her breasts, acting the debauched husband. Mia had borne it all with admirable flair, style, panache, confidence, dash, éclat—all of that and more. She had stunned him with her unabashed sensuality.

He leaned forward and passed her a brandy. "You have heard the term *auto-gratification* and understand its connotations?"

"It is the term the French use for sexual self-stimulation." He suspected she was not uncomfortable with the language as much as she was unhappy with what it implied.

"Mia, you need to work on this, especially if you're going to study in Boston. If you continue on—do your residency there you will spend years away from"—he stopped short of saying *me*—"you will be years away from home."

Her soft brown eyes grew wider. "You could come with me. You can do your research anywhere, America or London, what does it matter?"

"I also have commitments to Gaspar—to seeing that things are properly restored in both worlds. As you surmised earlier, there have been difficulties."

"What kind of difficulties?"

He sighed. "It's important we not change the subject. For now, I would like you to begin to touch yourself."

Mia nearly dribbled a sip of brandy. "Here, now?" She caught the drop of liquid with a finger and licked.

A trace of moisture on her bottom lip captured him momentarily. "Raise your skirt." His gaze eventually met hers.

She lifted layers of silk up long, shapely limbs—she wore pale stockings with delicate blue pinstripes. "Higher."

She uncovered pretty kneecaps and smooth thighs. He swallowed a gulp of brandy. The matching blue garters, with embroidered cornflowers, forced a quick adjustment to his trousers. "Place a limb over the arm of the chair and open your legs."

When she complied, there was a peek at her French pantalettes—the very brief ones with a saucy little bow closure at the slit. Exeter scratched the stubble along his jaw. Perhaps this wasn't such a good idea.

"Would you like me to untie the bow?" Holding her skirts up around her waist, she patiently awaited further instructions. Good God, what had he gotten himself into?

"Well, this is damned awkward." The very thing he had been trying to avoid—an erection was on near full display beneath his trousers.

Her gazed dropped to his rather prominent problem. "I see."

Exeter snorted softly and shook his head. "This exercise was supposed to be for you."

She dropped her skirts and stood up. "I shall retire to my room and undress. I will get into bed, pull the covers up to my chin—so there won't be any visual distraction. You will have another brandy, and then you come to my bedchamber and show me exactly what do with my hands."

She placed her open palm on his crotch and stroked. "If your hand is over the covers and mine is under—"

He grabbed hold mid-stroke and stopped her. "Let's give it a go."

She nearly collided with Mr. Tandi as she backed out the door. The dark-skinned servant held the door as Mia whisked past him. "Will you be needing anything else this evening, sir?"

"I don't believe so, we are both ready to retire." On the brink of dismissing his manservant, Exeter hesitated. "If you have a moment, Mr. Tandi? A few questions have popped up . . . about Mia."

Mr. Tandi closed the door and entered the room softly. Every gesture of this man was measured, gentle, every thought expressed, considerate. Exeter had never once heard Mr. Tandi raise his voice, though he had once taken a broom to an unruly scullery maid.

When Mia was very young, if she was badly behaved, a typical Mr. Tandi punishment consisted of a lengthy stint in the corner of the nursery, or the withholding of hot chocolate at teatime.

"Has Mia shared anything about her calling to medicine?"

"She will be an excellent healer. The Sky Father is pleased."

"It seems an American medical school has a slot open midyear. I know you're not keen on the country, but slavery is long past—by some twenty-five years. And the university is in Boston—duly civilized since the Tea Party."

Tandi clasped his hands behind his back, and many long strands of beads rustled from the movement. "It would be my honor to serve Miss Anatolia."

"Excellent. I worry about her.

"I have known Miss Anatolia since her birth. I gave the child her first bath, changed her wet nappies. I was there when she spoke her first word, took her first step. The month we were separated, I missed her as if she was my own child."

"You're saying . . ." Exeter switched his question mid sentence. "You never told me you were separated."

"Mia was taken to a hospital in Pretoria. She had contracted a fever. There were many small bites—insects, they said."

Exeter stared. "You say differently?"

"There is an old Zulu tale, one my people tell. About the evening panther—the black cat who is part human being. A creature with sharp, needle-like teeth, who travels in a dark mist. This being enters a hut during the night and shares his blood with another using a thousand bites."

Exeter fought to control his temper. "You might have said something earlier . . . Mia obviously survived."

Tandi's gaze was far away. "I stole away in the night, with a shaman's medicine. When I arrived at the hospital, Mrs. Chadwick was frantic. White doctors were of little use in the matter. The medicine I brought with me was potent—she could not hold it down, so we made a tea, and administered the brew over several days. On the fourth day, the child was better—in another week they sent us all home."

More than curious, Exeter pressed on. "Any arcane tribal wisdom you might share about her current condition?"

"A shaman might know more." His manservant met his gaze momentarily, as an equal. Tandi put his hands together in prayer. "What is done, is done."

"And we are far from the horn of Africa." Exeter frowned. This discussion felt like two men trying to sort through the care of a most cherished young woman, whom they both dearly loved. He found this new Mr. Tandi refreshing—as if the docile, reserved man was finally peeling off a few austere layers.

"Doubtful there would be anything in the library of secrets. Still, it's a lead of sorts, should we chance to run into a Zulu shaman." Exeter absently twisted a bottom lip. "Mia's beginning to fully integrate her cat side. She's making wonderful progress, but there is also another matter, and I'm dashed unhappy about it."

"You are unhappy, Om Asa, because you love her as a child." Tandi's piercing black eyes hardly blinked.

"Of course I love her." Exeter returned his stare. "Very much."

"And yet you would choose to let her go."

Tandi's flagrant impertinence was so unexpected, Exeter actually sputtered. He could not quite believe his ears. The amount of cheek from his manservant was unprecedented. "Why would you say such a thing?" Exeter protested.

"Because you do not face the truth in your heart."

Chapter Twenty-six

MIA SAT AT HER VANITY and peered at the young woman reflected in the mirror. Spending a few busy years in Boston might not be such a bad thing—in fact, it might be just the distance they both needed. She entertained a brief fantasy, and pictured a distraught Exeter, looking darkly handsome, as usual, and missing her terribly. More than he could have ever imagined.

Mia raised her chin, blinking rapidly. She would not cry—not again.

She tried to think of something cheerful—her newfound independence. The chance that she might have a new life in America. The picture in her mind quickly turned to a fledgling medical student alone in a strange country. Why, she didn't know a single solitary soul in Boston. A chill went through her, and then the longing for him returned. She had hungered for him before they were intimate, but not with this kind of intensity. At times it seemed as though she had yearned for him since . . .

Forever.

She had weighed her choices over and over these past weeks. If she stayed here in London, her life would be nothing short of a living torture. To live with a man she loved, who did not wish to be her husband or lover—but her guardian.

Mia shivered.

"Would you like a warmer dressing gown, Miss—the quilted

one perhaps?" The upstairs maid drew her from unhappy thoughts.

"I'm fine. Good night, Violet." The little maid padded out of the room. Absently, Mia heard the soft click as the door shut. She exhaled a sigh—more of a soft moan, wrenched from deep within her body. Dear God, how she would miss him.

Certainly, the young woman who returned her gaze in the mirror appeared older and wiser, or was that because she wanted to believe it so? Mia reached up to unpin her hair. "I would like to help you with that—if you would allow me."

She had thought the dark silhouette a mere shadow in the window. In the blink of an eye, he moved from her bedchamber to her dressing room. Mia stared at his reflection. "Good evening, Prospero."

"Mia." Their gaze met in the mirror. After every pin had been removed from her looped chignon, a mane of hair fell down her back, Gentle hands reached out and swept loose waves off her neck. Reverently, he bent and kissed her shoulder. "If I believed for a moment you could be mine, I would not hesitate to love you."

Her heart palpitated rapidly, not in the way it did for Exeter, but there was no denying the attraction. Something dark inside her—the cat in her, presumably—sparked to him. "How could you know?"

"I know only what I sense from your heart—" Prospero's breath drifted over her ear. "And your body. I have wanted you for some time now, Mia—to plunge deep inside you—feel those long legs wrapped around my waist."

Mia spun around and slapped his face. "Get out. Exeter will be here any minute."

The strangely handsome wizard stared—almost amused. Piercing silver black eyes squinted slightly as he evaluated her words. "He has not been in your bedchamber in weeks, why would he come tonight?"

She could feel him probe around in her thoughts, but he

could only go so deep. To know her innermost feelings, he would have to allow her into his mind, something he would never do.

Mia breathed a sigh of relief. She had left Exeter's study out of sorts and needlessly aroused. She had gone directly to her room, undressed, and waited for him to advise her on the finer points of pleasuring herself—not that she couldn't muddle her way through on her own—but if this was the only way to get him into her bedchamber it would have to do.

Whether he wished to admit it to himself or not, Exeter had become aroused in his study and was almost embarrassed by it. Frankly, that infuriated her more than anything. And now—here was Prospero, ready to make love to her. The wizard brushed his lips over the edge of her ear and nibbled.

Mia moistened her lips. She entertained a dangerous thought. According to her friend Phoebe, there were times when men needed to be jostled out of a stupor of indifference and taught a lesson.

Prospero met her gaze in the mirror. "As I said earlier, I would like to help you with that—if you would allow it." Mia wondered if she grasped his meaning—he understood her heartache and was willing help her.

"And what do you ask in return for such a favor?"

"You must convince Exeter to let me go free."

"But"—she looked him up and down—"you are here; you are free."

Prospero almost smiled. "A very persistent illusion."

She searched his face. So open and honest tonight. As though he had laid himself bare. "Why do they fear you so? What did you do to them that makes them so fearful of you?"

"It is not what I did to them. It is what they did to my people. They fear my retaliation."

"So you didn't create those Outremer dregs—Reapers, Grubbers . . . and the Skeezicks?"

"I had to survive. Oakley and his gang of corporate thugs sabotaged all my efforts to repair the unraveling. He even convinced Victor to blow up the aether plants. And now they have in their possession the temperamental Moonstone." He laced his gravely soft voice with an extra bit of irony. "It's almost amusing."

"Exeter mentioned problems." Her head whirled. She had not been privy to much information about these alternate-world moguls, apart from their great struggle for power.

Prospero suddenly swept her into his arms and carried her into the bedchamber. "He is coming."

He sat her on the bed and opened her dressing gown. She suffered an unexpected wave of modesty when he took a moment to admire her. "You've already seen me naked."

"Yes, I have." Prospero kissed her almost tenderly. "Forgive me, but I have to make this look good." He slapped her across the face and she cried out.

"Whatever happens, don't let the cat out," he whispered. "Trust me, please." He wrapped his fingers around her neck.

"Take your hands off her."

Mia glimpsed Exeter's tall silhouette enter the room. When she began to choke, Prospero lifted her up and flung himself behind her. "I go free and the girl goes free."

Mia nodded, the fear in her eyes just as real as it looked. As this was no doubt part of this scheming wizard's plan, she needed to be convincing. "Please, Exeter—he has promised to let me go."

"Oh, he will let you go, all right." Exeter fired a ball of violet-blue force much more powerful than he had used against Prospero in Paris, but then his energy had been drastically depleted by the explosion and cave-in. This time Exeter's blast hit Prospero squarely in the chest and sent him flying across the room.

Mia tugged her wrap back on and hid behind the open door of the armoire. What seemed endless was probably over in less than half an hour. The two men traded salvos of potent energy back and forth until they were both exhausted. Once the aether dust settled, a glance about the room revealed the devastation.

Furniture broken, windows shattered, shards of glass strewn about the floor from the bank of French doors. Tentatively, she ventured out from behind the safety of the wardrobe.

The Outremer wizard was the first to speak. "Cover your feet, Mia."

Exeter frowned. "You do not have the privilege of saying protective things to her—not after you hit her."

Prospero smiled this time. "I had to get you mad—fighting mad, deplete your energy so that you would have nothing left to force me back. You may have fooled everyone around you for years, Doctor Exeter—but you are a wizard. As powerful as I have ever seen and twice as intelligent. That is why I'm hoping you'll hear me out."

"But—" Exeter looked as though he might lunge at the man. "You were about to rape her."

Mia slipped on satin slippers. "Pish-posh, I'm perfectly fine."

She looked them over carefully. Both men had suffered bruises and scrapes but otherwise appeared relatively unharmed. She had to do something before one of them hurt the other, badly. "Hear him out, Exeter." She opened her bedroom door, and was surprised to see it didn't fall off its hinges. Mia tightened her wrapper. "Come along, gentlemen, I would like a cup of sweet spicy tea—and you both could use a relaxer."

The Outremer wizard raised both hands in surrender.

Exeter's glared softened. "No more games," he warned.

They picked up his medical kit on the way to the kitchen. Prospero sat quietly while Exeter examined him. "You need not worry about me. This"—Prospero pinched the torn flesh on his forearm—"is my double—a virtual copy."

"Do you self-repair? Or will you need someone over there to attend to your wounds?"

"Someone is already taking care of me. They scrutinize my every move; for the past hour they've been observing the original equipment get flung around the cell I'm locked in. They've already sent a team over to find out what I'm up to. We'll only have a few minutes to talk." Exeter removed his shirt and Mia dabbed tincture and bandaged cuts without too many hisses and yelps.

Prospero talked fast, starting with the story of an ancient struggle between two powerful families—vying tribes of a sort—and then a devastating loss of aether: enough to begin the unraveling of their world. Someone had to be blamed—and since Prospero was in possession of the remaining aether, he was forced to defend it.

"The Moonstone has restored equilibrium because it is the right thing to do, but the stone will not bend to either side's will. Oakley is trying to find a way to coerce me, bring us into some kind of false accord—but he fools no one, particularly the stone. Ask Phaeton. If you don't trust me, I believe you will trust his instincts."

Exeter's jaw muscle twitched as it always did when he was vexed or undecided on a matter. "You are correct about one thing. I don't trust you." He tossed back his whiskey. "But I will look into your story."

Mr. Tandi descended into the pantry. "There are three gentlemen in the foyer, looking for a—" He turned to Prospero and bowed. "This man."

The wizard pushed off his stool. "Please stay. Have your tea and drink your whiskey." He nodded to the black-skinned manservant. "With your escort, Mr. Tandi."

The Outremer wizard started up the stairs and turned back. " 'As I foretold you, were all spirits, melted into air, into thin air—yea all which it inherit, shall dissolve. And like this insubstantial pageant fade' "—Prospero's gaze traveled from Exeter to Mia. " 'We are such stuff as dreams are made on . . .' "

Exeter poured himself another whiskey. "A shot of this might help us both get some sleep tonight."

"Pour me a glass, then." Mia set down her teacup. "You must be exhausted—that was quite the battle of wizard wills, *Doctor* Exeter."

"Don't give too much credence to Prospero's assertions—I

am just a practitioner of the manipulation of powerful elements. The superstitious call them dark arts and attach names like sorcerer or wizard to those who apply them." Exeter finished the last of his whiskey. "The quote from Shakespeare was apt—most of it is theater."

Mia shot him a wary glance. "Those cuts and bruises are no such illusion. You're just being modest—or evasive." Swallowing half a dram, she hiccupped.

"Come—let's find you a place to sleep." Exeter reached for her hand and intertwined fingers. As they neared his bedchamber, he turned to her. "You can't sleep in your room—you'll catch a chill—then a cold." He opened his bedroom door. "Sleep in here tonight."

A good amount of heat radiated from the hearth, and his bed had been turned down. She untied her dressing gown and slipped under the covers. He caught a glimpse of long limbs as she tucked herself between the sheets. The moment her head touched the pillow there was a sensuous exhale. Exeter removed his waistcoat and shirt.

She cracked an eye open. "Where will you sleep?"

"Here, beside you." He sat down on the edge of the bed, bare-chested. "Here, Mia—beside you. Do you mind?"

She lifted the covers. "Come to bed and let me show you how much I have missed you, for I am more than ready." She stretched like a sleepy cat and curled up in his arms.

"Wet, are we?" His voice was soft and deep.

"Sopping." She rubbed his ruff of stubble with the palm of her hand. "How long until dawn?"

He inched the covers below her breasts and nibbled. "A few hours."

She moaned as he tongued a nipple. "Then we must make the most of this night together."

Exeter gently pulled the sheet past her belly, and let his hand travel farther, sliding down into her labia. He massaged gently, the kind of circling only he knew how to administer. He understood her subtle signals, what kind of rubbing she wanted, the rhythms and pressure to apply to the secret places that made her shudder and moan.

"I wish to reach my paroxysm with you inside me. Can we try?" Mia pushed the covers off and opened her legs wide—enough for him to view her pink folds of glistening flesh. Thoroughly aroused, Exeter dipped between her legs and gently licked as she squirmed with pleasure. Climbing over her, he held her arms at her sides while his tongue delved inside—in and out, laving broad strokes. He tickled her clitoris with his tongue and felt her shudder in response, as her sex grew swollen and her vagina flooded in readiness. Hovering above her for just a moment, he enjoyed the look of pure desire in her gaze. Firmly, he pushed inside the wet, warm sex of her, slippery with excitement.

"Slowly." She whispered.

This was only her third time. "Is it painful? I can stop if you wish." His voice was husky with desire.

"Don't stop. I want you to love me so that I will remember it for days and days," she ordered softly. She wrapped her legs up around his body and moaned; her breathing became harsh and rapid. With firm, deliberate strokes, he concentrated on her pleasure while building his own fervor a little at a time.

Exeter pushed his knees between her legs and without missing a single thrust, his hands reached under the small of her back and lifted her upright onto the tops of his thighs. Leaning back on his haunches, he impaled her on his penis and showed her how to rock her hips. He took a mouthful of breast and let their pleasure build to the next level.

"Good God, Mia." He kept it slow, and with each withdrawal, he pulled out enough to rub her swollen nub with the tip of his cock. He pressed his fingers into the flesh of her buttocks and brought himself deeper inside. His thrusts became rapid and violent as her trembling grew stronger until she responded with her blissful cry and shudder of release. "Oh . . . Asa." All she had to do was whisper his birth name, and his seed exploded into the depths of her body.

Exeter did not speak as he gasped for breath and chastised himself. He had become so highly aroused that he had not curtailed his behavior. He held her, clung to her, for he feared he had hurt her. She was not ready, yet, for such rough sex. Finally he managed an apology. "I'm so sorry. Are you well enough, Mia?"

"You must not treat me as though I am a piece of Royal Doulton china—brittle and easily broken," she chided.

He swept a few locks of hair over her shoulders and held her face in the palms of his hands. "No, you are brave and strong, and might I say so very delicious?"

"I came to pleasure with you inside me." Her chest rose and fell in soft slow intervals. Her nipples were relaxed, opalescent rose in color, and her skin glistened with the sheen of *lumière de l'amour.* He sometimes felt like he could drown himself in her body. He lifted a finger to the tip of her breast and watched it ruche in response to his circling.

There had been a kind of savage intimacy to their mating that felt as if their very souls had participated in a deep and profound intercourse. As it was, this night was to last in both their memories for a very long time, perhaps forever.

Epilogue

Pier 10, Southampton

MIA SWAYED as the hansom made a sharp turn onto the quay. Finally. She was to be away from England—and Exeter. She'd left London by train yesterday, accompanied by Mr. Tandi and a mountain of luggage. Their train had arrived in Southampton in time for a late supper. She hadn't slept particularly well; in fact, she'd tossed and turned most of the night. Troubling dreams had plagued her—Exeter chasing her through misty passageways. A hint of warm breath on her neck as she hid in the dark. Fear shuddered through her body as she turned to find Prospero standing behind her wearing that enigmatic half smile.

Twice she had been jolted awake, gasping for air, icy cold and trembling.

Shortly after breakfast, Mr. Tandi had informed her of a delay in departure. She'd spent most of the day pacing in her room. Finally, by late afternoon, word came the *SS Teutonic* was ready to board guests.

She'd left a rather hasty note for Exeter, who had attended a lecture at the Royal Society of Medicine and was expected to dine out with a colleague. It was better this way. No awkward good-byes, and no tears. Mia dipped her head for a better look at the sleek ocean liner. The cross-Atlantic voyage would take four days. They would arrive in New York, where she would have a brief visit, and then it was on to Boston, to start her new life.

She and Exeter had worked out an arrangement of sorts. He would visit during winter break and she would return home in summer. He assured her that medical school was an all-consuming experience and time would pass quickly.

The hansom stopped behind a long line of cabs and carriages, passengers alighting from all of them. The pier was a scene of mass confusion—a veritable uproar of passengers and baggage handlers all attempting to board ship at once. Stepping down from the cab, she paid the driver and began her search for Mr. Tandi, who had left the hotel well ahead of departure time with their luggage. Mia craned her neck looking for a tall, African man dressed in white. She wandered through a maze of trunks and suitcases being checked with porters.

There, just ahead—a tall man dressed in . . . Mia skirted a baggage trolley for a more advantageous view. The gentleman wore a top hat and traveling coat, certainly not Mr. Tandi. But there was something familiar about . . . he turned abruptly, and Mia gasped.

Exeter? On the pier in Southampton. Standing beside a pile of luggage and instrument cases. He spied her almost immediately and smiled from ear to ear—the rare grin that caused a dimple with a deep crease. The one that made her heart flutter.

Mia approached him slowly. "So, you missed me."

Exeter tilted his head slightly. "Did you know in French you don't really say, 'I miss you.' *Tu me manques* means, quite literally, 'you are missing from me.' "

She nodded. "'Tis how it feels."

He pulled her into his arms and kissed her in public. In front of all the passengers crowding the terminal and boarding the ship. And this was not a chaste public kiss—if there ever could be such a thing. This was a bedroom kiss, and she was flushed and breathless when he finished. "You are missing from me," he whispered.

Mia took a closer look at the stack of luggage and instrument cases surrounding them. "Does this mean you have changed your mind about living in Boston?"

"Rather apparent, I'd say."

"And what of your work in the Outremer?" she queried, arching a brow.

"Tim Noggy assures me there will soon be a portal in Boston proper." He continued to hold her close. "Mia, would you consider marrying me, on board ship, in approximately"—Exeter slipped his pocket watch from his waistcoat—"four hours' time?"

She stared, slightly openmouthed. "I had quite given up hope on this matter, Doctor Exeter. But it seems you have finally succeeded in collaring me."

His eyes crinkled, but he kept his tone solicitous. "I may have captured you, but I will spend my lifetime trying to tame you."

A tug on his lapels brought him close enough to kiss. "There are certain attributes we wish to remain animal and passionate—do we not?"

Turn the page for a special excerpt . . .

Chapter One

4 FEBRUARY 1889
SCOTLAND YARD, SECRET BRANCH
MEMORANDUM TO: E. CHILLCOTT
FROM: Z. FARRELL
RE: AGENT REASSIGNMENT

Believe I have located Phaeton Black. Appears to have let a flat below Madam Parker's brothel. Though the suggestion will undoubtedly cause you pain, I must continue to recommend Phaeton as the best man for this unusual case.

"OH, PLEASE NO, MADAM, HE IS A BEAST," THE HARLOT WAILED. "I beg of you, Mrs. Parker, do not send me down to Mr. Black."

Phaeton Black turned his back on the hubbub and paced the length of corridor between the foyer and staircase. A sultry sway of hip caught his eye. A luscious copper-colored wench descended the stairs. Her dark eyes lusty, curious, she ventured closer. "Fancy adding another dollymop, sir?"

Slouched against the stair rail, he swept a lazy gaze over her every curve. "Yes, why not? The more the merrier." He ducked his head around the corner and caught a glimpse of the bickering females in the salon. "We are waiting, my timid little sparrow."

The pretty whore beside him tilted an ear toward the clamor and quirked a brow. "Lucy?"

The din from the parlor hardly dampened his grin. "I believe so."

Right on cue, the reluctant whore let loose a shriek that pricked up the ears of every hound in the neighborhood. "I promise I'll work double the number of gents, just don't send me—"

"Hush, Lucy, before you have all the customers in an uproar." Esmeralda Parker stood just inside the parlor, arms crossed under an ample chest.

His stare trailed the baroque details of velvet flock-work wallpaper. "Does my reputation precede me?"

"Oh yes, something the size of an elephant's trunk, sir." The cocotte flashed a flirty smile.

He foraged back in his mind through a blur of absinthe and opium. "How long has it been since I rented the flat below stairs?"

"Near a week, Mr. Black."

He sighed. "I toss up a few petticoats, just to try out the wares, and already I am obliged to face down frightfully depraved and exaggerated rumors."

"Not a bad thing if you ask me, sir. Pay no mind to Lucy. She's a nervous little goose—believes everything she hears. Hasn't yet figured out a girl can pretty much work any size in, as long as she has a bit o' sloppy down there."

He dropped his head back against the wall, angling his gaze at the bronze beauty. He patted his leg. "Come closer."

She pressed against him and rubbed.

"Lovely."

The whining and whimpering from the parlor continued unabated.

"And your name is?"

"Mason, sir."

"What kind of a name is—?"

"Mason." She sucked in a breath and pushed her breasts up and out at him.

Mentally, he undressed her voluptuous curves. Cheeky toffer, this one.

"Named after me da, who was a stonemason by trade—all I

know of him." Her deep, coffee-colored eyes brightened. "Mrs. Parker calls me Layla."

"Ah, the ancient Persian tale, Layla and Majnun." The wanton strumpet brushed back and forth across his lower anatomy. "And do you promise to drive me mad, Layla?"

The parlor door rolled open and Madam Parker swept down the hall, dragging the miserable little tart behind her. He noted the vitality in Esmeralda Parker's determined stride; she was a fine-looking middle-aged woman. Truly a shame she had retired early to run one of the more reputable bawdy houses in town.

Things grew wonderfully cozy as two more women crowded onto the stairs. He inhaled the myriad scents of the female flesh surrounding him. "Esmeralda. Care to join?"

"Phaeton, be a dear and assure Lucy you will be reasonable with her."

Blinking back tears, the pretty whore shrank behind Madam's skirts.

He considered her again. Round bosom, tiny waist, lovely hips. Yes, there were very good reasons why he had selected her. "Lucy, might I assure you I am a man of . . . tolerable size, bone-hard?" He tucked a finger under her chin and tilted upward. "Though I am not entirely safe to play with, at the moment I am far from dangerous. In fact, it may take the two of you to flog me into a state of excitement."

Esmeralda snorted. "I imagine that will be quick work, ladies."

He held his hand out until Lucy placed a trembling, clammy palm in his. He frowned. "This one has been on the job how long?"

"She has a crippled brother and rummy father. Teach her well, Phaeton—she is their only means of support." Esmeralda stuck him with a fierce look before she turned to climb the stairs.

The sway of Mrs. Parker's bustle captivated him. He had attempted several times to lure her into his bed. So far, to no avail. With each refusal she became more attractive.

He cocked his head. "Any house credits for the instruction?" A faint echo of laughter and the muffled rumble of a door rolling shut answered the question.

Two delectable lovelies stood before him.

"Are you done crying and being afraid, Lucy?" In the darkened stairwell, he could just make out a nervous nod. A terrified doxy just wouldn't do.

"Suppose I make you a bargain. If, at any time during the frolicking and frivolity, you decide things have gotten a bit—"

"Whopping?" The copper-colored vixen offered.

He dipped his chin. "Do try to be helpful, Layla." He closed his eyes and inhaled a deep breath. "Now, where was I?" A hooded gaze shifted from one comely wench to the other. "If our interchange gets a bit too impassioned, shall we say? You may call a break in play. Exactly like a game of rugby—not entirely an unlike activity. What do you say, Lucy?"

"Very kind of you, Mr. Black."

"You're sure?"

Her eyes shone with relief. "Yes, sir."

He leaned closer. "Prove it with a kiss." He touched his mouth. "Here."

Tentative, soft lips pressed to his and shyly pulled back. "Charming." He pulled Layla close for a taste. Ah yes, sensuous lips with a bit of tongue. "Delightful."

"I believe this might turn out to be satisfying." Hands pressed to his lower back, he stretched. "Well then, shall we visit my den of iniquity? After you, ladies."

Descending into his flat, he opened the stove and poked at a few coals. The act of love should be something reasonably well-enjoyed by all participants. Even for ladies who made a living on their back. Phaeton bristled at the thought of Lucy's inexperience and terror. Well, he would make it a point to show her some pleasure. Pleasant enough duty.

"Madeira, or perhaps something stronger?" He perused several pantry shelves, upper and lower, and shuffled several packages and bottles about.

He passed through a cold spot and shivered. A low, unearthly vibrating snarl drifted up from below. The ghastly creature's purr was familiar enough. Phaeton took a peek at the girls. Predictably oblivious to his otherworld intruder. A shadow of movement swept past the corner of his eye. The end of a leathery scaled tail slithered around a cabinet opening. Phaeton stomped hard but missed. The fey creature disappeared into the blackness of the cupboard.

"Damned little demon."

"Rats, sir? Mrs. Parker set traps out just last week." Keen-eyed Layla dipped to get a look. He suspected she didn't miss much.

Phaeton kicked the lower door shut. "Harmless as a dormouse. Nothing to fear, ladies."

He decided to pour something stiff. A brief inspection of the young women had him imagining two sweet derrieres. "To a most favored position." He lifted his glass with a wink. "Bottoms up."

At the moment, his informal sitting room featured a single overstuffed club chair and a comfortable old chaise longue. Phaeton flopped onto the divan and reclined against a curvy pillowed end. He opened his arms wide. "I invite you to loose the dragon."

Reluctant Lucy made him grin, for she now eagerly climbed onto his lap. "Ah ah ah." He wagged a finger. "This teasing prelude has a caveat. For every button of mine undone, you must remove one article of clothing apiece."

He studied his evening's leisure through half-closed eyes. A man could be infinitely happy, at least for an hour or two, with a beauty settled on each knee. And the diversion was sorely needed. Purge the jabberwocky from his head and calm the racing thoughts that threatened to drive him round the bend. After a few hours of vigorous love play, he fancied himself dead to the world, thoroughly spent, snoring between two naked lovelies.

An ephemeral breeze bristled the hair on the back of his

neck. The subtle shift in air pressure signaled yet another presence. A shadow drifted overhead and the stairs creaked. Just above, in the darkness, something moved. His gaze shifted away from nubile flesh spilling out of unhooked corsets and untied petticoats. "Why, I believe we have a visitor, ladies. Care to join? One for each, I don't mind sharing."

The tall, dark-haired man on the landing frowned and continued his descent.

"Such unfortunate timing." Phaeton nuzzled a supple neck and groaned. "And I so dislike postponing pleasure."

He shifted both doxies off his lap. "I promise you will each have a turn on top of me." An exposed fanny invited a gentle smack. "Off you go."

The pretty trollops gathered a few undergarments and paused for a brazen inspection of the intruder before vanishing upstairs in a clamor of footsteps and twittering.

"Well, well. Scotland Yard's most celebrated agent, Zander Farrell, come calling." Phaeton buttoned his pants and settled back with a grin. "Something desperate has happened to bring you here, below stairs."

"I admit it took a bit of ferreting about." Zander ducked under a sagging floor joist. "You've made quite a comfortable nest for yourself down here." He lifted an aquiline nose and sniffed the air. "A bit moldy in winter, perhaps."

"Due to my recent loss of employment, I have found it necessary, indeed prudent, to conserve resources."

Never one for small talk, which Phaeton greatly appreciated, Zander got straight to it. "We appear to have another monstrous character about on a killing spree. Chilcott wants the case solved before the bloody press clobbers us. He'll not have another debacle like the Ripper."

"I can assure you Jack is gone. I took a stroll through Whitechapel just yesterday. Not a trace of the fiend's miasma."

Zander glared. "Exactly the kind of green fairy talk that got your contract canceled."

"Chilcott doesn't like me. Never has." Phaeton noted the barely perceptible clench in the man's jaw. Zander seemed strangely unnerved, a rare state of being for him. "Something's got you rattled. What is it?"

"There is some kind of beast or—vampire stalking the Strand."

Phaeton never laughed, a self-imposed rule that had remained unbroken for years. Otherwise, he would have been rolling all over the cold stone floor of his new flat at that very moment.

So he simply grinned. "Perhaps an actor costumed as *Varney the Vampire*? Or an Empusa. Might I look forward to a seduction by a bewitching female bloodsucker?"

Zander's glower gave way to a wide-eyed stare. "I thought you'd be pleased. You claim to believe in fairies and all that undead rubbish."

"My interest in the occult is not a matter of faith, actually." He rose off the couch and signaled Zander to follow. Rummaging through a set of pantry cabinets, he withdrew a bottle of liquor. "Nevertheless, I am honored and amused that Scotland Yard appears ready to consult the fey world."

He sensed darker undercurrents and listened momentarily to a fog of whispers. "The notion of an unearthly murderous evildoer is intriguing." He pulled out a chair. "Why don't you brief me while I *louche* us a glass?"

"Whiskey for me."

He swung back and raised a brow. "Certain about that? A bit of absinthe might help the investigation right about now."

Zander exhaled a bit too loudly. "As you wish, Mr. Black."

Phaeton set up two glasses and poured the dark green distillate. He angled slotted silver spoons etched with the likeness of a naked flying nymph across the rim of each vessel, and placed a lump of sugar on top.

The number-two Yard man leaned back in his chair. "Quite an elaborate ritual."

"Hmm, yes. I suppose it falls somewhere between a witches' Sabbath and the Eucharist." He retrieved a pitcher of iced water from a makeshift cold closet. "Just as the water looses the spirit of absinthe, so does the absinthe free the mind."

As the chilled liquid dripped slowly over the sugar cube, Zander's glass changed from deep emerald to a delicate, cloudy swirl of pale green elixir. "Ah, the transformation, when essential oils bloom and the fairy is released. To quote Rimbaud—"

"A meandering, scatological French poet." Zander huffed.

Undaunted, Phaeton poured a last splash over nearly dissolved sugar. "As I was saying: 'the poet's pain is soothed by a liquid jewel held in the sacred chalice, sanity surrendered, the soul spirals toward the murky depths, wherein lies the beautiful madness—absinthe.' "

He settled down and lifted his glass. "I know what they say about me at the Yard. Eccentric, when they're feeling charitable, a menace or madman otherwise."

"That's not true. Gabe Sterling thinks the world of you."

"Then you and he are the only ones."

"Not me, just Gabe." Zander sipped a taste before taking a swallow. "Frankly, I can't say enough about a man who can step into a crisis situation and disarm a Fenian bomb without a care. I don't know where that kind of courage comes from, Phaeton, and neither do a lot of other agents who would rather call you mad than try to understand a man who invites death and fears nothing."

Phaeton shrugged. More pale green potion slipped down his throat. "I miss those small hours of the morning. You know as well as I do, from all our evenings on surveillance, the coldest chill of night happens at the edge of dawn." His hazy gaze landed on Zander. "The time when shadows are not deep enough for spirits and abominations to hide in."

Zander leaned forward. "I need you back on the job. Murdering hobgoblin, vampire—whatever or whoever the killer turns out to be. Take the assignment, Phaeton. But don't do it to prove the other agents wrong."

Taken aback, Phaeton blinked. "Why not?"

"Because they're right."

"Bloody, thieving pirate."

America Jones's gaze fixed on Yanky Willem's every movement as he moved across the polished wood floor of the shipping office. The vile ship snatcher paused between secretary desks and curled back an upper lip.

Up until this night, she had merely been an annoyance to him. A pestering fly he could easily wave aside. But his nonchalance had served only to embolden her purpose. She had picked the door lock, and he had caught her, dead to rights, searching for proof of treachery. Now, quite suddenly, her circumstances had grown perilous. Eyes darting, she calculated the position of Willem's other lackeys stationed around the workplace. His men had not bound her as of yet. No doubt they thought her a helpless, frightened twat. Thickheaded cock-ups.

"Miss Jones." The Dutchman exhaled smoke as thick as his accent. His breath reeked of the black cigar clenched between his teeth. "Words cannot express how pleased I am to have you in my company this evening."

The captain's gaze traveled over every inch of her. "And my great-great-grandfather was a pirate, Miss Jones, but not I."

One day she'd wipe that smug grin off his face. Forever.

"I was obliged to take over your father's shipping business because he failed to make good on our loan arrangement."

She bit out a single word. "Liar." Quick as a strike from a snake, his hand lashed across her face. The blow jerked her head back, flooding her cheeks with heat. She licked dry lips and tasted blood at the corner of her mouth. Heart pounding, she blinked aside tears and retreated.

By the look in his eyes and the bulge in his pants, he would have her flat on her back soon enough. Then he would hand her off to his crew.

"I wager you'd all like a taste." She lifted her skirt and lace petticoats above the knee and made eyes at every surly mate.

Her sashay about the room revealed more and more leg. When she reached the tops of her stockings, their mouths dropped open.

Seductively, she slipped her hands between her thighs. Eyes wide with feigned surprise, she looked down, then up again with a wink. "Silly me."

In one swift motion, she loosed a derringer from one garter and a bowie knife from the other. Falling back toward the door, she brandished both weapons.

"If you value y'er jewels, I wouldn't make a move."

Chapter Two

"HOLD ON, MR. BLACK." The pretty harlot quickened her steps to match his longer strides. Phaeton grabbed her by the hand and wove a path between the fancy carriages and cabs queued along the Strand. Traffic would shortly become a mangle, as theatres began to let out. A frosty wind blew across the broad avenue, forcing them both to squint and hold onto their hats.

"Come along, Lizzie."

He quite enjoyed Miss Randall, whether she was on the job for Mrs. Parker or retained as a night crawler. He often used her for reconnaissance, a spotter who ably worked the streets or public houses.

At the corner of Savoy Row, he parked the tempting doxy by a lamppost. "Right here, love." A fine dusting of snow covered the cobblestone. Not enough to turn the ground white, but just enough to reveal a curious impression of footprints leading off down the row.

He directed his gaze after a diaphanous, almost imperceptible, flurry of snow. "I mean to follow a trace of vapor down the alley. I shan't be far off."

"A trace of vapor?"

He paused to think about his answer. "Do you believe in ghosts, Lizzie?

The girl scoffed. "No, sir."

"Phantasms with fangs who can pierce a vein and drain your body of vital fluids in mere moments?"

Eyes wider. "No, sir."

Phaeton leaned close and brushed her neck with his lips. "You will."

She shivered. "No need to frighten a girl, Mr. Black."

"I need you to keep a lookout. Act like a street whore—not terribly difficult. If any gents or goblins get too frisky, you scream bloody murder."

He swept a stray curl off her robust, pink cheek. "Lizzie dear, have I ever ventured into your lovely slit?"

She snorted. "A girl doesn't forget a poke like that, sir."

"Did I pleasure you?"

She batted dark lashes. "Yes, sir."

"I am so pleased to hear it." He tipped his hat and walked into the deeper shadows of the narrow lane.

The trail of impressions appeared cleanly made. Small feet, with steps placed far apart, as if whomever or whatever barely needed to touch ground. He followed the tracks down a curve in the row until the imprints grew so faint, they became all but invisible. He inhaled deeply. Snow and soot and something else, faintly . . . metallic. Again, Phaeton sniffed the air as he scanned the rooftops and lane ahead.

Aware of the faintest shift in atmosphere, he focused his search once more on the bricks below his feet. A tear-shaped drop fell onto the pavers.

Red. Warm. Ice crystals surrounding the drop melted.

There, another drop.

He looked up, but could make nothing out. A sudden spray of crimson drops scattered across the snow as a gust of wind blew off the Thames. A hiss of fine ice swirled into the air and traveled up past shop windows. A ghastly misshapen figure settled onto a window ledge close to the roof.

Phaeton froze. A large, birdlike entity formed out of ice crystals and gray speckled flakes, or were those feathers? Long, spindly legs, tucked against each side of a thin torso. As the creature struggled to gain its balance, a bloody appendage slipped off the window ledge. Pearlescent feathers ruffled as the rare bird retracted the crooked, gangly limb. A protective wing folded over the injury.

So, the owlish harpy appeared to suffer.

He stared hard at the apparition. Would the wraithlike specter ever fully materialize? The pale visage continued to reshape itself until it resolved into something more human than avifauna.

"Ah, there you are." He inched forward, mesmerized. "My high-strung, feathered"—the facial features were feminine, fragile; an enchanting, chimerical bird—"beauty."

The humanlike face swiveled and blinked. *Why do you not fear me?* The voice whispered in his head.

"You might try being more bloodcurdling. Bone-chilling. Hair-raising, perhaps?"

Another ruffle of ashen feathers. *Male, what is your name?*

"Phaeton Black." A wicked smile encouraged him to press forward for a closer look.

I do not like. The white bird hissed and drew away. Phaeton tilted his head to align his sights with her yellow-eyed stare. There, on the rooftop, the dark silhouette of a man gazed down on them.

He had to ask. "Friend of yours?"

A blast of air and cyclone of snow enveloped the harpy. A billow of white particles whirled off the ledge and vanished down the alleyway.

A chill shivered through his body. And a deep sorrow. Squinting through a tempest of frost, he swept the skyline for the stranger. Nothing.

Intrigued, he started after the small twister passing by several basement railings. He paused to stare at an odd finial post. The cast-iron head of a dog. Edging closer, he imagined the canine's upper lip curled back. How long had it been since his last glass of absinthe? Several hours ago with Zander. Any unearthly effects should have passed by now. He reached out his hand and the canine creature snapped.

"Ouch!" He put his finger to his mouth and sucked a very real scratch.

A faint tinkle of laughter. Crimson drops fell at his feet. Were they his? He guessed not. Wavering on the edge of hallucination, he traced bleeding drops of red over street pavers. Light snowfall dampened each footstep to a soft crunch. An icy stillness crept over the lane. Nothing but the sound of his inhale and exhale.

"Over here, lovey."

"Hav'a taste, handsome?"

A pair of street prostitutes stepped out of the shadows and beckoned to him.

"Evening, ladies." He noted a large dustbin just past the huddled women. Inexplicably drawn to the container, he reached for the lid and hesitated. A steady pulse of rapid heartbeats throbbed in his ears.

Lifting the cover, he examined ordinary contents. "Rags."

With a glance around the alley and a wink at one of the working girls, he edged closer. A rat leapt out of the pile of refuse. He dropped the lid, and it clattered to the ground. "Bloody hell."

Wait. Phaeton pivoted.

A presence lurked in the velvet black darkness of a niche between buildings. He leaned into the unknown. The cold steel of a large blade pressed against his neck.

"Do as I say, *mon ami*, and I won't cut your throat."

A feminine voice, with an accent. He swallowed. "I make it a point never to argue with a female wielding a knife." In the blackness, he could just make out luscious plump lips and almond-shaped eyes. Human. What a relief. And a good deal prettier than his recent encounters.

"Back me up—against the wall." She pressed the blade edge deeper into his flesh. A trickle of blood ran under his collar.

"Careful." Adhering faithfully to her instructions, he pressed her to the bricks.

"Any moment now, a number of pirates are going to round this corner. They wish to do me harm. I want you to convince them you are near to completing your satisfaction with a street doxy."

He grinned. He couldn't help it. "Allow me to do my best."

A clamor of hurried footsteps echoed off the row buildings. Racking up her skirt, he inserted a hand between her legs. "Hook a leg around me."

When she complied, he placed both hands under her buttocks and angled her against the wall.

"Oh my!" She cried. "What is that?"

Phaeton paused. "My cock, miss. What were you expecting?"

"But—" She gasped.

A few harried shouts came from several yards away. Quickly, he brought himself under her and worked her down onto his prick. He began his thrusts slowly. Not too deep, as yet, until he knew her body would receive him. "Make much ado, as if you are a pretty whore well paid for a quick tumble."

Buttons loosed, he nuzzled a firm, round breast and tasted salty sweat. He suckled a taut morsel of nipple through thin fabric and bit down. "Ahhh." She gasped. A flood of moisture drew him deeper.

"That's a girl. Louder. Tell me you want more." He drove in. "Do it."

Her words seethed between her teeth. "I will kill you for this."

"Must I remind you"—he gasped—"your blade remains at my throat." Gently, he began to withdraw from her. "In or out, love? Make up your mind."

A low mewl from this luscious alley cat accompanied a bold thrust of hips. Her cries were layered with mockery. "Oh yes, more of that—big man."

"I'll take that as a yes." This woman's sheath girdled him like some kind of heaven. "I have yet to play deep, miss. How much of me do you want?" His arousal was huge and satisfaction precipitous. He pumped into her, closing in on his own finish. "This is going to be fast."

"Deeper, lovey." She cried, urging him onward. Phaeton could just make out the shapes of several men. Her pursuers paused to listen to their heated sighs and muffled groans.

"Yes, oh yes—give it to me." Warm flesh quivered as her words gave way to lusty exhales.

"Happy to oblige." As he growled his lust like some kind of wild beast, his fingers pressed into the flesh of her buttocks.

Heavier footsteps this time and the harsh, exhausted breath of hunters in pursuit of runaway prey. The men circled closer, near enough to make out her features or wardrobe.

"Bugger off." Phaeton barked over his shoulder. "Get your own doxy, mate." Inarticulate grunts accompanied his intensified thrusts as her pursuers changed course and ran off toward the Embankment.

Arousal heightened by their public exhibitionism, the little minx moaned a fiery incantation. "Jesufina, Marianna, Josephina."

He was close. On the very edge of climax. He opened his eyes to view the beauty who had captured him. Her eyelids fluttered. Momentarily, she was incapacitated.

A fierce wave of pleasure slammed through his body. Phaeton let loose.

His prick throbbed inside her. A long moment passed before he remembered the blade. In one swift move, he grabbed the knife and twisted it out of her hands.

Those slightly exotic, almond-shaped eyes narrowed. "Get off me."

One last glimpse up and down the alley. "Very well." He kept her pressed to the wall and slipped out. "Lovely, unexpected diversion."

Pants buttoned, he looked up in time to avoid the blow of her fist. The ferocity of her swing caused a temporary loss of balance and the lady tumbled into an iron basement railing.

Phaeton leaned over. "Blimey, she's knocked out cold."

He had little choice but to pick her up and throw her over his shoulder. The pirates might double back this way. Pirates? Was she daft, or was he? More likely she was some kind of common street thief. He retraced his steps out of the row and onto the busy thoroughfare of the Strand. Lizzie, dear girl, stood under the street lamp right where he had left her.

Quickly, he settled both women into a waiting carriage. The coach lurched off, rocking Lizzie back and forth. She tilted her head and studied the young lady. "Who is she?"

"A mystery." Gaslight briefly lit the interior of the cabin. Enough for him to note his little cohort's sallow cheeks and red-rimmed eyes. "Lizzie, anything unusual to report this evening? Perhaps a flying phantasm or two?"

"Nothing much, sir." She hesitated.

Phaeton removed her gloves and chafed icy hands between his. "Tell me, Lizzie."

"Well, sir, a very beautiful woman approached me. Pale she was and stood real close, wanting a bit of warmth." Lizzie pulled at the collar of her dress and began a raspy struggle for air. "I don't remember much after—"

He pulled her onto his lap. Gently, he brushed back loose curls to expose a lissome neck and two perfectly dainty puncture wounds.

A dull ache of drums nagged at the back of her head. She moved to stretch and found her wrists tied to the arms of an oversized upholstered chair. Her pulse throbbed under the bindings. Assessing her circumstances, she closed her eyes and feigned a long awakening.

"Good morning, my dove."

She sensed the unmistakable power of his essence. He was a channeler. A mortal being haunted by demons, or enchanted by fairies. Hard to say which, perhaps both. Genteel society would likely call him a wretched man afflicted by a mental disorder. Wretched? Possibly. But a rare gent he was, and no doubt gifted in peculiar ways.

Aware of a bubbling teakettle and the familiar clink of china cups set on saucers, she opened an eye to observe the dark-haired man from last evening. The man who had thrust into her woman parts. Deep inside, she could still feel the effects of his churlish prick.

The shadowed niche of the alley had afforded scant illumination. This morning she revised her assessment of him. A bit swarthy, he hadn't shaved as yet and wore no cravat. His waistcoat remained unbuttoned, but she could see enough to know he was nicely made. Genuinely handsome, if a bit untamed.

His nose was strong and straight, but in profile appeared slightly beakish. His mouth was full and, yes, sensuous and kissable. Hair much too long to be fashionable, but there was something about the mode. Bohemian, perhaps? She examined his body as he moved around the stove. He was a nice size. Large enough but not imposing. And that rude shaft was plenty of male.

"If you are quite finished with your assessment of me, I would like to begin one of my own."

She closed her eye. Blood accelerated through every pathway in her body.

"You must know you have nothing to fear from me."

Still, a throb of alarm surged in her ears. She shifted her head and forced herself to open both eyes. He stood close by, scratching a raised brow.

"If I have nothing to fear, why have you made me your prisoner?"

"Ah, the ties." He tugged a side of his mouth upward. "For my own protection."

She strained against her bindings as he circled the chair. "While the Darjeeling steeps, why don't we revisit our precious moments together, last evening?"

He had a kind of unruffled, arrogant way about him. She squirmed in the chair. "I prefer an Oolong. Or a nice, smoky Lapsang Souchong."

His eyes crinkled, but his expression otherwise remained stoic. "You know your tea, Miss, but I shall not be diverted. Evening last, I was having a chase down Savoy Row after a pesky, flirty little phantasm when I was abducted by an equally trifling, yet forward olive-skinned maiden who put a dagger to my neck and proceeded to abuse me."

His gaze wandered between several undone buttons that exposed much of her flimsy chemise. "Care to explain?"

In the blink of an eye, she moved into a trance. Transporting herself back a few hours, she recalled a whisper of chimera and a tingle of demon. Her eyelashes dropped lower. "I sense unfathomable powers and yet almost unendurable exhaustion. Not death, but a weakness of spirit." She looked up into his eyes. "And great sadness."

He studied her. "You have abilities?

She nodded quickly and shook off the spell. "My mother had gifts. A Cajun witch, powerful, beautiful."

"A *Vauda*?"

She eyed him suspiciously before nodding. "You know the *sang mélangé français* ways?

"Your name, mademoiselle?"

"Why should I tell you my name? You hold me captive, sir. Why should I reveal anything to you?"

"Because I believe in civility." Caught in his own deceit, he shrugged. "Let's just say I prefer a name. If not possible before intercourse, after will do."

"I had no idea a man could get up a shag with a knife at his throat." Was that a smirk or a lopsided grin from him? "That wasn't a compliment," she growled.

"Honestly?" He tilted his head back. "Sounded like flattery."

"You raped me."

"You demanded it." He placed a hand on each chair arm and leaned forward. "Why didn't you cut me ear to ear?"

Her glare faltered. Why hadn't she killed him? The evidence of her knife was right in front of her. A fresh scar slashed across the side of his throat. If she had pressed harder, he would be dead.

She chose not to respond to his question because she didn't like the answer. How could she forget those intense waves of arousal? Pleasure that was both frightening and miraculous. She caught her bottom lip between her teeth.

His gaze lowered to rudely ogle her mouth. "Our first time was rushed, wouldn't you say?" Grazing the curve of her cheek, his lips brushed closer to her mouth.

Weakly, she parted her lips. "You took advantage of me, sir."

"I heard little protest." He held back, his words delivered as a soft caress. "Only oohs and aahs. Your hot, breathless words in my ear."

She curled the tip of her tongue over the edge of her upper lip. With his attention on her mouth, she furtively lifted a knee between them. "How could I complain with a band of filthy pirates after me?"

"Mmm, most taxing." His exhale buffeted softly over her cheek. "But, did you enjoy yourself, miss?"

"Yes." With one swift kick, she shoved him off.

He bellowed a hellish groan, as his hand flew to his crotch. Apparently she had clipped the jewels. Bent over, he walked off his agony by rubbing himself into impressive arousal.

"Happy now?" She braced for a beating. But none came.

Spurning the steeping teapot, he went straight for a bottle of whiskey and popped the cork. She gave him high marks for grog guzzling and pain tolerance.

He sputtered and coughed. "Delighted."

Phaeton and America's adventures continue in

The Moonstone and Miss Jones

Turn the page for a special excerpt . . .

Chapter One

FRANÇAIS TÉLÉGRAPHE AND CABLE
4 SEPTEMBER 1889 11:10 AM
DX MARSEILLES PHAETON BLACK
CPT AMERICA JONES
C/O CHERBOURG LE HAVRE CALAIS

SHANGHAIED IN SHANGHAI STOP MEET ME
BELOW STAIRS AT THE OLD FLAT

"I SWEAR I'LL SEE PHAETON BLACK HANG FROM A YARDARM." America Jones crushed the wire in her fist and tossed the message aside. The crumpled paper bounced along the bustling street of Le Havre in carefree ignorance of her angry heart.

Her boatswain, Ned McCafferty, flattened one side of his mouth into a thin line. She knew his grimace well. The very one he used to hide his amusement so as not to provoke her. "I wouldna' advise ye string up Mr. Black, Cap'ain Miss, not in y'er condition."

She sighed. "I suppose it defeats the purpose of chasing him halfway around the world. Perhaps I will torture him first." She'd do it, too, except the devilish man would have her strip down to camisole and pantalettes and swish a riding crop about.

America stepped off the curb and crossed Rue Dauphine. The harbor breeze stirred memories of Phaeton on a balmy Polynesian night. Bare-chested, a trickle of sweat ran down his torso. America caught her breath as a surge of arousal coursed through her body. "Drat!" He had entered her mind for a mere moment and rekindled her passion. And something else—an awful, unbearable yearning.

"First, I suggest ye catch him, lass." Ned purposely fell back and swept up the discarded telegram. He opened the crumpled paper and read aloud. "Shanghaied in Shanghai. Stop." His mumble followed on behind her as she turned the corner and set a brisk pace in the direction of the Port Authority. She tossed a glare over her shoulder. "I thank you kindly not to read my personal messages."

"Hold on there, Cap'ain. He might have been shanghaied—or worse."

She stopped in her tracks, brows knit together. "What are you saying, Ned?"

He removed his cap to scratch his head. "Stop and think now, Miss. Say your Mr. Black was kidnapped. Might of taken him a good while to get a message off ship."

"What if—might have? Just like a man to give Phaeton the benefit of the doubt." Hands on her hips, she leaned into Ned's face. "And he *might have* run off." America caught a lower lip under her teeth and chewed, a nervous habit that Phaeton often provoked, especially when she was cross. And she was thoroughly vexed at the moment.

Had Ned and Phaeton formed a bond during the voyage? She certainly hadn't noticed. But then why would she? She'd danced around the deck of the *Topaz* like a giddy young girl in love. Too deliriously happy, she supposed.

The wretched truth of it was she'd never been happier in her entire life. Not even when Papa was alive had she known such contentment and genuine affection from a man. While it lasted. America wound a circuitous path around dockworkers and drays. She missed him. These last weeks had been a misery without Phaeton by her side.

And in her bed.

America exhaled a deep sigh. Her eyes moistened and she

blinked hard, refusing to cry a single tear for the man. "I suppose we'll find out the truth soon enough."

For some weeks now she had sensed they were closing in on the rapscallion. Once aboard ship she'd give the order to make ready. They'd shove off under a full moon, have a skim across the channel, and up the Thames. The *Topaz* would make Port of London before morning—quick as you please.

Phaeton's wire had been held at the telegraph office for several days, but the cable had been sent from Marseilles. Might it be possible the *Topaz,* fast as she was, had nearly caught up with his ship? Her heart thumped erratically in her chest. She revisited his cryptic words. Shanghaied in Shanghai? It had been his first and only communication since his disappearance. What was she to make of such a message? Just like Phaeton to be clever in such a dire moment. In fact, the more life threatening the situation, the more amusing he often became.

Whether it be abandonment or abduction, she'd get to the bottom of his disappearance. She supposed she should be elated to know he was alive. To know she would once again be able to look into his devilish dark gaze. Eyes that bespoke a sharp mind and a lust for adventure.

As much as she was drawn to him, a fearful, nagging thought lingered. A worry that had never quite left her mind or her heart. Perhaps it wasn't possible to settle down with a man like Phaeton Black. Perhaps it might be better to move on and try to put him behind her. She swept a few unruly wisps of curl from her eyes and made her way down Pier 12.

Well, she had a great deal more than herself to think about now. She stepped around cargo nets and stacked barrels of stout. Up ahead, through a crisscross of masts and rigging, a blazing red sky framed the eye-catching merchant ship. America shaded her eyes from the low rays and inhaled a deep, cleansing breath. Even with sails furled, her sleek lines and proud stature made the *Topaz* the fairest ship in port. Ned hurried his pace and helped her onto the gangway. Single-file, they climbed the steep ramp.

Halfway up, she stopped and turned. "I caution you, Ned, not a word about my condition. 'Tis a secret between you and I. No one must know—especially Mr. Black."

Ned reached out to steady her. "If you say so, Cap'ain Miss."

She climbed the rest of the gangway stroking her barely swollen belly. "Forgive me, my little pea under the shell. Once we reach London, I fear you might well be fatherless."

"What can one say about you, Mr. Black? You are part devil and angel." The bold beauty stepped closer. Hair a honeyed shade of brown, a lovely aquiline nose, and eyes that sparkled like gemstones—green, he thought. No, blue.

No, green. The color of the seas off Crete.

Phaeton took another leisurely perusal of the young lady's wares. For the sparest of moments, he thought about warning off the intriguing girl. That was before his gaze lowered to her bosom. "I'd have to say largely devil."

Her pale hand swept over the buttons of his trousers. Brazen chit! Delicate fingers found what they searched for. "Largely, indeed." Her touch was light and fleeting, but the very notion that she dared such public foreplay cheered him greatly. Apparently, it also amused the naughty little vixen. Those astonishing aquamarine eyes traced the bulge in his pants. "Rumor has it you are made of wicked wood and when you play the seducer you are so very, very . . ."

A clearing of his throat ended in a grin. "Shocking?"

Her faraway glance about the room returned to him. "Sublime."

He quirked a brow, but otherwise kept his gaze steady. "Are we discussing length and breadth or technique?"

"Not sure." The wily minx tossed a wink over her shoulder and flounced away. "But I mean to find out." He watched the bob and sway of her bustle as she wove her retreat between chattering passengers.

They were nearing the dinner hour. The ship's salon swelled with first-class passengers swilling aperitifs. Phaeton drew in a breath and exhaled slowly. Miss Georgiana Ryder turned out to be a most charming ingénue with a saucy, hoyden-like quality about her. Quite irresistible, as were her siblings Velvet and Fleury, a delightful sisterly trio—each one as lovely as the next. He scanned the salon and found Velvet standing among a cluster of oglers. Her gleaming dark eyes and sultry pout beckoned without words. He met her gaze and lingered for a brief flirtation before he caught a blur of Fleury. The fey, dancing, wisp of a girl instantly distracted. Phaeton watched the youngest sibling flutter about the room, much like a hummingbird hovers and flits from daisy to delphinium.

"Are you enjoying the voyage, Mr. Black?"

"My return trip to London grows more diverting by the hour." Phaeton tore his eyes off the pretty chit and nodded a polite bow to the young lady's mother. "Mrs. Ryder." He feigned a pleasant expression. "Most especially since I have been fortunate enough to make acquaintance with you and your family."

If truth be told, he found the cloying mother barely tolerable and Mr. Ryder, the stout man slurping sherry in the corner, to be a degenerate troll who conducted himself as more of a procurer than a father anxious to see his daughters well spoken for. In point of fact, the entire family was odd. For one thing, they were inexplicably interested in him.

He had dressed early for dinner and entered the main salon in hopes of finding a tumbler of whiskey. The Ryder clan, which included the mister, missus, and assorted lovelies, had singled him out from a number of wealthy, titled gentlemen aboard the *RMS Empress of Asia*. He considered the obvious question—why?—and decided it could wait for later.

Yes, the voyage home was going to be interesting. The ocean journey that had once been tedious and despairing quite suddenly brimmed with intrigue. Phaeton nodded perfunctorily to the mother's ramblings, as the woman found it an unnecessary bother to pause or think between sentences.

He perused the room looking for his evening's distraction, Georgiana. The young lady's mother might indeed be a harpy in disguise and the father no better than a common pimp, but the eldest daughter? The bewitching dream of a young woman stood between two heavily whiskered gents whose eyes never left her astonishing assets.

Phaeton took another look for himself. There was nothing overly voluptuous or buxom about any part of her. It was just that all parts of her were so very . . . luscious. Aware of his attention, she turned and made eye contact across the crowded salon. Gazes locked, the little vixen opened her mouth ever so slightly. A pink tongue swept the underside of a peaked upper lip. The room, for a second, collapsed in size around them. The gesture caused a number of his vital organs to rush a surge of blood to his favorite extremity.

Phaeton tipped his glass for a last swallow.

A white-gloved steward entered the salon and rang a melodious set of chimes. The dinner bell. Another attendant, also liveried in a brass-buttoned jacket, opened a double set of doors. Georgiana turned to leave, but not in the direction of the dining room.

Peripherally, his gaze took in the delicate laces and bright colored silks of the fashionably attired as they drifted into supper. He dipped a nod, here and there, as the beau monde passed in a blur. A few oddly familiar faces, but for the life of him, he could not place the familiar spirits. He set his empty glass on a silver tray and wound his way through the room, in the opposite direction of sustenance. This evening his appetites lay elsewhere.

Phaeton stepped through the hatch onto the promenade deck. The night was clear and warm with a bit of moisture in the air. A sparkling carpet of stars swept across the sky overhead. He strolled toward the front of the ship and thought about a cigar, then thought better of it.

He found her standing near the starboard bow. He could have pressed close, but instead, kept some distance between them. She turned and struck a sultry pose with her back to the rail.

They were alone. He did not know how he knew this, for

he made no inspection of the deck. And frankly he did not care. Her gown rippled with the breeze. "Lift your skirt."

She tilted her head and rolled her eyes in the prettiest fashion. Not a refusal, but more of a flirtation. Her hand caressed a curve of hip and lifted her skirt enough to expose a dainty turn of ankle. His arousal was prodigious, yet he continued to trifle with her. He used two fingers to gesture upward.

Inch by inch, her skirt and petticoats rose. A delightful show of calf. A pretty knee. A silk-flowered garter. And above the top of her hose, a hint of peach-colored flesh.

With the slightest measure of control left, Phaeton closed the distance between them. He pressed her against the ship's rail. Not too hard. Certainly not as hard as his burgeoning need. "Georgiana?"

"Mr. Black?" Droplets of perspiration, like tiny diamonds, sparkled across her nose and cheeks.

"Please, call me Phaeton." He kissed the bridge of her nose and tasted salt—and a whiff of something spicy. The stubble of his beard brushed her cheekbone as he worked his way toward an earlobe. He reached under her gathered skirt and felt her body shudder. "Kiss me, Phaeton."

He lowered his gaze to her mouth. "And if I kiss you, what is my reward?"

He enjoyed the playful squint in her eyes and saucy turn to her chin almost more than her words. "As if a kiss is not reward enough? What do you desire?"

He slipped his hands under her bustle and rubbed gently, as softly as a balmy breeze off the East China Sea. "More."

The corners of her mouth lifted. She wrapped a limber leg around him. Good girl. "Then I shall see you snugly sheathed."

He found the ribbon on her lacy undergarment and pulled. Silk fabric slipped over a rounded cheek, exposing a lovely derriere. Firm with just the right amount of jiggle. He moved in-between her thighs and slipped the tips of his fingers along the sensitive inside flesh of her limbs. She spread her legs wider.

Phaeton smiled. He didn't even have to ask.

He caught a flash of scarlet in her eyes and caught his breath. Just a ripple of color, but even a hint of suspicion was bad enough. He quickly lifted silk pantalettes and retied the bow. "Arousing to see you again, Georgiana, or should I say *Mademoiselle Gorgós*?" He stepped away.

Deep crimson swirled behind midnight blue eyes. Her flesh took on a curiously ethereal form as something reptilian materialized before him. Scaly but feminine, with a pale luminescence. Her dress unraveled to lay bare high-set breasts and rounded hips. A gossamer snake of silk swirled over her nude form, entwining itself around voluptuous curves.

"Ah, there you are." Somewhat wistfully, one side of his lip curled upward.

Fully formed, she was feline and serpentine all at once. Her skin glistened with pearl-sized, translucent scales that rippled with each rise and fall of breath. Her new, darker gaze traveled the length of his frame, admiring, exploring. She grabbed hold of his lapels and pressed him back against the ship's rails. Every fiber of this female entity appeared to quake with anticipation. Sweeping aside her meandering skirt, she pressed his hand to her Venus mound, but his fingers retreated. In fact, his arm jerked backward. Awkward, even for Phaeton.

Regretfully, he stepped away. "Not that my soul is worth saving, but I make it a point never to lay with otherworld creatures." His *tsk* was more of a sigh. "Pity—you might have saved this for later—crawled into my berth for the suffocating climax?"

A shock wave of energy knocked him down and sent him sliding along the polished wood deck. He lay stunned momentarily, as the female demon swarmed over him, thrusting herself against his manly parts. He groaned. "Such a naughty succubus." Between caresses, this night creature would attempt to mount, then strangle him. There was nothing left to do but feign a struggle.

At some point he would have to extract himself from her

sexual alchemy. But not . . . immediately. He rather enjoyed this part of the macabre dance. There would soon come a delightful, helpless paralysis. He would chance a moment or two of pleasure before those invisible bonds took hold and began to choke.

Irises contracted into vertical slits as bulbous orbs swiveled up and down his torso. Georgiana had become decidedly less attractive.

The buttons on his trousers loosed. "Dangerous play, love."

Phaeton lifted his head as his cock sprung to life. It couldn't hurt to ask. "Might the naughty succubus swallow the dragon?"

Her answer came in the form of a pink tongue covered in shimmering scales and a long hiss. Soon, she would genuflect on his chest. With nostrils flared, bearing down hard, the she-devil would squeeze with all her considerable might and crush the air from his lungs, the living soul from his body.

Her scaled tongue lengthened and tickled his earlobe. Clawed fingers wrapped around his brick-hard prick and stroked. Good God, he ached for release.

The vixen's luscious mouth uttered a deep, throaty sigh and moved lower. "Cocks up, Mr. Black."

"Mmm, the pleasure is mine." He reached into thin air.

"Got nothing to do with your pleasure, sir. They're comin' fer ye. Shake a leg now and be quick about it. We made Port o'London last night."

Phaeton's eyelids flew open. The blurry visage of an old sea dog squinted down at him. He jerked awake at the sight of the gray-bearded geezer. "Crew sez they lost their share at cards last evening."

Phaeton rubbed his eyes.

His *tête-à-tête* with a night terror had been a stimulating hallucination—while it had lasted. He blinked again, and brought a wild bristle of chin hairs into focus. "Good God. That you, Mr. Grubb?" He barely recognized the croak in his own voice.

Rummy old Joe Grubb flattened weathered lips into a thin line. "Crew claims ye cheated 'em."

Despite the blistering hangover, he vaguely remembered a card game as well as a good deal of grog guzzling. "Preposterous." Lifting his pounding head, he reached down to scratch his crotch. A rat chewed on a trouser button.

Phaeton hurled himself out of his hammock. "Bloody hell." He caught a swinging length of knotted rope and managed to remain upright. The rodent skittered away into the deeper shadows of the crew's quarters. Listing to one side, he called after the creature. "Georgiana?"

He ventured a squint about his surroundings. "Where am I?" This was no luxury ocean liner but a rat hole in the bowels of a seagoing vessel. A listen to the chorus of snores indicated a number of men slept in the hammocks strung about the hold. He was in a cargo ship. But not the *Topaz*. And what had happened to America Jones?

He recalled making port in Shanghai. There had been a screeching argument, as well as a long, pointed weapon tossed at him. On further consideration—he shook his head—he was quite certain that the altercation between him and America had not been the cause of their separation. Again, Phaeton tried to shake the whiskey fog from his brain.

The gruff old seabird poked him in the rib. "Crew sez ye could see through their cards,"—his one good eye circled about—"as if by magic."

A blast of rotten breath sent Phaeton backward. "Possibly, but—"

Something surly and imposing stepped through the hatch tossing a cutlass back and forth between clenched hands. Good God. The ogre-sized sailor did seem familiar. Phaeton struggled to recall last evening through a cloud of smoke and spirits.

"Now see here—" He straightened up and backed away from the angry seaman. "Let me assure you, I have no peculiar ability at cards—luck of the draw." A broad swipe of the sailor's sword took out several hammocks, which fell onto a cold damp floor. Phaeton grimaced. More rudely awakened sailors with pockets lightened by grog and card play.

His heart rate and blood flow elevated to the correct level of alarm. He feigned a left and tilted sideways, barely avoiding the next slash of the blade. Phaeton retreated as a number of rousted sea dogs fell in behind the hovering thug with the menacing sword. Air buffeted past the end of his nose from yet another swing.

No time to lose.

Using a bit of potent lift, learned from a man full of such unearthly tricks, Phaeton flung himself into the air, banked off the ceiling, and landed atop a sleeping sailor. Arms out to his sides for balance, he grabbed hold of an overhead line and pushed off the grunting chest beneath his boots. He aimed straight for the seamen in pursuit, swinging across the barracks, head down, balls out, he struck the lead man. The rest of the crew toppled over like ninepins.

Phaeton released the rope and landed near the main hatch. He grabbed his hat from a nearby hook and scooped up the loose cutlass sliding across the floorboards.

Joe Grubb broadened a toothless grin. "Cut and run, Mr. Black."

Phaeton flicked the brim of his bowler. "Pricks to the wind, Chief."

He bolted down into the cargo hold, removing belaying pins as he ran. A flurry of cargo net enveloped, then whisked him up into the air above the cargo hatch. Several good swings of the blade loosed the web of rope and he dropped onto the wooden deck. Halfway across the gangplank, Phaeton glanced back. Christ.

He teetered precariously at the sight. The whole bloody lot of them were following on behind. He turned and made a dash along a pier stacked with cargo and crowded with dockworkers. Vaulting over large bales of cotton, he squeezed through stacks of tea chests and skirted cartloads of whiskey. A sprint over a footbridge led him away from the chaos of the docks and into the refuge of a covered alley.

He ducked into a dank niche off the lane and waited for his

pursuers to pass by. Once the seamen were well ahead, he darted back into the lane and made his way toward the cabstand on Westferry Road. Trotting along behind a loaded drayage cart, he was steps away from the bustling thoroughfare when one of the seamen gave a shout from behind.

Phaeton pivoted toward the surly bloke who came at him hoisting a belaying pin. He drew a pistol from his coat, knowing full well the chamber held no bullets. The sailor lunged just as a fast-moving carriage passed between them. The brief respite afforded him the opportunity to abandon all sense of propriety. He wrenched open the door of the passing vehicle and tossed himself inside.

From the floor of the carriage, amid a flutter of pretty lace ruffles and petticoats, Phaeton perused shapely legs covered in pale stockings. "My word, things are looking up."